Arak-An Angel's Story

By Morris Clark

Copyright

Foreword and Dedication

Possibilities...I was made to understand early on, this was what the following tale was really all about. Some of it might seem fanciful, perhaps even outrageous. But if you study Scripture long enough, you will find statements, references or small bits of information that will at least support the idea of...the possibility.

If you are a believer, you may feel like cheering at times. If not, you might cheer anyway. Life was meant to have some deep and true meaning. But, to find that, you often need to get off the beaten path of this "modern" society. Our cast will be venturing out into some of the lesser known places which may lead to that goal. I promise you, you will find yourself traveling with them.

There are references to actual places and a few events, but the characters are completely imaginary and do not represent any actual persons, living or deceased.

So enjoy it for what it is. A fanciful little narrative of how life might be if we had learned our lessons better regarding faith. Faith in Him...faith in each other...faith in ourselves.

Now prepare for a bit of a "ride" through just a fraction of that endless array of...

"Possibilities"

Dedicated to the memory of my son,

James Morris Clark III

Cast of Characters

Arak

Warrior angel whose original home planet is not Earth. On assignment to deliver a warning to one Amos Mikals.

Amos Mikals

Outspoken proponent of need for a "return to God"; nationally and inside the "church". Has recently started using the new Internet technology to make this message more widely known. Someone Lucifer has decided to silence...permanently.

Lucifer

A.k.a. Satan...Need I say more?

Buferan (Bu-fur-ahn)

High ranking demon prince. Currently assigned to obstruct Arak's mission to warn Amos of Lucifer's interest in him.

Jennifer Alexander, "Jenny"

Casual visitor to St. Peter's Basilica in Rome as part of her interest in the history of Christ's apostles. Her chance encounter with Arak will have widespread ramifications; both for her and numerous unsuspecting others.

Bubba

Amos' faithful canine.

Eddie Dormer

Amos's neer-do-well fellow worker at the "plant". Somewhat shiftless and self serving. Used to doing only what it takes to get by and head home for the next "good time".

The Arch Angel, Raphael

Arak's long time mentor and confidante. Also his normal "first contact" upon the completion of any mission.

James Alexander, "Jim"

Jenny's dad who has fostered and encouraged her Biblical pursuits since childhood. Also an outspoken critic of modern "religion" and its half-hearted practices.

Sammy

A.k.a. Samir; Mid-east terrorist on assignment to seek out U.S. targets of opportunity. A chance meeting with Eddie Dormer hatches the idea of manipulating him to cause a serious problem at the "plant".

Lonius

Arak's father on his home world of Deran.

Matt Robbins

Helicopter pilot for Nuclear Regulatory Commission. Flies in to the "plant" at regular intervals for mandatory inspections.

Peter

A.k.a. Pytor; Samir's fellow terrorist. Ex-Spetsnaz commando. The "muscle" of the team.

PROLOGUE

BUBBLE, BUBBLE, TOIL AND TROUBLE; sometimes it amazed even Him. It was also the source of much disappointment. As mankind stumbled and weaved through the current Earth age, his tendency always seemed to gravitate towards selfishness, greed and evil. As it had been before the flood, so it was once again. Sin was rampant throughout the Earth.

Naturally the Fallen Ones were right in the thick of the matter, that too was nothing new, but the level of surrender to their temptations had reached an all time high. The roll call of the resulting "crimes of godlessness" had also reached epic proportions.

The very leaders of the nations were among the most corrupt. They parlayed their positions into distorted, high level societies where they bargained with each other always seeking more personal power and gain. The same aphrodisiac that had seduced Lucifer. And now, that failed creature was steadily spreading the disease of his own downfall unto these to whom God had granted his own image.

With the leadership this foul, was it any surprise the citizens rushed to follow their example? When they awoke, their first thought was of self and gain; or of lust. The variations were endless as each raced into the new day eager to glean more and more for their own little kingdoms. They wrote songs about doing it "their way". They bragged of being "captain of their souls". To pass the time, when they were not scheming for more, they indulged in an ever expanding array of sin.

Drunkenness, sex and perversion of every variety had become the preferred methods of recreation. Partners were traded at the whim of whatever demon's voice the individual paid allegiance to at the moment. And all the while other deceiving voices, both broadcast and written, continued to proclaim the legitimacy of such moral recklessness.

They had even managed to contaminate the souls of the children. Into the minds of the young were poured the mantras of the adults. Through actions, words and the insidious media forms they were exposed to from infancy. Entertainment at nearly every level had become permeated with innuendos and filth. And now, the passage of time had seen that degradation reach down into the souls of the formerly innocent. The result was a polluted soul at an early age.

Without some awakening, some return to sanity, the physical destruction of their culture was certain to follow the moral one. The clock was ticking with a thunderous countdown...and no one was listening. Well, almost no one. As would always be, there was a remnant.

One such warrior had become a special target of enemy forces. Not only a target, but the focal point of some indiscretions that would have formerly brought severe reprisal. Yet, he was holding his own. Such men were indeed cast in David's image; after God's own heart. Even so, he was overmatched. There would be nothing fair in the fight Lucifer would bring to his door. The matter was deserving of special attention as it might well culminate in one of the more serious confrontations of the age.

And so it was decided; an emissary would be sent in. The only question was, who. It did not yet warrant an Arch intervention, but the level of demonic attention focused on the situation might well be more than a Third Rank angel could handle. A tiny smile formed in the mind above all minds. Arak, that boisterous Son of Deran. He had faced these enemies many times and his skill as a warrior was renowned. He had also experienced loss in this arena and knew to tread carefully through the snares of Earth. He was surely the best choice and there could be no delay.

For, as Lucifer's unorthodox attack against this lone believer began to mount, a large number of unwary souls were being slowly drawn toward an unscheduled appointment with a sudden and violent death.

CHAPTER 1

S AID MISSION, HOWEVER, had not begun well at all. And now the almost legendary Arak was furious...and fearful. Furious at his own carelessness, fearful of the repercussions that might result. He had been cleverly fooled during the dimensional transfer by none other than Buferan (Bu-fur-ahn) himself. With that single misstep both he and his mission were placed in serious jeopardy. Buferan had played this game for millennia and was, admittedly, good at it. But to be caught unaware, blindsided by some clever imitation, was not acceptable for one of Arak's rank and experience. He should have seen the little play act for what it was.

Demons of "military" standing would almost certainly not be sent to harass or interfere with a solitary First Rank report angel. But that was exactly the impersonation Buferan had tricked him with. Give him credit; he could do a masterful job of appearing to be something other than what he was...just like his boss. Now instead of coming to the rescue of a weaker member of his own forces, Arak was hemmed in by two undoubtedly powerful War demons, and their even more powerful commander.

A formidable and evil personality confined to this important theater known as Earth. One who was aptly compared to the Kingdom's own senior ranks. An ancient "Arch" creature that stood daily in the presence of his master, Lucifer, who had no doubt planned this little charade to obstruct any information or message Arak might be carrying. Now, as powerful as the Lord had granted him to be, he was clearly outgunned. And the Spirit could not intrude in his favor as no Earther of faith was actively involved. All three wore the baleful glare they used to intimidate and hide their expressions, but the first words from Buferan erased any doubt of the intent.

"Your stay might be somewhat extended eh, Arak."

So, just as he'd feared, they had amassed this muscle to attempt an imprisonment. All courier angels operated with knowledge of this risk but it was, in most cases, remote at best. Few messengers were deemed valuable enough to tempt these "Fallen Ones" into an open dispute that might ultimately engage Michael or one of the other Arch-rank angels. Arak, however, was such a prize and he knew he'd be expected to bring his own defensive force to bear on the situation before attempting to summon help. Help, it must be noted, that could not always be guaranteed.

Jehovah's thinking on such matters was not often fully understood by any other being except the Christ. And even he would tell you some matters and decisions rested solely with his Father. Being God meant operating on a timeline that could often exceed the imagination of even the original members of creation. The complete history of the galaxies was but a short story to the Lord. So, if there were some obscure reason that fit the Almighty's unimaginably long range plans, Arak could wind up in chains while those plans played out. Possibly in the company of that dubiously elite group of Fallens imprisoned during the original chaos which began this particular matter. The duration of that sentence would probably run till Earth's Armageddon. He was painfully aware that such tragedies did occur.

One of the War demons had produced a shackle and was brandishing it with a malignant delight. And they had begun to circle him like a pack of carnivores on Earth or Deran might some unfortunate creature they considered prey. In this case, however, those slow, gliding moves could transform into a strike velocity no predator on either world would ever match. Mind speed; the speed of thought. That strike would be designed to immobilize him just long enough for the shackle to be cast upon some vital point. Were they to succeed, there would be no escape...in either direction.

To return with the message undelivered was something all couriers strove mightily to avoid. But a reversal through Earth's atmosphere would at least give him a fresh shot at delivery; or a chance to request assistance. When the "fall" occurred, Lucifer, a.k.a. Satan, was said to have come down to the Earth "as a flash of lightning". That was before Arak's time but he did know when God cast you some-where, there you stayed. No demon ventured outside the atmospheric boundary of this little blue-green planet and their boss didn't do it except by permission.

On the other hand, to somehow forge past these three would give him the outside and risky chance of achieving a "sanctuary" position. Humans thought any church or religious location fit that scheme but, the fact was, bona fide refuge points were scarce. More so, in fact, than at any time in Earth's history. It was a side effect of the generally mediocre spiritual condition of the current inhabitants.

Arak's original, and intentionally deceptive, trajectory made it possible he could transfer to the interior of St. Peters Basilica on the continent called Europe. Probably one of Earth's most famous Christian sites, he knew it remained protected by Jehovah not for any piety or holiness the church might claim, but for simpler, even sentimental reasons. His son had friends whose earthly bodies were memorialized there; Peter being the obvious example.

A probing pulse emanated from the War with the shackle. Arak deflected it as easily as the feint it was. But a second stronger one blitzed in from Buferan. He grimaced with the effort but rolled it to one side like an ocean wave meeting a rocky shoreline. Any moment now the real attack would come. All three would strike trying to entangle and entrap his very mind and soul. First with lies and deceptions, then with an energy somehow linked to that shackle. Those deceptions would be skillfully formed around observed or surmised experiences of Arak's own existence. If he could be slowed or staggered long enough to secure it, the energy "chain" which developed would reach straight back to Lucifer. And that would be probably be that.

Even humans, familiar with Scripture, knew and respected the spiritual danger a creature as powerful as Lucifer represented. Michael, who had been face to face with him more than once, had counseled tiers of angels on the risk present in a confrontation. If the core knowledge of an angel could be subverted successfully, that unfortunate could be possessed as surely as a mortal. Earth stories that portrayed the idea of being turned to the "Dark Side" were closer to the truth than they suspected. That went for both humans and angels. But whereas a human could blunder into that disastrous state by sinfully misusing their free will, an angel could be coerced by deceit coupled with force. In addition, the trickery applied was specific to the origins and experience of the intended victim.

Arak had a history on his home world of Deran which was not fully known to these Fallens of Earth. However, long experience had taught them the array of similarities that could be drawn upon and cycled into an attack. No courier with Arak's mortal history was without chinks in the spiritual armor he wore into service. It was both the pride and the concern of any angel of mortal lineage. Every "life" was a mixture of triumphs, tragedies and the spectrum of experience common to the Lord's creations. The fact that you had passed the supreme test, and garnered this eternal one, did not diminish who you had always been. And none of your memories, good or bad, were taken from you. That meant your former regrets, heartaches and even pride could be brought before you as an object lesson or, as in the case at present, a weapon. Buferan already suspected what might work on Arak.

On a long ago mission he had paused and been irresistibly drawn to an unfolding tragedy. A military captain was schooling his adolescent son on chariot control. The lesson had gone awry when the team spooked and bolted. Before the soldier could regain control, his son had been catapulted out, landing badly on the hard packed arena earth. He died there in his fathers arms.

On Deran, Arak had suffered similarly; losing a child and having to wonder if you were ultimately to blame for it. As it was for humans, little a courier involved himself with while visiting the "air" of Earth went unnoticed. His interest in that situation was forever in Arak's "file".

Arak's own son, Donian, named after his famous maternal grandfather, had also met with tragedy. At the age of 12 suns, 18 years as reckoned on Earth, he had pleaded to enter the Christus Armaden. CA was an organized defense league built on the backs, minds and blood of true believers on Deran. Arak had served at a rank similar to Colonel for many suns. Those were dark times of conflict between the forces that worshipped and followed the pagan deity Agagal and the small contingent which subscribed to the teachings of the Christ. Ag devotees sought to impose their beliefs on the entire planet and, since they held the vast majority of leadership positions, it was not easy to resist. First with words...and later with blood.

Donian won out and entered service only to be quickly recruited as a "mogadin". A messenger that carried information, supplies and arms through the hostile traps and blinds that permeated the Ag lead society. It was the most dangerous assignment the CA had to offer and Arak's heart had turned cold at the news.

But his son was not to be denied, knowing the position was never offered unless the recipient was truly the best suited. Even Arak had to admit to a mixture of fear and pride that his son would possess the skills which set these particular warriors apart. Donian successfully completed seven assignments. On the eighth, he disappeared. That loss, followed by the ensuing suns of pain and misery, had left a scar on Arak's soul. This was a weakness the Fallens could now attempt to exploit.

If an angel's consciousness was forcefully warped far enough out of shape, all manner of doubt could be inserted and used against that which he knew to be true. This was a danger particularly pronounced when transferring to the Earth with its ever present spiritual warfare...and that situation had never been more intense. All courier and report angels were schooled regarding this. No one was ever taken truly by surprise. But the traps and distractions were constantly being altered in an attempt to come up with a fresh approach... Arak had just fallen for one.

Like a thunderous bolt of instant, agonizing misery the main attack came. Arak felt shame, guilt and hopelessness being slammed against his mind like molten projectiles from some hellish cauldron of white hot metal. Imagine taking the worst form of depression, multiplying it exponentially and inserting it surgically into a victims mind. A lesser angel would have been at least momentarily incapacitated and that would probably enable the capture to take place. Arak did reel with the broken floodgate of torment and as he did so, he felt the white hot touch of the shackle. The War demon had lunged in concert with the mental broadside but failed to get a lock. Just that grazing touch burned like a serpent bite.

Rumor had it the Fallens fashioned these shackles from chains which had previously held one of their own powerful brethren in the darkness mentioned in Earth Scripture. Whether that was true, and what had become of the original wearer, was a mystery which was not being explained to even a high placed servant like Arak. When he'd asked once about this, his mentor had smiled and quipped, "Arak, that's a little above your pay grade." At first he had not quite understood the term "pay grade", but it later became his favorite term to describe mysterious matters or inquiries that were often best left to faith. Till today, he hadn't given the shackle business much further thought. Now, that searing jolt brought him immediately back to the need to resist and he focused on the one thing that could save him; Truth.

All his Deran history, many suns of faith weathered in the face of towering adversities and losses. The centuries spent at the beck and call of Jehovah himself. And the endless council and love of the Arch and Elder angels; these could be his salvation yet again.

From deep inside his being an amber glow ignited. It coalesced and, like a bolt of its own, exploded into the dazzling, fiery gold aura many Earthers had described when recounting angel appearances. Instantly Arak was transformed into what must be termed a Creature of Light. The magnificent, powerful light of a Third Rank warrior angel.

Arak had not only passed his mortal Deran test, but had been granted ever more serious abilities and power by God himself. These demons were now entangled with one who had stood many times in Jehovah's own presence and been immersed in his love and good will as might a favorite son. He was certainly not an Arch, or in a class by himself, but he was of a class with serious, righteous power.

Now that power came to bear and the flashes and explosive cascades of light erupted like a display of rainbow birthed lightning strikes. Shockwaves of resistance streaked back at the ungodly trio and for a brief few seconds they were repulsed. But that would be over as soon as all three joined forces again. In those seconds he made his decision. Arak ended his defense with the favorite war cry of Michael,

"The Lord Jesus rebukes you!"

That did it. The power Father had placed in the Son's name was ever-present and just its mention momentarily added another stunning blow to the surprise his own resistance had already created. In that same micro-instant he continued the transfer unimpeded and with a blue-green crackling fire, like a million volts gone wild on a grid of high conductance filaments, he flashed directly into St. Peters.

In the next millisecond, Buferan and company materialized outside the massive cathedral in light speed pursuit. Arak felt their presence as they felt his. It was not possible to materialize in this realm undetected unless cloaked by permission in human form. And that was only permitted on the rare occasion of a long term assignment.

Buferan's sibilant voice came to him again, "Impressive Arak, but what now? My orders are to take all the time necessary. You may not remain in there beyond that which is allotted."

"Then I shall certainly summon assistance," replied Arak.

"Do not be so sure it will come. He has been known to withhold escalating these things before."

"True, but if He does not, is your infernal leader willing to risk it past the deadline?"

"Perhaps, since he believes you are intending to visit Amos Mikals."

Now, Arak was the one momentarily stunned. That was a shrewd piece of deduction. There wasn't any other explanation for Lucifer currently having that information. Amos was indeed his assignment. And it had been something of an honor to be chosen for the visit. The young man was of much interest in the Kingdom these days. On a world, seemingly gone mad morally, he stood out in his principality as a man of true faith.

Heaven knew, speaking literally, that in the Earth society he inhabited, such "warriors" were getting more difficult to find. In the last few suns, or years as they reckoned them here, Amos had turned his back on most of his mortal ambitions and sought to establish some sort of wake up call for Earth's dwindling and misled believers. Many astute humans surmised the possibility that a Laodicean style age might be upon them, but Mr. Mikals had become boisterously vocal about it. Hence, he'd also attracted the attention of the enemy camp...as further evidenced by this little drama.

In the massive cathedral complex around Arak, unaware of his presence, were the staffs of guards and clergy supplemented by sightseers and worshippers in large numbers. It was the Friday before Pentecost Sunday and the crowd was large and festive. After an initial survey, Arak settled his mind and called out to the Spirit, "Are any of yours here?"

A moment later, a slightly built young woman suddenly cocked her head, rotated slowly and focused directly on his back. She stared a moment in disbelief, gave a small gasp and sank fluidly to a kneeling position. The crowd around her took no notice. Just another visitor struck by her surroundings and caught up in prayer. Not this time.

Jennifer Alexander had come to this vaunted religious location more out of curiosity regarding its apostolic heritage than any proclaimed piety. Long years of Biblical study, tutoring and encouragement had taught her not to place an overly high value on the things which man thought impressive or sacred. This was indeed a big, pretty place but the history of those who controlled it was not marked by the leading of God's spirit, but by human ambition and selfishness.

None the less, either she was hallucinating or there was a giant, angelic looking man, sheathed in what seemed to be golden fire, standing not thirty feet away. He had a warrior style tunic with a large sash and heavy looking boots with straps laced up huge calves. And there really were large, powerful wings folded neatly against the massive, muscular back. Hanging gracefully across the upper portion of that back were long, gold-brown locks of hair like one would imagine on some Tarzan character.

Time suspended while she continued to stare in shock. Then the giant apparition began turning slowly in her direction. As he did so, the "fire" went out and a fleshly appearance replaced it. The face was one of genuine beauty yet with a solid look of strength and determination. But it was the eyes that again totally transfixed her. They seemed to gleam with an unearthly, jade green fire, yet still managed to look almost human. And now they were staring intently in her direction.

Jenny felt light headed and was shaking like the proverbial leaf. An unreasoning, visceral fright had begun welling up from the very center of her being. She was barely able to breathe. Then, with just the slightest tilt of that magnificent head, he found her face and those soul-piercing eyes aligned themselves with hers like a pair of lasers. She was paralyzed in absolute awe and fear.

Then he smiled, "Jenny, I am Arak."

CHAPTER 2

JENNY WAS ON HER KNEES, her mouth hanging open like a Hollywood cliché, her heart beating like a runaway rock drummer. The angel-giant had just said her name; in a voice that defied description as much as the rest of him. It had a bass timbre unlike any ever heard on Earth, yet it was gentle in her ears. Like an old friend calling from somewhere long ago.

She swallowed and croaked, "Uh...Eric?"

"Not exactly, but close enough for now."

"Are you real?" she asked, knowing how foolish it sounded even as she spoke.

"Very much so, I am afraid, and in need of your assistance."

Several people had taken notice of her apparent difficulty. A portly gentleman near her spoke up in a decidedly limey accent,

"I say young lady, are you feeling unwell?"

Jenny turned uncomprehendingly to him and stared up for a moment. From the corner of her eye the giant was motioning for her to stand. To her amazement she found she had the strength now to do so. As she did she said,

"Um, no sir, I think I'm OK." She was again looking at the angel though and not at the man himself.

"You're quite sure; you look as if you'd seen a ghost."

Jenny turned to him again, then burst into nervous laughter,

"I guess you could say that."

The man looked questioningly at her, then around at several others who were now watching and listening.

At that moment Arak spoke, "I'm sorry Jenny, but time is not on our side." He raised one huge arm as if placing a benediction on the small crowd. A strangely uncomfortable look appeared on the plump gentleman's face...then spread to the others as well.

"Just so," he muttered, "best be getting on then," and hurried away stopping only to glance back once over his shoulder. In fact, those closest to Jenny were melting furtively away like children trying to distance themselves from the scene of some mischief. The giant angel was still before her as clearly as before and he was softly shaking that beautiful head.

"How truly sad; they are uncomfortable in the presence of their own Creator's spirit."

"What?" Jenny asked.

"Nothing you don't already understand if you think about it," he said as he strode over to stand towering beside her.

"Ar...are you really an angel of God?"

"I am," he replied, "I am Arak of Deran, a Third Rank and a Destroyer; servant of the Most High God; follower of His son, the Christ."

"My dad will never believe this," Jenny muttered as she stared up at him.

At that, the angel smiled again, "Do not be so sure."

"Can anyone else see you...or hear you?" she asked.

"Only those the Spirit empowers, and that must come from within. I know you have questions and I will answer if it is permitted and such time is allotted, but at present, I must ask you to do as I request. Do you have your Scripture?"

"Scripture?" Jenny asked.

The angel seemed briefly puzzled, then, "A copy of the Earth Bible."

"Earth Bible??...Are there other kinds?"

An amused look fleeted across the giant face. "Ah, Jenny, that may be somewhat above your pay grade," and a deep bass chuckle escaped him. "Sorry, yes, a copy of the Bible."

It was her turn for a moment of puzzlement. "Not on me," she replied slowly thinking of the well worn copy in her room.

"Hmmm, surely in this place," said Arak as he began to rotate slowly scanning over the heads of the surging crowd. "Ah, see the display case?"

Jenny followed his gaze but couldn't see over the masses of people. "No, I don't have your height advantage," she smiled up at him. She could scarce believe how fast she was adjusting to the insanity of this situation. Or the fact that no one appeared to be paying any attention to what must look like a girl talking to herself.

Now the large eyes seemed to also twinkle with an emerald humor. "Follow me," and he set out in a gigantic stride towards something to her left. Jenny hurried to keep up and marveled that a path opened in front of them, yet the movement of the people seemed totally natural. Like some elaborate choreography was being acted out on perfect cue. She was preparing to ask about it when he stopped in front of a large, ancient looking, brass-bound display case. Beneath the thick glass was what appeared to be an even older book of some sort framed in an ornate leather binding. The weathered and worn looking pages contained three columns each of some strange lettering.

"Yes," said the angel after a moment, "A copy of the Codex Vatanicus."

"Which is?" Jenny queried.

"One of your early New Testaments. This one looks like a real papyrus copy."

"Eric, no disrespect, but I'm getting more and more lost here."

"Arak...two A's."

"A-R-A...K?"

"Yes, very good, and I'm sorry there is no time to explain fully. But since you are a child of faith, have some now."

"OK," said Jenny glancing around, "what about this Bible is important?"

"Offensive weaponry."

"What?"

"Ephesians, the Sword of the Spirit."

"Oh, right, the spiritual armor chapter...Uh, so I still don't understand what's going on."

Arak looked down intently into Jenny's eyes; it again froze her almost as completely as the initial shock had.

"If willing, my dear young lady, you are about to become Sword Bearer to Arak the Destroyer. Many would count it an honor."

Jenny tried to slow her thoughts and concentrate. This was really happening. She was now sure of that. And this massive, beautiful creature was really one of the Lord's angels. She was convinced of that as well. Where she fit in, she still had not a clue.

"Arak...I'm honored to even have laid eyes on you."

The smile again, "Do not misunderstand Jenny, I am the Lord's servant even as you are. Only I have been at it for quite some time. In your Earth years you would count it centuries. And the Deran conversion experience is different from that of the Earth. As I said, if we are granted time, I will tell that which is permitted. But right now I need you to take this Scripture in your hands."

Jenny paused a moment in thought...The Deran conversion? Then she turned her eyes to the golden cabinet, "Uh, this case looks pretty Jenny-proof Arak."

"Touch the surface"

She did; her hand went through the glass like it was water. She was looking at her own finger tips inside the ancient case. A quiet gasp escaped her. "B-But, how?"

"Third Ranks have some small measure of the Lord's control over that which, I believe you term, 'molecular matter'."

"Mommy, that lady's hand went through the glass and it didn't break," shrilled a young voice behind her.

Jenny snatched her hand to her side and pretended to be studying the Codex as she glanced back at the source. A small boy of nine or ten and his mother stood a few feet behind them. The boy was staring at her wide eyed. The mother smiled and said apologetically,

"Sorry, he's so excited about being here. He loves going to church and hearing about the things God's done. You know the Red Sea and all that. I think he's waiting every day to see a miracle of his own."

The boy was looking intently at Jenny, "I just saw one," he insisted, "Please ma'am, do it again."

"I uh," Jenny began, then the little guy's eyes suddenly flew open and his mouth dropped as hers had. He was now staring up over Jenny's shoulder and she thought, "Oh Lord, he sees Arak."

"It's...it's," he began stammering. Then in a flash his expression changed, a shy smile settled on his face and he nodded. Jenny followed his gaze upwards to find Arak, with a finger over his lips, shaking his big head from side to side. The gesture seemed so normal, and human, she had to suppress a laugh.

"Yes," his mother was saying, "I see it too."

Both Jenny and the young son turned to her questioningly.

"That painting up there, it's beautiful," she exclaimed.

As they turned and followed her eyes they saw, past Arak and high up on the cathedral wall, a large, tastefully done painting of angels. They appeared to be ministering to some saint or Bible character. Both youngsters looked back at Arak who just shrugged.

"Uh yes," Jenny said slowly, "you see things differently here," she glanced at Arak, "and maybe like you'd see them no where else."

As the mother continued to gaze at the painting, Jenny leaned down to the young man's ear, "He's in a hurry about something and we need to get on with it, can you take your mom somewhere else?"

The youngster stared at her for a moment then up at Arak who was nodding, "I guess so," he whispered, "do I have to?"

"Please trust me, it must be really important."

At that he looked up once more at Arak and said, "OK...I can do that." Then in a louder voice, "Mom, I need to find the restroom."

She looked down distractedly then said, "Oh, OK honey, I could use a stop too," then turning to Jenny, "Very sorry to interrupt you miss."

As mom scanned for a restroom location, the boy continued to stare, first at Arak, then at Jenny. His mother suddenly let out a small, satisfied exclamation, grasped his hand and began to stride away. The boy switched hands and pivoted so he was walking backward. "Hey, what's your name?" he called.

"Jenny...and thanks."

"And uh..." he said questioningly, staring at the giant angel.

"Arak," rumbled that powerful, friendly bass from beside her, "Go with God, Benjamin Markham."

"Yeah, I'm Ben," called the boy brightly, "I'll never forget you...either of you...bye," and they merged into the flowing crowd and disappeared.

Jenny turned to Arak, "Why could he see you but not the mom?"

"He still has child-like faith. Would that there were more like him here."

"You mean in the Basilica? That would start a riot."

"No Jenny," he said solemnly, "on the Earth."

"Oh... Yeah, I know what you mean."

Arak turned once again to the Codex. "Please remove the Scripture, Jenny." She turned and cautiously extended one hand to the glass surface. Once more it passed through effortlessly and she reached in with both hands and grasped the ancient writings. This time no one was paying any mind and she turned her attention to the pages before her. She carefully raised the volume and it also passed through the barrier with just the same resistance one might feel from water. Sea water at that; it had a strange but pleasant sensation on her skin.

"Am I ever going to wake up from this?" she mused out loud.

The deep chuckle, "Perhaps you have never been more awake."

Jenny stood looking, first at the indescribably aged material in her hands, then at her surroundings. She expected someone to notice what she was sure appeared to be the theft of a state treasure or something. But the swirling holiday throng was everywhere and she realized it was working to her advantage. Especially where the guards or security were concerned.

Arak's rumble came to her, "Please go to...hmmm," he stared thoughtfully at the old volume, "Go to Matthew chapter four."

She returned to a more serious scrutiny of the Codex and then looked up at Arak, "This is in Greek."

"Yes, it was commonly used at that time."

"I can't turn to what I can't understand. You needed my dad."

"Try."

She began to carefully lift the edges of the "page". It had a textured feel to it like canvas. She'd carefully leafed over only a few when Arak said,

"Stop, read."

Jenny looked doubtfully at the writing, then up at Arak with a half smile, "You've maybe not heard the saying, but, it's Greek to me."

"Read please"

She shrugged, "OK," and began to try the first pronunciation,

"tote o ihsouv anhcyh eiv thn erhmon upo tou pneumatov peirasyhnai upo tou diabolou"

Her eyes widened, "Wait a minute...I know what this says."

"Other tongues," said Arak, "say it in your language."

"Then was Jesus led up of the spirit into the wilderness to be tempted of the devil..."

"Oh man, this is getting too much," said Jenny and she folded the volume under one arm then bowed her head with tears glistening in her eyes. "Arak, why me, I'm no one. I'm not that great a person and this is starting to frighten me."

He looked down at her compassionately, "No Jenny...fear is not found in these words; fear on this world is of Lucifer. It is his lifelong attempt to disrupt your obedience and faith that you now feel. And you fail to see yourself sometimes as Jehovah sees you always. A grateful recipient of his highest act of love. An object of adoration as that of a favored child. He now sees you through a lens crafted by His own firstborn and sealed forever at the place you call Golgotha. You know the story so well, but it must live inside you. You must let it give you strength and peace, even unto death. For, I tell you this as solemnly as the Christ himself would...death can no longer hold you...so what is left to fear?"

Jenny had felt the Holy Spirit's presence many times. Sometimes it was stronger than others, but over the years it had become unmistakable. However, she had never felt the overpowering calm that was coursing into her soul as Arak spoke. An inner conviction, forged like titanium, of complete and absolute assurance that the very words of Eternal Truth were falling like benign projectiles from Heaven onto and into her being. It was beyond true description. She wiped at her eyes, looked up at the mighty warrior from God and said,

"You are so right, Arak the Destroyer; I lost sight...what do you require of me?"

Arak again looked into her face for a long moment, then spoke. "Listen well, little sister. Beyond these walls wait three emissaries from evil itself. Two are demons assigned to encourage and promote the act of war between the peoples of the Earth. Along side them is their superior, a demon of such power as to easily rival my own. Combined, they can overcome and confine me to a place of darkness till the end of this age. Thus preventing my efforts here on behalf and at the command of Jehovah himself. I am one of the first of Deran ever to courier to Earth. I can say that some true good has come from that for you and your fellow believers. I often see things through your eyes better than those who were never mortal. The assignment I am on may be the most important I have ever been given. I would rather be destroyed than fail. You can now be one of the keys to my success."

This speech had again widened Jenny's eyes. Even with the calm she was feeling, the information overload Arak was funneling into her brain was staggering. She paused and gazed at the masses undulating about them. Then, with a sudden look of determination, she turned back to the angel,

"Arak, I...um...Just tell me what to do."

He pointed over the crowd to where two massive oaken doors marked a main entry point, "We shall leave the sanctuary of this place through those doors. It will be necessary to create a diversion to enable you to carry out this Scripture without interference."

"Yeah," said Jenny, "and I'm stealing some valuable artifact, aren't I?"

"Do you not intend to return it?"

"How, without getting arrested or something? Wait a minute, you're a powerful angel, you have that all figured out don't you?" she said slyly. "Some crazy thing to match all this in reverse, right?"

Now the "mighty angel" appeared to have the questioning look,

"Uh, actually I thought perhaps you would employ the, as you say, Postal Service?"

Jenny stared blankly at him for a two count then burst into laughter.

Arak still seemed uncertain. One of the Lord's finest warriors with a child-like, raised eyebrow look of non-comprehension. Jenny could not contain herself. After several moments she glanced around and then looked up. In a voice, still punctuated with little gasp and giggles, she tried to explain,

"Arak, you pop into my life like some fiery giant from thin air, send people packing by raising your arm, turn glass into water and teach me Greek in nanoseconds...talk about other worlds and other conversions, then end up reminding me to use the Postal Service?"

She cackled again and Arak seemed to get the joke.

"Ah yes, I guess you were expecting everything to have the same uh, drama." A huge smile wreathed the beautiful face and another low, thunderous chuckle emerged. Then, "Actually, we try to avoid all this. I hope you do not think this is everyday assignment tactics."

"Oh, of that I have little doubt," said Jenny, once again wiping her eyes, "The National Enquirer would have it splattered all over their front....Hey, wait a minute," she said and stared up into Arak's face, "they haven't"...

"Not often," interrupted Arak, "and almost never with any accuracy."

Then he continued,

"You have a final choice to make Jenny, regarding your involvement with me and the beings that await. Already you have been exposed to more than many of His children will be required to experience in this life. Such exposure is a two edged sword. You may feel pride at some point because of it and thus dishonor the one whom you seek to worship. Or you may feel disappointment with everyday life and squander time in pursuit of another experience, thus thwarting the Spirit's plans on other matters. But perhaps the most dangerous side effect is that you will become a 'person of interest' to the powers of darkness."

"Here on the Earth, that power is significant and real. Even I cannot predict what form any attacks or reprisals might take. The 'Spiritual Armor' in Scripture, combined with true faith, makes you their equal in most any conflict. Even so, warriors, even those of Jehovah, are wounded and sometimes killed in battle. That outcome can be uncertain at times. What is not uncertain is the final destination of one who 'keeps the faith'. That I say with full authority as I am the result of such a destination birthed on Deran."

"Wait a minute Arak, you mean I could become an angel like you are someday?"

He paused in thought, "Ah, my understanding is that the Earth conversion does not involve such results. And the full facts on why and how it is that way," here he smiled that kindly smile again, "are above my own pay grade. That is one of those concerns best left in the hands of faith. The more crucial point right now, is outside those doors. If you accompany me, you will see them as you see me. If so, you must, I repeat must, not give in to the fear they will certainly try to induce in your soul."

Jenny felt the previous calmness of spirit descend once more, "Arak, the words of God and now the words of you, His servant, have changed me. My heart is beating fast and my nerves feel like razors, but I am not afraid. As the Lord is my witness, whatever waits beyond those doors will not face the same Jennifer Alexander."

"Well said little sister; welcome to the camp of Jehovah's own warriors. Let us go then, you and the Scripture before, I will follow." And with that they both faced the large doors and began the march toward an uncertain destiny.

CHAPTER 3

J ENNY WAS LEADING, per instruction, as the entryway
loomed closer. The crowd once again seemed to part
magically except for one instance when an elderly
man, who was slowly traversing the tile floor with his
walking cane, paused right in their path. He focused
curiously on Jenny for a moment, then up over her head.
"Uh-oh, another one," she thought, and looked up at Arak
who was calmly returning the old mans gaze. After a few
seconds the man nodded once to Arak and once to Jenny
then sedately continued on his way. Jenny turned again to
Arak who was following the man with those magical eyes.
After a moment he met her questioning look and said
simply,

"A Saint of God; lead on Jenny."

She turned and continued. The doors were very close
now and she glanced around nervously. Surely someone
would challenge her about the artifact under her arm. Then
a woman's scream erupted behind them and she spun to see
the old man lying face down on the floor. His cane had
landed off to one side and looked curiously alone as it lay on
the ornate tiles. A uniformed guard materialized from the

vicinity of the entry and began to hurry to where people were clustering around the old gentleman's still form. She couldn't clearly hear the conversations and for a moment felt the urge to rush over herself.

"Now," said Arak.

Jenny paused, and then it struck her. Something had passed between the old "saint" and the angel; he was the distraction. She stepped up and grabbed the huge brass handle with her free hand. As she touched it, her spirit discerned something she'd never felt before. A wary feeling gripped her heart; a premonition of danger. Like the cold chill from a ghost story. She looked up at her other worldly companion and saw there was a new look on the handsome face. One she'd only seen hinted at. This was the formidable look of strength and determination that seemed to shimmer below the good natured surface. In a flash she realized she was looking at the severe countenance of one of God's own warriors preparing for battle. It was now a face that would have truly frozen her, or anyone else, in their tracks. She shuddered involuntarily and pushed open one of the massive but smoothly functioning doors.

Bracing herself, she took a step out and at that moment a small incoming crowd thronged around her blocking her view. She was aware it was still sunny and probably in the sixties, but couldn't clearly see the surrounding courtyard. She glanced back and saw Arak had remained inside the oversize threshold, the people seeming now to pass through him like some ghostly apparition. The feeling of foreboding grew stronger. Not something her imagination had cobbled up but a real, palpable compression of the atmosphere. Like an aircraft pressurizing itself with a mist made from your worst nightmares. Then it came. A voice so malignant to the ears as to defy description.

"Does the mighty warrior from Deran shield himself with little girls?"

It seemed to surround her coming from everywhere at once. Arak had warned her to be prepared for the "appearing" of this trio of evil, but even though the incoming people had passed, nothing visual was to be seen. Only the horrid voice and the pernicious spirit of oppression which felt like some fog from, well, hell. That was pretty close she realized; it felt like she was standing in a fog from hell. Yet no one amongst the few streaming to and fro seemed aware of it. She was squeezing the Codex to her side and drawing quick, short breaths. From behind her came the rumble of Arak's voice, only this time it truly sounded like a general or some commanding officer,

"Face the enemy, face your fears, keep the faith."

As Jenny was turning to ask what was there to face, she caught a strange glint out of the corner of her eye. She rotated quickly and then recoiled as she looked up into a glowering face towering right beside her. She felt a bolt of panic and quickly quelled it. The entity was not looking at her but had locked eyes with the angel. She also knew instinctively this was not the source of the "voice". It was about the same size as Arak, a good ten feet tall, but there the similarity ended. This looked like a giant metal clad soldier from some conquering Roman army.

There was a helmet peaked with a long deadly looking spike which was topped off with a tassel. The "body" was concealed behind huge breastplates and armored arm and leg coverings. There were gloves and boots that resembled chain mail. And at the side hung an evil looking, strangely twisted sword, like something fashioned from a giant Eland horn.

The "metal" was all the same hue, a bronze finish that had a glimmer but looked opaque and flat at the same time. The face was hidden behind an evilly fanged, gladiator style mask but the eyes shown clearly from the openings. They resembled the orange flames that flicker and dance inside the sockets of a jack-o-lantern yet had distinct pupils of pure black. Emotionless black centers like the eyes of a man eating shark. "This," she acknowledged in her mind, "is a Demon of War."

Time seemed suspended again but her mind was racing with unfamiliar clarity. He said two War Demons she thought and quickly tuned to check the other side of the door way. Sure enough, the second monster was placed identically and opposite the first.

"They really mean to trap Arak," she thought and suddenly an infant spark turned into a growing flame of anger in her heart. With a sense of wonder, bordering shock, she realized she loved Arak with all the purity and devotion that Christ had ordered his followers to have for one another. The thought seemed to implode like a reverse nova in her mind "My God; I'm willing to die for him." And with that, her righteous rage was complete.

Like a high speed reel, a kaleidoscope of scenes from newscast and documentaries, showing the true face of war, streaked through her consciousness. And here before her stood representatives of the force responsible for encouraging that unimaginable crime and horror throughout the Earth. Yes, man was ultimately culpable, but many of those men had allied themselves with, and maybe even been driven by, these assassins from hell; knowingly or not. And now they wanted to destroy this "creature of light" who was Jehovah's own messenger sent to counteract this scourge. Her mind was actually casting about for some way to attack when the terrible voice once again assaulted her senses.

"Ah, his influence allows you to see us. How touching. Does the little maiden have a name?"

The statement dripped with sarcastic malice and somewhere down deep a small tumbler seemed to click and lock. For the first time, Jennifer Alexander clearly understood the complete hatred and disdain Satan felt for every member of the human race. God's special creations given a will to choose their own way; untouchable by force from either side. And, as suddenly, she realized the true scope of the massive campaign being mounted to subvert the creations from the Creator. "The preachers call it a war all the time," she thought, "but they haven't a clue how accurate that really is." She again experienced that calm assurance from the Spirit and looked carefully around the area. And there it was. The source of that scathingly contemptuous sound... and he was indeed terrible to behold.

Half again as large as the others, he looked like a cross between some giant venomous serpent and a mutated great ape. The "skin", or outer surface, had a definite reptilian, scaly appearance overlain with a dark, oily looking aura. There were huge, muscular legs, a heavy torso and large powerful arms which ended in wicked looking, long fingered claws. The face was that of a deformed snake with a jutting jaw and over lapping fangs but with a bulging cranium shaped like that of a giant primate. The top of this misshapen skull was crowned with a ridgeline and along it were what looked like dragon's spikes. From the heavily over-browed eye sockets, huge glaring eyes were riveted on Jenny. They were an almost incandescent ruby red accented with slit-like pupils of ebony black; like those of some giant underworld cobra. They seemed to emanate the hatred and disrespect the voice embodied and now it came again,

"The last mortal to behold me is still quite beyond treatment. And since you will no doubt soon join him, at least leave us with the memory of your name."

Arak's stentorian rumble came from behind her, "You over reach yourself Buferan, she belongs to the Christ."

Jenny thought she saw a momentary flinch in the monstrous apparition. And the shock of seeing that unearthly appearance was wavering in the face of her righteous indignation. An indignation which it now seemed was being fanned internally by the Holy Spirit into a well stoked furnace. She squared her shoulders towards the awful Buferan and said clearly,

"My name is Jennifer Alexander, daughter to James Alexander, follower of Jesus Christ for seventeen years on the Earth and now Sword Bearer to Arak the Destroyer of Deran."

Even as she heard the words she wondered where they were coming from. Just as quick she remembered the Scripture in Luke which said not to worry about what to say if brought before kings or rulers. Wow, it worked before evil, underworld rulers too! Buferan had seemed to lose stature before these words but now he retorted,

"Oddly, I don't see the wonderful 'Son of God' coming to the rescue here. And as you well know Arak, time is running..."

"She said Sword Bearer, Buferan," interrupted Arak, "You never did pay enough attention to the details."

The malevolent eyes narrowed and re-focused as if seeing Jenny for the first time. At the same moment Arak said quietly, "Open the Scripture."

Jenny brought the Codex out in front of her and opened to the page she had kept marked with her finger. Immediately there was a keening sound mixed with what sounded like metal being ground at high speed. It was worse than the proverbial chalkboard and sent ripples across her taut nerves. She looked about and saw that both War Demons were backing away.

This produced a moment's satisfaction but at that same instant the courtyard suddenly erupted into chaos. It was as if a small tornado had touched down center stage. Scraps of paper, mixed with leaves and dust, swirled viciously in every direction. Luckily there had been few occupants but she heard some yells and one scream as those in the vicinity raced to distance themselves. One couple appeared from nowhere and almost bowled her over as they charged through the doorway. She sidestepped them and returned to the confrontation squinting as she tried to see through the noisy mini-maelstrom.

Then behind her Arak's voice roared, "Enough."

Motion ceased. The bushels of debris caught in the swirling vortex froze in place for an instant while a bluish green fire seemed to cast an outline around every separate item or piece; even the dust. The next second it all began fluttering back to earth as an eerie silence settled over the scene. All that could be heard was the patter of leaves and scraps raining softly onto the cobblestones.

"Jenny, read," commanded Arak.

She blinked and without a pause began to intone...in Greek,

"tote o ihsouv anhcyh eiv thn erhmon upo tou pneumatov peirasyhnai upo tou diabolou."

("Then was Jesus led up of the Spirit into the wilderness to be tempted of the devil.")

The grinding sound of the War Demons commenced again and from Buferan's direction came something between a snarl and a cry of pain.

"kai nhsteusav hmerav tessarakonta kai nuktav tessarakonta usteron epeinasen."

("And when he had fasted forty days and forty nights, he was afterward an hungered.")

The sound of the War Demons shot to a crescendo, then abruptly ceased. Without even looking, she knew they had gone. Gone where was probably above her "pay grade", but she could none the less physically and spiritually discern their absence. She read on,

"kai proselywn autw o peirazwn eipen ei uiov ei tou yeou eipe ina oi liyoi outoi artoi genwntai."

("And when the tempter came to him, he said, 'If thou be the Son of God, command that these stones be made bread.'")

A guttural roar of pain and rage issued from Buferan's direction.

"o de apokriyeiv eipen gegraptai ouk ep artw monw zhsetai anyrwpov all epi panti rhmati ekporeu-omenw dia stomatov yeou."

(But he answered and said, "It is written, Man shall not live by bread alone, but by every word that pro-ceedeth out of the mouth of God.")

The roar became an ear pounding shriek and at the same time Arak appeared in front of her with one mighty arm raised. "Listen well, Demon, to the words of the One who will cast you into the pit."

Jenny looked up. Buferan had become misshapen. The evil, but regal, appearance had slumped into something revolting; like a wax figure settling under the noonday sun. What appeared to be a crackling, reddish energy bolt leapt from the monster straight at Arak who calmly captured it with his huge upraised hand and then hurled it back at the distorted figure. The impact produced another shriek and the whole image of the demon wavered and seemingly began to evaporate into the air. The vile voice, filled with hatred, echoed about the square as if from a distance,

"You know this is not over Arak."

"But it is over for now Demon, return to the rage of your master."

And at that, all was calm. Nothing moved. No sound could be heard. Jenny stood rooted, her mind in overload trying to categorize the unbelievable things impacting her senses. She turned haltingly to look up at Arak even as the other large oaken door began to creak softly open behind her.

"Arak, I think I'm going to…

"Peace, little sister, you have earned the right. I cannot tarry. Remember the name Amos Mikals."

He was suddenly enveloped in some charged looking, bluish-green haze that crackled like high voltage and the next second...he was no longer there. She swayed and turned her eyes to the doorway only to be met by the open mouthed face of little Benjamin Markham.

"Wow," he said quietly.

"W-Wow is right," stuttered Jenny and slumped to the ground unconscious. The Codex hit the stones beside her...still turned to Matthew, chapter four.

CHAPTER 4

A MOS WAS DEFINITELY TIRED...but it was a pleasant kind of weary. A day spent prospecting his favorite dive spots, or "holes" as the locals called them, had left him sun baked, salty and ready for some down time. Unfortunately there was a lot of hardware to be rinsed and stored before that was going to happen. Not to mention two nice grouper to be filleted. That it was worth it wasn't in question. Friends and family alike knew that one of the things that "defined" Amos' life was spear fishing. The other was a passion for the Scriptures and their author. To Amos, the vast, shallow expanse of the Gulf of Mexico off Crystal River contained some great elements of both.

He often marveled that today's believers didn't seem to understand the need for alone time with God. Amos didn't think the venue mattered much as long as it got you out of the mainstream hustle and bustle called modern life. Hence, getting you somewhat out of range of the Satanic influence and chaos which was unavoidable in heavily populated areas. Areas filled not only with the human denizens, but also their demonic counter parts. Satan's league of henchmen who were always observing, and often on "assignment", seeking clever and subtle ways to encourage human character and morals to new lows. Even a brief examination of society testified to the success the other team was currently enjoying.

The alone time thing was certainly not his idea. Scripture clearly related the emphasis Jesus put on going off alone into the wilderness to pray. Several places in the Bible had God telling prophets to specifically go here or there alone to meet and talk; usually a mountain, desert or some other isolated place. Amos had just picked up on it during his own studies and imitated the idea. He had discovered God was still out there waiting for those who would answer the call to "be still and know". Apparently that number was decreasing with each generation. Things must be desperate indeed if he was one of the few left willing to give the Almighty a chance for some private fellowship. That not withstanding, he also knew he would gladly trade his entire mortal life for the experience it had become.

Bubba collided companionably with his legs and brought him back to the business at hand. A seventy to eighty pound brindle bulldog with a white chest blaze, Bubba's face left little doubt as to his occupation prior to that of being Amos' confidante and personal dive partner. The muzzle scars and notched places on his ears were testimony to a mutt that had "been in some rumbles". Amos had been introduced to him at the first (and only) organized dog fight he'd ever witnessed. It was a story that would sell well in some places but not one he told much. Still, despite his underworld history, Bubba was a handsome rascal that loved kids and never offered harm to anyone or anything that didn't mess with one of them first. Well, there were a few exceptions. Lightning strikes, blue crabs and loud machinery were notable examples. In fact, no one watching the relaxed way he spent hours out on the Gulf would believe how his first boat ride began.

Loaded onto a seventeen foot Trembley "well" boat, Bubba had pounced and attached himself to the forty horse Evinrude as soon as it fired up. Despite the fact his eyeballs were practically being rattled out of his head, his over trained jaw couldn't be removed from the cowling. A problem they'd finally solved by simply turning the motor off. Convinced he'd done the right thing to stop the danger, Bubba had looked surprised and then "hang dog" at the lecture Amos had given him. He had also never repeated the performance. Bubba was, for Amos' money, the most thinking, intelligent four legged creature he'd ever encountered.

The sun had begun another command performance out over the Gulf by the time everything was rinsed and put away. Amos stood on the dock cleaning his grouper and watching the show with an appreciative eye. No matter how many sunsets you saw, each had its own particular splendor. Then his mind began to wander as he wielded his old black fillet knife.

The Holy Spirit had seemed very manifest the last few days. At first he thought it might be a comfort thing. Once again he'd met with a church leader, voiced his heartfelt concerns and, pretty much, been politely "shown the door". That wasn't new; he was yet to find a so called "pastor" who was more interested in the hard truth than the pew count and offering plate. Between the lack of concern on the new

internet bulletin boards and the on-going local rejection, he
felt he was wearing a little thin. The truth of the Scripture
in First John was painfully evident to him; if a message is
from God, the world won't listen to it. Never the less, truth
was truth and Amos knew the things God had enlightened
him about were stone cold fact.

"Fat lot of good it does me," he thought. Then after a
moment he glanced skyward, "Sorry, I shouldn't feel that
way."

Tossing the remains to the crabs, he picked up the platter of fillets, then walked over and sat it down on an old
picnic table near the edge of his property. A sigh escaped
him as he turned to briefly enjoy the "million dollar" view.

Amos' residence was a cozy three bedroom mobile home
on the north bank of Fish Creek in a small island chain
hamlet called Ozello, Florida. His small back yard faced the
vast expanse of estuarial needle grass plains which
stretched south towards Homosassa Springs. The lot to his
west contained another small trailer whose owners rarely
visited. To the east were several acres housing a two story
Jim Walter vacation home belonging to a northern owner
who also made very infrequent appearances. To say he had
solitude would be an understatement...and he loved it.

Bubba had trailed along and settled comfortably at his
feet but suddenly he sprang up and stared out over the
creek. Amos glanced around, "What's up bud, boat coming?"

Bubba raced each and every boat that shot out of a
main canal just east of their place. The locals, particularly
the commercial guys, always willingly participated. As they
made the turn into the small bay they would drop the
hammer and the race was on. Over the first hundred feet or
so, Bubba was king. After that the boats would gradually

build enough speed to start catching up. Just in time to disappear around the sweeping left turn at the far end of the bay, and for Bubba to pull up short of plunging into the next canal. Amos could rarely pick the winner from his vantage point.

But this time Amos didn't hear a boat and it was late for most of the guys to be heading out. Never the less, his dog was on full alert; something he knew well enough not to ignore. He didn't seem combative or tense, just intently interested in something out on the bay. He did a quick three-sixty scan of the properties but everything seemed normal. For all intents he could be the only human on the planet.

Then, as he turned back to examine Bubba's point of interest, there was a loud crackling sound and, out about fifty feet, the mirror smooth surface of the water suddenly erupted into large, concentric rings of ripples. The next instant a cloud-like haze of blue-green sparks formed out of nowhere and sparkled like a small fireworks display. Two seconds later, Amos' mouth literally fell open. A fiery gold giant flashed into being right in the center of the ripples.

A charged sensation began at the base of his spine and shot upwards. His mind reeled trying to acclimate what he was seeing. Time itself seemed to suspend as he stared in disbelief. The huge, brilliant figure was facing the sunset as if in contemplation or thought. Another tremor struck Amos mind as he realized he was looking at large folded wings in profile on the oversize back. "Oh dear God...an angel?!" As if reading his thoughts the huge head rotated slowly and faced him. He could truly be described as beautiful but there was nothing weak or feminine about him. The eyes were that same blue-green color and had a subdued glitter like a firefly captured against a night sky. It felt like they were burning into his soul. Amos was entranced and a little terrified at the same time. Then it spoke,

"Forgive me Amos; I have not seen this beauty for some time now."

The voice was like gentle, far away thunder and began to dispel the shock that had paralyzed him.

"I-I," Amos stuttered. He tried to collect his racing thoughts. "I...uh, sir, you must be an angel of God. I have heard tell of you but have never seen one of you myself. Forgive me for my fear and foolishness."

The angel looked intently back at him for a few moments, then smiled,

"You have been observed to be neither fearful nor foolish. And the true source of forgiveness, you and I both subscribe to...I am Arak."

"And are you an angel from...Him?"

"Where else would...ah, yes, I was briefed on your habit of caution. Yes, I am in the service of Jehovah himself...Lucifer cannot and would not attempt this particular deception."

A low grunt from Bubba reached Amos' ears. He looked down to find the animal sitting calmly on his haunches with his habitual canine grin on his face.

"My dog obviously trusts you," he commented.

The spectral eyes shifted in Bubba's direction, "Yes, I've noticed the creatures here adopt something from their master's way of living and thinking. Another place I might get a more alarmed reaction."

With that, the aura of fire seemed to go out, a fleshly appearance replaced it, and he strode across the water's surface towards them without leaving a trace. At its edge, he stepped up on the low rock seawall as naturally as any human; only larger.

Amos had experienced a thrill of sensation at this approach. As he looked up into those unearthly eyes, his nerves all seemed to be singing like guitar strings. But this time it was a pleasant sensation with none of the misgivings he'd first experienced.

"Wow, you are not what I would have expected...you're huge," he exclaimed.

There was a low sound that had to be a chuckle, "Amos Mikals, I am Arak of Deran. A Third Rank in the service of Almighty God and a Destroyer. You are an Earth believer whose faith and message have resulted in this coming together. I bring you greetings of love from both the Father and the Son."

Amos' knees gave out and he slumped slowly to the ground next to Bubba, who was also staring intently up into the oversize face. "Oh Lord...is this real?" His head slumped over and he was silent. After a few moments he looked back up. The giant had not moved, or disappeared, but was looking down at him with compassion.

"All is well Amos; I have memory of this also. Knowing of something is not the same as seeing it."

Amos nodded his head and cleared his throat, "No, it isn't; I've seen some pretty amazing things over the years, but nothing to compare to you." He got partially to his feet and slid weakly onto the bench seat facing the angel.

"I ah... imagine you didn't just drop by...what did you say your name was?"

"Arak, two A's, and you surmise correctly. I am here at His behest. First to strengthen your resolve and second to warn you. I have battled one great prince and his minions to get here and may have to do so again. Although I have employed some distortion of your 'time', they may unravel my trail before we finish. If that occurs do only and exactly as I say...agreed?"

Amos stared at him..."Ah, yes sir...I understand...I think."

The angel smiled again, "Truly Amos, the sir is not fitting. I was once as you are and we serve the same master and purpose. We are brothers, call me Arak."

"Yes s...uh, OK Arak, my brain is still trying to catch up here...You say you were once as I am? How is that possible?"

The low rumbly chuckle came again, "Your perusal of Scripture is well known and I am sure I create many questions. Sadly time will not permit a lengthy discussion. Let me say only that you are correct about 'the other sheep pens.'"

Amos paused, "I knew it", and his fist smacked his palm. Bubba jumped to his feet at the sound and eyed the angel, Amos and the surrounding area. Amos reached over and patted the large head absentmindedly. Then he looked back up at Arak, "Who flies that stuff we see out here?"

The angel seemed mildly taken aback, "I tell you I carry a warning yet you would rather unravel mysteries?"

"Oh, uh...yeah, sorry about that, what's the warning?"

"Do not misunderstand, but you surprise me. Most Earthers think first and foremost of their own well being."

Again Amos paused quietly for a moment, "Arak, my well being has been in His hands for so long, I guess I don't worry much about it anymore. What's an Earther, a human?"

"Yes, a member of your race here on Earth. It is a, how do you put it, 'slang term', but with no disrespect."

"OK, just curious. It's no secret though. When I moved here, I heard constantly about the UFOs. Some pretty wild stuff. But these old fishermen didn't seem like ones to tell tales. At least not that kind. Then I saw them for myself; I mean all the time. We have nothing that can maneuver like that. A human would be flattened at those speeds to stop or change direction like they do. And I haven't seen them come down and draw water from the Gulf like the guys talk about, but I've seen the colored lights reflecting down low in the clouds during storms. So is somebody else up there or not?"

The giant angel was silent for several moments. "I could have used you on Deran," he mused quietly, then to Amos, "My young friend, you truly amaze me. And I would enjoy telling you all that is permitted and fellowshipping, but at this time, it cannot be. Trust Jehovah has all these things orchestrated in his Great Plan which is beyond our limited understanding," he paused again then chuckled once more, "no...let us say some things about it are 'above our pay grades' during certain phases." Here he looked skyward and closed those glittering eyes for a moment, "That's pretty close, isn't it Father?"

As if on cue, the sound of distant thunder growled in from the southwest where towering thunderheads could be seen reflecting the glory of the setting sun. Both Arak and Amos looked at each other and broke into grins.

"Yes," said Amos quietly, "I've heard Him do that many times. It's as the Scriptures say,

"His voice is in the thunders."

Another quiet pause and Arak said, "To my purpose. You need to know that the disregard others have for your message does not reduce its importance...nor accuracy. You continue to plant the seed, trust the Spirit to tend the cultivation. Do not grow faint or weary of the assignment and you will receive the reward."

Amos thought a second, "I'm not really doing it for a reward. Truth is its own reward."

"Even so young Amos, if God himself suggest you be rewarded, will you tell Him no?"

Amos again bowed his head a moment then looked up, "Only a foolish pot would argue with the potter."

The angel nodded, "That is so."

Arak continued, "Secondly, as you are well aware, there are forces in play on your world against anything that is of God. Having watched your Earth 'history' for some time now, I also am aware things seem headed for some climax or conclusion. I have marveled, as I see the rampant sin, that His hand has stayed even to this point. No doubt He hopes messages like yours will reach some who can be saved. Eternal suffering in a living death is not something He has ever wished for His creations. But, as you also know, Lucifer has members of your race who have surrendered their will to him. Some knowingly, others not. You are in contact with a number of them each day you go to the place you work for your money. What you call, the Plant."

Amos eyes narrowed, "Crystal River Three?"

"Yes."

"Arak, are you saying the warning involves the nuclear power plant?"

"Yes."

Amos was momentarily stunned. The job at the generating facility had been a godsend in most every way. It had come out of nowhere at a time he was praying to find a new job and leave the occupationally uncertain world of Land Surveying. It turned out a neighbor had high level contacts inside the "plant" and had gotten him a slot in the two day testing required for clearance into a nuclear facility. He remembered with humor one question on the psychological evaluation,

"I am a special agent of God"...T/F. He had laughed mentally and noted every Christian should choose true. However, knowing what the testers were looking for, he had answered false. Whether that one response would have sunk his chances or not he was unsure, but suspected it might have had a negative impact.

After acceptance, there was more schooling on rules, regulations and procedures. Then assignment to an entry level maintenance position. Maintenance, it turned out, meant more than dealing with the mundane details of keeping the place neat and clean. It also entailed handling high radiation waste and clean-up situations where sometimes a "spacesuit" was needed. He loved it.

From the first visit to the turbine deck, then the "auxiliary" side and finally through the air lock into the reactor area itself, Amos was fascinated by the massive high tech gadgetry involved. He told friends and family, "It's like Star Wars every day." To add to the pleasure, the pay was great and he was assigned to the three to midnight shift. This meant some mornings could be spent on his beloved fishing grounds and still be home in plenty of time for work. Life, in some respects, had never been better.

He had also been raised with an old fashioned work ethic where you gave your employer an honest day for the wages. Turned out that wasn't the norm and it didn't take long for his superiors to notice. In short order he'd been made lead man for the shift and relieved from the usual routine of assigned chores. He found himself with the run of the plant, keys to the restricted areas and a telescoping Geiger counter to ensure he didn't blunder into a "high dose" area.

At least one dosimeter and often multiple ones traveled with every hot side employee. They were checked and logged daily by the Health Physics technicians and anyone exceeding the allowable exposure rate was deemed "burned out". This meant being sent to the cold side, or possibly even home, till a new period began. For lots of reasons, it was best to avoid burning out.

And, if you used your head, it was easy to do. The auxiliary and reactor sides were built like mazes. There were multi-sided warrens of concrete and lead designed to help contain the rays and particles. A little common sense taught you to keep the walls and even the various devices and equipment between you and a "source". In his first six months, Amos had accumulated the same exposure as a set of dental x-rays. Not bad for a rookie. However, after that time period, his opportunities for a higher rate were increased dramatically.

Fact was, the hiring period that allowed Amos to get on board had been prompted by a mishap at the plant. In the early part of the year, faulty instrumentation had caused a reactor "trip" from near one hundred percent power. Crystal River Three was a Babcock-Wilcox plant, built by the same firm that constructed the Three Mile Island facility. Operators, fearing a similar situation to the over-heat and core damage suffered by that sister reactor, had proceeded to input so much cooling water that, at some points, it had reached three feet on the reactor building walls. This inundated areas and equipment not designed for that environment and prompted a massive clean up and general overhaul.

Besides the clean up, which often required laying down resin to absorb and capture the radioactive particle pollu-tion, it was also decided to do a re-fuel and control rod drive rebuild. This meant the head would be off the reactor and the core visible from up on the walkways. Both were sights Amos had never dreamt of seeing. He also never suspected how close a look he'd actually get.

About half way through the planned work it became apparent that the skilled guys doing the hands on technical efforts were insufficient to finish the job. At the present rate, the available number would obviously burn out well before the project conclusion. This despite the fact that B/W had sent in their crew of specialists, some of whom had also handled the Three Mile incident. The records were hastily searched and employees whose resume' contained any mechanical skills were encouraged to move to an apprentice position on a reactor crew.

Just after high school, Amos had worked for a major Caterpillar dealership in the engine overhaul shop. His extensive experience tinkering with hot rods and race cars would have gone unnoticed, but not that job period of his resume'. An early afternoon call, received on one of the plant lines, had resulted in his now being classified as ANM; Apprentice Nuclear Mechanic. This brought even more income to his table but some increased risk and exposure as well.

The main job was to remove the large control rod drive units from the head for inspection and possible refurbishing. This meant disengaging the massive bolt structure using oversize wrenches and bars, and then raising them out with the giant R/B (Reactor Building) polar crane. The drive tips, which were in contact with the fuel cells, were radioactively "hot"; way hot. Personnel who were not not directly involved, didn't get anywhere near one of these operations.

After removal, individual units were hoisted over to where a special "building" had been constructed on the R/B floor. A two story, frame work affair built on scaffolding, it measured about ten feet square and was enclosed using clear plastic sheeting. The interior housed a stack of fifty five gallon drums, each with a hollow core surrounded with leaded concrete. A work deck had been constructed encircling the upper drum. Each drive assembly was lowered in through a slit in the roof and a mechanic, fully space-suited and supplied with ankle, wrist and chest dosimeters, entered through another slit which acted as a door.

He relayed directions to the crane operator and guided the tip into the barrel core. After the desired position was reached, the first job was to stack lead pellet pouches around the base where the drive went into the barrel orifice to further suppress the radiation. After that, he went swiftly to work scraping and cleaning the gasket surface where the unit bolted to the head. It could have been suffocatingly hot work as well were it not for the conditioned, purified air being piped in through the suit helmet.

In the midst of such activity, there was enough latent danger. Amos didn't want to think what a warning from God himself through this mighty messenger might indicate was afoot.

"OK, you definitely have my attention Arak, please define 'warning'."

"Amos, you regularly venture into an environment where humans seek to control one of the Lord's own 'building blocks' of creation."

"I understand...I've referred to it as God's play dough myself." Amos smiled, "I imagine the technical details are above my pay grade."

The towering Arak grinned back, "Not necessarily, just beyond our allotted time at present. The best way to defeat any effect of your message is to remove you."

"Remove me?" interrupted Amos, "As in do away with, assassinate?"

"Yes," replied Arak evenly, "You yourself often point out the growing animosity toward all things Christian in this land. Be aware that Lucifer is riding the tide he has helped create and enjoying his increased influence over those without Truth. I have been permitted to watch this activity involving some who work, as you do, in the Plant".

"Can you tell me who you refer to?" asked Amos.

"Truthfully, I cannot. Interaction here has limitations dictated by the 'free will' aspect of the Lord's decrees. I was told only to say that all who are friendly are not your friends and any efforts made to silence you could also be at the expense of many others."

Amos stared pensively out over the island dotted expanse towards the massive hydrogen-helium ball which was slowly blazing its way into the horizon. After a few moments he turned to the angel,

"Arak, I'm trying to take all this in with the kind of faith I know He expects. So let me try a recap...I'm face to face with a ten foot tall angel of fire...who says he was once as I am...sent to tell me to keep up with the Lord's message...but be aware that someone in the 'service of Satan', who apparently also has access to the nuclear plant, might try to get rid of me?"

"I fear that is accurate Amos."

Amos was silent for another long moment, "How would I defend against this person...or persons?"

"All I may add is this. Listen to the Spirit as never before. Do not waste even a moment being cautious or doubting if, inside, you know it is He."

Amos thought again, then, "Alright...I thank you and the Father for this...visit. I'll treasure it always. And I will do as you suggest to the best of my ability. I also trust when this is over, you and I will get to see more of each other?"

Arak smiled down at him, "The pleasure has been mine Amos Mikals. And only the Lord knows if we will meet again here or there...but meet we shall. I have been fortunate to avoid the enemy even these few moments and must depart. I leave you only one further thought, and this one is my own. If a fellow believer should ever cross your path with details of this visit, that person can be relied upon. It may never happen...but if it should."

"Another mystery Arak? Well, at least that person wouldn't think I was crazy."

"Be of good cheer Amos. In time, all mysteries and questions will be answered. Farewell, little brother."

There was a flash of the blue-green fire and sparks, accompanied by a loud snapping sound like a downed power line, and suddenly, he was not there. Bubba leaped to his feet and stared intently at the empty spot for a moment then looked up at Amos. Amos also stared at the empty space then looked down at his four legged best friend,

"Bubba, tell me that really happened." Bubba gave Amos a soulful look for a moment then broke into his usual grin. Amos smiled back then burst into a cheering whoop as he sprang to his feet dancing toward the creek bank.

"Thank you Lord", he shouted, "that was the coolest thing I have ever seen." He stood at the shore's edge with his hands raised skyward whispering words of praise and thanks. Bubba had followed and was eying him with mild concern. After a minute Amos wiped his eyes and looked down,

"Yeah buddy, I know; not all of that was good news." He paused again, looked around and then muttered to himself, "Who else, I wonder, could possibly know anything about this?"

He continued eyeing the surroundings briefly then looked again at Bubba,

"Come on old man, guess we better tend to these fish."

With that he gathered up the utensils and platter, then headed for the back door...unaware that a similar batch of ripples had suddenly sprung into being on the quiet, still surface of this isolated little bayou.

CHAPTER 5

T HE PANORAMA WAS BRILLIANT; the colors far more vivid than any she'd ever seen on Earth. Now, how did she know that? This wasn't Earth. Yet it was very Earth-like. Her vision was focused a towering peak, some distance away, which glistened with a cap of pristine white snow. Then, as her eye wandered down slope, the snow gave way to greenery. Patchy and small at first, as the view descended, it blossomed into larger stands of trees and undergrowth. By half way down, some of the trees were tremendous and reminded her of the towering Redwoods of home.

Home...Earth was home. Who was she? Her mind whirred trying to find an answer while her eyes continued to drink in the overpowering beauty. To her left, the slopes gave way to flatlands which resembled those she had seen only in books and films; the plains of Africa. There were vast expanses of grassland dotted with islands of undergrowth and trees. Some of these were also of impressive size and height, unlike the low hanging versions on those plains of memory. The similarity was complete with herds of grazing animals. Large herds that stretched over impressive segments of the vast horizon. For some reason though, they didn't fit with anything she recalled from pictorial visits to the "Dark Continent". These more resembled...resembled what? It hit her; even at this distance, they seemed to mimic the legendary herds of Earth buffalo.

Jenny...her name was Jenny. Momentarily satisfied, she resumed her long distance inspection of the awe inspiring view. To the right the mountain appeared to tumble all the way to the sea; and what a sea it was. Emerald blue-green, it transcended any travel brochure she'd ever seen. At several places the mountain's craggy landscape tumbled to meet the shore and ended abruptly in towering waterside cliffs. At two of these she could see giant waterfalls cascading over the lip and into the waters below. Other sections marched in a more orderly fashion down to wide, creamy colored beaches. Several of these locations were fringed with giant palm-like trees. This side was like Hawaii re-imagined by some genius sculptor.

Nearer her position, the vast plains also descended to the beachfront. At some points great rolling breakers cascaded over unseen obstacles below and raced foaming onto the shoreline. Yet, just a little further on, the same waters seemed to nestle against the shore in a clam, placid fashion. That's odd she thought, waves one place, calm waters another.

Her eye suddenly focused on a small detail; a sail. Out off the distant beach she could plainly see a sail. No wait, there were several dotted at different ranges. There were people here. She scrutinized the shoreline once more. No mistake, there were what looked to be dwellings scattered unevenly along it. They appeared to be made primarily of stone-work trimmed with sections of timber. Some looked fairly large and elaborate, others were small and simple.

Her mind found a new gear. I must go and meet the people that live in such a beautiful place. She made an effort to move. Nothing happened. It was as if she were frozen in place. She tried again; with no more success than before. Now she heard a new sound. Sound...she'd been watching the majestic scene before her, but there had been no sound. This sound seemed familiar somehow. Of course...it was calling her name.

"Jenny, Jenny," a youngish voice was intoning.

She tried to focus her eyes to see who owned the voice. Now the panorama was gone and her vision seemed to be alternating between light and dark. She felt herself squint then opened her eyes as wide as she could. A brick? No, lots of them. She was lying on her side, face canted downward and her view was comprised of old, weathered stones or bricks. With a groan she managed to rotate her head slightly. A young face, somehow familiar, swam into view.

"Are you alright?"

She tried her voice, "I...I," it wasn't working. She tried harder. "Wh...Where am I? Where's the mountain?"

"The mountain?" echoed the young voice, "Jenny, it's me Ben."

She focused on the boy's face as he continued in a quieter tone, "Ben...Ben and Arak...remember?"

Arak! Her brain sprang into action. It all came rushing back. It was real. It had happened. Where was he? Was he alright? Buferan...the terrible war demons...that had been reality. The mountain. The sea with sails on it. Where was that beautiful place? What in the world was...

She felt herself gently shaken. "Jenny, people are coming. Can you sit up?"

With Ben's help she struggled upright. Her eye lit on the Codex lying next to her. "Ben, I need you to do something else for us."

"OK, what?"

"Give them this book back."

"Sure, no problem," he smiled slyly, "bet they can't put it back the way you took it out."

Jenny got shakily to her feet and smiled back, "No, I'd bet not."

"There you are," came his mom's voice from the doorway, "I thought you were right behind me. At least that old gentleman seems to be OK. Unlike those two youngsters who are still babbling about the tornado. Pah, look at this weather. You see any tornadoes?"

Ben and Jenny eyed each other, "No ma'am, not that I see," offered Jenny.

Several others came into view coming slowly out of the entry way. They looked curiously around...one was saying, "I swear; it was like a small hurricane or something."

Ben had picked up the Codex. His mom suddenly noticed it and her eyes opened in surprise, "Isn't that the book from the case?"

Jenny hurried to intervene, "Yes, and your son had just offered to return it for me."

"I, uh, didn't realize they loaned those out," she said suspiciously.

Jenny looked at Ben who was obviously becoming worried. She sighed, "No ma'am they don't. I just needed it for an emergency; but now I'm done. Please let Ben handle giving it back."

Another thought struck her, "Ma'am didn't you mention you attend church at home?"

"Yes," the mother replied, "First Baptist of Chattanooga. What's that got to do with this?"

Jenny looked directly into the woman's eyes,

"I give you my word, in the name of our Lord Jesus Christ, that what transpired here was sanctioned by God himself and is directly connected to His work here on Earth." Wow, there was that authoritative sounding language coming out again.

Mom looked taken aback for a moment and Ben's voice piped up, "Mom, you had best believe what she says, it's absolutely true. And we need to do whatever He wants us to."

Both women looked down at Ben and after a few seconds mom looked back at Jenny and sighed,

"OK, I feel it too. I don't know what went on here but I'll play along."

"Ma'am," Jenny began "I can't tha..."

"I'm not ma'am," she interrupted, "I'm Irene. And you're, what, Janey?"

"Close, Jenny, and I thank you with all my heart."

At that moment a security guard materialized in the doorway and began scrutinizing the area. Ben spun so the Codex was on his far side, "Uh, Jenny, you might wanna' go."

Both women looked back, "Yes, you are so right about that," said Jenny, "I love you both and I hope we meet again."

"It's guaranteed," said Ben and smiled up at her.

Jenny paused, "That it is," she grinned back, "Guys, I'm outta' here."

"Bye," they chorused together and Jenny headed away at the most normal pace her nerves would allow.

As she traversed the byways heading for the Ottaviano metro stop, she had time to try and assess what she'd just been through. Along with the cascading images and flashes of memory coursed another thought. Wonder what Dad would say to this. What were the rules on sharing something so...profound...and crazy sounding? Then it dawned clearly. The Holy Spirit would have to be the judge of that. That settled she went back to replaying some of the moments.

Arak...what a magnificent representative of God. And what love and compassion for Him to send Arak to...wait a minute, why was Arak here? What had he said...courier.

"That's some courier," she thought out loud.

What else was it he said? At the end...remember a name...Amos...Amos Michaels. Why does that sound vaguely familiar?

She strode on more purposefully now. After all, if a being like Arak told you to remember someone's name, it must be important. With that thought her mind slowed and peace settled over her thinking. No doubt about it, I'm coming clean with Dad and see what he makes of all this. Whatever else, he'll be the only one who'll believe me.

THE STERN FACED security guard towered over Ben and Irene Markham. Ringed around them were several curious onlookers including the "tornado" couple. In a less than friendly tone he asked again,

"Let me get this straight madam, your youngster just happened to be in possession of a priceless Church artifact when you walked out here?"

"Uh, yes sir, as crazy as it sounds, it's true."

He turned to Ben who was looking somewhat distressed but not for reasons the guard would ever have suspected, "And you, young sir, what's your version?"

Ben had been experiencing something different inside himself. Never an overly bold boy, he'd gathered confidence throughout this experience. A source that seemed to reside in his heart was emanating a sense of peace regarding the whole matter.

"Sir, I don't think I can say anything more about it ri…"

"You haven't said a bloody thing yet son," the guard interrupted, "I'm all ears and you're in deep trouble."

"What do you mean trouble," interjected Irene, "the book's fine and he's returning it."

The guard held up his hand silencing her. "I'm waiting son."

Ben sighed, "The fact is sir, if I tell you the truth, you won't believe me…so what's the point. Can't we just put it back?"

"Very well, have it your way. Both of you come with me. I'll take that," and folding the Codex carefully under one big arm he grasped Ben's hand with the other.

"Wait a minute," protested Irene.

"Wait not at all madam, right now it's voluntary, another word and I'll have you both arrested."

Ben looked up at his mom, winked and nodded.

"OK, OK, fine. Let's talk to someone else about this."

"That would be the Captain and that's where you're headed," affirmed the uniformed potentate.

With the hapless duo in tow he broke ranks with the small crowd and headed for the entry way. They had gone only a few steps when the oaken doors again went into motion. First one robed priest and then a second appeared as they swung both large doors to full open position. Revealed in the threshold were a number of plainly dressed folks, presumably tourists, and one tall, impressively robed clerical figure. Their attendant security person stopped dead in his tracks and swept off his uniform cap. He seemed to come to attention, "Your Excellency," he exclaimed with a trace of disbelief in his voice.

"Ah...Officer DiPaggio isn't it; what seems to be the problem here," his eyes widened slightly "and what in His name are you doing with the Codex?"

"Your Excellency, I have retrieved it from this young fellow and am taking the boy and his mother to the Captain for further questioning on the matter."

The intimidating robed figure turned his attention to Ben and his mom. "I am Archbishop Cantelli," he stated informally, "and you are?"

Ben was surprised to see his mom make a polite curtsy and say, "I am Irene Markham of Chattanooga, Tennessee and this is my son, Ben."

"Pleased to meet you both," he paused, "you're here for Pentecost Sunday?"

"Uh, not exactly sir, we are in town with my husband on business and just wanted to see the famous church."

"I trust you've not been disappointed?"

Ben and his mom eyed each other briefly, "Most certainly not," she said.

"Wonderful," said the dignified figure in his deep authoritative voice. Then he turned his attention directly to

Ben, "How is it young sir that you had the Codex in your possession?"

The boy looked uncomfortably around at the crowd which had begun to increase noticeably with the presence of the church officials.

"Sir, may I tell you in private?"

Now the Archbishop paused and also eyed the growing numbers, "Ah, yes you may," he stated, "let us take a short walk together. I would ask you ma'am and you officer to please wait a moment here with the Fathers."

Irene watched apprehensively as the tall figure led Ben towards an ornate marble bench strategically placed under a small group of flowering trees. She realized that she didn't have a clue herself what the actual story was.

The two of them arrived at the bench and sat down together. At first it was obvious the cleric was asking questions of Ben. Then the boy seemed to be opening up and his expressions and gestures became more animated. The Archbishop gave away nothing facially, except a slight widening of the eyes once or twice, and one instance when he pointedly looked up and surveyed the surrounding area with obvious interest.

By the time they finished most of the onlookers had become bored and wandered on. The guard had been engaging the Fathers in polite conversation but Irene hadn't noticed much of the content. The majestic looking Archbishop led Ben back to the group and then turned to Officer DiPaggio,

"Let us return to the display case with the relic officer."

The two priests fell into the lead and again held the doors open as the little entourage re-entered the complex. It was a short walk to the large, ornate home of the Codex and soon they were all gazing at the empty space inside. There, in a light layer of dust, was a perfect outline of the ancient volume replete with small smudges on both sides where it had obviously been lifted by someone.

"DiPaggio, how is this entered?" asked the Archbishop.

"I'm not sure Excellency; we've never had the need before."

The cleric glanced down and gave Ben a confidential look, "So how do you suppose this young man was able to borrow it?"

Irene noted his use of the term borrow with some relief.

"Ah...I've truly no idea Excellency, there must be an access behind that drapery back drop; but it would take at least three or four of us to move this."

The stately religious leader eyed the case quietly for a moment then gently placed his fingertips on the glass top. He seemed to be in deep thought, maybe even prayer. The little entourage waited respectfully for the better part of a minute and then he looked up, first at the large painting overhead and then at Ben. After another pause,

"What we shall do officer, is summon the required help to examine the back of the case for an entry, which I'm sure we will find. I will take possession of the Codex, if you please."

"Yes, Excellency," he said as he carefully handed the priceless volume over. "And what of these two?"

The arch bishop turned to Ben and Irene, "I'm not sure. Young Ben, is there anything further I can do for you or your mother?"

The two exchanged glances and Irene spoke up, "Your Excellency, I believe you've done exactly what was needed."

"I'd like to believe that as well," said the Archbishop. He turned to one of the Fathers, "Anthony, may I have one of the cards with the diocese numbers, and a pen, if you would."

He took the proffered card and implement and wrote carefully on the back for several moments. He handed the card to Irene while meeting eyes with Ben. "Do not hesitate if I can be of any further use to you during your stay."

"You mean we're free to go?" she asked.

"But your Excellency, they...," began the guard.

"DiPaggio, were you not summoning help?" the cleric asked somewhat sternly.

The officer sighed, "Yes Excellency." He gave the two perpetrators a narrow glance and hastened away.

"This is somewhat unorthodox but I perceive it has been an unorthodox day," so saying the Archbishop made the sign, then placed one hand on each of their heads, "Go with the protection of Our Lord into whatever awaits you."

All three looked quietly at each other for several moments then Ben said quietly, "Amen."

"Amen indeed, and now, if you will excuse me, duty insists that I return to it." Then turning to the priest, "Fathers, if you please."

And with a wink at Ben he strode regally off towards the massive interior.

They both stood watching him go for several seconds. Then Ben turned to find his mom staring intently at the case.

"Her fingers really did go through the glass," she murmured, then turning to him, "Ben what in the world went on here?"

"OK Mom, I guess I can tell you what I know, but let's get out of here before Mr. DiPaggio gets back, huh?"

"Oh, yeah, good idea."

They began retracing their steps to the doors and his mother said, "Now, tell me."

"Mom, your not gonna believe this but..." Ben began.

"Ben," his mom interrupted, "you just tell me the facts and let me worry about believing, OK?"

"Alright," Ben said with a twinkle in his eye. Then they passed through the great doors for the last time and out into the bright, sun-lit courtyard.

CHAPTER 6

EDDIE DORMER SMILED TO HIMSELF as he cleared the security station exiting the Crystal River nuclear facility. For all the yak-yak about procedures that prevented material and contamination from leaving the premises, it was no big deal to defeat them. His collection of contraband included "Radioactive Waste" bags, one vinyl outer "space suit", a pocket dosimeter and numerous tools and bits his friend Charlie had slipped to him. Charlie was a tool room assistant on second shift and had access to some really cool stuff. Yeah, they'd freak if they knew how easy it was.

Most of the items had simply been carried out in his lunch box. But with the reactor rebuild and all the clean up, a new and ingenious way to get even larger stuff out had appeared. Almost every night there was a dump run where the "cold side" debris was taken to a collection point outside the main perimeter. There it would either be hauled away or incinerated on site. He had played Mikals for several weeks now working hard and even volunteering for some of the more hazardous details. Like the filter change on the R/B exhaust unit. It had been brutal, and dangerous, but even McMillan had to admit he'd more than carried his share. And it had certainly been worth the effort. When he asked Amos to post him on the dump run so he could get outside once in a while, he'd made it happen. Now to figure the best way to make use of the situation.

He knew McMillan was suspicious. Eddie had worked under his supervision for two years and always been something of a slacker. It was just plain luck Mr. Goody-Two Shoes had taken over lead for second shift. First it was all that "lead by example" crap, practically doing the work of two and encouraging the others to do the same. That didn't go over so well with the old hands who were used to leaving a lot of the dirtier work for third shift. (Why not, first shift did it to them all the time.) But you had to admit, Mikals didn't ask anyone to do anything he wouldn't do himself. All well and good, Eddie knew hiding places all over the plant...But then had come the big bust in the D-Ring.

There was a dungeon like area deep alongside the reactor containment vessel shaped like a large "D" and called just that; the D-Ring. It was accessed through a hatch and long climb down a steel ladder system. Eddie assumed it was there to inspect the vessel walls and piping but the guys had turned it into a hideaway to hang out and generally goof off. Mikals had been perplexed, after he first took over, at how short handed he often stayed during a shift. Only to have a complete crew show up at checkout time, usually claiming to have been here or there on other duties. It worked for several reasons. One; a nuclear complex like this was a massive, confusing, multi-storied maze. And two; Mikals hadn't been there long enough to know his way around much of it. But someone must have snitched.

Fortunately, Eddie had been absent from the group that night. Several of the guys had been playing cards and one even asleep in a hammock, cleverly made from a couple of XL cotton suit liners, when Mikals suddenly appeared at the foot of the ladder. He didn't say a word at first, just casually walked around taking in the makeshift clubhouse arrangements. Then he tapped poor sleeping Dennis on the shoulder giving him one serious shock. He simply said, "Clean it all out and get back to work." Then it was waiting on pins and needles for him to turn it over to McMillan. That their jobs were in jeopardy was pretty obvious.

The couple of roughnecks involved chose not to bluff or try threats on Mikals. He wasn't a big guy but he had a muscled, athletic look and had won several fun bets proving he could do one arm pull ups with either hand. It was also rumored he had some kind of martial arts background. Whatever the case, no one felt like putting it to the test in what would probably be a losing cause anyway. There were people lined up wanting these jobs and chances were McMillan would can the lot of them...But that wasn't what happened.

When they gathered at 11:30 for checkout, Mikals had already asked McMillan to let him speak to the men privately. What they got was a lecture on the lack of integrity it took to take anyone's money for doing nothing. It had made quite a few of the crew squirm, but no one interrupted. He ended, memorably, by stating anyone that low rent should turn backwards when they got their check and not look the paymaster in the eyes.

Officially McMillan never got into the picture but it was later revealed he had hidden around the corner and listened to the whole thing. No one lost their job, the D-ring club was closed and, overall, the men responded surprisingly well. Instead of becoming a pariah, Mikals stock went up in the opinion of most. Maybe there was something to that Christian stuff he was known to promote.

None of that mattered to Eddie. His plans for mischief were unchanged. In fact, lately it was like some little voice rode around in his head coming up with better ideas all the time. Like...if you could get stuff out, why not stuff in? He had no idea what he would want to sneak in but it was a novel thought and a challenge. His latest method of passing the time and entertaining himself, however, had been to invent the "Wolf Man".

There were multiple phone stations on every deck in both the hot and cold sides. In fact, there were so many, he wasn't sure anyone knew what the actual count was. Some were in isolated areas and probably never saw much use. Others were in high traffic zones and were used many times per shift. Most inter-plant business was relayed or conducted over this system. There were two lines, "Plant Line 1" and "Plant line 2". Both lines activated an equally large number of strategically placed loud speakers. Loud enough to be heard over even some of the mind numbing noise and roars present while under power. A typical message would start out with the individuals name and a request to pick up "PL 1" or "PL 2". Eddie had invented another use for them.

At first it was a spur of the moment thing. He was alone in a remote location and noticed the phone station. Glancing around he lifted the receiver and did his best wolf howl imitation at full volume. The result was an ear splitting cacophony that echoed throughout the entire plant. There was much chatter that night and, on subsequent evenings, a few imitations. Swiftly though, word came down from on high to knock it off. Then to knock it off "or else".

Perceiving he had not only touched a nerve, but that it was reflecting back on McMillan, Eddie had a new hobby. Nightly, and often more than once, he managed to repeat the performance. The vastness and complexity of the plant made detection nearly impossible. The frustration level in the front office escalated to the point a reward was in place for the snitch and the offender was guaranteed to be history. Eddie confided in no one and all the attention only heightened the thrill. So, for the time being, the "Wolf Man" was part of daily life on second shift.

UNKNOWN TO EDDIE, he was also being "played". Normally a non-Christian didn't figure very prominently on the radar of so exalted a demon as Buferan. They were rarely, if ever, a threat to the "Master Plan" and were, in fact, viewed more as POW's in the warfare on Earth. That all changed when one appeared to be steerable toward the means to counter or neutralize one of the true threats. Amos Mikals had become just such a threat. He had been opposition for a number of his years, but the last few had seen him turn the corner towards a much more serious irritant. A purveyor of something cleverly hidden over a vast period of human history. Something his boss, Lucifer, least wanted exposed to the race called human; the truth.

Half truths were ok, genuine falsehoods were better, but a shiny, realistic looking counterfeit was best of all. A rapidly growing number of His little churches were falling ever deeper into the latter category. These fools, they termed pastors, would preach right by a verse in the wretched book that exposed important facts. Facts that were affecting and sometimes decimating the very group they claimed to be leading. It had become almost too easy to waylay these "men of God" into looking the other way using the standard techniques that worked on everyone else. By far self ambition was number one. Anything that smelled of controversy, or wasn't "politically correct", was treated like it didn't exist. That is to say, if it didn't keep the pew and the plate filled, it was deemed inconsequential by these "Titan's of Truth".

Many centuries of effort, some of which he had person- ally directed, had gone into diluting the religious establishments to this point. And no upstart like young Mikals was going to be throwing sand on his well function- ing gears. In fact, this qualified as a special pursuit's case. Mr. Mikals was just liable to find conversations with his God much more personal. It would have to be cleverly orchestrated, but it might be a game they could win. And this one, Dormer, was well placed to be used in the effort. But, to achieve the best results, he would have to gain Mikals trust. That might be the tricky part.

Buferan had already made another personal visit to ob- serve Mikals. In fact he had barely missed confronting that great pain in the posterior, Arak, right at Mikals back door. It seemed the message had gotten through. He would give an acre of souls to know the exact content. Lucifer wasn't the only one closely watching this drama. The Unmention- able One himself had sent the Deran derelict on that mission. And maybe worst of all, Mikals with his continuing faith, was keeping the influence of the dreaded Presence charged up. Not even Lucifer could predict what direction that might take at any given moment. In concert with these "re-born" types, he had ruined many a well laid plan.

So the risk was high, but so were the stakes. It was time to re-group and get some input from his underlings regarding others involved in this scenario. He already knew one preacher in Crystal River that bore watching closely as he'd wavered under Mikals presentation. And he would have to appear before Lucifer and tell of the success of Arak's little foray. That was going to be painful; but not near as much so as he intended to make it for the mortals involved...No matter how long it took.

ARAK TOO PREPARED to stand before his master; a presence mere words could not convey. He was surrounded by numerous other beings. Some powerful, some carefully cultivating that power and others in various stages of service or training. But all with the same thing in common; adoration of, and loyalty to, Him who had created them. He often wondered deeply that this was not universally so.

What went wrong in the mind of beings, both in spirit and in the flesh, which made them quest after their own glory? He had come to believe that even creatures as willfully far from the truth as Lucifer could not adequately explain their motivations. And, as far as the misguided Deranians he had known, and the Earthers he now observed, he imagined they might have even less to offer on the subject. One thing did seem clear, in any such case, a switch to worship of ones self and your own existence seemed to be a common denominator. Greed and selfishness replaced love and kindness as the prime factor or touchstone by which "life" was measured. Such an inverse pursuit was hard to comprehend from this vantage point.

The great throne room was, as always, a busy yet harmonious place. The dazzling bright aura and splendor were balanced by the presence of not only love, but its author. He truly was the source of all that was good and that fact permeated the atmosphere with an undertone like the ultimate spring day. So what might seem initially intimidating, what with the torches of "The Spirits" and the majestic many eyed creatures, not to mention the presence of so many renowned Archs and Elders, became somewhat mitigated and normalized for the newcomer or visitor by that benign warmth. But the underlying sense of awe at being in "His" presence, never changed or diminished.

There were marvels here, some hidden since ages long past. And entities worthy of the highest and humblest regard. There was the glorious presence of Jesus himself, operating with Father's full authority, to help oversee things being coordinated from this, the ultimate command post. Certainly things no mortal mind had ever imagined. Although, Arak thought anyone observing even a slice of the so called "known universe", shouldn't have been surprised. A being exponentially vast enough in power and intellect to have set such a thing in motion, just for the pleasure of it, was also sure to have things just as vast and incomprehensible playing out across that endless and eternal arena.

But the reality of His presence completely overshadowed all of this. Even after countless visits and secure in the love that mighty hand held forth, Arak knew that to adequately portray the majesty of Jehovah God to another mind was impossible. And every entry here was like the first. You had to acclimate to the stunning and immeasurable impact of that presence, then regain your senses and remember why you'd come. And so it was now. Even after all this "time", which was also a relative term here, Arak could only shake his head lost in wonder at the unfathomable affection and power that had reached out to such a puny, erroneous thing as himself and said "I made you, I love you." It was the most humbling thing in all of Creation...and the most precious.

Finally he glanced around and nodded to several fellows with whom he had worked or helped to train. And to others who had helped and trained him. Michael was absent, probably in pursuit of some goal beyond Arak's imaginings. Nor was Gabriel to be found at the moment. However, his long time mentor, Raphael, was in attendance and he was motioning to Arak; undoubtedly to get a report on this latest Earth mission. As he approached the venerable elder, Raphael held his fist to his heart then extended it toward Arak. It never ceased to amuse Arak that he'd seen this motion imitated in less than hallowed circumstances on the Earth. He also knew the imitators had no clue whom they were mimicking. He returned the salutation.

"Arak, my child, it's good to see you safe. Father informed me of your scrape with Buferan."

"Yes sir, I fear he did fool me rather shrewdly."

"Many others have suffered similar deceptions; it is more important that you evaded the snare and gained wisdom from it." The giant Arch looked thoughtful, "That would seem much like the trickery used to waylay your brother, Kurtanus. I am both proud and relieved to have you home."

"I am always honored to do His bidding whatever the risk."

"Yes, and you are always a credit to us my warrior minded little brother. But now, tell me all that transpired. Father will want to hear more of it, but he's still dealing directly with some irrational business Michael has uncovered. I fear those involved may see His wrathful side if they have not a credible explanation for such misadventure."

Arak had only seen the Lord truly angry on one occasion over all the period of heavens history he had been privy to. Why anything with a thought in its head would risk that was beyond him now. Although he realized that, on Deran, he too had probably attracted a little of Father's negative attention in his younger suns.

"Sir, it was actually, ah, somewhat illuminating. Because of Buferan, I had occasion to interact with a number of the saints and one young believer pure in heart. They accept our presence more swiftly in this generation...though the initial shock is still pronounced. In order to thwart his trap, I had to request a young woman act as 'Bearer' with an older copy of the Earth Scripture. The outcome might have been quite different without her...as well as one or two others. The whole thing again made me look forward to that time when their war is over and we are united."

Raphael said thoughtfully, "As do we all young Arak, as do we all. Tell me your impression of Amos."

"He is all I was told and more. His interest was less in the threat to himself than to ask questions regarding matters he has pondered during his suns there. He asked me quite pointedly about the 'craft' observed within his area. I wish I could have told him more. But there is no doubt he feels his mission is of Father and worthy of sacrifice. I must say sir, in that brief encounter, I came to truly feel like brothers of long standing. I would request permission to remain courier to his situation should the need continue."

Raphael had paused again in thought, then, "I will ask that option be left open. How would you assess the danger where the 'others' are concerned?"

"They are following quite closely. Lucifer had already, somehow, intuited the target of my visit."

"Indeed, are you sure?"

"Buferan stated as much when we clashed."

"That is worrisome. I needn't tell you that, should anything happen to Amos, there is virtually none at present to carry on in that section of his principality."

Arak contemplated this a moment, "When you view the numbers present, that is sometimes hard to fathom. It would seem Lucifer has had more influence over them than the Ags' ever exerted on the population of Deran."

"Perhaps so...Father has let this conflict wear on far longer than I supposed it might. The ratio in each generation seems to feed upon itself as the Fallens foster the greed and selfishness that so attracts man. Remember, Jesus himself observed this when he asked them if he would even find faith upon his return."

Arak again thought a moment, "My impression is that he will, but it will be a very small number. I fear the 'narrow gate' will receive little use in the suns to come. There is a sense of spiritual immorality and deceit on every continent I touched."

Raphael nodded solemnly, "I have felt it myself...back to Amos. It still appears they may try to use something at that power facility to place him at risk?"

"Yes, they are barely able to contain the minute quantities which they have appropriated. Any disruption of the cooling or safeguards would place many mortal lives at risk, including Amos."

"Have your observations singled out any likely to cooperate in such a scheme?"

"Two, sir, one with adequate knowledge and access to the mechanics involved and another, a member of the Eastern Fanatics, assigned to the area. Both exhibit the lack of moral restraint and order common to those beguiled by a demon. Although I was unable to witness it first hand, I fear Buferan's involvement with both."

"In this case that probably goes without saying. You will notice that what seems a Special Pursuits case has not been approached through those channels. Lucifer is grown bold with his successes. If it is Buferan manipulating matters, instead of one of his underlings, things are going to reach a critical juncture very quickly."

Arak paused, "Raphael, why does He not just let me tell Amos the facts if he is so crucial? Especially in light of the destination that awaits their deceived. Surely one like Amos might reach out and help deliver some of them."

"My son, the conditions on Earth are different than those you experienced on Deran. It is true you dealt with perverted natures that could be called evil, but the true originator of that behavior is Lucifer himself. And he was never actually present on your world. The mortals on Earth have been subjected to him almost from their beginning. That is one obvious reason for Father's reluctance to end the age there. He wishes to give every possible opportunity, for those who will, to accept His plan.

"And, as you know, it is the only stage where He has allowed the actual "physical" involvement of the Christ. You think you comprehend the reasons why Earth is such a focal point in the endless reaches, but I assure you that not Gabriel, I, nor any of the others completely understand those things. And that is as it should be; no mind can fully align itself with His.

"It is true, as Jesus portrayed it to the Jewish leaders, he and Father will always remain "one". But, as you are aware, that is in purpose and procedure, not power and authority. There are sometimes things that even he is not privy to...beyond such matters as the hour of his return and such."

This speech again left Arak in contemplation, "I thought I somewhat understood Earth's importance to Him, but I think perhaps I underestimate it. It is as if He threw down a gauntlet to Lucifer and dared him to try and consolidate the Earthers under his banners. But why only now seems to come into focus. In that state of 'will', are they not more like Father than any others?"

"They are truly in His image...you begin to understand. Look, He's finished and, thankfully, no fireworks. Let us lay this before Him and seek His guidance on the matter. It is one of the things He is most interested in at present."

With that Arak and Raphael repeated the familiar steps they had taken many times in approaching "The Great I Am". And, as always, the awe glittered and cascaded through Arak's whole being as he drew near. In all of Creation, with its countless, mind numbing secrets and glories, there was nothing to compare with Almighty God face to face…There never would be.

JUST AS HE'D FEARED, "His Exaltedness" was furious.

"How could you three let that ex-mortal, alien, puffed up toad out flank and out think you? You had enough firepower to capture two of him."

"My Lord, we were very nearly successful during his transfer, as you so wisely foresaw. And we did have him cornered in Rome. We could have forced him to the deadline and completed the capture…or sent him slinking back without making contact…"

"Buferan," roared Lucifer, "I care not what you might have accomplished, why did you let him leave that sanctimonious palace of fools in one piece? And where are Sardon and Atreus?"

"Ah, sir, I sent them back to Israel with instructions to observe the situation, query their lieutenants and bring you their reports. They will not be long."

"That, at least, is acceptable. I cannot have two of their caliber off on any more bungled attempts to counter this interfering Deranian. What exactly went wrong?"

Buferan hesitated. This was the part he hated to admit to. "Ah, a 'follower' showed up my Lord; a real one."

"What…how many mortals were present?"

"Not so many at the moment you would expect it to be so but, none the less, it occurred."

"Judas riding a goat, for millennia I have worked to pare their numbers and still they pop up. And always at the worst times. How did he come to interfere?"

"Ah... not a he sir, a she, a younger female."

A pause, "This gets worse and worse. So you were thwarted by a girl? Who managed to engage you in what, some cleverness developed by the busy body 'Presence'? I mean, Buferan, I would think yourself and two Wars should be able to counter that; explain."

The mighty sub-prince of darkness shrugged his massive, reptilian shoulders, "My Lord she appeared before us and not only knew we were there, she saw us."

"WHAT," roared Lucifer again, "She looked upon the three of you? And it had no effect?"

"Sire, it was clearly the influence of the Deranian."

"Yes and YOU let him get through to Mikals! If he can exert that much influence over some chance encounter with a mere girl, what effect do you think he will have on him?...Wait....Just what did this femme fatale do that succeeded in freeing Arak from your trap?"

For once Buferan looked his master straight in the eye, "She carried a 'copy' out of the sanctuary...She quoted both of you..."

Understanding settled on the countenance that had once graced heaven but now sought its destruction.

"She became his Bearer." stated Buferan flatly.

Lucifer was silent for some time. "I see," he said finally. Then more silence. Suddenly, "This thing is reaching what those idiots call critical mass. After all these ages, with victory seemingly where I can touch it, the influence of that 'One' still manages to frustrate too many of my plans."

He sank back in deep thought for several moments. Then, "You have contingencies concerning Mikals, do you not." It was a statement rather than question.

"I do My Lord. I have groomed one that is in close proximity to him. My influences are willingly becoming his own. I have at least one other nearby and a few further placed...but useful none the less."

"What is the substance of this plan? Is it likely to bring the verdamnt 'Archs' into the picture?"

"That depends oh Majestic One; do you deem this a 'Special Pursuits' engagement?"

The ruler of all evil paused again in thought. "Buferan, I have no intention of seeking permission this time. Those days have expired."

"I suspected as much sir, therefore we must consider the possibility that an Arch may be sent in at some point. Or it may provoke another incursion by the Deranian. Something I would actually relish, if I may say so."

"You are overly bold for one who has had his tail pulled more than once by this adversary, Buferan."

"Sire, his luck will run out. He takes too many chances that remind me of another of his ilk; one who was eventually neutralized as I recall."

"Do you recall as well what a near thing it was for us?"

"You deemed it worth the risk on that occasion, Highness, only you can do so now. I await your consent or command," and he bowed his massive frame low before the mighty King of Chaos.

"Leave me. I will give it consideration. Go to Israel and be sure your underlings are not bungling that assignment as well."

"As you wish, My Lord," said Buferan and he vanished in the same dazzling, electrical manner as an angel...but with a hue that would best be described as, "Black Fire".

CHAPTER 7

JENNY TRUDGED UP HER FATHERS' STEPS, her suitcase feeling like the proverbial lead weight. She tried the door and, as usual, found it unlocked. Dad had never figured out this little Jacksonville neighborhood wasn't the same place he remembered. Years ago he'd been a child here and sometimes, she thought, he still acted like one. She'd tried to win that argument more than once.

"Child-like faith is one thing," she'd offer, "but foolishness is something else."

"What foolishness," her father would ask with one eyebrow raised.

"Dad, there are bad people living near this neighborhood now. They rob and steal pretty often around here. Don't you watch the news? What if one of them just walks in here sometime cause' you won't lock the door during the daytime?"

"'Tis the sick that need the doctor."

"You'll be the one needing the doctor," Jenny had retorted.

But now, in the period of her life she'd begun to think of as "Post Arak", she considered a different possibility. Her father was one of the most sincere men of God she'd ever encountered. And not just because he was her dad. His intensity concerning things Scriptural was a daily pursuit and she had watched the changes in him over her own lifetime. Not many years ago an intruder here would undoubtedly have been met with deadly force. Despite his Christianity, he'd always been prepared to protect either of them physically or with firearms. But apparently he had come to some conclusion that it just wasn't necessary; at least not as a first step. She knew those weapons still lingered here, but she was also sure they had been relegated to "last resort" status. Now another possibility had come to abrupt and amazing light.

Did he have some confidence that the Holy Spirit would actively warn and protect him? Had something happened to strengthen that conviction or was it just spiritual maturity? Her mind never stopped replaying segments of the encounter with Arak and she remembered that when she remarked about her dad not believing this, his response had been, "Don't be so sure". That was worth pursuing, but at the moment, she was just too tired. As she slowly made her way across the living room, the back door leading to her fathers shop opened and James Alexander appeared in the dining area of his small home.

Six foot three but weighing a mere one eighty five on average, Jims friends and family had long ago borrowed the famous football players nickname and often referred to him as the Mad Stork. There were multiple lines of reasoning behind this blatant plagiarism.

The tales of her father's youth revealed an exuberance for life that frequently led to minor scrapes and mischief.

He and his buddies were nearly legendary because of misadventures and pranks which they either perpetrated or were in cooperation with. The mysterious re-opening of the high school gymnasium for come one, come all sports nights. Motorcycles driven down the school hallways. A boa constrictor in the girl's locker room...the school days list was long and well remembered. The post high school tales lost some of their "innocence", but nothing in the telling. Then, at a certain well defined point, they were all eclipsed by her dad's introduction to the Gospel of Jesus Christ. Or as he put it, his serious one.

Jim's church experiences as a youngster led him to believe he'd accepted Christ at an early age and nothing he did or didn't do after that was really pertinent to his salvation. He walked the aisle, got baptized and figured his "fire insurance" was in place. But one summer night he picked up his Bible and was confronted with the Scripture in Matthew 7 about the narrow gate and how few found it. He realized that he was, more than likely, not one of those few. His life's focus had thus far been on self and a good time; not service to, or interest in, God. That epiphany cost him some friends and changed his thinking and lifestyle but now, many years later, he'd tell you his only regret was...it didn't come sooner.

These days Jenny would place her father in a category shared by few when it came to knowledge of, or faith in, God. Some serious and high ranking church leaders, and a few self proclaimed prophets, had walked away in deep thought, or disturbed indignation, over his observations on current "Christian" policies and practices. But not one had ever looked him in the eye and said, "You're wrong."

He swept her into an embrace, "It's always a relief when you're actually here safe and sound. Did you walk in the apostle's footsteps around Rome?"

She smiled up at him, "It's a relief to stop moving and rushing to the next stop too. But dad, this trip yielded a lot more than just a look at where Peter and Paul are supposed to have been executed."

He eyed her curiously, "You met Mr. Right?"

Jenny looked surprised then began to laugh, "That's very funny dad. No I didn't meet 'the' man...but I sure met someone."

He released her and stepped back as his face sobered somewhat, "I suppose you should probably take some time to rest and then tell me about it."

Jenny felt the urge to blurt out the Arak chronicle but she too realized the wisdom of waiting till she rested up, "As always, oh dad of mine, you have the better idea."

"Hmph...I wish that were so, but...there's something going on here. And your look tells me it's important."

"Dad, you are so right, this is as major as anything I..."

He raised his hand, "Jen, just wait a few. Maybe take a short nap and then have a bite. Or are you hungry now?"

She paused thoughtfully, "I'm hungry but the nap sounds like a real winner. My eyes feel like lead. Besides, you always say don't rush things...this might be one of those times."

Nearly three hours later, she groggily opened those eyes to the familiar sights of her childhood bedroom. Problem was, it wasn't supposed to be so dark. How long had she slept? She creaked into a sitting position and stared down at the hardwood floor and her favorite old throw rug with its worn Navaho design. She'd been back on the "mountain" at some point in her dreams. Where was that place? And why was it haunting her? It couldn't be real...could it? The amazing Rome adventure began flitting through her still viscous mind.

Here I sit on my old bed like nothing's happened...but things can never be the same. I see why he warned me about looking for other "experiences". This existence seems to be on some wavelength of boredom after St. Peters. Oh well, it's time to uncork the genie and tell dad.

Jenny found him out back in one of his favorite states; fiddling around with something mechanical in his elaborate little work shop. His back was to her and he was absorbed with some small, noisy tool as he moved it in a gyrating fashion inside what she recognized as an automotive cylinder head.

"Dad"...no response..."DAD"...he turned, smiled, then switched off the little noise maker. It sounded like a small jet turbine spooling down.

"Wondered when you'd return to Earth."

That gave her a moment's pause, "Uh, why do you say that?"

Now Jim looked quizzical, "Well...wake up, revive, return...you know."

"Oh...yeah, it's just that...I've been dreaming about someplace and it's not Earth."

"Really?" he looked interested, "where then?"

"Wish I knew, it's the most beautiful planet I ever saw...Hmmm, that's the first time I've really acknowledged outright it could be another plan-...Whoa...Wait just a second...Oh dear God, what if it's this Deran?"

She rarely found her dad in total surprise or without words but he just stared at her in silence for a few seconds. Then,

"Jennifer Alexander, what in the world are you talking about?"

"Ok dad, you might want to sit down...I do."

He absentmindedly corralled his old swivel office chair and then retrieved the "guest" version from under the corner of one workbench. When they were seated comfortably face to face he looked at her and said,

"Ok daughter of mine, spill it."

Jenny drew a breath, "Dad, I know you've seen miracles from God right? I mean, I know the ones you've told me about, but that's not all of them is it?"

He thought a moment "Jen, some aren't meant for sharing; they're between you and Him. I think the same applies to most believers."

"Well, at first I wasn't sure about this one, but I feel the Holy Spirit has okayed it for you and me...Besides there were a few others involved anyway," she paused thinking of Ben and Irene. "...how do I begin this..."

"What say we try the beginning?"

"OK," she sighed, "Here goes...Dad, I was in St. Peters' just looking around, you know...sightseeing. Not praying or feeling real 'religious' or anything. But you know that chill you get sometimes when the Holy Spirit is saying something or trying to get your attention; I never felt one this strong. Like my whole back was...like I had my back to some high powered electrical current and it was making static race up and down my spine. So I turned around and, dad...there was an angel...A huge angel...Just standing there about, I don't know, I guess eight or ten yards from where I was...And fire, he looked like he was coated in golden fire with the wings and everything...Dad...he was more beautiful than we have words to describe..."

She paused and realized she was half-stepping breathlessly through the opening of her story. Her father was sitting wide eyed and she watched him blink once or twice like someone trying to wake up. She reached out and grabbed his hand.

"Dad, I know it sounds crazy but it's true."

He paused, still looking a little shocked, "Jen...I'm not doubting you, I know you'd never make up something like this...But wow." He was silent, again in thought, "I'm also wondering why he was there or what was going on. I mean, the Bible seems to indicate that when they come here there's a reason...or assignment."

"Well, I know why he was there. I...," she thought a moment, "I do know why he was in St. Peters I mean...But, you know...I have no idea why he was here in the first place."

"How do you know why he was in the Cathedral?"

"Well, he told me most of it...I mean he, being Arak, needed some help and of all things Dad, I was it."

Jim slumped heavily back in his chair, "Jenny, you talked to this angel...what'd you call him, Erok?"

"A-r-a-k dad, yeah I spent quite some time...no, actually it all happened in like, wow...that whole thing was probably only something like eight or ten minutes." she paused reflectively.

Her dad sat forward, "OK, hold the phone here. This is much more than I expected. Catch a breath and start over...Slowly with all the details, alright?"

"Yeah, I need to go over some of this myself...It does seem unreal now that I sit here so far away. But, dad, it was more real than anything I've ever experienced. OK, when I turned and saw him, my legs felt like jello and I wound up on my knees. And I have to admit I was a little terrified...no, a lot terrified. Then this awesome, powerful looking person or spirit or whatever looks right down at me and smiles...then says hello...No, not hello, he says my name and tells me his...

TO THE SOUTH, Amos was distractedly going about his routine in "the plant" while mentally canvassing his own stunning visit from the same source. The following morning it had seemed like a vision or dream was the best explanation. But as he reclined against his headboard, coffee in hand, Bible open in his lap and gazed out at the marshes, he knew better. It had been real; perhaps the most "real" thing he'd yet experienced in this journey called life. With that acceptance came the ominous realization that the warning had been real too. Danger would be stalking him now. And it stalked in an arena already fraught with enough potential peril.

He had long understood that all mankind was under the observation of demonic forces. Also that those forces had to, by nature, be most interested in individuals participating actively against the plans of Satan. Plans to encourage the soul of man to ever lower levels of degradation and sin. Without realizing it most humans were cooperating with their worst enemy. Amos had spent time in that category himself. He knew the false gods that overtook the minds of those who failed to resist. But now the mechanics were reversed. He had attracted enough of the "other side's" attention to garner some fleshly enemies...as well as the spirit ones. Worse yet, those involved placed no premium on human life and would take out innocents in their zeal to silence him. He thought about the vast complex of structure and machinery that spread out around, above and below him right now. It was like a multi-storied labyrinth. Any military man would have to describe it as a "death trap".

Death; that was the most terrifying word mentionable to most people. Far too many would keep that appointment without seeking knowledge of, or considering the second one that lay beyond. How had Jesus put it, Fear not him who can kill only the body, fear Him who has power to destroy both body and soul in hell. The point being, much greater horrors than the grave awaited those who rejected the call to righteousness through Christ. That second one now held no fear for Amos. The trick was to avoid letting this unknown adversary speed his acquaintance with the first.

He glanced at the various door ways and passages leading from his current location in the Auxiliary building. It would be no great contest to waylay an individual in such a setting. But that would most likely not result in harm to others if done "hit" style. Arak had warned that the approach taken might cause danger to the lives of those around him. What would fit that scenario? Well, the obvious thing was the nuclear component. If you tampered with the systems managing cooling and containment you could endanger everyone in the plant. Heck, you could endanger the west coast of Florida. His eyes widened.

Oh man, the core was exposed for the reactor work and it was being refueled. There must be opportunities galore to cause problems. And as "lead" Amos would feel obligated to enter the affected area, assess the situation and report to the control room. Worse yet, during the periods he was acting as ANM, McMillan was letting second shift function on it's own till he returned. Primarily because the fuss about work ethics and the D-ring episode had produced some positive results among the crew.

Now that could prove a double edged sword, assuming the threat originated on second shift. If it did, then whoever was involved would have an even freer reign while he was ensconced in a full exposure suit and trapped in a "high-rad" work area. For that matter, wouldn't that be a great time to create some accident which resulted in a terminal exposure rate.

This was maddening. The opportunities and scenarios were countless. When Arak had said listen like never before for the Spirit's voice, he wasn't kidding. It appeared the other guy's had outside influence and support, Amos was going to need the same to have any hope of mounting a defense. He paused and offered up a short prayer,

"Father...sometimes I just don't know how or what to say...My life seems to take more unexpected turns all the time...I definitely didn't see Arak coming, but thank you again...And thanks for trying to give me a heads up...But Lord, this place seems...indefensible...Without your help, I'm afraid of what could happen here..."

He paused...now that was exactly what the Scriptures constantly taught. Man was largely helpless against the unforeseen events of life...And therefore needed to rely on his Creator for guidance and comfort...

"OK Father, I need to let you handle this by your spirit...We both know I'm sometimes clumsy at that...But I will try to keep my thoughts neutral and not waste time worrying...And to show no cowardice when the time comes...Grant me the strength to do that...And the wisdom to detect Satan's activity...For the sake of your Son's name...Amen."

The words were barely out when Eddie Dormer popped around the corner and abruptly halted face to face with Amos.

"Eddie, I thought you were in the R/B?"

"Uh, yeah, I'm actually on my way...But I left a box of rem bags somewhere up here and thought I'd get em."

Rem bags were the slang term for the yellow, oversized vinyl waste bags that were marked with the radiation level of the material inside. It was pretty flimsy that anyone would need to look for a box to take into the R/B as there were more than enough already present within.

"Eddie, that's kind of wasting time. You know there are plenty of those in there already."

Eddie looked uncomfortable and glanced briefly at his shoes, "Uh, yeah, I know...actually I was hoping I'd run into you," this was a lie, but circumstances had provided an opportunity and Eddies little voice was telling him to take advantage.

"Are you making a jump tonight?" Another slang term for suiting up and entering a really hot zone.

"Not tonight, why?"

"It's just that...man, I need to get ahead on things. My landlord is talking about raising the rent. My ex is always on my case for extras. I just don't seem to make enough to meet it all."

These statements hardly matched the facts, but Eddie was gratified at how well he made them sound. The truth was, the landlord was after him for unpaid rent and there was no payment owed his former spouse. Just a casual girlfriend with champagne taste making short work of his beer pocketbook. The primary reason the rent was late...again.

Amos antennae were always active when he talked to Dormer. The guy had a checkered past with McMillan and he sensed the man did nothing without an agenda. True, he had made serious improvements of late, but still, Amos suspected he would be in error to let his guard down. Then a sudden thought stuck him; what if the warning involved Eddie? Nah, the guy was somewhat shiftless, but a, well...terrorist? That word hadn't entered his thinking till now either. Any act against a US nuclear plant was a clear case of terrorism. Any crime committed within the confines of such a facility might be viewed or construed to be likewise. He pushed the thought aside and eyed Dormer.

"Sorry to hear that Eddie but what is it you think I can do?"

"Well, I have experience with mechanical stuff too. Could I get a shot at an ANM assignment? I mean, we all know they're burning you guys out pretty fast."

Amos thought a moment, "What kind of experience...is it in your file?"

"Uh, actually it's bikes man. Motorcycles, I been wrenching on them since I was a kid."

"You mean adjusting the chain, changing sprockets...what?"

"Figured you might know something about them too. Nah, I do full rebuilds; motor work, frames, everything. But

I never put it in my application stuff...didn't think it meant much till now."

Amos thought a moment. That level of experience would indeed make Dormer suitable for many of the reactor assignments.

"OK Eddie; that might be something worth looking into. Let me talk to Fitzgerald, he's in charge of crew planning."

"Fitz" as he was known was one of Babcock's top men. He'd been in nuclear power forever and had headed the team that bored through and sent cameras into the Three Mile Island containment facility. He often enthralled Amos with tales, some harrowing, from his years of experience in the nuke world. Thanks to him, Amos knew details the public might never hear.

"I appreciate it, Amos."

"You know McMillan will have to OK it too, right?" Everyone was aware of Mac's distaste for Dormer and his previous work habits.

"Uh, yeah, well he listens to you man. See if you can get me a break. You know I been trying."

"I do know that Eddie. That's why I'm willing to look into it. Call it a small case of reaping what you sow."

Eddie seemed nonplussed for a moment, "Yeah man, I guess."

"Now, how about heading for the R/B and help Jimmy on the north generator; Fitz wants it ready for that tube sheet jump by tomorrow. That means all the lumber not in use and other loose stuff has got to go. Mark it up and put it by the fans but not anywhere in front, OK?"

"You got it." And Dormer headed back into the maze of hallways enroute to the pressurization hatch that serviced the reactor area.

Amos stood reflectively rubbing his chin and pondered the conversation. There was a familiar undercurrent to his thoughts; that still small voice that originated outside his own consciousness. But the impulse was not what he might have expected. He wasn't looking for clues or warnings regarding Dormer's possible culpability, he was thinking of the hopelessness of his life and final destination.

Amos had come to accept the fact that Americans were hardened to the Gospel of Christ. The percentage of people, who would give it a fair hearing when the subject came up, hovered at around two percent by most theologian's calculations. This was borne out by his personal experience as well. Therefore Amos had long since backed away from trying to "force feed" Jesus to anyone. Certainly the few times Eddie had been present when anything religious was said, had shown clearly he was, at best, disinterested. But now it seemed something had sparked the Spirit's interest in him.

Brother, things were just getting stranger and stranger. OK, so first chance he would try engaging him on the subject. But what about putting him on a reactor crew; probably his own. Did he want such a man involved in what could, at any time, turn into an extremely dangerous, potentially lethal situation?

"Ah Lord," he sighed, "I said I'd look into it, that's what I'll do." And he resumed his patrol through what he sometimes humorously thought of as, "The Valley of the Shadow of Contamination".

An outsider would not have found it all that funny.

CHAPTER 8

ARAK TOO WAS HEADED OUT on patrol, but he suspected it was mostly a "busy-work" assignment. Something the Lord, and perhaps Raphael, had cooked up to distract him from his preoccupation with the unfolding events on Earth. Still, it did give him an excuse to visit Deran and actually see friends and family. That was always welcome, although transferring back to his home world often left him somewhat disoriented. Even after such a lengthy period he still couldn't quite get used to it.

Deran bore little resemblance to the chaotic, strife filled planet he had once "lived" on. Instead it now boasted all the positive values and resources that had lain at its core, refined and glorified by the particular plan blueprinted for its rebirth when the original stars were young. As he prepared for the event that would take him almost instantly there, he marveled again at the scope and kindness which were the hallmarks of Almighty God. And the incomprehensible power and thinking that brought such plans to fruition across this unending vastness. A vastness that only He himself could truly know or be familiar with.

Deran lay at the outer limit of the transferrable Cosmos with which Arak had any experience. He well knew that within that boundary, while supported by the authority granted him, he could reach any approved destination traveling virtually at the speed of thought. That too had, at first, been beyond his comprehension. And the fact was, such transfers were not everyday occurrences. True, many assignments began with one, but after that there was usually some effort to be made, work to be performed, or maybe just information to be gathered. This involved differing lengths of absence depending on the intensity of whatever activity was required on Father's behalf. It never failed to be illuminating or informative on some level.

The area in play was beyond massive and here he liked the Earth nomenclature; millions and millions of light years. Initially, the sheer distance that implied had been a daunting thing and, as a First Rank, he had never been truly comfortable venturing out into such a limitless void. In time though, he found void was not an apt description.

There were worlds and marvels, fit to unhinge a mortal mind, scattered like diamond dust across the shimmering, galactic immensity. Time, physics, dimensional placement, any of the "cornerstones" God's various creations observed or postulated to explain "existence", were subject to cancellation, rearrangement, or both, depending on where you went. Arak had the audacity in his younger suns to consider one concept he felt was a shortcoming involving this eternal life discussed amongst the Deran believers. What, he had wondered, was one to occupy themselves with...well, forever? Such a thought now brought a smile. It would take what he had once considered "forever" to begin to know this small corner of reality. That was what awaited those who accepted and obeyed Jehovah God...the true reality. Comparing ones brief mortal life to this immortal one was like standing a small candle next to a Supernova.

Speaking of which, one huge star, in a remote section of his patrol zone, was inversely gathering energy at its core and would assault the local galaxy with one of those unparalleled energy releases when that core eventually collapsed. It would be quite the thing to transfer to center stage and see the action as it cataclysmically imploded and departed one dimension for the next.

On Deran, Arak had never really been the astronomer type. However, the CA had required that all members possess basic navigational skills and this had caused him to maintain a layman's interest in the space surrounding his dear planet. Now, however, he could not only witness the mechanics of the various systems he visited, but appreciate them with an understanding and admiration greater than that which existed on any of the currently "occupied" worlds. No matter how advanced a life form considered itself, the shock that true knowledge, imparted directly from the Creator, would cause your mind to go through was another of those afterlife experiences that could not be adequately described. All these, and more, Arak lumped into a category he had heard Peter describe as...Uber-Cool. Little brother Amos would someday be here to share them and Arak already looked forward to his company.

Amos...What was it about Amos...Well, for one thing, he had courage. Donian's kind of courage. Sadly, that courage would surely be tested if the animosity towards the Christ burgeoned on Earth as it had on his home world. And the fact was, all the indicators were heading in that direction. Many on Deran had learned what it meant to die for your beliefs. Amos could ultimately be tried in that crucible as well.

His earthly life was even now in jeopardy and Arak could not evade the sense of involvement their meeting had generated. Very similar to that which tortured his thinking when Donian had walked a similar valley. A sigh escaped him; many souls contemplated this reality thinking it was some kind of candy-coated existence where every thought was sublime and nothing of concern would ever intrude on your perpetual state of bliss. Frankly, that sounded a little monotonous to Arak, and he was glad that it was somewhat in error.

True, no evil entered the Kingdom, except by permission, and the condition of being eternally secure underscored every matter that came up or required your involvement. But, as he well knew, Jehovah had a plan that covered not only your mortal life, but the immortal one as well. He would see to it that your time, or more correctly "being", was used fruitfully in one of His myriad undertakings or missions. He would also see that you were constantly stretched and conditioned towards his purposes which He now considered you a partner in. It was mind-boggling for Arak and he was actively participating. There was no method or way to explain it to mortals.

On Earth they read the Scripture that said, *No eye has seen, no ear has heard, no mind has conceived what God has prepared for those who love him*, but that was insufficient to hint at even the most elementary wonders that lay in wait. Take your best shot, dream huge, and then multiply it exponentially...you wouldn't even be close. The great tragedy, he now realized, were the many beings that rejected that truth and wound up inheriting the same eternity in surroundings whose grimness and horror were equally impossible to describe. The title, Second Death, seemed inadequate in some ways...but was ultimately accurate.

His musings were interrupted by the arrival of Damius, a senior Third Rank, "Greetings brother Arak, are you preparing for your little sojourn?"

Arak looked up in surprise, "Raphael told you this?"

"He did; even asked me to encourage you to be at peace while you are away."

"Aahh, he knows me too well. I cannot help but wonder how the one called Amos is doing."

"I'm sure that's why he sent me...I once felt that way about Daniel."

Arak stared, "You couriered to *the* Daniel of Earth?"

"Umm, not as you did with Amos. Daniel and I never talked face to face when he was mortal. I did however lead two counterstrikes when Lucifer came at him through channels Father deemed forbidden."

"So you found yourself concerned with his state even after the defenses were made?"

"I did; it is most natural to view these men of Earth as our brothers. They fight the Lords battles, as we do, holding onto faith in something higher than themselves. But they, for the most part, never view the physical side of this reality during that life. You, Amos and those you met in St. Peters, are of a rare group indeed."

"Yes, Raphael reminded me of this. Still, he too thinks the events of Earth could be turning toward finality."

"That may well be brother Arak. But let me say that I thought this same thing when I watched Daniel earlier in the age. Prophecy there is so constructed that, at any given point, Father may proceed to fulfill their destiny, yet never vary from Scripture. It is a mystery but it keeps each generation aware of the possibility and undergirds their faith."

"Yes, mystery upon mystery it often seems. Who could possibly have imagined all that there is to know or learn or even adjust to. I had the thought earlier that eternity is the right word. It will take me that long to understand my own part in it."

Damius smiled, "Longer, I am afraid. But I do have some encouragement. Father has doubled the First Ranks on Amos and I overheard Raphael suggest to him that he send you in should further intervention be required. A possibility none of us are wagering against."

Arak allowed a smile, "That is welcome news. Who are the First Ranks reporting to?"

"That is something which surprises even me. I saw Father bring one directly before him on arrival. Although I don't imagine they are all reporting personally, it is more evidence He shares your interest...or rather vice-versa.

"Yes, Raphael assures me He has been watching the situation for some time now. Certainly well before I was introduced into it. Do you know if the Spirit has added anything directly to the First Rank reports?"

"Ha, I am reminded of that worn out phrase you are so fond of...That, my friend is above my pay grade."

Fearsome, imposing warriors of God looked squarely at each other...and burst into laughter. When he regained himself, Arak reached out with a massive, arm and gently patted an equally impressive shoulder, "Thank you brother Damius...for everything. I will make the patrol and try not to dwell on these things."

"Farewell brother Arak, I hope you find all is well wherever you go. We are up to our ears in 'excitement' over
several dimensions; even without the constant warfare and
chaos of Earth. I almost envy you."

Their eyes locked again, each held a fist to his chest and
then extended it so that they met knuckle to knuckle. A
long moment passed and then a virtual explosion of com-
pressed, blue-green energy enveloped Arak...and Arak was
no longer there.

JENNY'S NARRATIVE concluded and she and Jim sat alternating between moments of deep thought and
observations or questions regarding her unimaginable
experience.

"Dad, I don't think there was any rhyme or reason to it.
I think I just happened to be there at that particular point.
But already I see he was correct about seeking more of the
same. It could be futile or frustrating at best...and maybe
destructive at worst."

Jim thought a moment, "Jen, any pursuit of such matters should have obvious input from the Spirit himself. If
we try to operate minus that, it likely means one of two
things. First, and worse-case-scenario, you're not really His
and don't know his voice; no matter what you think your
track record is as a 'believer'. Or second, you're off chasing
after something He hasn't ordained for you. I didn't realize
the seriousness of that when I was your age."

"How do you mean, serious?"

Jim drew a deep breath and sighed, "Sweetheart, you're
one of the few I know who seem to really 'get it'. It, being

the fact that God will not participate in a part time business that you operate when church is in session or when you think it's convenient. I tried that without even realizing that's what I was doing. I was fortunate to have wiser followers tell me things that I could ponder and learn from."

"Like?"

"You already know most of them...the one about I'd 'see God in everything or I'd see Him in nothing'. And maybe more important, 'I'd never know God any better than I knew his word or His word any better than I knew Him'. When I examined my life and motives honestly, I realized I wasn't looking for His input into my whole life, just where I thought it was needed. That will always end in failure. Now, the answer you have to seek, is what, if anything, does He further require from you in this instance? In all such matters the Spirit takes an interest. I think maybe He left you a clue through your friend Arak."

"A clue...what clue?"

"He said to remember a name."

"Yeah, Amos Michaels. It's stuck in my head like it was carved in stone."

Jim thought silently for a moment with an odd little smile on his face, "I think that Michaels is spelled M-i-k-a-l-s, and I think I know who he is."

Jenny's face relaxed in amazement. "You know who he's talking about?"

"I think I know of him; I've even mentioned him to you once or twice."

"But"...she stopped, "you know...that name was vaguely familiar...why?"

Once again Jim was quiet and Jenny imagined she could smell the wiring getting hot as his mind raced around collating her crazy sounding story with something he already had an insight on.

He looked up at her, "I'm pretty sure he's posted some very pointed things on a few of the Internet bulletin boards. He's definitely right wing Christianity, or fundamentalist, as much as that word gets abused."

"Not one of those 'I know the date' types."

"Not at all; in fact I agree with his stuff I've seen. His biggest point seems to be the 'Laodicean' spirit in today's churches. Say's were not doing it by The Book anymore."

"Well, that does sound like a kindred spirit. How long have you known about him?"

"Little over a year I think; I don't remember exactly when...Oh yeah...I do remember. He posted some little write-up about caring for our cars like we do our bodies. Said a lot of Americans would be ride-less in short order if their cars were abused in the same way. I think it was an expose' on fat church goers."

"Bet that went over well."

"I remember being surprised at the lack of reaction. I never saw anyone post in opposition to it. It was really hard to argue with...and that made it stick in my mind. Fact is, we do abuse our 'temples' a lot in this generation. Heck, we've been doing it for a long time in this country."

Now Jenny was the one in thought. Finally she said, "An angel, a huge, powerful angel, who's in a big hurry, takes time to tell me to remember this guy's name...why? Should I try to write him, find his number, you know, communicate? Or is that pushing against the warning not to pursue other experiences?"

"It's not another experience Jen, it's the same one."

She gazed at her Dad, "You're right...This might all be related somehow. See, I knew I had to tell it to you. No one understands this stuff like you do."

"I doubt that, but thanks for the confidence. So what do you think you might do about it?"

"Pray, sleep on it, I don't know. Guess it would be wise to find out where he's located. Could be outer Siberia or somewhere."

Her dad again smiled mischievously, "That's the easy part, first thing I noticed was he was a fellow Floridian."

"What?" Jenny bounced straight up onto her feet, "I go half way around the world to run into this, this...'experience' and the guy in the dialogue winds up being in my own home state?!"

"He do work in mysterious ways, don't He?" grinned her father.

Jenny's eyes narrowed, "You already know where he is, don't you."

"Not exactly, it was somewhere near Tampa I think."

Jenny collapsed back into her chair. "This is getting even weirder. I mean, how is all this tied together, and is it related or not? Dad, Arak changed the way I view everything I thought I knew about God, but is He really all that interested..." she just stopped. Then, her voice barely audible, "We don't deserve His interest in our lives, do we?"

"Never have, never will, that's the real magic of it."

"Arak...he said something about that...he said God views us through a lens from Golgotha."

"The meaning's obvious isn't it?"

Jenny gave a small sniff, "He views our faults and failures through the sacrifice made by Jesus."

"And secondly" prompted her dad.

"As a Father who loves you...but will correct you if you need it."

"Bingo, this one isn't about correction I think; looks more like obedience to me."

"You think I need to make contact with this guy, don't you."

"I think it's a strong possibility, but I suggest you give it the twenty four hours."

"Yeah, make no major decision in a hurry. I bet that gets violated all the time."

"It does," Jim replied, "Often with consequences."

He unfolded his lanky frame from the chair and looked affectionately down at his daughter. "Let it rest for now Jen. You need to go home and get your feet under you before anything else. Let's eat and you get a night's rest. Besides, I bet Martha's tired of taking care of Mr. Bones."

Jenny smiled, "Once again your wisdom shines forth, oh father, is that the age thing coming to the surface?"

"Only as old as you feel," he quipped, "bet I feel younger than you right now."

"You can definitely get an amen to that, lead me to the feast so I can restore myself."

And with that they wandered contentedly towards the small kitchen. Unaware that, beyond the dimensional wall, unseen eyes and ears had managed to take in much of the discussion.

AN OCEAN AWAY from the focal point of all this activity, Felim stood and stared pensively out across a vast expanse of the Sahara desert. A desert whose fringes seemed to encroach a little more each year on this small Nigerian town. As his eye distractedly calculated the advance, his mind was gnawing on the latest request from his superiors. He had received an unusual amount of specifics regarding this one...and that made him wary. It was a definite breach of established security practices. Someone was perhaps being careless. Or there was always the possibility he was being set up. But he could honestly think of no reason for that to be so. Maybe the extreme distance, and lack of association, were deemed insular enough to avoid scrutiny by outside forces. Personally, he did not care to take such chances.

For Felim was an assassin. One who used poison on his victims with a most fearsome method of delivery. His targets usually died in excruciating pain combined with an agony of terror. In the circles where his name was most often whispered, he was known as "The Keeper of Serpents". Not just any serpents; only those whose venom possessed an extreme lethality due to toxicity or volume. Some of his "weapons of destruction" carried relatively small doses of very powerful toxins. Others produced less virulent levels of liquid death, but made up for it in the massive quantities delivered by oversize venom glands and large rapier-like fangs.

A Saw Scaled viper usually topped out at two feet, but its bite was invariably fatal. The larger, often six foot, Inland Taipan of Australia provided enough poison in a single bite to kill one hundred humans. But they had become difficult to acquire. The tried and true Black Mamba was easy to get, delivered a terrible load of venom and was prone to be very aggressive when cornered or frightened. That was probably the best choice for this assignment.

A Mamba packaged tightly and delivered as some innocuous, brown papered gift, perhaps bearing an innocent electronics logo, would undoubtedly get the job done. Felim had methods to immobilize the reptile quietly until the packaging was fully opened. At which point, it would come powering out like some jack-in-the-box from hell. And in a most foul frame of mind. Even if not bitten immediately, which was more than likely, anyone in the immediate vicinity would be viciously pursued, like some doomed rodent, and probably bitten repeatedly.

Chances were good the recipient would experience both of these horrors. It was an ugly death and when someone ordered these type "hits", Felim knew that often more than just the dispatch of the target was involved. It was personal; someone wanted to make a statement, scare the competition or realize revenge for some act or treachery. These matters, however, were of little concern to him.

This being a very long range delivery, a drop would have to be employed that allowed access to overnight shipping. Enough time to seriously agitate the serpent but not reduce its aggressiveness through fluid loss or exposure. He already had contacts that could make that happen, as well as bypassing some of the normal out of country shipping safeguards.

Felim wandered over to one of several large terrarium-like units and opened an upper hatch. Grasping a small staff, he inserted the tip slowly toward a seven foot Mamba that, to all appearances, was dead or sleeping. Then with a flick of his wrist he prodded and whirled the staff amongst the snake's coils. The reaction was gratifying. It shot toward the glass front then reared up cobra-like hissing loudly. She was ready for instant defense or combat, all the while looking Felim directly in the eye. There was no doubt; this one would love to kill him. He aggravated it daily as a sort of training regimen and he thought he could actually see the hate in her cold expressionless eyes. He would have to be on his guard when packaging time came. After that, a certain individual in the Great Satan was slated to have a very bad day. It would be their last.

TUBE SHEET JUMP; that's what the Nuclear Mechanic guy's called it. This one was on the upper level of the northernmost steam generator. These giant heat exchangers also acted as the last line of defense in the separation of radioactively contaminated, high pressure core water from the steam that actually drove the giant generating assemblies. The Turbine Deck was never supposed to see primary water or steam; it was part of the "cold side". However, fate had intervened and now those massive turbines were ringed with radiation hazard tape making it the only "crapped up" unit currently in the industry.

To say that the powers above were not happy was gifted understatement. The owners and shareholders were already unhappy that the mega-watt generating facility was out of action and inhaling massive quantities of cash instead of creating them. The plant management and staff were equally unhappy since the focus was on them 24/7 to make repairs and get things moving. The NRC (Nuclear Regulatory Commission) was unhappy because they had to police all this activity which strained the manpower available from an already inadequate supply.

And now this. Apparently a control rod drive had shed a gear at some point. Said gear had catapulted into the system and taken up residence on this upper tube sheet. Here, where the multitude of three quarter inch tubes were welded around the neck with their bell shaped openings facing up to receive the torrent of super heated core water.

The fact was, some weeks before the actual "scram", the computers had picked up the noise, diagnosed the possibility and relayed the info to operations. But no one was willing to order a shut down, on an otherwise operational unit, for some "suspected" gear malfunction. This would have raised hackles in several venues but nothing had been made public. So the gear had remained atop the sheet, whirling in the maelstrom of hellishly hot water and steam, while the dollars continued to roll in. However, the piper's bill was now due. Personnel were dispatched to view and photograph the effects and, with the more experienced guys almost at burn-out, the first man in would be Amos.

He stood on large scaffolding, built to reach the inspection hatch, fully suited and festooned with dosimeters. HP technicians fussed around his suit and air supply double checking the fittings and safety gear. A reinforced plastic sheet was installed as a "door" over the hatch to act as containment, but the crew members nearest the opening were outfitted with respirators none the less. Also in attendance was Eddie Dormer. True to his word, Amos had reasoned with Mac regarding the need for more crew and managed to persuade him on the matter. Neither of them was totally convinced of the man's sincerity, but the pressure to get back on line was increasing daily and no stone could be left unturned. Fitzgerald, who was desperate for manpower, had been no problem at all.

As for Eddie, he was a little awed by the scope of things in-play around him. Not that he would admit it. Only last night he'd bragged to his newfound drinking buddy, Sammy, about making a jump into the reactor head. The "jump", so far, was in his own head, but he had actually watched from the sidelines while Amos guided and prepped one of the Drive units through the first stages needed to get it ready for a return to action. The complex work inside the head itself was yet to come and Eddie knew, at some point, they'd have to use him too.

It was thrilling to walk by the other maintenance guys during the shift swaggering with his new importance and invulnerability to the mundane task they were continuing to perform. For unlike Amos, and most other draftees, Eddie sought to distance himself from his usual task when not involved on the rebuild teams. He accomplished this by first professing an infatuation with the nuts and bolts of whatever phase was being worked and hanging around to watch. And secondly, knowing where the others were assigned and avoiding those areas.

The exception was when a dump run was scheduled. He almost always managed to be available to go outside with that crew. Since Amos had previously OK'ed it, no one asked questions. Oddly, when he'd mentioned it during the boisterous conversations at the local watering hole, Sammy had seemed fascinated that they actually had the opportunity to take breaks in the "fresh air" outside the restricted perimeter.

"Yeah, I get to watch the sunset some evenings and still drag down the same ANM pay as if I were inside," Eddie boasted.

"Wow, you have got it made over there," Sammy had praised in his light sing-song accent.

"Hate to admit it, but yeah...maybe you should put in an application dude, you got any mechanical background?"

"Ah, no, I always worked in my father's grocery before I decided to leave Miami."

"Too bad, we're gonna burn out everybody we got before this thing's over."

"It is all so fascinating; and you get to go outside for breaks as well. Do you have to go back through the clearance procedures when that happens?"

"Nah, not so you'd notice. The security guys are so used to it they just give us the once over. Maybe stick a mirror under the truck. But mostly it's just names out and names in."

"Yes, I can see why it would be like that. After all, you are actually working inside the reactor; you are much more trusted and important than they are."

Such music to Eddie's ears. His life had not been one to garner him much praise or acclaim. Mostly the opposite; but he was finding his "new" self pretty impressive in his own eyes too.

Other eyes and ears were focused on these conversations as well. But not even Sammy, also known as Samir, with all his training and instruction, would have understood or believed the array of forces gathering around this little scenario. Not so, on the other side of the "wall", where both camps were intensely watching and gauging each other. Each side had been in these situations before.

Every so often mortal history approached one of these crossroads and, with the increased participation, came unexpected, sometimes baffling and occasionally deadly results. These members of the human race, with their complex thinking and attached free will, were rarely what you could call "under control"...by either side.

CHAPTER 9

CRYSTAL WAVELETS DANCED A syncopated rhythm against the pale shoreline. Their reflections flashed multi-faceted traces of the midday sun in a riotous dance creating a sparkling symphony between sea and sky. Great and small seabirds soared above these dazzling waters, pausing occasionally to plummet down and snare stray or unwary minnows known here as Gobaions. They were an important link in the food chain housed in these wonderfully clear waters. Waters that represented merely one of the great oceans the planet was home to.

A wide belt of sugar white sand girdled the waters edge. It blended out into the depths producing broad, sloping aqua-marine shallows punctuated by a profusion of coral heads and rock formations. Easily visible in the clear waters, schools of Gobaions flickered and soared endlessly through these sanctuaries often followed by their larger, sometimes multi-colored, cousins.

Shoreward, the brilliant sand gave way to soil more suited to vegetation. Large bands of towering, palm-like trees were thronged in stately groups and meandered along this irregular boundary. The land beyond sloped gently upward to what appeared to be plains or grasslands. These were dotted intermittently with "islands", large and small, made up of robust combinations of shrub and tree growth. These leafy outposts teemed with diverse varieties of bird and animal life, each seeming a small community unto itself.

On taking all this in, one might think you had arrived in some form of paradise. Oddly enough, you would be right; this was Deran.

Unnoticed at first, a tall figure leaned casually against one of the palms. Tanned and athletic, with a mane of lightly graying dark hair, he would have caught the eye more quickly in other surroundings. The relaxed posture failed to diminish the regality of bearing that seemed to accompany his person. This was even more surprising given the humble clothing with which he was adorned. He was clad only in a pair of well worn shorts and a sleeveless t-shirt. The feet were bare but, even so, he stood something over seven feet tall. He fit this setting so well, the scenario seemed to again echo that unobtrusive aura of perfection.

You could somehow sense he was a person of knowledge, and possibly power. There was ample reason for this; for he was Lonius, (Lon-eye-us), father of Arak the Destroyer, servant of the Most High God and a leading citizen of this shimmering place. One of the Lord's crown jewels in this sector of forever. A reborn planet populated by those who had won their individual victories over self and doubt in the Ag wars of the distant past. Each one also reborn in the same perfect, eternal state as their home world.

Now, with all this perfection, you would probably also think nothing worrisome intruded on the thoughts and minds of the inhabitants of such wonders. On this, you would be mistaken.

Lonius thoughts were on Arak who had "enlisted" in the Lords army, so many suns ago. Such volunteers became a much expanded version of being taking the actual title, Angel. To his discomfort, his "angel" had become somewhat renowned for his daring and risk-taking in pursuit of Father's purposes. Purposes on such far flung places as the world called Earth, where the population had the dubious distinction of being harassed non stop by a powerful demi-god known as Lucifer. In addition, or perhaps because of this, it was also a legendary focal point in the entirety of all Creation. The one place where the "Righteous One", the Firstborn of all that is, had taken on flesh...and subsequently had that fleshly container murdered by the inhabitants.

Though he knew it to be true, he could still scarce credit it. The very concept sent a cold feeling through the center of his being. And Arak, his own "firstborn", was known to engage in contest with the minions of this demonic Earth-God. Contest, which he now painfully understood, carried risk even to one as powerful as a Third Rank angel. After all they had endured, he had to deal constantly with this new and unforeseen possibility. Having the thought processes natural to his state of perfected existence did not blunt the barb of a fathers care and concern for his offspring.

So he waited here at one of their favorite locations to, at long last, enjoy a short reunion with that offspring. When Arak had communicated the news of an impending visit, he also warned of its brief nature and against getting the other family members involved. To Lonius this meant his son had something on his mind and wished to confer. That was not the least bit unusual either.

All completed beings partook of the Lord's wisdom in their own character and style. It often seemed Jehovah had set it up this way to insure the continuation of long standing, beneficial relationships which supported the backbone of love shared between citizens in these Kingdom realms. Despite some involved members frequenting the very throne room, Father would often leave a solution, conclusion, or the parameters surrounding one, to be explored and discussed in a most natural fashion. It would be far from the first time the two of them had bent their heads over some such concern...in this life or the previous one.

His mind had wandered off onto more local interest, when he was snapped back to the moment by the familiar, but always awe inspiring, sound of the dimensional fabric being powered open. Like the splitting of the first atom magnified a hundred-fold. First, the air took on a charged feeling; the next second blue-green, crackling "fire" erupted and assumed the massive shape of a warrior angel arrived directly from Heaven itself. After another moment, the intensity of the fireworks subsided and a flickering, golden hued fire took its place.

It never failed to raise the hair on Lonius' neck and send an indescribable sensation up his spine. One second Arak towered there before him encased in golden flames and the next, the fire seemed to turn in on itself and vanish. Now he appeared in his perfect, solid form, an angel of "fleshly beauty" if such a term could be applied.

He had materialized looking out to sea and, after a moment, turned and spied his father. Their eyes met and both smiled simultaneously,

"Honored Father, I bring you greetings from the Lord."

Lonius bowed his head slightly then looked up at this familiar giant, "As always, the honor is mine. Welcome home my son."

"It is like the proverbial breath of fresh air father. I never imagined involvement in Father's undertakings could leave me wishing for a sabbatical, but it is so."

"Yes, but I gather this is to be an abbreviated one?"

"I fear that is correct, though I will tarry as long as possible."

"Your mother would like that and I can give you what news I have of Donian."

"No need really, Raphael informed me that he is with Michael attending to some business which has drawn Father's attention to a world of which I have never even heard."

"Did he also mention his interest in meeting you here at the earliest opportunity?"

"Uh, no, I don't imagine he had such news. When did Donian indicate this?"

"According to your mother he spoke to her, in that mysterious fashion of his, morning last. He also said it was not an emergency or related to any Kingdom business. To tell you the truth, I think he just yearns to see you and probably to do some more exploring of the new Deran. Neither of you has stopped talking about the visit two suns ago."

Another smile lit Araks countenance, "Yes, we had never seen those species you are now familiar with...Nor had we imagined the size of them; truly magnificent."

"And you have not seen the best of them yet, my son…But you have not come regarding such pleasures, have you?"

"Ah, no father, I have not." He paused and glanced back out to sea, then turned again to Lonius. "The Lord has involved me in a situation on the Earth and then seen fit to send me off with instructions not to concern myself with it. The problem is, I cannot seem to do that…though I try."

"Hmmm…If I correctly recall, there have been several incidents where the elders thought you involved yourself more deeply than the assignment required."

Arak sighed, "Yes, Peter says it is both my strength and my weakness. He fears that Lucifer will exploit it…as he did with Kurtanus."

A shudder coursed through Lonius, "Arak, does no one know what Kurtanus situation is, or what his fate may be?"

A scowl creased his sons face, "Of course the Lord himself knows…or knows the array of possibilities, but he is not inclined to be questioned about them. I know this straight from the Christ himself, who apparently also does not share that particular knowledge. Therefore I do not pursue it."

Lonius was silent for long moments, then, "It is the very thing I fear for you."

Arak reached out and rested a massive hand on his fathers shoulder, "I know father. I never meant for our concerns to carry over this way. After all we endured it seemed the price had been fully paid. But I must confess, I never imagined a place like Earth."

"Earth," Lonius shook his head, "on the one hand it sounds much like Deran, but on the other, I cannot fathom this Lucifer creature. Are you certain he was once as you are?"

Arak thought for a moment, "No, not as I...different and definitely more powerful...but yes, at one time, a trusted servant of God. More than servant actually; he was either an Arch or possibly something beyond that. I have dared to wonder if he was a step closer to the caliber of the Christ himself than to an Arch. I can say this; the senior ranks do not speak of him lightly or as one with whom they were equals. It is another of those mysteries that is not up for much discussion. Father gets that look in his eye if you push him on it."

Lonius chuckled, "I am quite familiar with that look. I saw it once or twice on his early visits to Deran."

Arak nodded, "Which is why I'm a little torn over this Amos business. I do not wish to hurt Father's trust, but something tells me we are missing some vital point in the game Lucifer is playing."

"Amos...what is Amos?"

"Not what, father, who...an Earther of real faith and purpose to whom I couriered a message...actually a warning."

"A warning; something to do with this Lucifer I wager."

"All conflicts on the Earth involve him in some fashion. But rarely is it this pronounced towards a single individual. He means to silence Amos' efforts by ending his mortal life. Something he would not previously have dared to precipitate on his own authority. Yet Father forbids interference; except at the most basic level."

Lonius rubbed his chin thoughtfully, "Father does nothing without purpose, why would he limit things so on this matter?"

Arak sighed, "Largely, I believe it is because of their state of will. I seem to learn more all the time regarding Earth and much of it is surprising...even disturbing. During their suns as mortals there, they are entirely autonomous in spirit. They may say no to anything or anyone completely based on preference. This includes not only each other, but both Lucifer and Father. They may also adjust their compliance to some stated belief on a daily, if not hourly, basis."

"What," Lonius blurted out, "they may switch camps at will?"

"Not just camps, as you speak of, but camps within camps. They call the following there Church, or sometimes, Body of the Christ. Yet, within these very groups are endless variations which differ from each other on some point or points, both large and small."

"But that would lead to chaos...and their own downfall."

"And who, dear father, do you think promotes and encourages these frictions at every opportunity?"

A pause, "Lucifer again," said Lonius quietly, "but I thought they could deny him."

"As best I can tell, the strength to do so issues directly from Father's Spirit of Truth. Only the true followers receive him...and this has been the case for a relatively short period. It began after Lucifer's attempted assassination of Jesus. A gift of sorts purchased at the cost of that suffering. Minus this condition, the Earthers seem to behave almost identically to the Ags. They pursue self and lust in countless variations, each following their own particular dictates. But frequently in greater or lesser agreement with others who also choose to deify their own existence."

A mournful gaze appeared on Lonius' face, "It does sound much like Ag philosophies under a different banner."

"Yes, the similarity is pronounced. But, if anything, more intense because of the continual war waged behind the scenes to influence those involved. Each one is contested for with fervor but that fervor is magnified in cases like Amos."

"What of the ones who are already of an opposite mind to Father?"

"They are largely ignored...unless they are used as pawns against the true followers."

"What is attracting such attention to this 'Amos'?"

"Ah Father, that most elusive element which we also contested night and day for...the Truth."

Lonius paused in thought, "This Amos then, is a harbinger of the truth governing Father's will for their world?"

"To that end he has searched and applied himself; and as you might expect, few are concerned. It also resembles our past in that respect."

"Well, if he has little effect, why the effort to silence him?"

"Lucifer's most consistent goal is to do away with the thing he hates most; and that is Truth. Earth Scripture clearly states this, but most have abandoned it and seek their 'truth' in other places. Places he is happy to provide. He is a master deceiver and counterfeiter; to the extent that many of his victories are inside the very groups which claim Father's name."

Lonius again looked thoughtful, "So, your Amos, and now you my son, are embroiled in a contest to protect Fathers truth for these who, by and large, do not really care that such truth exists? I fear I miss your point somewhat.

When the Ags rejected the truths presented us, it was a much more straightforward position. Perhaps because we were unencumbered by one such as this Lucifer. But still... since both societies seem governed ultimately by faith, I must question why you have become so intent on the outcome for these particular ones. Why not just let them reach their own conclusions and be done with it?"

Arak stared downward for a moment, obviously in serious thought. Then he gazed back at his father with a strange look on his face. Finally he let out another sigh...

"What I tell you now I do not definitely know is permitted. I do not detect any direct interference, so I will relate it...but to you only. The end that awaits those who reject Truth on their world is nothing like that of Deran. The main reason Lucifer fights with such fury, is because there is a place that Father has ordained as his destination at the end of the age there. I have no idea where or how it exists. Indeed, I am unsure how many in the Kingdom, beyond Father, have much knowledge of it. I believe the original ranks all have some insight as to its purpose and substance; but I know not to what degree. They are reluctant to discuss it, therefore it is rarely spoken of. What I do know, is that it exceeds all horrors of which I am aware. And I have been privy to some very unpleasant things.

"The Earth Scriptures refer to it variously as, place of damnation, place of torment, lake of fire and several others. I once heard Michael refer to it as "the pit". All are indicative of a misery and pain beyond calculation. Earthers refer to it mostly as, Hell. Those Scriptures further indicate this existence is prepared for Lucifer, his Fallens and all those souls of the Earth who have lived their lives contaminated by his disobedience and evil. Especially those who have heard and rejected Father's message to them through Jesus."

Lonius was staring at Arak dumbfounded. After a moment he asked in a quiet voice, "Father has prepared such a place? A...a what, prison, for the Fallens and the Earthers alike?"

"More than a prison. Far beyond anything such a term might imply. As I say, I have studied it to the extent permitted. This is a sentence of misery, pain and hopelessness the likes of which exist nowhere else in all the universes. It is total separation from God. Creations who have rejected their creator and, in turn, are ultimately rejected by Him."

The shock on his fathers face was unabated, "I...I don't know what to say...to think. This is true? Well yes, considering who you are...who we are...I just..." he faltered to a stop.

The towering Arak stood there and wondered if he had perhaps made a serious error in judgment. But then the color seemed to return to Lonius face and he looked up at his son,

"I am sorry...nothing has shocked me in longer than I can recall...but this truly does. How long will Father require these unrepentant ones to languish in that...state?"

Arak hesitated another long moment, then, "Forever." And the color, again, drained from his father's face. His eyes grew wide and his lower jaw relaxed in shock. His mouth was open but no sound issued forth.

"Eternity" stated Arak flatly, "There is no appeal...There is no release...There is no hope."

The two of them stood there, eyes locked, one in utter disbelief, and the other in uncomfortable silence. Finally

Lonius found his voice, "Arak, why must this be? Are the creatures there so far beyond redemption as to require this...this place? Why would Father send his own offspring into such a...condition?"

The mighty angel's voice took on a stern tone, "The truth is, Father sends no one to this place, not even Lucifer. It is a sentence that must be earned. For Earthers, their state of will is truly a terrible, two edged sword. But they are not left to ignorantly fend against this.

"The original tribe, to whom Father gave dictates regarding conduct, morality and spiritual fidelity, wrote voluminously of it in their early writings. Warnings dictated to them by the Spirit of Truth himself. When it became apparent that these beings would not summon the strength to overcome themselves, or the influence of the Fallens, He instituted an incredible "master plan". One apparently reserved for these willful and misguided Earthers. The only beings who would ever see the Firstborn over all Creation willingly leave his post at Father's side and become clothed in the same flesh as they. Many to actually hear his voice and see the power at his command. To be informed and shown first hand that everything they wished their "lives" to be, could be accomplished simply through love. Love of their Creator...love for one another...love of Truth. He willingly became and walked as one of them, showed them the ways and power of Father himself and, as you are already aware, in return, they brutally executed him."

Lonius nodded grimly. That piece of the story was legend...even here.

Arak continued, "You would have thought this would bring Father's wrath instantly down upon them...resulting in their utter destruction. Instead he had planned to let His own words sent through this 'Son of Man' stand for all time as the beacon of true light. A light shown, once and for all, to attract those who would be drawn. Think of it father, Almighty God, our God, watched as seemingly insignificant creations willfully spilled the blood of His own chosen 'firstborn', on the ground of their wretched little world.

"And as this transpired, Lucifer rejoiced thinking he had finally put an end to even The Great I Am meddling in his plans. Plans to unite these creatures under his own banner. One of self, greed, lust and every form of spiritual or physical perversion and disobedience. But, this 'Master' plan of Father's, which Jesus had tried to tell them plainly of, was in effect long before he agreed to enter their world as Father's emissary."

Arak looked intently into his father's eyes...Lonius appeared spellbound. "The very blood they shed became the answer to their plight. With their state of 'free will' each could choose whether to believe the outcome of this saga...or not. For after lying dead for three days, Father recalled the spirit to this 'body' of the Christ and he arose. Once again the Firstborn, this time in fleshly eternal power from among the dead of the world called Earth. He arose to be seen by many, written about by countless others and to completely rearrange their history. And then, as you know, to resume his place at Father's side. But, he is not only Lord of all, with Father's full authority resting upon him, he is also a personal mediator for these new brothers of Earth.

"And all, father, all who existed from that time and, in some fashion I don't truly understand, every soul that had previously inhabited this place, even before He came, were invited to repent of their evil and pledge their allegiance to this 'sacrifice' on their behalf. And if the invitation is truly and honestly accepted, He pronounces them not guilty. Freed completely and finally from their previous sins and crimes before Him."

"What...there is no accounting afterwards?"

"Not as you speak of. And, to support them in this effort, they receive that marvelous, internal connection to the Spirit of Truth himself. He provides them the strength and authority to follow after the dictates of the true God and not the false one of their world. The few that are faithful to this call, walk in an ever maturing state of spirit and are no longer easy prey for Lucifer and his minions. Thus, the ever present onslaught to influence and counter them and the message they carry. Because they are representatives of all which he hates, he unleashes his fury against them without respite."

Arak paused and again gazed silently out over the crystal blue sea; Lonius waited in patient silence. When he resumed, his voice was quiet...almost reverential.

"Let me attest to you father...I have been allowed to see some of these battles and I am deeply involved in this present one. I realize now, little of the wonders I have seen is more glorious than watching one of these small, finite mortals take a stand against the very 'power of darkness' which infects their world...and yet prevail. Even as they do so, they know not the respect and rejoicing that goes on in some parts of the Kingdom. They do not hear the conversations regarding their actions. The cheers at their successes or the sadness at their defeats."

"Defeats?"

"Yes, Lucifer wins some of the battles even after the chosen ones are sworn. Particularly in the early stages. But those who remain true imitate the Righteous One...and they also get up. They learn from their wounds, from Father's words and the lessons of the Spirit...and they grow. They repent, gather themselves and re-engage the fight. All of this without ever seeing or experiencing the promises Jesus delivered them. Most having never actually seen their Savior and King with mortal eyes. They press on and are carried forward by faith alone. It is this faith which sets them apart...and is so treasured by Father.

"It is true, as you may have heard rumored, He has interacted directly with some of them during their history. And many of us have been sent to certain warriors and followers; sometimes at crucial moments. But most often this occurs well after they have established themselves as the bona-fides. These ones of whom I speak, have paid their dues and often been crushed and tested by trials and hardships that might have destroyed many a Deranian.

"They do not know it, father, but while they are 'walking the fire', we who are allowed to watch, admire them. We applaud them with all the honest respect we possess. For we acknowledge that given their circumstance, some of us may well have fallen short.

"And this Amos is a worthy representative of those of whom I speak. In one brief meeting he garnered my loyalty with no direct influence from Father or the Spirit. His heart is lacking the fear that stifles and way-lays most of his Earthly brethren. A fear Lucifer diabolically employs to keep them cowed and concerned over their own little existences. It works, like the twisted charm it is, to make them selfish. It keeps their eyes turned in and down, never to look up or out and realize the awesome scope of the 'game' in which they have been called to play."

Arak paused several long moments in thought and Lonius again watched his face quietly.

"And there is one thing further, peculiar, I believe, to Amos. It seems his well intentioned, but often clumsy, wanderings in search of truth were inspired early on by his parents and later more pointedly by his grandmother. She is also of some renown in the Kingdom. But, apparently, in his early, and sometimes rebellious period, some act of disobedience directly aroused Father's ire. I do not know the details, but He had a very special message delivered to dear Amos. A most unpleasant one I gather. The facts are known to only a few, but when Father assigned me to the task, He said that some of Amos' conviction and effectiveness stemmed from...having seen the very portal to Hell."

Arak paused again in his soliloquy, then "I am unaware of any other being that can make that claim. Indeed, I would much like to question Amos about it if we again meet on the Earth...and He will permit. But such an experience would make him unique by that world's standard...or perhaps any other. So my father, I have probably violated some protocol by divulging all this, but perhaps you can better understand my fascination with the assignment and the individual."

Lonius blinked for a moment as if waking from a dream,

"Never had I imagined such things. And, truthfully, it is no wonder they are not widely known. Many have suspected Father's interest in that world was couched in some mystery, but this...this Hell, is the most terrifying thing I have ever heard of."

His son replied, "It is saying a lot, but my truest belief is that this Hell may well be the most terrifying thing that ever has or ever will exist. Except for my authorization to peruse Earth Scripture, and Father's counsel, I would know only the rumors. And indeed, the rumors do not do it justice. And last, yet most obvious father...this must remain between us two."

Lonius sighed, "As so many things have eh, my son. But I will attest; this is a troubling knowledge to possess. I could wish I had never heard it...No, that is untrue; if it helps your cause to share such a burden, I will gladly do so. But what now? Father has apparently seen fit to disengage you from the battle."

Angelic scowl would seem to be an oxy-moron but that is exactly the look that now creased his son's face, "I do not know father, and I do not understand all that He may have in play. We have both experienced the complexity and incomprehensible design inherent in Father's ways. But, of one thing I am sure. Suddenly, after all this 'time', and all the battles that have raged throughout their history...Lucifer has begun to break the rules."

CHAPTER 10

HOWEVER, Lucifer's chief "rule-breaker" was currently nowhere near the scene of the proposed crime. He was instead doing the work of a lower rank and quietly observing a single human target; Felim. The impulses that initiated the targeting, which had so concerned the "Keeper", had their origins in a place that would have surprised even the already subverted minds of those involved.

Neither Felim nor his masters could be said to be overly devout and any suggestion that they could be swayed or led by some outside spirit agency would have been met with amusement. The perfect environment for Buferan to work his quiet, deadly bedazzlement. Generating an irrational hatred of anything Christian had always been easy in these quarters. Introducing his intended target had only required some well directed, fanciful browsing of websites known to promote the theology of the "One". After that, bringing Amos to the forefront of his subject's mind was simplicity itself.

Any human psyche, absent the dreaded "Presence", was no match for the influence of a master of hate and deception. And that hate could be focused relentlessly, driving the recipient into a sort of mental, or spiritual, madness bordering obsession. Such was the condition of the superior in authority above Felim.

Buferan had observed Felim's efforts with an appreciative eye for some time. After all, what was more poetic than a serpent when involved with these "ones of belief"? Did not their own teachings credit a "Serpent" with the mechanization of their earliest failure and downfall? What a delight it would be to see that irritating pipsqueak silenced by a most dreadful representative of the same breed. In fact, just watching the preparations gave him a thrill of anticipation. Human suffering was one of the end game goals which every being in Lucifer's camp worked in harmony toward. And best of all was the suffering of a so called "Saint".

Felim had finished preparation of his containment device and the time had come. The Mamba' hatch was open and he was inserting a long handled capture device to snare and control the business end of this messenger of death. However, he had no sooner begun his initial move when she suddenly hissed loudly and shot straight up from her coils going instantly into aggressor mode. He barely had time to react as she lunged through the opening directly at his face.

The noose clattered to the floor as Felim danced back trying to gain separation from the very monster he himself had created. The snake was now half way out, reared up on the edge of the hatch and glaring down into his eyes. Her mouth was open exposing the dark lining that gave her species the "black" part of their name. The death, he had so assiduously cultivated for others, was staring him in the face and he felt a sudden cold sense of dread and fear. Panic was but a moment away as every impulse screamed flee, flee for your life. But Felim was the "Keeper" and honor dictated otherwise.

Instead he spun and raced towards a small closet door. Snatching it open he fumbled among the various shapes and handles stored within. The sound of the heavy body thumping to the floor announced the Mamba's arrival to continue the confrontation. Looking wide eyed over his shoulder he saw her gather into a striking position, then spy him and uncoil immediately to race in his direction. The head stood nearly waist high and the hissing was nonstop. She meant to kill him.

Never had he seen such vengeful thinking and malignant intent from a reptile. But there was no time to marvel at the insane ferocity of the attack. His trembling fingers closed on the desired handle and he snatched an aluminum tong assembly free scattering several other items haphazardly across the area in his haste. This proved to be his salvation. One small length of broom handle spun directly into the path of the enraged reptile distracting her. She halted momentarily and focused suspiciously on this new adversary. But after only seconds of examination she ignored it and resumed her charge for the hapless Felim. Felim was ready.

Now armed with a four foot scissoring pair of capture tongs, he fended the large head deftly to one side while attempting to close the hook-nosed jaws around the thick neck. But, as the snake felt the pressure, she suddenly withdrew downward evading the capture and shot forward striking at Felim's leg. She barely missed. He reeled backwards only to come solidly up against the wall adjacent to the narrow closet door; trapped. Supercharged by adrenaline and terror he cart wheeled gymnastically up and outward in a pivot while leaving the tongs planted on the floor as support. The serpent followed this aerial progress and, as he landed, she turned to continue the attack. But Felim had managed to regain his balance and place the tongs between them.

Holding the snake's malevolent glare, he danced back a step to gain maneuvering room. Unfortunately his foot landed squarely on the errant piece of broom handle causing his leg to shoot instantly out from under him. He landed heavily on his side still grasping the tongs defensively in front. Now he was eye to eye, mere feet from a sudden and unholy death. The reptile seemed to gloat as she reared up to deliver the coup-de-grace. At that same instant he snatched the hinged vee section of the tongs directly up under the jaw and closed it firmly around her neck. All hell broke loose.

His arms were jerked violently from side to side as the reptile exploded in a frenzy of writhing and thrashing. The hisses came in irregular grunt-like efforts and he was forced to close his eyes as flecks of venom spattered from the gaping mouth. Maintaining his grip he pulled one knee under himself and then used his elbows to lever to a crawl position. Through squinted eyes he tried to keep watch on the maw and fangs. He was now perched on his knees and elbows face to face with her. But the violence of the struggles had started to abate. Her cold-blooded energy level was beginning to wane.

Holding the trigger firmly with one hand Felim reached out and grabbed for the back half of the undulating coils. He lost his grip on the first attempt and the Mamba reignited her efforts forcing him to briefly use both hands on the tongs. But she soon began to slow once more and his next effort was rewarded with a firm grasp of the thick body two feet from the tail.

Both Felim and the snake were blowing hard and he grunted with the effort of coming to his knees while maintaining his tenuous control. For several long moments the combatants puffed in unison and eyed each other. She snapped her jaws at him halfheartedly once or twice but was clearly out of gas. Pressing his advantage, Felim placed one knee on her back freeing that hand to help with his final move.

Controlling the "close" trigger with his left hand, he slid his right up under the tong jaws and locked his fist around the muscular neck. He let the apparatus clatter to the floor and was now in the position he'd originally tried to achieve. Problem was...his nerves were shot. He was trembling with adrenaline and fear and wanted nothing more than to throw the snake bodily back into her terrarium. But he could feel she was also spent and if he did so, this effort would have to be repeated. Frankly, it was now or never. He did not want to tangle again with this particular specimen. In addition, he knew she might regain enough strength for round two at any moment. He carried the temporarily vanquished Mamba swiftly to his packaging table.

A deep rectangular box stood on end with the upper flaps open. Inside was a tube made of large, dryer vent looking material surrounded by a special insulating collar and Styrofoam peanuts. Into said "tube" Felim began inserting the snake tail first. She resumed her struggles, but she was still tired and he was in control. He wound her tightly into the cylindrical hollow till only the last twelve inches and head remained free. He had calculated well; it was a good fit. Stuffing the last section into the remaining space, he picked up a heavy cardboard disk with a small plastic handle in its center. It fit the diameter of the tubing perfectly and carried a freight sticker clearly marked "open this end". He suddenly released her head and inserted the disk, spiraling it down two turns of the wire frame supporting the vinyl sheeting. She was trapped. Felim drew his first semi-relaxed breath since this debacle began.

Without hesitation he poured more peanuts into the upper void and then folded the flaps trapping the whole "snake cocoon" securely within. The final taping and brown paper wrap took a little time as he had to make sure his small, camouflaged air vents were open. After that, he finally allowed himself the luxury of a few minutes recuperation. Slumping heavily into an old chair, he sat drawing quick breaths while staring vacantly at the wall.

Suddenly a gale of laughter roared out of him. The combination of pure joy at being alive, and relief at having the "snake from hell" packaged, all came together at once. What I would give, he thought, for a video of that affair. Of course that would be creating evidence but, in this case, I would risk it. Never will there be her equal. However, this was not the time to relive the insanity of those minutes. This serpent, from the Keeper of Serpents, had a destiny to fulfill...and it was time she caught her flight.

On the other side of the dimensional wall, having watched one of his well laid plans dangle perilously close to disaster, even Buferan had to admit to a sense of relief.

THE TWO ALEXANDER'S were seated in Jim's small office in front of an early IBM PC desktop. Its dated appearance belied the internal improvements added over the last couple of years. Only the color display provided a hint that things weren't as they seemed. It looked like an old chevy sedan, but ran like a Corvette.

"Ozello...who ever heard of Ozello?" exclaimed Jenny.

"Well, actually, I've heard of it," replied Jim, "just never talked to anyone who's been there."

"Sounds like some kind of dessert."

"No, apparently, it's an old fishing village on the edge of the Gulf just south of Crystal River. And look here, he's listed in this address directory. Some street called South Osprey Point...no phone though."

"Hmph, I'm almost relieved. Dad, this guy will probably think I'm nuts."

"Well, look, we both know you can't just blurt out your story, but up till now you've wanted to follow up on this thing...why the hesitation."

Jenny stared amusedly at her father,

"Let me see...the plan here is to cold call some strange man, planning to unload the most insane sounding story he's likely ever heard, adding that this same 'angel' told me to remember his name. Considering that I'm a younger female, with no real credentials in his world, you think he might get the wrong idea?"

"Credentials...his world...what are you talking about?"

"Dad, I've just read this guys stuff; he sounds like the real deal. I mean a real 'Man of God'. That also means he's probably somewhat like you. You might not have noticed it but I've watched you all these years. You're a nice person and I'm proud of you in all kinds of ways, but Dad, you have no patience with people who waste your time on frivolous arguments...or off-beat religious stuff."

Jim was eyeing his daughter as if from a different point of view, "Uhmm, yeah I do know what you're saying....truth is I consider it one of my shortcomings. I know I can appear brusque at times"

"Bible says we all must bear some faults dad, but you could exercise more patience with some of the folks that seem out in left field to you."

Jim was in thought for several moments,

"Sweetheart, don't misunderstand what I'm about to say. I know full well I could be more 'warm and fuzzy' even when I don't feel like it. And patience and kindness are virtues we should all strive for daily. But you may have also noticed the ones I'm sometimes a little short with, are often the so called leaders who can't seem to see the forest for the trees. I used to really beat myself up over it till one night He reminded me that Jesus ticked off almost every religious leader of his day. In fact his message offended nearly everyone who wouldn't accept it."

He continued, "Now, I'm not making excuses...I could do better lots of times, but don't fall into what I call the 'marshmallow trap' where Jesus is concerned. Mainstream religion paints Christ as this wimpy, almost effeminate individual in a snowy robe scattering petals everywhere he went. Couldn't be further from the truth. He was an outspoken critic of the sin and wrong he observed and a stern voice of warning as to where those actions would lead. He offended the Pharisees and the other sect leaders almost every time he opened his mouth. You know why, because from then till now, the one thing that cuts like a razor, is truth; God's truth. And it sometimes seems we're not much closer in our so called churches today."

He thought a moment, then continued, "Love and truth are inseparable. If you love someone you'll be truthful with them," here he smiled, "like you're being with me. But no matter how gently you phrase it, sometimes the truth hurts. I think it's how we handle the ones that are uncomfortable that best show our character. And I have to admit, some of the more painful things I've had said to me, have come from those who I am certain love me the most…including Him.

"What I try to emulate when that happens is the Scripture that says '*a wise man rebuked will love you all the more*'. I try to be wise about it. Now, forgive the speech, I do understand what you're saying…and he might react that way, but what other options are there?"

"What about contacting him through one of those bulletin board things?" she asked.

"Thought hard about that, Spirit seemed to squash it. I guess this is to remain as private as possible."

"OK, but we're just talking about making contact, not telling the story…right?"

"The feeling, or sense, I get is we don't want our names connected with his in any public fashion. That sort of jives up with what the angel said about 'person of interest'. I think we need to avoid drawing attention from any outside source as much as possible; at least for now."

"Uh, OK, I can see that…but what does that leave?"

"Hasn't He given you any input on this? You usually hear pretty clearly for yourself. Any impressions at all?"

Jenny seemed perplexed, then sighed and looked at her feet for a moment,

"One picture does keep appearing in my mind. I'm driving...driving to wherever this guy lives; which I now know is this...Ozello. And I can see myself walking up to a house, I guess it's his. I even know somehow there are two or three concrete steps...and what I think are sliding glass doors. I'm uncomfortable with it but it's popped into my head maybe three times now."

"There's your answer."

"Oh Dad, I don't really want to do that."

"Ever notice how often it works that way? If God isn't getting a believer out of their comfort zone fairly regular, that believer may be stagnant."

"Great...so what if I do all that without contacting him first and he's not home or something?"

Jim flashed a mischievous grin "What if we just follow the leading and see how it works out?"

"We...we...are you going with me? Oh dad, that would be great. That would be different," Jenny beamed back at him.

"You involved me in this dear daughter, and I can't sense any reason not to stay in it. We both have the time free. Martha OK with Mr. Bones a while longer?"

"Martha'd like to adopt him. He's such a schmoozer, he's wrapped her around his paw already."

Jim laughed, "Yeah, elegant and alley cat don't get mentioned much together, but he's definitely one example."

Jenny laughed with him, "One of a kind...we hope. OK, what next pop?"

"Hmm...It's off season; maybe we can get a room on Crystal River. Let's look on here for a map to this Wallace Point, and then see what we can book for tomorrow. With luck we can take off first light."

Jenny thought a moment and then shook her head, "So the adventure continues." She looked at her father with a serious expression, "You didn't see them dad, but there are some really scary players involved in this thing."

"Are you afraid?"

"Not really...Arak got me past that...but I do respect their power and influence. I mean, they may be here right now."

"No, probably not at the moment. Spirit's too involved between us. You know, two or more are gathered."

"Oh...yeah, you're probably right. Besides, I think I would sort of sense it if they were near. That's a feeling I'll never forget...ever. But you don't seriously think we can go find him in his home town and the demons not know it?"

Jim sighed, "No, not really. But they rely on human agents for the physical work just like God relies on us. It would be pretty far fetched to think an episode as unusual as you had, with the two camps so openly pitted against each other, doesn't have a counterpart or two involved somewhere out here."

Jenny looked baffled for a moment, "You mean 'real world' bad guys in league with the demons?"

"Look at history...has it ever been otherwise?"

She was silent again, considering his words, then, "I hadn't thought of it that way...it's always like that isn't it?"

"From Judas to Hitler."

"You know, I'm around you all the time and you still amaze me the way you see things."

"Humph, the only amazement is that it takes most of us so many years to finally stop and view the world as it is. It's the spirit side of life that's reality. The nonsense we're exposed to everyday is mostly a carefully counterfeited lie.

It keeps most folks looking at the surface without ever considering what's going on behind the scenes...spiritual smoke and mirrors."

"Well this girl has been inoculated against that forever. In Rome, I got a look behind the scenes. I consider myself a believer and it still blows my mind. Oh dad, we have to be careful, those things are playing for keeps. I never understood the...the purity of Satan's hatred towards us...and God. It sounds like a cliché, but it really does chill my soul when I think about it."

Jim smiled, "It would probably chill mine too, but I have a famous 'sword bearer' to travel with."

Jenny stared at him a moment then broke into laughter, "That's me, Jenny the Bearer...and my dad the Prophet."

Jim joined in the laughter then wiped his eyes, "Well it's time this dynamic duo got some rest, but let's bring this before Him first."

With that, they knelt side by side, bowed their heads and began a short petition for protection and guidance.

IN THE ARENA where that prayer was aimed, Raphael stood surrounded by the ultimate glory to be found in any corner of creation...and was totally oblivious. The reports accumulating on the Mikals situation were beginning to somewhat consume his thinking as they were Araks'. It was obvious Lucifer was organizing a multi-pronged offensive against this lone believer; he'd seen that before. But the apparent urgency involved meant the adversary was also looking at the situation on the Earth and wondering if that long awaited D-day might be in the offing.

In addition, Father was allowing him to operate outside established channels with apparent unconcern for the breach...or the growing danger to young Amos. Both sides were breaking some new ground here and Raphael had nothing in his vast, timeless experience to compare it with.

Arak had "checked in" on departing Deran and apprised him of Lonius newly imparted knowledge regarding the deadly spiritual accounting facing the entities of Earth. He couldn't fault the youngster, nor was he surprised at the effect it had on his father. He had always been glad this was a one-off creation. Even after observing its history, he sometimes questioned whether he would have the temerity to see it through in the end...as he was certain Father would. In a Cosmos where many dangers and unpleasant surprises could sometimes be found, Hell stood alone like a city on a hilltop as the most shocking and horrible conclusion any living thing would ever be subjected to.

Were it not for the other side of that coin, the "escape clause", you would have to say the sentence was unjust. However, those with knowledge of the basics regarding this particular plan had to admit, it was a deal that would have been hard to resist; even with the danger.

For God himself was filtering through these on the Earth looking for true loyalty and obedience from beings that were of His own image in self will. Something which had evaded him with Lucifer. Raphael knew that this was a great heartache to the Almighty One. He also knew the wrath attached to such disobedience would be second to none as well. Hell was surely second to nothing for horror, pain and punishment; but the reward offered was also second to absolutely nothing.

Those coming out of the firestorm of trials and temptations Lucifer rained down on their short mortal lives, attained a status no other living creatures would ever see. "Brothers and sisters" of the Christ; Jehovah's own children in the strictest sense of the word...with eternity in the bargain. The joy's that stretched forth from that moment, no one adequately perceived.

Most of mankind longed for acceptance, peer support, accolades...glory. The glory promised these over-comers was the shared glory of Jesus granted by God himself. Each and every believer, who made the pasage through "the narrow gate", would individually take that bow on the center stage of Heaven itself. Standing square on the focal point of everything known or imagined, past or present. And they would do it before an audience of numbers and prestige the likes of which they could not possibly conceive. The roars of approval would rock the constellations. The tumult of celebration would never be equaled...and all this would appear only once in all of eternity.

As Creation was God's own masterpiece reflecting the glory of Him, these finite mortals would ascend to the very forefront of that masterpiece. Priceless jewels to glitter endlessly in honor of their God and Father. Even for an Arch, it defied description.

All well and good, but without ones like Amos, some who might have evaded Lucifer's snares would certainly fall short. Father was not willing that any face that final death of soul while some stone of realization was left unturned. Before the constant "giving in", to the demons work, hardened their heart past the point of redemption. For it was well stated that the Spirit *"would not strive forever with man."*

In fact, in Raphael's experience, most current members living in Amos' principality, would come in contact with a serious "religious" experience an average of three times. That number was probably not coincidence. Exposure to Amos' efforts and words was always one possibility; one that was worth protecting...but how. Any move outside His dictates would be foolishness itself and might subject the offender to wrath and chastisement on a scale with infinity...no way to measure it. He sighed; there was no choice but to trust again in the unlimited thinking of Father. No matter how bad things were beginning to look from here.

SAMMY SIDLED UP to a barstool beside Eddie in the taproom of the old Orange Blossom Inn. The grandiose name might have meant more in decades past, but today it was just another of the struggling small enterprises left adrift by the arrival of the federal interstate system. Perched on US 41, a little north of the beaten path that comprised the Crystal River "metro" area, it had definitely seen better days...better clientele too.

Eddie looked over as he sat down, "Hey dude, what's up?"

"Just passing by, saw your truck; thought I would say hi."

The bartender came and took Sammy's request, then he turned back to Eddie, "So my friend, get to watch that sunset tonight?"

"Nah, tube sheet stuff is keeping us pretty busy."

"Tube sheet?" he feigned ignorance.

"Ah, crap…I think I'm not supposed to talk about it."

"Sorry, it is none of my business anyway."

"Not your fault man; anyway I know I can trust you. I got this, like, sixth sense."

Samir suppressed a smile at that, "Thank you, I am honored you feel that way. I sometimes get the other reaction. All my people do. But we understand…no offense taken."

If Eddie was honest, his trust was as much founded on Sammy's willingness to buy rounds as it was any instinct. This despite the fact the man never seemed to finish the first drink of his own.

"Yeah, well it's no biggie between you and me. Fact is, they got contamination in places they shouldn't have and there's a big push to get it cleaned up and repaired."

"I guess I am like everyone else, those plants both frighten and fascinate me. I cannot imagine working inside the actual reactor."

"The 'sheet's' not part of the actual reactor, it's an end piece of a big heat exchanger that sends steam to the turbines."

"Oh, so I take it this piece has developed some problem that requires the attention of you and your team."

Eddie's ego was again feeling those signs of inflation that went along with Sammy's attitude, which often seemed akin to a small degree of hero worship. He went ahead and told the gear drive story while playing up the dangers and difficulties involved. His partner's eyes grew suitably wide at all the right places and between that, and the alcohol in his system, he was once again feeling pretty splendid about the "new" Eddie.

"Truly an amazing device. I had never thought about how one of them actually made the power generate," another falsehood.

"Pretty intense stuff alright, you sure you don't want to apply?"

"No, my friend, my hat is off to you. My nerves could not take it. What will happen when everything is returned to working condition?"

"I guess we'll get back to making electricity for the masses."

"You said they hired many of you just for this work, yes?"

That caused a moments pause, "You mean will we all have jobs then? Good question, the newbie's will all be gone pretty quick. Rumor is they'll scale down maintenance some too."

"Surely not someone such as yourself?"

Eddie looked thoughtful for a moment, "Nah, they need the old hands like us to keep the thing running," he said, while a completely different train of thought ran through his head. The fact was McMillan would likely use that opportunity to "can" him. A very unpleasant scenario indeed.

Sammy, aka Samir, was unobtrusively watching his reaction, "Ah, it is too bad then, many of your comrades will be back out looking for work in this terrible job market."

Eddie was still pensive considering the possibility he might be leading the pack, "Uh, yeah...too bad about that. They'll never match this pay anywhere around here."

His friend let out a long sigh, "Yes, unfortunate; one could wish the work could go on."

Now Eddie looked back at him, "Well pal, that ain't gonna happen. Big bucks involved in this game. I heard that sucker pulls down over a 400K a day."

Sammy whistled, "Wow, you are right. No wonder they rush things. Still, when matters are rushed, sometimes things go wrong. Would you care for another?"

Eddie was still absently mulling the cloud of uncertainty that had arrived on station over his own future.

"Nah, thanks anyway...I better get moving."

Samir said nothing further. That was how these things worked. From small seeds, great plants may grow. Even nuclear plants, he thought...and smiled.

CHAPTER 11

THE UPS DRIVER stopped his "brown" panel truck, shut off the diesel engine and gave the area a slow visual scan. Amos' own truck was typically absent, for this time of day, but he suspected eyes were following him none the less. Nothing moved or made a sound. He sighed; so that was how it was going to be. Remaining watchful he backed into the cargo area and retrieved the rectangular package with Mikals name on it. Then, as he paused in the doorway, he again slowly rotated his head looking for any sign of movement. He knew it would be a predatory, cat-like momentum that was hard to detect...nothing.

He glanced at the package which was fair sized but not particularly heavy. There was a sticker on one end marked "This end up" which bore the Sony electronics logo. There were also several tears in the outer wrapping and one of the corners was rounded from pressure. It seemed to have had a rough ride. He hoped the baggage gorillas hadn't created a problem for the company; or the customer. He also wondered what Amos was up to now?

Over the years he'd delivered everything from automotive racing parts to Bibles and Christian DVD's. He knew these things because of the casual friendship that had developed with Mr. Mikals. He was an interesting guy; even if you didn't subscribe to his "church" views. And, although he was persistent about those, he was never pushy. It was safe to say he liked Amos. It was also safe to say he liked Bubba...even that Bubba liked him. But that rascally pit bull's idea of fun was an ambush. The first time it happened had taken a couple of years off his life.

As he exited his truck that first day, he'd caught a movement out of the corner of his eye. Turning, he found himself face to face with a big, stocky, brindle pit bull. One with the eyes and scars of a killer. The dog had not made a sound. The wicked looking stare, combined with an absence of any barking or growling, had nearly made him soil himself. This "stand off" had seemed to last forever but was probably only a few seconds long. Then without warning the animal had exploded in his direction with a speed that left him no time to react. The scream was still forming in his throat when the blur that was Bubba veered around his legs, brushing him soundly. The animal continued some five or ten feet then spun around facing the hapless driver; who barely had time to pivot himself, while holding his package in front like a shield.

It took several seconds to overcome the wide-eyed panic and adrenaline. Then he realized the fearsome countenance had been replaced with a nearly human expression of merriment attached to what could only be called a canine grin. He didn't need a dog psychiatrist or interpreter to read the message. The eyes sparkled with the unspoken "Gotcha". Holy cow; he'd never imagined anything like it.

His knees were like jelly but he slowly put the package down and held out a tentative hand. Neither party made a sound till Bubba calmly walked over and accepted a few shaky pats. Then the man suddenly burst into laughter and reached down to seriously pet the big, grizzly head. He could see the perpetrator shared his humor. It was the darndest behavior he'd ever witnessed...and the beginning of a friendship. Now once again, his mission was to reach the front steps without being surprised by you-know-who.

It wasn't more than forty feet to said steps but there was cover scattered on both sides. An observer would have been totally confused by the driver's actions. It looked more like a hunter on safari, creeping towards a would-be target, than a UPS delivery. Sweat trickled down his neck and the prickly feeling increased. He could feel Bubba watching, but where the heck was he?

The first step was within reach now. His reflection peered back at him from the mirrored glass doors. Nothing else moved in the background. Then, as he was cautiously lowering the package, another image seemed to materialize directly behind him...and as quickly vanish. He dropped the package and spun only to face...emptiness. Whatever it was, it wasn't Bubba. It was huge and ugly and...gone. What the??? He shook his head and rubbed his eyes in the classic fashion of disbelief.

The heat that had seemed to oppress him was strangely absent; a cold inner chill had over-ridden it. Goose bumps raced up and down like a wave over his skin. His pulse had gone from quickened by the game with the dog, to racing with adrenaline and fright.

"Man, if I didn't know better, I'd say I just saw the world's scariest ghost," he muttered to himself. "This has to be one of Amos' tricks or experiments or something."

He turned back towards the steps to examine the glass door for any gadgetry, then yelped in alarm. Bubba was sitting on the top step like another ghost materializing from nothingness.

"Dammit, Bubba," he began then stopped. Bubba wasn't looking or paying attention. His big, gold-brown, cat-eyes were riveted on the delivery. He looked again at the package. The labeling and stampings indicated it had traveled a long distance in a short time. He gave it a gentle shake but nothing was loose.

"What is it boy?"

Bubba glanced up at him, then back at the package. There was a look of concern on the scarred, handsome face but, as usual, not a sound came from the ex-prizefighter. What Ted, for that was his name, did not know, was that Amos had been catching and releasing snakes for years. In his youth he and his brother were regular wildlife relocation agents. Even to the point of removing problem alligators from residential areas. Sometimes with the clandestine, but sincere, appreciation of local wildlife officers.

So, naturally, Bubba had been exposed to many of the species Florida had to offer. He'd been with Amos when they tackled everything from Red Rat Snakes to Cottonmouths and Diamondbacks. He was well schooled in the danger the venomous ones represented; even to "tough guys" like he and Amos. There was no way to fool his senses as to what this package contained. But this was a new and strange variety laced with something that seemed to surround the area with a vapor of things bad. If Bubba had understood evil, that's the word he'd have chosen.

Ted looked back into the reflective glass remembering the apparition from moments ago. He could see nothing that would explain how such a monstrosity could be projected onto its surface.

"Look Bubba, I don't know what's going on here, but I've got to get moving."

The animal glanced up, then pirouetted off the steps like a jaguar. He landed next to Ted and looked purposefully around the immediate area. Not only was there something not right about this box, he could sense that other foul presence that had appeared once before. The night the big man with wings had walked across the water and become their friend. Amos seemed not to notice, but Bubba had his back on such matters. If it was looking for trouble, it had come to the right place.

Ted started for the panel-van and Bubba fell into step. Ted was a friend too. If this thing attacked, it was going to have to fight both of them. However, nothing untoward occurred or appeared. Ted looked down a last time and said, "I don't know boy, just keep an eye on things till Amos gets home; I'll see ya."

With that he fired up the diesel and motored around the lime rock cul-de-sac returning to his route. Bubba gave the area another meaningful scrutiny, then turned and headed back towards the package. None of these creatures had ever been delivered to them before. Always the incidents were accidental or random. Then the snake wound up in a sack until Amos took them out for a ride and released it. Bubbas' favorite part, a trip to the forest and some hiking along the dirt roads and trails. But this situation didn't fit. He returned to the steps, which were shaded by an aluminum overhang, settled back on his muscular haunches and sat eyeing the package with a suspicious glare.

"WHAT DO YOU MEAN VISIBLE?"

"Just that, My Lord, the human clearly saw me. It was momentary, but the reaction was unmistakable."

"That's just not possible. Why would He allow one of his own stupid 'laws' to be broken? Was this another of these believers?"

"Absolutely not; I had been watching him at close range for some time with no interference."

Lucifer paused in deep thought, then "It must have something to do with Mikals. After all, you were both on his ground were you not?"

"True enough sir, but Mikals was nowhere near. And the 'Presence' was not there either."

"Buferan, do not state the obvious. Had He been present, you would not have been. Unless in the escort of one of those repulsive 'followers', He has no hesitation in lashing out. Such a confrontation is not a thing you would survive if you venture beyond the boundaries...yet."

The master of evil was silent for a long moment. Then, "What was this man doing on Mikals ground?"

"Ah...that is the good news of the matter. He is part of the secondary plan I told you of."

"You didn't 'tell' me anything. You affirmed there was a back up."

Now Buferan proceeded to fill his boss in on the details of Felim's little enterprise; leaving out the specifics of his near disaster with the packaging. For once, even the awful Lucifer seemed pleased.

"Appropriate indeed Buferan, I give you that. But it had better work. There are some important threads that cannot be pulled until this matter is concluded successfully. Do not turn your attentions away from the first situation either. In fact, even if this little gambit silences Mikals, I wish to proceed with the other effort as well. Re-assign Manoc to the peripheral humans involved. It's his principality; let him coordinate some of the lesser details. Devote your attention to Mikals."

"Ah, My Lord, forgive me, but are we not already treading in Arch territory?"

"I will tread much further before this matter concludes."

Buferan decided to risk a question, "So the day approaches?"

Lucifer eyed his subordinate until the mighty demon began to fidget nervously, "Would that change anything? You are to do as told regardless."

"Always Highness, I ask only because I have not your magnificence or insight. I humbly apologize for any offense."

The even mightier "God of Chaos" actually sighed, "No offense Buferan, you have always served well. That is why you are leading this mission...on which much may depend. Listen to me; this Mikals reminds me of one of my favorite things...a virus. Only this virus has the potential to do *us* much harm. And yet, He holds back while we weave the noose closer and tighter. Why? Already there is sufficient violation to demand an accounting. You are also aware of these things. Is it not cause for some question?"

Buferan had never had a conversation like this with his master. Millennia of service had been rendered with no gratitude or explanation expected or given. Only rants and threats when things went awry. The situation must be more serious than he had imagined.

"Ah, Majesty, I have thought these things but do not question your wisdom on how they should be handled."

"Are you familiar with the human term 'sucking up'?"

Buferan's huge reptilian eyes widened in surprise. "I understand it, sir"

"Then quit it. These matters are racing ahead at a pace I don't think even the others expected. He is either toying with us or some very significant events are in the offing. I order you to keep abreast of it and to inform me of any and all occurrences affecting this Mikals business; without all the simpering. As they like to say, give it to me straight. And if something catches your eye that you are unsure of, tell me anyway."

Buferan's eyes remained widened, "Ah, yes sir...I, uh, will endeavor to do...that."

"Fine, now get out of here and get on it...and send Atreus back here, I want to know where those idiots in Jerusalem are on the temple matter."

"At once...uh, sir." And in a "black fire" flash he vanished.

Lucifer glared at the lesser ranks that had reappeared with the exit of the famous under-lord, "Get out of here," he snarled, "and let me think."

They vanished like mist.

"I will have Earth's throne," he muttered to no one, "I will ascend and I will control. And I will rid myself of this Mikals and any of his ilk as the beginning of your end here. You may restrain your hand...I will not."

Evil incarnate had spoken.

"THIS PLACE IS BEAUTIFUL", exclaimed Jenny.

"Yeah, I'm actually glad things were jammed up on Crystal River."

"H-o-m-o-s-a-s-s-a...Homosassa...Wonder what exactly does that mean?"

"You're gonna love it," replied her father "it's a Creek Indian name for, Place of many Pepper Plants."

She examined her fathers face to see if he was serious, "And you just happen to know this how?"

"I read the sign", stated Jim turning to point at a large brass "State Historical Site" plaque posted behind them. "Says it was at the center of a sugar producing concern before the Civil War, and then got destroyed by the Union army for supplying sugar to the Rebs. Same old story with much of the South; a lot of history got eradicated in the name of one side or the other."

Jenny eyed their surroundings, "Well, it seems like time has been kind to it since then. Look at these oak trees. They may have been here for some of that."

"Pretty place alright, let's check out the river."

They meandered towards a lengthy dock which ran in front of an equally impressive row of covered boat moorings.

As they got closer Jenny exclaimed once more, "Look at that water; it's clear as glass. And look at all the fish."

It was true; under the dock and around every piling were schools of minnows, bream and small bass flitting and cruising in apparent aimlessness. At the approach of the two Alexander's, they seemed to undulate in a choreographed fashion towards where they were standing.

Jim eyed them and said, "Well, it's obvious these guys get fed by the tourist."

"Yeah…Oh wow, check out that one."

Sure enough a much larger version of bass had materialized from the shadows under the dock.

"Yeah buddy," exclaimed her father, "that's an eight or ten pounder."

"What do you feed one that big?"

"Look's to me like he's got his eye on the one's being fed."

Jenny chuckled, "Reminds me of the bumper sticker with little fish getting eaten by the big fish, getting eaten by the bigger fish…"

"Yep, a regular little food chain; let's go check out the room and find a fishing pole."

Jenny eyed him curiously.

"Just kidding, that would probably get us lynched."

They turned and began the walk towards the rustic looking McRae's Hotel and Bait House nestled under some of those same mighty oaks. What they found was a large, comfy room with double queen beds and a view of the river. Jenny sat on one bed with a pensive look on her face.

"Nervous?"

She looked up at Jim and sighed, "Dad, is it normal for this thing to keep, uh…I'm not sure how to put it…"

Jim said nothing, just waited patiently.

"I guess the best way to describe it, is...it seems to fade in and out of reality."

"Go on."

"I have no idea how many people have seen what I saw in Rome, but I bet it's not many. So there's no 'data' on what to think...or even feel."

"How's it making you feel?"

She paused again, then, "Actually...different at different times...I think it's linked to how close I'm 'walking with the Spirit'. Don't we all fluctuate some in our spiritual attention spans?" Without waiting she continued, "OK, I go through the amazement phase and the feeling that I've been allowed to experience something...profound, but then later I feel uncertain as to...things."

"Things like?"

Another sigh escaped her, "Things like...why me. I look inside and think that, for the most part, I've honestly tried to do what you've taught...put Him first. But dad, I've never gotten that exactly right 24/7. OK, I'll just say it...I feel unworthy."

Her dad was quiet, eyeing his only child thoughtfully; finally, "Jen, we both know that, technically, we are 'unworthy'. But the longer I'm in this fight, the more I think that this 'spirit' of unworthiness, is one of Satan's highlight tools. It's worked on me too, but that makes you take your eyes off the Truth. And that can lead to quenching the very Spirit Jesus promised would come and be your guide. But let's look at the 'mechanics' involved here. You'll have to be my questionee, so let me ask you a few 'Kindergarten Christian' questions."

Jenny looked quizzical for a moment then shrugged, "OK."

Jim repositioned himself on his own bed and began, "Have you accepted Christ as the atonement for your sins, transgression...all the stuff you built up between you and God?"

"Yes"

"Does that mean those things are forgiven?"

"Well...yes."

"Did that change your heart?"

"Absolutely"

"OK, does that heart have any willful sins that now stand between you and Him? Anything God would point out to you"

She paused..."Not that I," another pause..."no, nothing I'm aware of."

"So, you have forgiveness for those sins of the past; and you don't have any un-confessed or unrepentant sin lingering now between you and God. Christ paid the price for any errant, transgressions you may commit later on. And God is now absolutely the biggest, most important thing in your life...you want what He wants."

Another short pause, then, "I would have to say yes."

"Then quit letting Satan distract you from what He wants here. I can assure you, whatever this is all about...the devil doesn't want you to complete the task."

Jenny sat a little stunned, "You are my own father and once again I'm amazed at the way you see things."

Jim smiled, "You don't really have that correct you know. Sometimes, in fact most times, I'm surprised too. What he does is let His spirit work, in those who are willing...to inform, edify, whatever you choose to term it."

"Thanks Dad...Thank you Lord...I'm willing. You know I hadn't really looked at all this as a 'task' before. Something Arak said comes back to me. He said he'd rather be destroyed than fail God. I realize now how deep that thought must have been embedded inside him...and dad, he was beyond awesome in every way. Can I possibly commit any less?"

It was Jim's turn to stare at his daughter, he shook his head softly, "You also remarked he welcomed you into the camp of Jehovah's own warriors. You make me proud."

Jenny's countenance suddenly took on a calm, almost serene look, "Dad, let's tackle this thing and make Him proud."

All her father could say to that was, "Amen." Then, "You ready to see Mr. Mikals?"

"As ready as I'll ever be I think."

"Want me along?"

Jenny closed her eyes and was silent for some seconds, "I guess this step I have to take alone."

"I think so," and Jim handed her the car keys, "Map's in the console."

Their eyes met briefly and Jenny turned and walked out. Jim closed the door behind her, sat on the edge of his bed...and bowed his head.

CHAPTER 12

A BOUT THE TIME JENNY began her drive to Ozello, Amos was exiting the large pressurization hatch which provided access into the reactor area. He felt distracted. Something was nagging at the back of his mind. He thought it might involve, or perhaps be related to, an odd-ball dream that had unexpectedly launched his pre-dawn day. In it, the angel, Arak, had again been trying to tell him something but Amos could never quite hear him. It had been a maddening loop that seemed to play for hours. While he was pondering this little mystery, that tell-tale shiver suddenly ran in reverse down his spine.

"That's strange," he thought and stopped dead in his tracks. He was almost run over by one of the HP techs also coming out of the hatch.

"Oof," they collided lightly. Amos turned and was face to face with his friend, and sometimes guardian, Health Physics Technician, Ron Bennett. An Aussie, who was nicknamed R.B. after his initials which matched those used for the containment building.

"Sorry, R.B."

"No worries mate. What's up, forget something?"

"No, not exactly," Amos said distractedly.

R.B. was immediately in "HP" mode, "Amos, you feeling crook?"

Amos looked at him blankly.

"Sorry, are you feeling OK?"

"Uh, yeah I'm fine R.B."

"Got a jump going?"

"No, not tonight."

"Good, can't tell if you've seen a ghost or what."

"That's it," said Amos quietly.

Now R.B. had the blank look.

Amos glanced at his face, "Nah, R.B., really I'm fine, I just remembered something I have to do on the Aux side."

Amos clapped his friend on the shoulder and started back the way he'd come. He returned to the hatch which looked like a cross-section from a submarine had been installed in the wall of the Reactor Building. Ron watched him for a moment more, still wearing a look of concern, then shrugged and continued on his way.

Meanwhile Amos had begun to put two and two together. Arak had mentioned listening like never before. That familiar voice was trying to get his attention; pretty determinedly. In fact, he had the strangest sense of himself taking the rest of the day off. Now why would he do that, the day just started? It wasn't even four in the afternoon. Not that it would be a problem.

As he'd told R.B., he wasn't scheduled for anything ANM related tonight and was on his way to help the guys with the routine stuff that comprised the first few hours of a shift. And since they were working seven day weeks, it was not unusual to take some time off once in a while to catch up on life outside this demanding, often stressful, drama they were all playing parts in.

Amos tried to get ten days in before taking a break, and since he didn't check in till three p.m., even Sundays hadn't been much of a problem. Management seemed to have formed a favorable opinion of his work and leadership and he was secretly glad he'd never had to enforce his commitment not to work during morning worship hours...except in real emergencies. The powers running this show thought the whole thing was one big emergency. But that was a reflection of the money involved more than anything else. He knew, in some ways, that "priority" overrode the actual safety of the individuals involved. He also knew this was common corporate thinking and didn't take it personally. None the less, he kept an eye on his crew and McMillan stayed on them constantly about proper procedures and safety. Still, a place like this could only be just so "safe".

He sat through the pressurization cycle with numerous fellow workers swarming in and out like bees serving in a hive. The premonition of needing to be home would not abate. He wished there were someone he could call to ask if things seemed normal, but most of the neighbors hadn't been around for months. The place was a ghost town, with the exception of Jerry, and he was off traveling on business. In fact, Amos was the one they counted on to watch their places when they were absent. OK, no use fighting it; he'd check his guys one time and let Mac know he was taking off. With the decision made, his step quickened and the sense of urgency, if anything, increased.

THE MAMBA FELT the changes that occurred. All the various temperature and scent inputs, as well as the vibratory impulses that passed for sound in her world, registered upon her sensory systems. But there was nothing she could do to respond; and this infuriated her. The months of ill handling, culminating in the unsuccessful battle with Felim, and her subsequent even more restrictive imprisonment, had left her in a state of uncontrolled fury. The flight part of her "fight or flight" programming, was pretty much cancelled. Now she lay cramped in a coiled spring position with only one reaction available to her rudimentary reptilian mind; kill.

She was aware of the current mammalian scent nearby and the others that had come and gone. Her only goal was to inflict enough punishment to insure that none of these creatures intruded upon her again. And she was mightily equipped to do so. A new possibility had registered alongside this vengeful thought pattern. The air-flow had noticeably increased bringing with it a renewed hope of escape from this tomb-like enclosure. She could not know this was due to the insults and mishandlings inflicted upon Felim's package during its travels; nor would she have cared. But it caught her notice and she began to exert pressure against the strange material comprising her prison. And the cardboard plug slipped...just a little.

Bubba too, was aware of the change. The crawling one in the package was making sounds now. Every imprisoned snake, in his experience, had done similarly. They were always looking for a way out of the box or linen sack that constrained them, both for their well being and that of the individuals in their vicinity. He sensed that letting this strange new specimen extricate itself from the box would be a bad thing. But Amos was not present to notice if he sounded the alarm and Jerry was not home to come investigate if he did so either. For now, Bubba felt sentinel duty was his only option.

If this one got out he would have to decide whether to try to kill it or let it escape. It had that scent of the ones that could kill with their bite, but not the same as the Rattlers and Cottonmouths he had experience with...He wished Amos were here.

JENNY HAD NEVER SEEN, much less driven, a road like this. It had obviously been laid out in an effort to take advantage of every piece of dry land that hop-scotched across the vast marshes. Shortly after departing Highway 19, the two lane black-top had begun to meander like a drunken sailor. State Road 494, the only roadway in or out of Ozello, promised to do nothing to detract from the "adventure" aspect of the day.

She was at the wheel of her dad's Nissan 200SX, a vehicle entirely suited for just such a task. He'd made an exception in his love of the American V-8 and turned this into his "economy" hot rod; reworking and upgrading it like he did most everything else. The end result was a powerful little sedan sporting a classy pinstripe paint job and an additional one hundred turbocharged horsepower. She'd been in the SX several times when Jim had "let it out"; the little sports car was part projectile. On this particular stretch, you could see the roadway undulating across the marshes from island to island and clearly spot traffic. She smiled to herself, "Dad see's this, we're in trouble." Even she couldn't resist setting the speed at a constant number and twisting the little rocket through some of the turns. But, after a few twisty miles, the landscape began to change.

There were more frequent, and larger, islands separated by clearly navigable waterways. These were spanned by raised bridges of increased stature as well. Soon, even houses and side roads began popping up at irregular intervals. She was eyeing her dad's little print-out and looking for South Osprey Point, but it appeared it would be a challenge. Only a few of the side roads had signs and none matched her map, which also didn't have every street labeled. Ozello was off the beaten track in more ways than one.

She passed a small, dilapidated looking mom and pop grocery store and thought of asking for directions. But it was gone around a sharp bend in the roadway before she could decide. Another half mile and she saw a sign advertising a marina and boat launch. It looked about a hundred years old and had no info for the street name. She continued on and was suddenly in a much more populous area which sported yet another small grocery establishment, this time with gas pumps.

"Time to ask for help," she muttered.

She pulled into the lime rock parking area, got out and headed for the old style double doors. There was one "local" pumping gas and two or three more clustered off to one side amidst a group of weathered looking pick up trucks. They all gave her an appraising look but were politely silent. It seemed pretty busy for such a remote area and suddenly she remembered why; it was right about quitting time.

Oh man, bet they don't get this too often. She was kind of "done up", wearing her best jeans with a fluffy sleeved top that had a bow on the back. Her long, ebony hair was pulled into a pony tail with a turquoise and silver clip producing what her dad termed her "Iroquois" look. Add the fact she was tooling around in the snarly sounding little sports car and she realized she had unwittingly "made an entrance".

She pushed through the double doors and was confronted with a typical coastal town convenience stop; everything from groceries and snacks to cast nets and fishing tackle. On a rotating rack by the door were multi-colored t-shirts with what looked like a cypress bayou scene outlined on the front. Underneath, emblazoned in large letters was, "Where in the hell is Ozello?" She had to smile, "That pretty much does say it all," she thought. There were more locals perusing the aisles and it seemed they all gave her the once over.

Jenny also looked things over for a moment. There was a formidable looking, large economy size woman of about middle age working the counter. Her hair was pulled into a "tail" like Jenny's, but there the resemblance ended. She would make more than two of her and was built like a lady wrestler. So she was surprised to hear a clear, high, sweet voice when she looked at Jenny and asked,

"Hey there little un', you lost?"

Jenny was caught by surprise, "Uh…yes ma'am…How'd you know that?"

"Hon, everbody' comes out here gets lost. What's a little sparkler like you doin' this far out anyway?"

"Ummm, I'm looking for a friend…well not friend…an acquaintance…sort of."

The lady reassessed her suspiciously for a moment, "You a re-porter?"

Jenny's eyes went wide, "Oh...Oh no, I'm just...I just need to find South Osprey Point."

Another pause, then, "South Osprey...child, who could you possibly know on South Osprey?"

Jenny hadn't meant to start out with subterfuge, but she was a naturally private person and didn't normally share her business with many. This time however, she didn't need a sixth sense to know that any further appearance of dissembling would not yield positive results. Everyone in the place was paying attention now.

She sighed, "I just need to find Amos Mikals."

"Amos...not to be overly nosy, but what you need to find 'Preacher' for?"

"Preacher?"

"You ever hear that boy get wound up about God?"

"Uh, no...that's sort of why I'm here."

"OK, honey, you gotta forgive us if we pry, but everbody's about tired of the whole UFO thing."

Jenny went totally blank again and it showed.

"Never you mind dear, you probly' don't need to know. If you do, stick around till after dark. You want to find Amos' place, just go back to the marina road, that's South Osprey. Bear right all the way to the end, you'll be parked in Amos' driveway."

"Oh, OK, thanks...I saw it but there wasn't a street sign."

The woman thought a second, "Can't remember a time there ever was one. Mos' folks just call it Marina Road."

"Well thank you, I guess I better get moving."

"No need to rush dear, you won't find Amos there right now anyhow."

Jenny paused, "Uh...no? Will he return soon?"

"Bout' midnight-thirty I guess."

Jenny's blank look again.

"He just started work about a hour ago. He don't get off till midnight."

"Oh, I see, where does he work, maybe I could have a word with him there."

"Not less' you got a Guvermint' noo-cle-ur clearance."

Jenny had been fielding all this information on the fly as best she could, but this was getting crazy.

After several moments thought she looked up at the woman, "OK, I'm sorry, did you say 'nuclear clearance'?"

"Of course dear; you really don't know Amos at all do you?"

Jenny sighed, "No ma'am, I don't...but I really need to talk with him."

"Little sparkler like you, he'd be nuts not to want to talk to you too. But sweetheart, they ain't gonna let you any-wheres' near that nuke plant. Specially' with all they got goin' on in there right now."

"Nuke plant...nuke plant?" Jenny heard herself echo.

"Of course dear, Crystal River Three. You never heard of it?"

Jenny actually slapped her hand lightly to her forehead, "Oh...I'm sorry...Yes I did know there was one near here somewhere...So, Mr. Mikals works there...I never even considered it."

"Yeah, well that's one of the best places round' here for decent pay and they got half the men workin' out there now for the big re-fuall."

"Uh...re-fuel?"

"Yep, they are takin' all them radiashun' rods out and puttin' new ones in."

Jenny assessed this for a moment, "Wow...yeah, I bet they don't want visitors around all that."

"Hon, you don't wanna be round' it neither. Those boys are wearin' all kinds of doodads to measure how much they get cooked ever' shift. My own fool brother is out there cause' of the big money...He's a welder."

"So Mr...ah, Amos is part of all that as well?"

"Shoot dear, Tom says Amos gets in a space suit near ever' day and walks around inside the reacter' doing stuff. Says he trust God to protect him from the cookin' rays comin' off that thing. Me, that's a test I'll not be puttin' the Lord to any time soon."

Jenny stood a moment perplexed. After all the hype and build-up, most of which she admitted was in her own mind, Mikals wasn't even home. And wouldn't be, really, until in the morning. She wondered if he slept late because of his hours.

"Ma'am...I'm sorry, my name is Jennifer Alexander...Jenny."

"Clarice Bowmar miss' Jenny, nice to make your acquaintance."

"So...Clarice...if I want to talk to Mr. Mikals tomorrow, how early could I come out?"

"Best be early dear. Always the chance Preacher and that dog of his will take off out in the Gulf shootin' grouper."

"Shooting grouper...shooting at fish?"

"Not with a firearm dear, with a spear gun. Shucks, I don't know how many of the guys round' here he's got infected with that business. These ol' boys thought they knew this area purty well. Your man Amos has taught them a few tricks about findin' grouper holes. I seen a twenty three pound black myself that he shot in only five feet of water off the Bird Racks last year."

Jenny lapsed into silence, trying to think all this info through. I come all the way here, because of Rome and some "religious" writing on the internet, expecting to meet some cerebral Professor of Divinity. The guy is walking around in a nuclear reactor and assassinating big fish for a hobby. Sounds more like a cross between Tarzan and Johnny Quest.

Looking back up at Clarice she said, "I can't thank you enough ma'am. I'll try to catch him tomorrow fairly early then."

"Yore' more'n welcome miss' Jenny...You get a chance tomorrow, drop over and bring Preacher. You get him and Tom tellin' UFO stories or talkin' religion and you'll never forget some of it."

Jenny smiled, "I might just take you up on that...and bring my dad. He's not someone you'll forget too quickly either."

"Sounds like a date to me hon, I'll be lookin' for you folks."

"Bye," said Jenny and headed out the swinging doors to the SX.

She got in and sat there, again trying to assimilate the info provided by her new friend. Now that's unusual, she thought. When's the last time you had a five minute conversation and really felt like you'd really found a friend. This was turning out to be an interesting place in more ways than one. It was disappointing to have missed Mikals, but the trip had been worthwhile just the same. She looked forward to telling her dad about it.

BUFERAN WAS RARELY surprised by human actions. And he didn't remember ever being surprised by the same human twice. Perhaps that was because of the latent danger involved with attracting his attention in the first place. But *she* was not someone who would ever again be able to enter his presence without detection. The same little female that helped devastate his plans in Rome, was now scampering around on Mikals home ground.

Impossible...no not impossible he chided himself, don't get in any deeper than you will be when Lucifer finds out. He said get the facts and report. Fact one, that Deranian has got to be in this somewhere. But the only other presence, currently, was the One feared above all and he too was hovering closely as if watching the girl. Well too bad; Buferan had done his homework well and Mikals trip on the Earth was about to be over. It was the anticipation of this positive report that led now to his personal visit and this unsettling discovery.

Too late he realized he should have assigned more watchers to those involved in Europe. Let this be a lesson not repeated. He would have Manoc locate the woman and child as well. The after reports also mentioned an old man; he too should come under some scrutiny. But for now, this was the arena that would yield results. Any other attempts at reprisal would pale next to eliminating Mikals.

He observed the girl re-enter her vehicle. There was one bystander under the adjacent trees who could be counted on to react to promptings of lust or lewdness. But, with the dreaded Presence following so closely, it might backfire. Better to stay in the background unless challenged. He would monitor her while awaiting Mikals and assign a watcher once he saw what direction things took from there.

She began her vehicular travel back the way she had come and Buferan prepared to glide along the dimensional wall, at a safe distance, following her. Then at that moment, his senses alerted him to yet another familiar presence. A nondescript sedan had arrived in the same parking zone and there was little doubt who was on board. As he watched, Samir got out of this one and also sauntered into the supplies building. Well, well, as the idiots often proclaimed, small world. One they would lose ownership of soon enough. He nodded to the watcher following in "Sammy's" wake and continued his pursuit of Jenny.

JENNY SLOWED as she approached the ancient looking marina sign, and then suddenly decided to turn onto what she now knew was South Osprey Point. Might as well take a look while I'm here, she thought. The asphalt ended, or rather turned hard left, at a point where a huge culvert had been installed to allow a tributary to carry boat traffic out into an adjacent bay. This bay was visible through the trees but still a couple of hundred feet away. It appeared South Osprey went right and became a lime rock drive on the other side of the culvert. The asphalt continued, she guessed, to the marina. She took the turn over the large hump and continued on.

A nicely appointed double wide appeared on her left sitting on a canal that fed straight out to the bay. A little farther, there was a small concrete block home on a large piece of semi-cleared property. It was perched on the north bank facing southerly over the open water. To her right were only undeveloped woodlands. Some weathered "For Sale" signs sprouted here and there indicating lots were available on that side. Just past the little CBS home, the lime rock roadway became a distorted cul-de-sac with the straight portion turning into a curved driveway of sorts. This must be the place.

There were grasses, palmettos and evergreens blocking any view of the dwelling, so she pulled in a little way to finally see where this guy actually lived. As she rounded the short bend she came to a sudden stop. She was looking down the left side of an ordinary looking mobile home, but directly behind it, filling the view from that point, was a panorama that would never be considered ordinary. She was seeing it through a natural alley created by the mobile on the right and the undergrowth on the left, but the narrow out-take was beautiful.

Vast needle grass plains stretched to the horizon peppered haphazardly with islands supporting groups of pines, palms and palmettos. In the forefront, the bay itself, some two hundred or so feet across, danced and glittered in the afternoon sunlight. Without conscious thought, she shut off the SX, opened her door and walked dream-like towards the spectacle before her. As the view opened up, she realized she had trespassed onto what must be Amos Mikals' backyard. Wow...what a view. She was standing near a strategically placed picnic table and just sort of slumped down on one side. She let out a small laugh, man, it's not the "dream world", but it ain't bad.

A rock sea wall ran both ways in front of her going back towards the little block house, part of which was now distantly visible, and along the bank of what must be the rest of his backyard. About half way across there was a compact dock with a table built on one side, obviously used for cleaning your catch. She tore her eyes off the scenery and glanced around the small yard area. Everything was neat and trimmed. With a sudden sense of guilt, she realized she was making herself at home without permission. She turned to look back where she'd left the car...and froze.

Directly between the vehicle and her position, stood a dog; a big, scary looking one. Her blood turned to ice water. It was a brindle bulldog with a white chest blaze and white socks. Muscles bulged prominently over the entire body and the head was huge, with a grizzly bear shape to it. It ended in a scarred looking muzzle also blazed with white. But it was the eyes that instantly set her heart racing. More like something you'd see on a lion than a dog. And they had her pinned in their sights like the scope of some big game rifle.

The animal hadn't moved, hadn't barked and didn't even blink. Terror spawned adrenaline was coursing through her body and she mentally gauged the distance to the sea wall. It was perhaps her only means of escape; maybe even survival. Those scars could only mean one thing; this was a fighting Pit. Everyone in Jacksonville knew of them. There was a little town outside Fernandina that got rousted regularly for holding the fights. She'd even seen a few pictures in the newspapers...and this looked like the real deal.

Neither party flinched. Jenny couldn't even draw enough breath to pray. Now it fleeted through her mind attached to the opening "Oh dear God". She tried to draw in another gasp to help her pounding heart. He just stood there, like some terrifying statue, not twelve feet away. She tried her voice and failed. She swallowed, concentrated and then squeaked,

"Good boy."

What a lame attempt at saving one's life. It had no apparent effect either. She cleared her throat as quietly as possible.

"Hey boy, I'm sorry. I shouldn't come on your place without permission."

The head gave a slight tilt and one eyebrow went up. Another time it would have been hilarious. It looked like a canine imitation of Mr. Spock. Then the large head rolled upright and the jaw muscles relaxed releasing a big pink tongue. The frightening, predatory expression was transformed into what could only be called a grin. She took hope.

"Oh God, I hope you're friendly," and she shakily reached out her hand.

The animal released from his stance and strode purposefully over to within two feet of her unprotected legs. He was looking directly into her eyes the whole time. There would be no escape if this went wrong. She reached out a little further and was rewarded with a short sniff and a few wags of the thick stub of a tail. Gathering her courage, she eased her hand up to pat the big, bear looking head. He accepted this graciously, and eased over, almost against her leg, while shifting his gaze out over the bay.

Jenny drew her first complete breath. "Oh, thank you God," she breathed.

At the sound of her voice he looked back up and wagged the stub a few more times. This time Jenny gave him a serious petting and scratched a little behind the floppy ears. He really was a magnificent looking animal.

"I would never be afraid with you on watch," she grinned. Then she looked around again and said, "I guess Amos isn't either".

At the sound of "Amos" his head snapped back in her direction.

"Yeah...Amos, I need to see him too."

The happy grin became more pronounced as if he understood perfectly.

Jenny laughed out loud, "You are something else, I wish I knew your name."

She placed her hands on either side of his head and looked into the big, gold eyes, "I'm Jenny and we are going to be friends."

He flopped down on those muscled haunches apparently content to have as much conversation as she felt necessary. Her breathing was finally returning to near normal. She gave a sigh of relief and shifted her gaze back to the marshes, while she continued to softly run her fingertips behind the big guy's ears.

"What a day. Heck, what a week. I don't know where this is all going, but I wouldn't miss it for anything."

That enthusiasm would be short lived.

CHAPTER 13

T HE EXHAUSTS ON AMOS' TRUCK were singing one of his favorite songs; the warbling, deep throated roar of a big Chevy engine "doing its thing". It went totally unnoticed. His thoughts were consumed by an urgency that seemed to emanate from his very center. He had clocked out without question and was thundering down Highway 19 at a pace moderately above the posted limits. Never one to needlessly antagonize local law enforcement, Amos was using a level of restraint that would evaporate as soon as he made the turn onto 494. And that point was now clearly in view.

Whisking past the local airstrip, he began braking then down shifted the Muncie transmission into third, then into second. He took the turn off at twice his accustomed rate. Upon application of power, the 496 cubic inch, Amos-built, "stroker" over powered the tires. He absently brought the power slide around to the desired angle and short shifted up to third. The hot rod pick-up slammed into alignment with the center line and shot forward snarling its defiant tone like a charging dinosaur. The view of oncoming roadway was clear and he whispered a thank you; nothing in sight.

Both driver and vehicle were now in their element. Without conscious thought, Amos was laying out the twisting ribbon of black top before him, calculating the lines and apex points of a road he knew he could drive in his sleep. Problem was, he would never have attempted this under normal circumstances. Any error and he would end his run in a canal or wrapped around some palm tree. And there were blind spots that would require a much slower approach and exit. Still, in a few miles he'd be able to see across the marshes in the direction of his place. A sick feeling in the pit of his stomach prepared him for the possibility of smoke.

It was the only thing he could think of that would cause such unprecedented activity in his spirit, literally driving him to return home. Someone was ransacking or burning his house. Those enemies, Arak had warned of, must want to silence his writing and Internet activity as well. That would be an effective way to accomplish such a goal quickly.

Another pickup appeared on the straight stretch before him. It looked like Gilberts old step-side Ford. Amos' closure rate from behind was fast, but Gil would beat him to the corner and then be blocking him through the two blind turns that crossed one of the forested islands. Instantly he down shifted to third and fire-walled the throttle.

The secondaries on the 850 Holley filled the cab with the groan of their massive inhalation. At the same time the sound through the Hooker exhaust system exploded in an imitation of afterburners engaging on a jet fighter. The Ford came at him like a filmstrip put in fast forward. As he shot past, Amos was slamming fourth and their passing sounded, and felt like, a sonic shock wave. Seconds later he was downshifting into the turn. The thought of Gil's face flashed through his mind, but he'd have to laugh later; and explain.

Hard on the brakes now, as there was danger from on-coming traffic. Then, as the way opened up, another angular slide into the next straight section. At last, the view across the open spaces towards home. No smoke?? He'd felt that had to be it. Was this all some wild goose chase brought on by bad nerves related to Arak and the "warning"? If so, he was making a dangerous fool of himself and breaking some personal conduct rules. Gil wouldn't be the only one to observe this mad dash, and most of them expected better of "Preacher".

But the sensation of impending danger would not be denied. If anything, it was worse...what the devil was going on. Amos felt like someone else was inside him giving the orders. Hard on the throttle and away down the homestretch. The confused pilot and his thunderous steed were back in unison and covering the ground like a high octane banshee.

SUCCESS... The snake could see light. The formidable strength in her seven foot frame, combined with the weak-ening damage done by the handlers, had finally overpowered Felim's packaged imprisonment. It was only a matter of time now before the cardboard outer shell was breached. She wormed her snout against the small speck of daylight in front of her and even flicked her long, forked tongue through the opening "tasting" for the enemy's presence. Currently, things were quiet, with none of the tell-tale vibrations or scent in the vicinity. Soon...Soon she would bring the fight back to the one who had tormented her for so long.

JENNY GAVE the dog's big head a last pat and stood up, "Well boy, I guess I'll have to say good bye till tomorrow. I hope your Amos is as much of a gentleman as you are."

Bubba listened attentively to this little speech. Not only did he find this girl instantly likeable, she aroused his protective qualities as if they'd been acquainted for years. He hadn't forgotten the snake parked on his doorstep. In fact, it was time to take up the vigil again. It would be a long evening waiting for Amos, but he was determined to stay close enough to keep an eye on that strange smelling harbinger of death.

She paused for a long, last look out over the marshes, which were starting to take on a golden late afternoon glow, and drew in a deep breath of the clean, salt charged air. Finally she began re-tracing her steps accompanied by her latest "new friend". Passing the corner of the mobile, she was glancing appreciatively at her dad's SX, when a motion caught the corner of her eye. She turned to look and froze. For a second her mind refused to accept what her eyes were telling her. There was a snake crawling out of a large cardboard container which was lying at the base of a set of concrete steps. Somewhere in her subconscious, the familiarity of the steps and glass doors registered but there was no time to give it a second thought.

As it continued to emerge she realized it was huge and nearly as big around as her forearm. Her brain raced trying to identify the type, but drew a blank. It had almost the grey-brown of a Coachwhip but was more heavy bodied and had a strange, almost rectangular head. Then it spied her. The free section of body suddenly stood up waist high to Jenny and the mouth opened in a threatening display while releasing a loud guttural hiss. The inside was an inky black instead of white adding to the already menacing image it presented. She sensed the dog moving, but was transfixed by the terrible, mind numbing spectacle before her. Suddenly he appeared in the forefront between her and the reptile. She snapped out of it and reached down to restrain him. Her mind was screaming this thing was venomous. But he just placed himself between them and made no move to attack.

The snake stopped and re-focused on this activity as well. The two locked eyes momentarily neither making a sound or movement. Bubba was sure now about the danger from this one. The snake too, was trying to categorize this strange looking mammal. Then it resumed extricating the remainder of its length from the ruptured packaging and Bubba released a low growl; it was free.

Time seemed to suspend for Jenny. She was beset with flashes of thought ranging from run to attack. She did not want the dog to charge in and get bit, but he was not giving any appearance of doing so. More like he was establishing a boundary in front of her and warning the snake to respect it. She let her eyes roam the area for weapons. There was nothing she could see and she didn't want to turn her head or even flinch and attract the vipers' attention back to her.

There was also an approaching roar which she realized had been in the background for some time now. But it was reaching a crescendo somewhere near their vicinity. The dog's ears were standing up as if he was listening to it as well. With her background around her dad, it was easy to classify the sound as a "healthy" engine at some pretty serious RPM's. It was beginning to sound as if they were perched on the center of a drag strip instead of the bank of some Florida creek. Even the reptile seemed to pick up the vibration and turned its head momentarily in that direction. The roar had reached near deafening proportions. Then there was a sudden cessation of the thunder and the clear sound of tires locked and sliding on the lime rock drive behind the shrubbery.

At that point the scene, which had seemed to be in suspended animation for those few seconds...exploded. The snake came towards the dog at an incredible speed for such a large animal and struck at its face. The wily canine sidestepped at the last possible instant and lunged at the back of the head. His return strike missed as well, but you could hear the shock of those jaws coming together. She reared, with her head still almost three feet above the ground, and whirled on the dog hissing furiously. Only to have him nimbly dance back out of range. This macabre little waltz left the angry serpent far too close to Jenny. As she took her first step backwards, the malignant glare of the furious Mamba came to rest square on her. It struck.

Jenny was already stumbling backwards in high gear. The strike came up short. At the same moment Bubba landed on the tail section trying to get a grip on the twisting, angry reptile. The Mamba again pivoted to engage this second enemy and he was forced to dance clear once more.

Then, without a moment's hesitation, it turned again on Jenny.

This only made sense in her limited reptilian thinking. The insults and harms visited upon her had been exclusively at the hands of a humanoid. In her present enraged and confused state, there was not the slightest chance of her re-thinking the attack. It was kill or be killed from here on out. No one was returning her to any type of captivity or torment. And besides, any programming for flight or escape had been brutally conditioned out of her for Felim's purposes. Jennifer Alexander was mere seconds from receiving the terrible ending which had been concocted for Amos.

If the next few seconds were slowed down and examined, a fantastic ballet of events would be on display. But they happened with the same over-clocked speed which was now consuming every member of the frightful little drama.

Jenny continued to pedal backwards faster than humanly possible, thanks to her own adrenaline charge. The snake, in her state of fury, accelerated to close the small gap and deliver the coup-de-grace'. Bubba regrouped and prepared to go ahead and sacrifice himself by latching on to whatever piece of the hellious serpent he reached first. It would then be forced to abandon the girl and clamp it's fangs down into him. He really was that grand and fine thinking an animal...But, again, in slower motion, it would play out like this.

There was a stentorian roar behind Jenny that sounded like the words, "Bubba OFF!" At almost that same instant her back collided with the unmistakable form of a fellow human and the snake launched its second strike in her direction. Only to find itself blocked and entangled in what appeared to be a gardening rake which was thrust suddenly in front of her from her right. In one fluid motion she was forcefully tossed aside and landed splayed in one of the stunted evergreens on the east side of the drive. Even as she was semi-flying backwards, she watched the scene before her undergo a dramatic change.

There was now a young man in combat stance, holding a rake and taking her place before the enraged reptile. With that speed, which only thought can produce, her mind apprised her this must be Amos Mikals, that he was handsome and then, in the same millisecond, that he was about to die. The rake in his hands did not seem adequate to fend off the large, insanely attacking snake for long. The dog was dancing back and forth behind it, in what appeared to be a waiting mode. He was shadowing each move or twitch with an adjustment of his own jockeying to stay in the snake's blind zone. It was hardly necessary at this point.

Felim and his associates, both seen and unseen, would be gratified to see the Mamba had fully engaged their original target. The confrontation with a stick-like device combined with physical contact, had completed his image into that of her recent antagonist. All the hatred and ferocity, stored formerly for her terrorist master, would be unleashed on this hapless American after all.

She withdrew from the tines of the rake and circled to the left. Amos rotated smoothly keeping the tool between them. Suddenly the head dropped to the ground and she shot under the defensive perimeter at an unbelievable rate. Having no reason to be intimately familiar with a Black

Mamba, none of the parties knew they are considered one of the fastest snakes on Earth. She had closed the gap.

She reared instantly up to deliver the strike as Amos was attempting to rotate the rake back into a defensive position. Jenny let out a small scream as she realized it would be too late. There was an explosion of sound, more like a roar than a growl, and the snake was jerked backwards right at the instant she struck. The downward momentum impacted the head on top of Amos' boot where she sank her fangs and held on for a moment. Then she was again jerked in reverse losing the grip and sliding away from her intended victim. Bubba had her by the tail. She reacted instantly and turned her rage again on the meddling mammal. In an instant she had poised herself to once and for all do away with Bubba.

Amos' reaction was not much slower. As the gaping mouth and extended fangs descended towards his dog's unprotected face, she was again brought up short by the sudden appearance of the rake between her and her target. The "Off" command was repeated and Bubba used the interruption to cheat death one more time. The pain from his fang punctures registered in her cold blooded consciousness and she was forced to pause momentarily, undecided which attacker should be dealt with first. It was all the break Amos needed.

He brought the rake suddenly down gathering her upper neck area under the flat surface supporting the tines. The would-be assassin found herself forcibly pinned to the ground with only six inches of her neck free. She writhed and snapped with all her might, but this battle had once again begun to drain her reptilian energy level. Amos watched for an opening and brought his boot down firmly on the remaining six inches pressing the large coffin shaped head to the ground. Kneeling, he grabbed the snake directly behind the jaws and, at the same instant, placed the other foot firmly on the struggling body.

"Man", he thought through the haze of shock and adrenaline, "big snake."

His mind further registered, however, that it did not possess the power of a similar sized Diamondback, a welcome observation. He captured the undulating body with his free hand and then folded part of it under his arm for containment.

The "Serpent from Hell" was once more, a prisoner. Amos stood holding the captive monster and tried to slow his heart and breathing. Sweat had started to impair his vision, but there was not much help for it. He raised the hand controlling the fanged end and tried rubbing his eyes against the back of his forearm. Then he looked down at Bubba who had been on station, per usual, during the final act.

"Boy, I think you just saved my life."

Bubba gave him his happy-dog grin. Then he turned to look at Jenny who was still lying caught in the evergreen branches with her mouth hanging open. Amos now hazily recalled his original mission to save his home and focused a narrow gaze on her as well, "You...what are you doing here?"

Then he rotated carefully scanning the area for accomplices. An unspoken glance passed between him and Bubba. It was reassurance from his faithful canine that there were no other dangers at present...an opinion Amos had learned to regard as "gospel".

Jenny hadn't been able to utter a sound. Amos strode over to her and looked down at the hapless form, lying amongst the braches, seemingly frozen with shock. She couldn't tear her eyes off the snake which was, for the moment, surprisingly calm in the grasp of this muscular stranger.

"Who are you with," he demanded.

A squeak issued forth, and then she cleared her throat, "No one...just me. I uh, I'm sorry...I was petting your dog and...and...uh," she seemed to run out of gas. Then she said weakly, "You're getting blood on your shirt."

Amos looked down. Sure enough, the punctures near the tail, where Bubba had attempted his self sacrifice, were leaking a few drops on his clothing. Without warning the hilarity, and femaleness, of such an observation, especially in light of the last few minutes, overcame him. He burst into laughter and, after a few seconds shock at his reaction, Jenny got it too. She giggled at first and then joined in the comedy full song. Bubba eyed them both with concern, not considering any of the afternoon's activities to be all that mirthful.

After some seconds, Amos caught himself, "Look, I need your help to bag this thing."

Jenny stifled a last set of giggles and looked questioningly at him, "Bag it?"

"Yeah, by the way, is that your car in my drive?"

"Uh, yeah, sorry."

"No matter, but in back of you is my truck. Look behind the driver's seat and get the big cloth bag; might as well get the stick too. Looks like a golf club."

Jenny was carefully freeing herself from the evergreen. Her hair was caught and she was covered in little brown needles. With that same female ability to blend fashion with near disaster, she thought how awful she must look. Amos, as if seeing her for the first time, was thinking just the opposite.

"OW...Ow...Those little needles hurt."

"Umm, yeah, sorry about that."

Jenny stood brushing at herself and looked up at him, "You're kidding, right?"

She looked over at Bubba and then at the Mamba who was once again showing signs of agitation.

"He might have just saved your life, but if that thing's poisonous, you just saved mine."

Amos too looked down at the large squarish head he held imprisoned, "Point taken; let's get my stuff. I have a suspicion what this is, but I've only seen them on TV and in books."

All four participants were now heading for said truck. A Kodak moment that would most likely never be repeated in this neck of the woods...Maybe anywhere else for that matter.

Amos directed Jenny's retrieval of his snake stick and capture bag, then walked her through holding it open while he loaded the body. With the major portion encapsulated, he took over and, holding the corner of the bag in one hand, placed the business end in the bag's opening, still firmly in his grasp. Kneeling so that the bag was laid out on the ground with the snake inside, Amos placed his snake stick, which had, in fact, originally been a golf club, length wise across the neck opening. He snatched his hand free, while pressing the stick down, effectively trapping Miss Mamba inside. Placing one booted foot on the stick to maintain the pressure, he doubled the neck over and proceeded to use the tie strings to lash it securely closed. He stood up holding the once more reluctant captive, albeit under more humane circumstances, at arms length. Then the three of them shared a look that conveyed a feeling of relief comparable to soldiers after a fire fight.

Jenny had wisely decided to hold her council unless Amos asked anything directly. During the somewhat decompressing activities of bagging the snake, he seemed to have accepted her presence as some kind of mischance comprised of just being in the wrong place at the wrong time. What she couldn't know, was he was listening carefully for the small, still, authoritative voice of the Holy Spirit. He absently picked up his garden rake and placed it back in the truck bed, but his mind was elsewhere.

Only now was the wild flight from work crystallizing as the obvious mission from on-high it must be. But why; people met unexpected deaths all the time without any directed salvation coming to their rescue. He hadn't yet begun to categorize the disturbing nuances involved in having a deadly African snake dropped on your door step. For he was certain this was a Mamba. Nothing else had that black inner lining in the mouth. Under different circumstances, he'd have been honored to be offered one.

He was still glad for one thing. If the monster in the bag was built to the same specs as a Diamondback, it would have been twice as hard to contain. That notwithstanding, your chances of surviving rattler bites were a hundred times better than with a Mamba. So who had placed it on his property?

He turned to Jenny, "You say you saw this thing come out of a box?"

They were standing beside the 1972 Chevy step-side, which was still ticking and clacking as the running gear temperatures subsided after Amos' mad charge across the marshes. The shrubs and foliage, along with a certain Nissan, blocked the view of ground zero where the whole crazy drama had begun.

"Yes, it was almost out when I came around the corner planning to leave."

"Which brings me back to the question of what you're doing here...and who are you?"

Jenny looked down at her feet for a few seconds, then met his eyes "Amos Mikals, you are not what I was expecting."

Amos looked at her blankly for a second then his eyes narrowed once more, "How do you know my name?"

Jenny felt that little stir now in her own consciousness. This thing had certainly not turned out as planned, but the reasoning had not changed. It was time to "test the spiritual waters" and see what reaction she got. She sighed internally and thought; OK...here we go,

"Arak told me."

For a few seconds the blank look returned, followed by a slow burn of comprehension. Then he carefully set the Mamba down and settled into a seated position on the stepside portion of his pick-up. His face had the far away look of someone remembering a dream.

He slowly looked up at Jenny in that dazed condition, "You're the one he...oh man...I never expected there'd be anyone who'd believe me."

CHAPTER 14

"**Y**OU FAILED...AGAIN?"

Lucifer's quiet, deadly tone caused Buferan to wince even more than his usual roarings did.

"Lord, I cannot offer excuse or explanation."

It was time to test that camaraderie His Excellency had initiated during the last report. Any lame mutterings this time might be met with serious punishment. The most malignant glare in the known universe continued to rest on the hapless under-prince.

"You had best offer some details."

The thing he least wanted to do, "Ah, Your Worship, I must regretfully report something that has not occurred before."

He paused but the glare was unchanged; only a stony silence accompanied it.

"One of the players that helped spoil the Rome situation, has surfaced in Mikals' principality."

If anything the glare intensified and the giant, cold, slitted eyes seemed to bulge slightly.

"What are you saying Buferan...spit it out."

"Your Lordship, the girl from St. Peters has appeared...uh, actually, on his home ground."

Lucifer digested this, "That would seem most unlikely, would it not?"

"My thoughts also sir, but I wish only to report the facts...as instructed."

"The Deranian is clearly not here...the 'Presence' rarely orchestrates such matters directly...yet it must have been he."

It was time for Buferan to figuratively "step out on the limb". "If I may Your Highness, there is one other possibility."

"Such as?"

"I suspect the Deranian gave this girl information concerning Mikals while in Rome."

"Not possible; it would never be permitted. He can only relay message details to the recipient. Even a 'real' Third Rank cannot venture outside those guidelines...much less one of these half-breed imitations."

Well here goes, thought Buferan, if Lucifer took this the wrong way it was going to be quite painful. "Forgive me Sire, but, as you pointed out, many things we ourselves have put in play would not normally go unchallenged. Is it possible this is being reflected in the activity of the 'others' as well?"

His boss lost some of the glare and he dared to hope. Then, "Buferan, are you saying He would allow infractions amongst his own because we are committing some?"

The lack of venom in the tone encouraged him, "Your Lordship, I could not presume to instruct you, but please consider it might be possible...under the present conditions."

Now there was a real silence and Buferan could see this thought caused even the Great One concern. At last he looked at his subordinate and when he spoke the tone seemed more like their last discussion,

"One of the safeguards in contesting for these humans has always been His unchanging predictability. I do not care to think where this is leading if he rescinds those controls. But you may be correct; He is perhaps going to treat this like one of those brush wars Atreus has been so successful with."

Buferan thought a moment, "So, He will respond to our 'transgressions' by permitting similar ones among those assigned to thwart us?"

"It would seem possible," said Lucifer thoughtfully, "this is actually not the first example I had noted."

"Then...does that not return some of the predictability to the matter?"

"It does...we have some measure of control, it would seem, over how far to push certain parameters. And that may prove to finally be this Deranian's undoing."

The reptilious Buferan nearly salivated at the thought, "May I be so bold as to ask how?"

"Listen, what is the common denominator running through your encounters with not only Arak, but with Kurtanus as well? What ultimately resulted in his capture?"

He studied on this for a moment; His Highness had seemed to have an uncanny ability to "predict" Kurtanus movements. He had been close with Arak last time as well. Was it possible he had inside information? Then the light went on...and the glowing ruby eyes of the sub-prince of darkness actually increased in wattage as a slow, fanged smile appeared on the unearthly countenance, "Sire, that's diabolical."

"You're welcome, I'm sure," smirked Lucifer.

"WHAT?" Arak asked wide eyed.

He had only recently "materialized" from the patrol that had offered the chance to visit Deran. His intention had been to unwind a short while before seeking out Raphael, but a First Rank had quickly come calling to his "mansion". However, in this case, it was more a glorified apartment. He had sectioned off a small work/retreat area for himself and let several of the Deranian First Ranks in training have the run of the remainder. It was not uncommon for a Deranian high rank to do this for a couple of reasons.

One, they were on frequent or extended patrol far more often than any other branch of Jehovah's service. Two, when present, they were expected to take up training duties with their under brethren. These First Ranks were Arak's wards and pupils as much as they were those of the instructors from the other levels. The common mortal bond also linked them somewhat differently than most and such experience often helped to get vital points across. Had he been Father himself, he could not love them more. Their enthusiasm and innocence brought him back to earlier times and rekindled the memories of his reunion with Donian. Mere words would not explain those emotions.

Now he was once again in conversation with Raphael and learning of the misadventures on Earth in his absence.

"Yes, they played this serpent gambit very cleverly. Lucifer did a good job distracting the First Ranks with a feint involving a co-worker."

"And Jenny has actually contacted Amos," he asked incredulously, looking up at his friend and mentor.

Raphael smiled, "You could say that. But for Amos sense of obedience, she might be telling you this story herself."

"Are both safe?"

"For the time being. Buferan thinks we are in the dark regarding details of another prong of his current plan, but Father has outlined the array of paths it will most likely take. We must hope that young Amos holds fast to what he has experienced thus far. Particularly where it involves the Spirit's 'leading'. That is all that saved the situation this time."

"Am I permitted to know these other details?"

"Perhaps soon. As you'd hoped, He has left the door open for your involvement if this madness on Lucifer's part continues."

Arak thought for a moment, "Sir, are the efforts against Amos affecting his message?"

"They have caused him some distress, but your visit has more than made up for it. He continues to readily accept the 'prompt' when in the presence of those deemed approachable. One of Buferan's own henchmen has weakened to a degree under the influence of his sense of fair play. Even I am surprised."

"There is nothing I am aware of that offers more unpredictability than these Earthers."

Raphael eyed him mildly, "Little brother, you have no idea. Come let us seek some refreshment and I shall tell you the tale."

TO SAY THAT JIM was incredulous didn't do it justice. To say that a cold hand clutched his heart at the thought of the danger his daughter had faced, would also not fully describe his feelings. But old habits die hard and the underlying theme in his mind was to somehow acquire a "personal" meeting with the perpetrators.

"A Mamba...a Mamba...What in God's own name is a Mamba doing loose in Florida?"

"Dad, calm down...I'm OK...I know what you're thinking...There's no one to go after...at least not yet. None of the markings on the box make much sense. It's like someone shipped it to and fro around the world. But Amos thinks the snake would not have been in such fresh condition if that was true. It also has some high-tech insulation, like you'd find at NASA, which might be traceable. But it was definitely delivered UPS and the delivery guy is a friend of his. He's trying to find him, but it'll probably be tomorrow at the soonest."

The steely glint in Jim's ordinarily friendly eyes was still in place, "What about the law?"

Jenny sighed, "On that, you and Amos think a lot alike. He says it would be worthless...no, he said futile."

She paused in thought for several long seconds, then began solemnly,

"Dad, you should have seen his face when I said Arak's name. I watched him go through the shock, and then you could almost see his thoughts racing around calculating the possibilities all this is piling up. But the first thing he asked was who else had knowledge. Then when I told him you, he said it had to go no further. Not even the authorities. He sounds like you in person too, Dad; he says this fight isn't actually against flesh and blood."

Jim's countenance had relaxed to a more thoughtful pose. He digested Jenny's statement then said, "I guess I always picked up on that fact when I read his stuff. He's no dummy to start with and I really believe God has given him wisdom beyond his years."

"Yeah, well I can't argue that. And I don't want to sound like a starry eyed little teenager, but Dad...this guy went toe to toe against that snake for someone he didn't even know. In fact, he was coming to save his house and writings and stuff. When he saw the SX, he thought it must be the bad guys. That rake in his truck bed was the only weapon he could think of. He was going into combat, with people Arak told him are out to silence him, with a garden rake."

Jim had to smile, "I guess we better add courage to wisdom." Then a bigger grin creased his face, "So, this knight came to the damsel's defense against the fierce serpent with only a garden rake? How often you hear a story like that anymore?" Then he grew serious, "I owe him more than I can repay for saving your life little girl."

Jenny felt a little misty eyed too, "I've only known him a few hours and I can guarantee he wouldn't accept a thing. If you want to thank him, just do it once. I think it really embarrasses him to be considered a hero."

"Isn't he one though?"

"From now till eternity," she stated quietly. "You know he had us kneel at the picnic table and thank God for saving us both. It was one of the most wonderful prayers I'll ever hear. I think even the dog was chiming in. He just sits and concentrates like he understands the whole thing. And if you want to get down to 'brass tacks', I think he saved us both as well."

Again her father looked thoughtful, "I'm just thinking...back when you planned the Rome thing, I knew it was something beneficial. An experience you'd learn from and carry the rest of your life. I even felt that God had okayed it. Now look where it's taken you...us...an angel of all things. People would give a lot to see one. I would...much less speak with one. But all this...Jen, it looks like we're deep into one of the Lord's own battles. I mean, who on Earth would really believe such a thing anymore."

He paused, "The truth is, I feel honored. And that's not easy to say when I think of you in harms way. But I better understand what you and Arak meant. I'd be willing to give it all on this one too. And it looks like that option is going to stay on the table. So just in case, I want you to remember one thing...I love you with all my heart."

They came together in an unspoken embrace; some tears flowed freely but with no sadness. After a few minutes they held each other at arms length sniffling a little.

"Wow," said Jenny.

"Yeah, wow..."

They both grinned and Jim said. "So when do I meet Sir Lancelot?"

"First thing tomorrow, he's offered to fix breakfast at his place."

"On top of it all he can cook?"

"Tell you the truth Dad, I get the feeling we've just scratched the surface on this guy. I mean, if nothing else, he's really the catalyst behind all this. He's the one Arak was coming to see...and the one who Satan wants to permanently silence. And he fits the bill so well. He's an unassuming guy, but he's got something that kind of hangs around him. At first I thought I was just reacting to being saved, but as we talked, I felt it. His spirit has a different sense to it. An authority, like he knows so much more than he's telling...or something. It sounds corny, but man, he's 'heavy'."

Jim laughed, "I was just thinking...a real spiritual heavyweight."

Jenny giggled herself. Then, "No matter what, Dad, two things; I'm not sorry were in this and you're my biggest hero; always will be."

"Thank you o' daughter, you're mine too. But even heroes gotta eat. Want to sample the grouper in the restaurant?"

"Thought you'd never ask."

"How about another thank you prayer first?"

Jenny nodded, "Absolutely."

Several minutes were spent in heartfelt gratitude to God. Then, with uplifted spirits and countenances, they left the room and sashayed arm in arm towards the brightly lit fish house.

Other eyes taking in this scenario were not as light hearted or optimistic...they weren't even human.

ARAK RESEMBLED SOME magnificent statue cast in a moment of introspection. The sheer intensity of events unfolding on the Earth was once more monopolizing his thoughts. His soul ached to join the fray, but he was honest enough to admit he didn't know exactly what he could do. Already things were so far outside the boundaries and protocols of the eons that it seemed almost like Heaven itself was holding its breath waiting on some gathering storm. All except Father, who would apparently not be engaged on the subject no matter what your rank or assignment. Even Jesus had little to say, beyond what was currently shared between the involved entities, except to remind them, "Have faith."

Arak well knew it was not his faith that was wavering, it was his patience. In mortal life he'd been a man of action. Father had customized this "perfect" existence to coincide with that fact. It was the same with almost all the members of the various corps with whom he shared counsel. Not only Kurtanus, may he be well wherever he was, and Zantar, also of Deran, but Peter, David and many of Earth's "graduates", shared a similar warrior mentality. Now these brothers in arms could only look at each other and shrug. Father would do what Father would do. Chafing would only make the wait harder. Trouble was, he feared little brother Amos was running out of time.

At the moment he stood poised in a typically gorgeous setting near his home that could be loosely compared to a park on Earth. He was absently watching two of the Deran First Ranks attempt to master an elementary stage of transfer. Another time he would have had a good laugh at some of their antics. Having succeeded in the ability to transpose from one location to another, they were enthusiastically attempting to surprise each other by doing so suddenly. Only to reappear behind or even suspended over the head of their fellow student. A cat and mouse game you could observe nowhere else in the Cosmos.

How proud they made him, yet now, how concerned. He could remember when he and Kurtanus had played similar pranks on one another. All the while content in the knowledge that eternity was securely supported around them by the mighty hand of God himself. But now the whereabouts and condition of that brother Deranian were shrouded in some deep mystery. Such a possibility would not have occurred to either of them during that early rambunctious period. But, at that point, the thought of acting as a courier in the Earth battle had never crossed their minds either.

Now he understood that these lessons, by necessity, were still colored with some of the stigma and stain of the spiritual danger that permeated Lucifer's place of confinement. The little blue marble, spinning brightly on the shooting board of space and time, had long ago lost its innocence. Only Father knew or suspected where these new trails would ultimately lead. He was sure the outcome would follow the dictates of Earth prophecy and that all should be well, but for now, the war raged on. And Arak was in it, as Lonius would say, up to his eyeballs. He wondered what Amos and Jenny were doing...and how their spirits were holding up under the constant oppression by the godless "God" of their world.

CHAPTER 15

NEXT MORNING, Jim got his first look at the madly winding road leading to Ozello. Jenny smiled mischievously when she saw his eyes widen. As they finished the first series of short blind turns and saw the twisting ribbon of asphalt stretching away over the first set of marshes, all he said was,

"Cool."

"Cool?...Cool?...Dad no one's said 'cool' in about a hundred years."

"Well how would you describe it?"

Jenny glanced at the road and back at Jim, then laughed, "OK, it's pretty cool."

"I rest my case," he said and notched the transmission down a gear which caused the rpm's and turbo whine to jump.

"Dad, you're not gonna..."

"Nah, don't know the road. But hang on."

Jenny was treated to an upgraded version of the tactic she had employed herself. Jim set the little speedster at a moderate velocity and tried to maintain it with a minimum of brake or throttle adjustment. In her dad's experienced hands, the re-engineered SX took the road like a slightly tamed version of a one dimensional roller coaster. She felt the G-forces sway her from side to side against the belts and settled back to enjoy the ride.

Actually, she acknowledged...she was enjoying being alive. Funny the clarity of thinking that could result from a "near death experience". The treasure granted each person, which was called "life", often went unnoticed or appreciated; sometimes for long periods. She'd been a victim of that mindset herself. Now she wondered why. Even though it was never perfect, she sensed God meant for every day to mean something to your soul. Maybe more like a variety of something's. Why do we lapse from that intent so easily she wondered? Worries...Satan?

Meanwhile, they had reached the first of the forested islands and Jim resumed a more pedestrian driving style. He too was stealing more glances at his surroundings. As they cleared these, the full majesty of the salt water plains opened up before them. Cast in the golden light of early morning, the beauty of Creation was truly stunning.

"Wow," said her dad.

"Yeah pops, I lost count of my 'wows' on the way out yesterday. Wait till you see Amos' back yard."

"This reminds me of Lochloosa prairie, only bigger."

Jenny thought a moment, "The one north of Ocala?"

"Yeah, they're fresh water though. This is a whole nuther' animal. Can you imagine the life cycles playing out in these estuaries."

"Well, I got the impression there's some pretty serious life cycles playing out in the Gulf off here too. Amos says it's a shark nursery part of the year and you can see schools of the babies sometimes; he calls them pups. And he's had some run-ins with mamas longer than his boat."

"How big's his boat?"

"Twelve foot."

Jim turned and looked straight at her, "That's a lot of mama."

They resumed their enjoyment of the green and gold panorama and Jim forgot all about playing sports car. They were barely at the posted limit when the marina road appeared.

"How far does this go?" he asked as they took the left turn off the main drag.

"Uh, don't know really. There's that little store about a half mile further; that's as far as I got."

Jenny guided them in to the same spot she had stopped on her first visit. It had been less than twenty four hours, yet somehow seemed a lifetime ago. So much had transpired, she felt her senses were becoming a little numb. They got out and stood staring at the same view that had first greeted her. In the morning light it was, if anything, better.

Jim gazed a minute at the salt water vista, then turned to Jenny. His question froze in his throat. His daughter was in a semi-crouch staring at a big, husky brute that had to be Bubba. The dog had materialized maybe ten feet from her and looked like some over-size mutant cat getting ready to pounce. The eyes were eerily appropriate for that description. He felt the rest of him momentarily frozen as well.

Then Jenny thrust her arms forward and let out a loud "Boo". The bulldog catapulted out of his crouch and was on her in an instant. Well, not on her; he was more all around her ducking and dancing while his daughter did her level best to grab hold. Then suddenly he allowed himself to be "collared" and the two tumbled to the ground. She crouched nose to nose, with both hands on his big, muscled cheeks, chortling "Gotcha, gotcha, gotcha."

Then, as if suddenly remembering her dad, she looked up to find him staring uncertainly at the two of them. Bubba went still too and focused on Jim. What a picture.

"Oh, sorry about that...Dad, meet Bubba...Bubba...Dad."

She stood as Bubba bounced up and gave himself a good shake to clear the grass clippings. Then he strode over to Jim all the while looking intently into his face.

He reached down and said, "Nice to meet ya' boy."

Bubba reached up to sniff his hand and the stub tail wagged happily. Jim stroked the back of his head and said to Jenny,

"Guess any friend of yours is a friend of his. What was that all about?"

"Part game, part something in his nature; Amos calls it the 'Ambush Game'. No matter who comes on the property, he never barks. You don't know he's there till it's too late."

She looked at Bubba who was enjoying Jim's petting then said loudly, "Just like someone did to me yesterday...and took several years off my life."

With her change in pitch, the animal broke contact with Jim and ambled over to Jenny with a questioning look.

"Amos' big worry is he'll give someone a heart attack. You should hear a couple of the stories about strangers and delivery people."

"I don't wonder," said her father. "That'd spook most anybody. You were right though, even with the battle scars, that's a good looking animal."

"Yeah, well let's take 'Mr. Wonderful' here and go find his master."

They turned the first corner of the brushy perimeter and Jim stopped in his tracks, "That's the pick-up?"

"Yeah, nice paint huh, you should hear it run."

"Well, you said hot rod truck; I was expecting a rat rod. That's a semi-collector job there...this guy's just full of surprises."

"The surprise is he's not out here already." Jenny raised her voice, "Amos?"

A shout reached them from the back yard.

The trio of father, daughter and Bubba trooped around the corner into Amos' backyard. They found him clad only in a pair of cut-off jeans, standing at the dock's little table cleaning a fish. A small V-hull aluminum boat with a fifteen horse Suzuki outboard was nestled against the pilings. Some snorkeling gear, along with a serious looking spear gun, were laid out neatly on the planking. There was a glass casserole tray, half full of water containing some fillets and chunks of ice, sitting next to the cutting board. Said board still held a partly cleaned fish of a variety with black and white stripes. Amos took a garden hose nozzle hanging at his elbow, vigorously sprayed his hands, then reached out to Jim.

"Sorry about the fish smell."

Jim smiled, "Won't be the first time. Glad to meet you Mr. Mikals."

Amos grinned back, "Just Amos, please."

"Amos it is..."

Both Amos and Jim were thinking much the same thing; Jenny's description was pretty good. Here before Jim was a wavy haired, tan, mid-sized guy with enough muscle mass that no one would mistake him for a push over. And Amos was immediately drawn back to Jenny's moniker "Mad Stork" but with a slant of his own. Jim reminded him of a tall, lanky, square jawed cowboy. Complete with the drawl and the gunfighter eyes. A good man to have on *your* side, he thought.

"Amos, did you go out and get these this morning?" asked Jenny.

"Um, yeah, just to the mouth of the creek. There's a big hole there full of mangrove snapper and sheep heads."

Jim cast a knowing eye at the cleaning board, "Thought that's what they were. Those are good sized ones."

Amos nodded appreciatively, "And the guy's around here mostly leave them alone. Say they taste too fishy."

Jenny was eyeing the table with less enthusiasm than the men, "Do they?"

He smiled at her, "The secret is in the tray there. Icy cold salt water for a half hour and you'll think its grouper."

"Uh...are they breakfast?"

"Yep, just trust me."

Jim watched this little interplay with a smile tugging at the corners of his mouth. His daughter let out a sigh, "Amos Mikals, so far there's not much I wouldn't trust you about."

Jim broke in, "Amos...I don't really have the words...but thank you for yesterday."

"Mr. Alexander," he began...

"Just Jim too, OK?"

"Ok...Jim...sir, it happened too fast to think about. I guess Jenny told you most of it."

"All we talked about last night...that and Arak."

Amos looked intently at Jim then turned and gazed out over the southerly wetlands. The others joined him and there was a contemplative silence for several long moments.

"I had just done this same thing; cleaned a couple of fish. Got done, was heading in, and then stopped at the picnic table to watch the sunset." He shook his head, "You know, Bubba knew something was up almost thirty seconds before it happened. I thought he heard a boat...then wham, there's this... electrical crackling, and the next second...the world changed."

Jenny said thoughtfully, "You know dad, that's a good way to describe it. In Rome my world changed in a split second."

"Yeah," said Amos, "he...Arak, said that knowing of something isn't the same as seeing it. Man, you can believe that; the seeing part will scramble your head pretty good."

"But what an honor," said Jim quietly.

Amos turned again to him, "Yes sir, it's definitely that...In my case the honor has a few strings attached."

"You mean as in large poisonous ones?"

"Well, yeah, that was pretty tricky, but to be honest, I'd rather they tried it like that."

"I understand; Jen told me you've been handling them since way back. Do you think the enemy had any knowledge of that?"

Amos paused, "Enemy...the enemy...guess I better start thinking like that, huh? Till now I just considered it the possibility of some poor misguided soul under Satan's spell. I have no idea if they knew about the snakes. The way they packaged that one, it could've easily surprised me. Most anybody probably; wanna' see it?"

Jenny's eyes widened a little, "Amos where did you put it?"

He grinned, "You'll never meet a Mikals who doesn't have a few cages or aquariums hanging around."

"That would be interesting," said Jim, "but on the 'enemy' thing, I guess Jen told you about the demons in Rome?"

"Yeah, I had a time getting my head around Arak; I can't imagine the 'overload' that would cause."

Jenny actually gave a small shiver, "It was a lot easier to face them with Arak right there. It will take all your faith if you go up against them on your own."

Amos smiled, "I don't have to go it alone anymore."

She thought a moment "That's true; the Holy Spirit seems pretty intense about all this. But he relies on us just like Satan...er, Lucifer, Arak kept calling him that, relies on humans too. I mean, somebody flesh and blood set you up with that snake."

He was still smiling a small, knowing smile but saying nothing.

"Oh...You mean...Well yeah, we're here...But we have to get back to Jacksonville tomorrow..." She trailed off as both men were now looking at her with the same amused look.

Once more Jenny's eyes widened a little, "Dad, are we staying?"

Both young people were watching Jim expectantly.

"Tell you what, let's help Amos get breakfast and talk about it; agreed?"

"O...K", said his daughter a little slowly. Then she looked over at Bubba who had been sitting quietly listening to the whole dialogue, "Can Bubba show me the kitchen? And what do you want to have with those, uh, fish?"

"Come on," said Amos, "we'll both show you. What we need is a pot of grits and some home fries."

With that, the little band surged across the lawn to the small screen lanai adjacent to the now famous picnic table. As will always be likely, in Earth's present age, their conversation and actions were followed as closely as possible by "the other sides". However, in this case, both sides had a great deal more knowledge and experience concerning this scenario than would have been considered historically normal. Fitting, since considerably more than "normal" matters now hung in the balance.

LATER THAT SAME MORNING, Eddie was seated with Samir at the "Inn" planning on an early beer and some lunch. However, a small glitch had just affected his appetite.

"Are you crazy," he asked, staring at Samir through narrowed eyes.

"I am sorry...It was a stupid idea."

"Yeah man, I have to agree with you there. You don't screw around with one of these plants. We're talking serious jail time bro."

Sammy sighed, "As I said, it was not my idea. I have some, uh, recently acquainted friends who are benefiting somehow by the current lack of operation at this plant. They mentioned it."

Eddie just stared at him, unaware these friends were totally imaginary.

Sammy leaned in close, "It has some nonsense to do with a stock buy-out, but that part is mostly over my head.

All I know is we were talking about the power plant and I happened to mention I knew one of the head mechanics. They asked me a bunch of questions, which I mostly could not answer. Then out of nowhere they wanted to know if it would benefit anyone if the re-start date was delayed. I remembered our conversation about your men being out of work and admitted it might. That's when they asked if you would be willing to participate in something to perhaps help foster such a delay. That is all there was to it; except for the money."

It was Eddies turn to lean in, "What money?"

"Well, when they were trying to explain the stock thing, they said the delay would be worth a great deal. Being only human, I asked how much?"

"And."

"It boggled me, I tell you. They said someone higher up would pay fifty thousand dollars to see it out of action for another thirty days."

Eddie was momentarily speechless; finally, "Fifty thousand bucks?"

"So the man said. But now, I think maybe they were having a joke at my expense. It is probably a big nothing. I am too gullible by far."

Samir feigned the appropriate chagrin as he covertly watched Eddie's wheels turning. As for Eddie, he was still trying to overcome the dazzle that much money created in his mind.

He finally turned to Sammy, "Do you think it was a hoax?"

He looked surprised, "Uh, I cannot say for sure now that I have heard your input. But I must admit they seemed very serious."

"How'd you run into these guys anyway?"

"The restaurant at the Holiday Inn. I had gone there to see about maybe picking up some extra work but they were not hiring. I decided to have lunch at the counter and these men were seated next to me. It was quite accidental."

"You get their names?"

"Only the first ones; John and Sam."

"Yeah, John and Sam, sounds a little fishy already. They give you a card or anything?"

"No, they wrote a number on a napkin."

Samir fished a wrinkled napkin out of his pocket and handed it to Eddie. Inwardly he smiled at the thought that this was actually a number that might be the catalyst for one of the greatest triumphs of all time against these hated Americans.

Eddie eyed it briefly then looked up at him, "If these guys know so much, did they suggest anything that might be doable to cause this...delay?"

Samir held out his hand and Eddie absently handed him back the number. It would not be wise to let him have even that bit of history...untraceable though it should be.

"Ah, no, and I did not share with them anything we have discussed either."

Eddie looked blank.

"You know, the tube thing you were talking about."

"Oh, yeah, well thanks for that. Don't matter much though, that piece is already screwed up enough to use up a couple of weeks."

"I'm sorry, Edward, but are you actually considering this?"

"Probably not, but fifty grand will make a man think of things differently."

"Yes, I suppose. Many things are possible for someone with that much cash in the economy of today. But, as long as you are playing 'devil's advocate', how would anyone add to the delay of such a place. They did not offer any advice but you know much more than they. How could such a thing even be done?"

Eddie was already lost in thought regarding that exact matter. What was it McMillan was yapping about the other night? Some big test of a major system was coming up. Samir quietly waited. He had his fish nibbling but it was too early to try setting the hook.

"Tell you what Sammy, can you make sure these guys are the real deal and meet me here tomorrow night?"

"Ah…I suppose, but Edward, what are you thinking? I do not wish to get in any trouble either."

"Look dude, you're the contact guy. Anything comes of this, you're already in, get it. But if these guys offered that much there's bound to be plenty more. OK, look here, you get hold of them and say you just have a few questions. One, how do you know they'll pay up? Two, they gotta ante up for your help if the thing flies. Name a price, if they balk, we forget it."

"But, I don't know what we are forgetting. Do you know some way to cause such a delay?"

"I got an idea, but I need to think it over and look at some things."

"I don't know, perhaps I should not have said anything."

Eddie was being overpowered by one of Lucifer's all time favorite ploys; greed. The lust the thought of all that cash generated in his soul was beginning to cloud his already fuzzy moral judgment.

"Sammy, all you're asking for is some kind of...assurance. Don't say anything about actually taking the job, just ask. Pretend you're an undercover guy or something. Ask without incriminating, get it?"

"OK, if you say so, I will try."

"Good, now I got the day off, let's have another round and order some lunch to go with it. And no more talk about this for now, deal?"

Sammy sighed, "Deal," and motioned to the bartender.

Had the old Orange Blossom Inn been in another phase dimensionally, then this conversation would have been recognized as having royalty present. For Buferan himself listened closely as Samir, for all intents, acted as his agent. He already enjoyed the atmosphere these "bars" were permeated with, but listening to these stupid humans plan each others demise certainly added a nice spice to it.

And this was even better. To watch things unfold aimed at snuffing out an irritable bedbug like Mikals, currently had little to equal it as far as pleasing this prince among the demons. Although...the wave of human destruction that little weasel Samir was trying to orchestrate wasn't half bad either.

CHAPTER 16

EARLY AFTERNOON found Amos and company again
seated in his small kitchen...and ready for another
meal. Their day had consisted of an in depth tour of
Ozello by both land and water. This had included a spirited
half hour with Clarice who warned them repeatedly about
the "noo-clee-ur" dangers Amos and Tom were fooling with
in that "plant". Also included was a face to face with Miss
Mamba, who was now housed in a large, wooden, glass
front cage. She had not lost much of her fury over the
indignant handling of the previous day.

But it was the boating that was most captivating. Upon
seeing the marvels, so vividly clear in the crystal shallows
of Amos' beloved hunting grounds, it was no effort to
appreciate his affection for both the marine environment
and the art of taking meals from it. He explained his
conservation technique of taking only what was needed,
rarely more than one fish per hole, and spreading the
hunting "zone" over the seventeen of those he had so far
charted.

"Sometimes I won't see the same hole for a month or
more. By that time there's always newcomers and surprises

down there. It's funny," he continued, "when I stumbled across the first one and saw the size of the grouper, I figured the locals must be all over them. Turned out you can hardly ever get a fish up because they snag the line in the caves. A spear gun is about the only answer, but most of them won't get in the water because of the sharks."

"If that hammerhead was a medium one, I don't blame them," said Jenny flatly.

"That was maybe an eight or nine footer. They come way bigger sometimes. Not usually a problem though, if you aren't shooting. They do get frisky if there's blood in the water. But since I normally don't shoot any hole more than once, I'm always moving on about the time they show up. Been a few interesting moments, but not often."

Jim spoke up, "Amos, are you going to work this afternoon?"

"Yes sir, there's a lot going on and they're counting on me for a jump tonight."

"A jump?" queried Jenny.

"Uh, a 'work event'. You get suited up and do a pre-planned job inside one of the hot zones."

"How dangerous is it?"

Amos paused, "I don't know...one to ten I'd say a five...if it's done by the book. The HP guy's are pretty sharp and they watch you like hawks; it's not that big a deal."

"Hmph," intoned Jenny, "that's not what Clarice said."

Amos laughed, "Clarice is all worried over Tom being in the reactor area. Truth is, he's not even in the ones where you need respirators, let alone a full suit. But you'll never convince her anything about it is safe."

Jim broke in again, "What are you doing tonight on this 'jump'?"

Again Amos paused before answering, "Well, they're a little twitchy about that one. We have a situation where some damage allowed contamination into areas where it was never intended; the turbine deck to be exact. But let's keep that between us, OK. NRC is all over us about it and operations is paranoid someone will play it up for more than it is. Nuclear power has enemies that know nothing about it, but love to sensationalize anything they can get their hands on."

"Guess we can thank Three Mile for that huh?"

"Yeah, 'fraid so. Now, that was a mess. We didn't get even close to the temps they experienced on that one."

"How do you know that", Jenny asked, "Have you been up there too?"

He smiled, "No...No way, I'm pretty much a newbie. But there are still some members of that original crew working here with us. We're a sister plant to that one."

"You mean you had the same problem?"

"Not even close. We did have a major scram, but it was never really out of control. CR-3 is the same design by the same engineers as Three Mile, Babcock Wilcox."

Jenny looked perplexed, "A scram...as in scram, get out of here, run for it?"

Another laugh, "No, scram is when all the rods are dropped back into the core to shut down the reaction. It's an acronym left over from the forties. Supposedly, on early nuke test, the rod was raised and suspended by a rope and they had a guy standing by with an axe to cut it if things went wrong. They called him the Safety Control Rod Axe Man. SCRAM's been with us ever since."

"Now there's a piece of trivia I could win a bet with," remarked her dad, "OK, you two, what say we let Amos get ready for work, then we'll head in and get some barbe-que...my treat."

"Mr...uh Jim sir, you have a deal."

Jenny eyed Amos with an impish grin, "Jim...Sir...Jim sir...You've been saying that all day...Can't bring yourself to just say Jim?"

He looked sheepish, "Nah...not really. It's hard to over-come some habits. My upbringing was always sir and ma'am, and then all the years in the martial world the instructors and high ranks were always sirs too...I think it's something I'm stuck with."

"Aha, I told you dad. Just the way he moved yesterday with that snake, I'd have bet on it. Dad's no stranger to that world either."

"Really...what style sir?"

Jim glanced at Jenny. She raised an eyebrow, "Go on."

"Oh well, Korean stuff, Tae-Kwon-Do and Tang-soo-do...at different times over the years."

"Tell him the good stuff," she said.

"Nah, old guys always want to brag about their hey-days. Makes people tired."

"Hah...OK...In the good old days of the sixties, dad was a 'contact' fighter. Got a closet full of trophies at home."

"Wow, that's cool sir, those were some serious years. Bill Wallace, Chuck Norris."

"You two and cool...I guess I'm going to have to be cool to hang out with you."

Amos looked at Jim and then at Jenny, "Well, that would be really cool."

Jim laughed, Jenny rolled her eyes and Amos just grinned. It was on this light note they began their trip back into town for the promised barbeque.

Later, as they concluded this mini-feast, Jenny glanced around making note they were in a fairly private location.

"This has been a great day Amos, thanks for everything, but aren't we ignoring what started all this? And the unpleasant stuff that may still be ahead?"

Jim fielded the remark, "Jen, I doubt that fact has strayed far from the back of any of our minds."

"Well, shouldn't we have a plan or something?"

Amos spoke up, "This thing really has only one plan possible." He also glanced around, "The 'big guy' said listen to the Spirit as never before. I have to wonder, if not for that remark, would I have made it to the house in time yesterday?"

A silence settled, and then Jim said, "Other than keeping the weather eye open, that's going to be our best and maybe only shot. That and the fact that the demons do their work through humans too. This 'prince' Jenny saw with the other two in Rome, is no doubt a formidable creature. And he may well know everything we're doing even now, but he's limited as to any interference in the matter. Both by our wills and that of any henchmen he's scrounged up."

Amos settled into another silence that lasted till both father and daughter looked inquiringly at him.

"What," asked Jenny?

After another short period of apparent contemplation Amos spoke, "I haven't wanted to discuss this till we got to know each other a little better...And yes, I know God's hand is on this and I can trust you two."

He looked at each of them...the expression on their faces had begun to mirror concern. Obviously something important was afoot. And if there was something more serious to this story than had already been revealed, it must be major. They were tactfully silent.

After a moment Amos continued; his expression grave, "I said to you this morning there were strings attached to my...visit."

They both nodded.

"I wasn't really thinking about the snake. That was bad, but like I said, I'd prefer that was the method they took towards silencing me. With Arak, that one never came up...What came up, was Crystal River 3."

There was a moment as the other two computed and then a dawn of comprehension hit them almost simultaneously.

"What," hissed Jenny?

"Wait a minute," said Jim at the same time.

Amos raised his hand shushing them.

Jim was the first to speak, "Amos, what did he say?"

After another circuitous glance, he continued, "Basically, he said to watch out for persons who seemed to be my friend but weren't; and I think he meant inside the facility. He also said that efforts to silence me could be at the expense of many others."

Jim fell back against his seat staring at Amos. Jenny alternately looked at both of them for a second with her mouth still open in an "O" of surprise.

Then, "Oh dear God...Do you...Could he..." she collected her thoughts, "Amos, could he mean they'd cause a problem in a nuclear power plant just to get rid of you?"

Her dad looked at her, "Jen, do you think the Devil cares what the cost is?"

"No...," she said slowly, "I've never had a clearer idea of what he's up to...or capable of."

Jim met Amos' eyes, "Amos, this was bad before...but that...that's more frightening than anything I could have imagined."

Amos let out a sigh, "Don't I know it. I mean, I walk around that place every night and realize it would be a snap to waylay someone in there. It's worse than a maze...it's a multi-storied maze. I don't think any one person knows all of it."

"Ok, yeah, that's a bad spot, but if they went after you like that how could it involve many others?"

"I don't know. I'm not sure if it was done that way, it could."

Jenny spoke up, "Ok, if the plan was to trap you in this maze, who would do it? I mean is there anyone you're suspicious of?"

"Not really. I've made some waves for some of the guys who were goofing off, but no one reacted that badly; not that shows anyway."

Jim was absently rubbing his chin; a habit Jenny knew meant the wheels were turning. Then he said almost to himself, "Of all the worst case scenarios. I mean if this is a real possibility, and we have to assume it is, then we're in possession of information that amounts to a terrorist threat to a US nuke plant...and we can't tell anyone."

Amos nodded, "My thoughts too. I mean, can you see the sheriff or agents face...Yeah, a ten foot tall, flaming angel told me. That would get a trip to the asylum."

Jenny said, "What if you didn't go to the plant any-more?"

"Thought of that...move the fight to safer ground. Pon-dered and prayed and did it over again. I can't get any peace about it. Finally it sort of hit me. What if something's in the works that doesn't fully depend on my being there?"

"I don't get it."

"Ok...that snake trick didn't happen suddenly. It was well concocted and thought out; pro stuff. What if there's something else that has already been put into play; something that can't be shut down or turned off?"

"You don't have any way of knowing that...or finding out?"

"No, trust me, I've asked...Let's face it, we've already seen more involvement by spirit agencies than in some books of the Bible."

Jim nodded, "You have that one right."

"So, at some point I...we, just have to operate on faith. And since He won't green-light my absence from the plant, I have to stay. It seems almost like roads or trails of some kind lead there...or maybe intersect there. And what if it's something I could affect positively, but I'm off hiding out?

Jenny slumped forward and rested her forehead on her arms against the table top. Both men waited and watched.

After a moment she looked up, "I was so thrilled about Rome...after it was over. Now I'm trying to take all this in...snakes, nuclear plants, terrorist plots and it just gets worse and worse. But the hardest thing is feeling helpless, like it's out of control."

"I know," said Amos, "trust me, I know. But if He has enough confidence in us to allow the miracles we've seen already, how can we lose heart and still be worthy of the honor?"

"We can't," stated Jim, "and now it's bigger than all of us together. There are a whole lot of people going on about their daily lives right now that would freak out if they knew any of this. And most of them are not in the same camp we are. Our job has always been to represent Him so that some might turn and be saved. We agree on that?"

"Absolutely," said Amos as Jenny nodded.

"Then keep in mind, if anything even remotely cata-strophic happens at that plant, there could be a long list of human souls whose opportunity to make that decision...has expired."

Both youngsters stared at Jim thoughtfully. Then Jen-ny sighed,

"We're not going home are we?"

"Not in a million years," said her dad.

"I better call Martha."

"And it's time I headed for the Valley of the Shadow," said Amos.

They all looked at each other in total silence for several long moments, then Jim said, "Pray first?"

And they did.

CHAPTER 17

MATT ROBBINS EXECUTED a sweeping, banked turn and brought the NRC's Bell 407 helicopter to an upwind heading. Seconds later he began his descent into the Crystal River 3 reactor compound. There was plenty of room on the large concrete apron that fronted the main access hatch and he had lost count of the landings here since repairs began. Under his expert touch the skids touched down as lightly as a falling leaf.

The problems inside seemed to be escalating these days and his boss was in and out of the place regularly. His chief responsibility was to inspect and advise on the various repair phases and operations underway. And, although they were striving to be on the same page, he wondered if the in-house personnel weren't a little tired of all the over the shoulder coaching.

Not his worry he thought as he watched Charlie hunch over and hustle away from the chopper. The turbine began spooling down and the blade rotation commenced its transition from a thunderous blur to something akin to a giant ceiling fan. Matt eyed the instrument panel for several moments then glanced out at the now familiar surroundings. The weather was pleasant enough and his job was to wait. Might as well wait here where the view was great too.

He'd had opportunity to meet some of the people involved and even renew friendships from past encounters and misadventures. Fitz was, as usual, heading up the teams doing the "hot" work. What that guy didn't know about these systems didn't amount to much. He was often referred to as "the Guru of Gamma". Some of the new players were becoming friends, instead of just acquaintances, as well. The lead kid on second shift always said hi to him and often asked some good questions about his helicopter. His name was Amos, something or other, and he had apparently been around aircraft at some point. Matt was well aware that once flying caught your interest, it would likely last a lifetime. A gorgeous piece of machinery, like the 407, would naturally attract such a person.

Matt referred to her as "Red Bird". She was a bright, cardinal shade of that color with the NRC logo prominently displayed on the fuselage in contrasting, glossy black. He'd been flying her for almost four years now. It was good work and decent pay, especially in comparison to doing the same job for some law enforcement agency. The Commission didn't do much night flying and no one was tempted to take a shot at you for shining the light on them. The only thing he'd never really gotten comfortable with were the facilities themselves.

They were huge labyrinths of loud, powerful machinery which always seemed to be on the edge of man's ability to control them. With his inside relationship, he knew stories of a few mishaps that would never be made public. No matter what they espoused to the civilians, these monsters would always pose some latent dangers. However, he also had to admit that a well run plant, under proper supervision, was a great alternative to being held hostage to the Mid-East oil barons.

All that was well and good. He'd gladly fly you into the area and wait somewhere outside the "hot" zone till you were done. Matt could count his own trips into reactor containment buildings on his fingers. And several of those were the familiarization visits dictated by job training. He could tell the Auxiliary side from the R/B side and even describe the steam generators and massive negative pressure fan systems; but that was about all he needed to know. He tipped his hat to the guy's suiting up and doing the really hot work on the reactors themselves. Spending your days, or nights as the case may be, tap dancing around an open core or climbing around inside the actual head of the beast itself...nah, they didn't have enough money to entice this mama's son into that world. And speaking of that particular breed of wild man, Amos himself was approaching.

"Hiya Matt."

"Hey yourself Amos...How's things in hell town."

Amos grinned, "Aw, it's not that bad Matt. Those of us who can't fly gotta do something for a living."

"Well, I must say, you picked a pretty scary something."

Amos paused and looked thoughtful, "You know Matt, you're right. It is getting scarier around here. That latest crack has me a little worried. Matter of fact, I'm surprised Fitz let you guy's land here. This is exactly the spot we were getting the highest readings."

Robbins face took on a shade that almost matched the concrete beneath him.

"What the devil...Amos, are you serious?"

Amos had a tough time keeping a straight face, "Why do you think I'm out here? I have a Hi-Rad team on their way out to try and pin down the source. When I saw the Bird, I thought I'd better come see if any of the paint was peeling off."

For just a moment Robbins looked like a man about to choke on his own tongue. Then Amos couldn't take it any longer and broke into laughter. Robbins face magically went from white to beet red. He pulled off his ball cap and hurled it at Amos who unconsciously caught it in one hand while holding his side with the other.

"That's not funny Amos. You damn near gave me a heart attack." But he was starting to grin too.

Amos gasped out, "I thought you pilot guys had to stay in better shape than that," then lapsed back into almost tearful mirth. He wiped his eyes and looked at Matt who was canvassing the area to see if anyone else had seen him being played like the proverbial fish. For the moment, they were alone on the large, raised escarpment which comprised the reactor's back yard. The only spectators were the vast expanse of sky and Gulf.

He finally grinned back at Amos and said,

"Please remind me to give you a ride sometime...one you'll never forget."

Amos had regained most of his composure and straightened right out at this remark, "Oh man, don't I wish."

"Wish what, that I introduce you to six ways to use a barf bag?"

"It'd be worth it Matt, I'd take a ride in the Bird any time."

Matt eyed the muscular young man before him. He always got good vibes off this guy and couldn't say exactly why. He just seemed like an old fashioned straight shooter. Like some character out of a forgotten John Wayne script.

"You know, I believe you would."

Amos had fully recovered and as he handed back the cap he said wistfully, "Believe me, nothing I'd like better."

"Well if you're that interested, why don't you take lessons?"

"Did once during high school; actually made it to my solo flight in a PA-2 'Trauma Hawk'. But then we moved and I just never got back into it. Now, I don't have the time."

"Should have plenty when this beastie goes back on line."

There was a sudden pause and an odd expression fleeted across Amos' face. Then he said, "The beastie's not really the issue."

"Well, what is, if I might ask? You'd obviously like to fly something."

Amos again listened quietly inside for a moment. Yep, there it was. That light mental tap on the shoulder only had one source. He turned his eyes back to the pilot,

"God is the issue, Matt."

Robbins stared for a moment then his face again paled, "Umm...sorry?"

"I have a job to do for Him."

Their eyes locked, and then Matt said quietly, "You're serious aren't you."

"Very".

"Can you tell me about it?"

"Be glad too...if you want to hear."

There was another lengthy pause; then Matt said, "Amos, I just this morning picked up a Bible after almost fifteen years. Now some guy, I barely know, tells me he works for God. I'm dumb, but I ain't stupid. I can take a hint."

Amos was thoughtful in turn for a moment, "That's a good start, Matt. God works like that sometimes...for those whose hearts turn to Him. I get the impression yours has decided to take another look?"

The pilot turned and stared out over the Gulf with a far away gaze.

"When I woke up this morning, I kept seeing scenes from this really weird dream I had. I was on a busy street in some hell-hole, like New York or somewhere, trying to catch a cab. Something I've never actually done in real life, and two pulled up at the same time. One was black, the other was white. Both drivers were trying to get me to use theirs. There was someone I should have known already sitting in the white one but I couldn't see them clearly.

"In my mind I knew the choice I made was more important than just a ride. It had that life or death feel to it and I was afraid to choose. Then it ended. When I woke up, I went all through the house looking for a Bible and found my mom's old wore out one. She used to read it to me till I wouldn't listen anymore. That's when I realized the person in the white cab was her. She's been gone seven years."

"What did you read?"

Matt turned to him with no hesitation, "Mark chapter four; the part about the seeds falling on different types of ground."

Amos looked intently at the man, "I guess you understand the ground represents your heart?"

He sighed, "Yeah, and I'm afraid the thorny ground fits mine. I've been too busy living and doing it my way to notice God."

"It would seem He's noticed you. The cab thing is pretty obvious."

His eyes met Amos' once more, "Yeah man; it is. I don't want to make the wrong choice...I'd like to see my mom again."

"That's a decision we all have to make, Matt. And it does always start with the heart. God is either going to be number one there...or he will be absent."

The man gave another sigh, "He's been absent; I know that."

Amos' gaze lasted another long moment, "I'm going to tell you some hard truths. I pray right now that God's own Spirit of Truth will testify of them to you."

It was Matt's turn for another lengthy pause then he shrugged and said quietly, "OK"

"At this point many church folks would have you recite a little prayer saying you accept Jesus as savior."

He nodded, "I did that when I was a kid."

"Can we agree that if you can feel God's absence, it didn't quite work?"

Another nod.

"Then this is my prayer for you. Right now I ask God to allow His spirit to again touch that heart. When he does he'll remind you of the sin in your life. The things God hates, yet we find excuses to keep doing. Does that sound familiar?"

"You have no idea."

"Actually, I do. This inner knowledge of how I've disappointed the very one who made me, is often termed conviction. If I remain in that state, I am going to be just that, convicted...and condemned. No matter what prayers I may recite, or what I might accomplish as a churchgoer, if that sin remains in me, and between me and God, we will never be friends, only relatives."

"What...what do you mean relatives?"

"Matt, nothing in all the universe can change the fact that God is technically your Father. He's the father of us all. What we need is to make Jesus our Savior...and our brother."

Matt looked a little stupefied, "How can He be a brother to someone like me?"

"He can't. He can only be a brother to the new you."

Another wide eyed pause, "The new me?"

"God's own words teach that when someone surrenders their heart back to Him, some wonderful things happen. Your past life with all its sin and activity of the 'flesh', that kept you and God apart, is forgiven, gone forever. That's the sacrifice Jesus provided. You are remade in the spiritual image of your new brother and Lord, Christ himself. Old things pass away and all things are made new. You have a clean slate. And you receive the gift of the Holy Spirit; the Counselor. Even Jesus depended on that Spirit to operate in this sinful world and yet defeat that sin at every turn. His sacrifice then opened the way for God to send that same Spirit to you and me."

"And this may be the part mainstream religion fails to understand or teach. If you are now truly housing God's own Spirit of Truth, you can also learn to defeat sin. You will gain the strength to obey God's dictates on how to conduct your life. You probably won't be suddenly perfect, but you will show steady growth in that new character. And this world will start to lose its appeal; at every level."

Matt's eyes had about doubled in size. None of this matched up with what he remembered from his old forays into church; mostly at Easter and Christmas.

"Amos, I can barely control the bad habits I have now. You make it sound like a person can become some kind of saint."

"Yep, that's what He calls us in Scripture, Saints of God. But you will never control anything, least of all yourself. You will choose to be controlled by one or the other; God or Satan. And Satan is synonymous with self. Many times what you think you're doing all on your own, is actually the result of who has the overriding influence in your heart."

"We're back to my heart again."

"Yeah, and right now God has sent that Son to knock on your heart's door. But I tell you ahead of time, he's not coming to offer you a rose garden. To truly accept the gift of Jesus is to step back in line with God, his Father. And to know Christ often means to know his suffering; trust me."

"I gotta be honest Amos, that's not how I remember it. What happened to the peace and joy and all that?"

"Oh it's still there. In fact it's magnified if you know God's words on the matter. If you do then you're not disappointed every time life doesn't go the way you think it should. Every little complication doesn't get laid at God's door like He's some kind of genie in your personal lamp. True friendship with God makes you the enemy of this world. That means the enemy of its false god too. You will take up fresh residence in a world that has conclusively proven it hates everything you will now speak out and stand for."

"Man, that is not what I've heard preached. That would scare most people off, buddy."

"Only if they didn't hear or understand the other side of the story."

"Which is...?"

Amos paused thoughtfully once more, "Matt, I'd like you to give me two numbers. Let's call them price tags. But first, relax your mind. Get it out of 'worldly' mode. Try to put it in eternal mode. The Bible says, God has planted eternity into the heart of man. Think about, and consider for a moment, all that suggests and implies...

"Now, the first price tag is the one you think a person should put on actually knowing God and even being His friend. Think seriously about that and give me a number."

He barely paused, "Amos, you and I both know there's no price for something like that."

"OK, agreed...How about life eternal...Not some cloud and a harp but real, meaningful existence in the company of both our Lord and his Father. To be reunited with loved ones and saints from all the ages, with purpose and fulfill-ment in the bargain."

Matt's eyes looked a little glazed. "I...I don't think...I'm not sure I can get my head around all that."

"And yet that, when all the man-made dust of religion gets blown off, is what we're talking about. What Jesus was sent to offer us. Can you place a realistic value on that?"

"No...from that viewpoint there's not enough in the whole world to match it."

"Is there anything life could throw at you that wouldn't be worth enduring if that's your final destination?"

"No... nothing."

"Now consider this...what kind of love would someone have to feel for you to make you an offer like that?"

Matt's head slumped over a little, "More than I deserve."

"What kind of love and loyalty should I feel for someone who would actually make it happen, who would provide that kind of future for me? Should I be willing to die for him like those old Samurai warriors in Japan would for their Lord? Like Peter, Paul and countless others have done for theirs?"

Matt looked up and met his eyes squarely, "Yeah...yeah Amos, I guess anybody should."

Amos softened his voice, "Well Matt, that's where you stand today. God has gotten your attention and wants you to consider His offer. But He wants you to understand that to be His you have to have the same heart his Son had when he was here. The same allegiance and loyalty Jesus had for the Father while he walked this very ball of dust. To truly belong to God, you have to be willing to die for God. And the first thing you have to die to, is yourself...still want to pray that prayer?"

Matt stood erect and squared his shoulders, "I do."

Amos reached out slowly and shook the man's hand, then turned and knelt in the shadow of the "Red Bird". Matt knelt beside him and there, on a man made hill overlooking a fine example of God's creation, next to one of the most volatile examples of man's creation, Matt Robbins changed his eternal destiny.

Neither was aware of how close destiny had begun breathing down their necks.

CHAPTER 18

"SAY AGAIN, FALCON." The connection was terrible. It was one thing to be stuck in such primitive conditions as part of team security measures; it was an entirely different matter to attempt to conduct operations under those same circumstances. Samir's scratchy dialogue commenced once more, ending with, "Falcon request Car 54 verification."

This time the "Car 54" cryptonym came through clearly and Pytor's eyes widened in surprise. Without a pause he hung up the archaic landline and walked out of the decrepit looking office attached to an equally haggard looking hangar. Dust devils were swirling lazily along the packed dirt runway which stretched north and south in front of the abandoned looking structure. His pulse had initiated a rapid upbeat as soon as the innocuous phrase penetrated his thought patterns.

Car 54 was "crypto" for the Mk 54 SADM (Special Atomic Demolition Munition). A sixteen by twelve inch cylindrical package, in a casing weighing only a hundred and fifty pounds, it was the most compact nuclear device ever successfully tested. None the less, some models were touted to be well beyond the kiloton range for yield. It was gratifying to be in pseudo-possession of such a weapon, but the inherent security measures surrounding such knowledge were indeed formidable.

The "Car 54" was a play on an aged American sitcom; something to do with a spoof against their police forces. All well and good, but the forces the Americans could bring to bear on a suspected terror situation, were not at all amusing. He didn't even like the fact that the 54 of the nomenclature was factual.

Pytor wandered over to the remains of an old wooden table parked under some scraggly looking trees, which barely provided any relief from the scorching midday sun. Sweat trickled freely from his pores trying vainly to keep his body's cooling system on a par with the intense heat. His physiological reaction to Samir's query probably wasn't helping any. It was one thing to cluster in a group of like minded mercenaries and boast of what terrible plans they had for the hated Americans. It was another matter, when trapped in less than secure circumstances, to face the reality of attempting to infiltrate a nuclear device into that same society. If the code phrase resulted in an actual verification, meaning Samir had a suitable target in his sights, the powers above would order them to try and accomplish just that.

The risks were indeed high. Rumor had it there were US spy satellites that could detect fissile material from orbit. That wasn't much of a threat at this location, which was among the numerous abandoned uranium mining sites in northwest New Mexico. The greatest danger would involve the multi-state transit required to reach Samir's current stalking grounds. Having taken these people's money, and seen second hand how they dealt with internal problems, Pytor knew he would be bound by both honor, and survival interest, to make the attempt. But not to get the cart before the horse. The actual process of an operational go-ahead was something that had to be handled first.

Re-tracing his steps into the office, he walked to the back wall and stared down at a pile of crusty tarpaulins. They appeared to have been used as painting drop cloths ages ago. Grabbing a lower edge he dragged them to one side, reached into his pocket and brought out a small folding knife. One that would never get you in trouble on a routine traffic stop but something that Pytor, with his years of east-bloc training, could use to take a life in almost any circumstance. Including a throw distance up to thirty feet. This time, however, he simply located an indentation in one narrow board and used the innocent looking knife to pry the edge up. Using his fingertips, he completed the removal of first one, then two other similarly crafted floor boards. The masterful way they meshed together was another testament to the skills ingrained in these increasingly unemployed operatives.

There, in the void beneath, lay a state of the art Harden Fr-210 encrypted satellite phone. Using the device was restricted to events such as those unfolding today. The fact that the Inmarsat system didn't support Doppler shift tracking was not completely fail safe as far as being triangulated on by some snooping entity. Any signal that was "securitized" might be enough to warrant a second look by one of the numerous agencies eavesdropping on every wave length used for communications. But the Harden was great tech and the call would be short and nonsensical in nature. It was doubtful any array was currently configured to triangulate in this remote area, but that was a chance that must be taken. Pytor would most likely be relocating after the call anyway.

He removed the Sat-phone from its hideaway and made his way back to the old table under the trees. His thoughts were still racing in several directions seeking to coordinate security considerations with potential tactical actions. Finally he gave a sigh, extended the antennae and powered up. When three indicator lights turned green, he keyed in an alpha-numeric password which armed the encryption package. After a brief wait, a second set of two amber indicators lit up confirming full operation. Inputting his personal security code, he then initiated a pre-programmed dial out with one key. The intended party answered in seconds.

"Go," was the only word spoken.

"We have Car 54 verification request from Falcon."

A momentary silence ensued and Pytor imagined the fat Iranian's mind turning the same somersaults his had. There was a terse, single word statement, "Proceed," the signal collapsed and Pytor quickly powered down.

In the space of those few seconds, an untold number of lives were suddenly placed in a most terrifying state of jeopardy.

"SO THAT'S IT, HUH," said Jenny.

"Yeah, I take it that big round structure houses the reactor."

"Man, this place is huge. What are all those other buildings and stuff farther out?"

"The ones to the west have got to be the coal fired plants. I'd say this complex is generating a lot of power."

"And Amos is in that round one?"

"Could be," said her dad, "but I take it they move around the plant a lot...when they're not doing those 'jumps.' That big attached area must be the auxiliary side. I'd guess that's where the turbines are."

Jenny could see why Amos had jokingly referred to it as Dracula's Castle. There was something foreboding about the huge, cylindrical tower that housed man's ultimate power source. The sheer size, of both it and the surrounding compounds of steel and concrete, made the task before them seem impossible. And she was seeing it from a distance.

While, under normal circumstances, they might have arranged for a tour of the cold side, it was obvious that activity in the facility was at a level which would certainly prohibit casual visitors. There were trucks and forklifts moving to and fro inside the fenced perimeter and the lattice of a large crane boom could be seen towering on the far side of the reactor building. That was probably the location of the "hatch" Amos said was used to transfer the larger components in or out. A number of workers were visible in matching blue jumpsuits and reminded her of ants scurrying around a gigantic ant hill. In the background, steam or smoke poured from numerous candy striped towers adding to the overall impression of massive forces in motion.

"OK Dad, this re-fuel is a big deal. That goes without saying, I guess. But if it's this busy outside, what's it like inside where Amos is?"

"Gotta be similar I imagine. Listening to him I get the idea there's more of a controlled or contained atmosphere though. You can't charge around inside someplace where radiation is present like you can a regular construction site."

Jenny was quiet for several long moments, "How are we supposed to be any help from way out here. I mean, not that I really have some great desire to go inside one of those things, but we're the only others aware of what may be happening and we can't get near the place."

"I know. I've never been much of a sideline guy either," he caught himself and grinned at his daughter who was looking at him with an "eye-rolling" expression. "Guess I don't have to explain that to you, huh."

"Hardly pop; I'm half afraid you'll charge the place and half ready to go with you."

"Listen Jen, we wanted to see the reactor site; now we have. I admit it's intimidating. Hard to even imagine we could ever get inside." He paused, "Actually, I'm not even sure that's in the cards..."

They were silent, both lost in thought, then,

"I wonder if Mom sees any of this."

"I don't know honey. I hope she's not watching this one, it'd really worry her."

"It really worries me."

"I guess we'd be nuts not to feel a little of that."

"Know what I hate worse...feeling helpless...like right now."

Jim nodded in agreement, "You're right there, let's head back to town, we can't do anything out here."

They'd been sitting unobtrusively in a remote parking area that was full of other cars. Jim fired the raucous little SX up and they made their way out to the long access road that ran east back to Highway 19. Sometime later, just north of the Crystal River "metro" area, Jim's attention was drawn to a faded looking establishment proclaiming itself the Orange Blossom Inn. He slowed as they passed and Jenny looked curiously at him.

"What?"

After a moment he said, "I don't know...something about that place...probably nothing." But he continued to eye it in the mirror as they rolled on.

The Holy Spirit was again making His presence felt.

ELSEWHERE, beyond this dimensional realm, far less than "holy" spirits had reconvened as well.

"So, Buferan, I trust you bring better news this time."

Still unused to this "new" Lucifer, Buferan nodded as he spoke, "Yes Sire, the original participant, most closely placed to Mikals, is reacting favorably. The Eastern Fanatic has placed the bait before him and he has engaged himself toward acquiring it."

"What see you regarding the others?"

He knew what his master was most concerned with, "All channels seem normal at the moment sir. There is the same overage of First Ranks in the principality, but the 'Presence' has been quiet of late."

"I need not remind you against being lulled?"

"No Your Lordship, I have watchers in place on all concerned. It is only when they approach the girl that He stirs, so I have instructed extra distance be kept...for now."

"What of Mikals himself...any change?"

The huge overlord actually seemed to sigh, "Sir, the hedge about him is as before. I confess we have not managed to shake him...thus far."

Lucifer raised one mighty appendage and waved it dismissively, "It will be of little consequence if your plan succeeds." He thought a moment, "I must admit the idea of turning such a one is appealing. It would rival the destruction of those fools on their airwaves. In fact it would be better. This one is cutting far too close to the bone on matters that have required most of this age to secure."

Buferan knew his boss was thinking of other glory days when a number of "TV" preachers had dropped their guards long enough to be seduced into fatal errors. Errors that effectively neutralized much of their efforts. He also knew the factual level of those efforts, while more widely circulated, lacked some of the deadly accuracy that Mikals brought to the table. Accuracy that would not be permitted to expand beyond the point where this massive effort to silence him culminated. It was also evidence of where these creatures were going with this so called "Internet" technology. Rarely, if ever, had one this physically removed from the public eye become a danger which could not be ignored.

It was again time to test this new confidentiality,

"Sire, we are still very much treading in what was once Arch territory and yet things remain silent. If it continues, will the Deranian reappear?"

Lucifer again eyed him but without the old malice, "You are much concerned over this Arak."

Buferan cast his own glowing, venomous eyes downward, "It is where I most recently failed you Highness, I admit to a thirst for vengeance."

"You apprehended the legendary Kurtanus. That is a great sorrow for Him and a great victory for us. Is it not enough?"

"The thought of his imprisonment gives me endless pleasure," and here he raised his eyes once more, "but I am aware that Kurtanus was much tutored by this other, who seems not only more powerful, but more clever as well. As long as he is in play, does not the Mikals threat have a much sharper edge to it?"

His boss ignored this, "Admit it Buferan, you wish to involve yourself in preparations for the snare we spoke of."

"I do sir, Sardon can oversee matters here can he not?"

Lucifer was again thoughtful for a time, "It is a gamble, even with the knowledge we possess. As you say, this Deranian is a troublesome adversary. You will need a diversion in that principality to somewhat explain your presence. If He suspects things so seemingly distant are again related it might finally result in the appearance of an Arch."

"Are we prepared for that as well?"

"At the moment I would say, partially. If things remain as unbalanced as they have become, we will have quite the surprise for whoever shows up; Deranian or Arch."

"Forgive me Sire, but how confident can we be regarding the Deranian?"

"Buferan, you have always been ahead of most on these things. Think again of what worked with Kurtanus."

"Uh…You, sir, seemed to know what he was going to do before he did it. Your trap was a masterpiece."

"Yes, but how was it laid in the first place?"

The reptilious features of the awful visage took on a perplexed look, "I have never been sure of that, Sire."

"And there is no time now to explain it. Go to Maktou. Tell him of the basics but nothing further...only that the operation is under your guidance. Place watchers at all six corners of the province...no, place a pair, and then send a report back to me. Do nothing to attract His untoward interest. And do not allow any harassment of their First Ranks...for the time being."

"Consider it done, My Lord."

And with another black, imploding fireball, Buferan vanished.

AMOS ENTERED THE BREAK AREA on floor two of the Auxiliary building and took a moment to mop his forehead. Even with the conditioned air, those suits could get hot. Then a smile crossed his features. He was still feeling the exhilaration of the surprise encounter with the NRC pilot. Nothing life had to offer compared with seeing a fellow human escape the Second Death. He hoped to spend some more time with Matt in the upcoming days.

McMillan's office was empty and none of the crew were present; not that unusual for this time of evening. The tube sheet jump had gone off without a hitch, but there was a lot more to be done. He'd taken additional photos of the ring that the errant gear had gouged in the finely machined surface and the damage to the bell-ends protruding above it. Some of the shavings and chips were still lodged in various crevices and cracks. It would require several additional jumps to completely clean these out before repairs could commence. It also looked like Eddie would get his shot at actual ANM work pretty soon. The guys were accumulating a lot of Milli-Rems on their dosimeters and some new help would be required.

Mr. Dormer had called in requesting a day off, but that was no longer as suspicious as it had once been. His work ethic had much improved and he'd been on nearly two weeks straight. He still caused a "tingle" in Amos's spirit when they talked and he had tried to examine that objectively. Initially he wondered seriously if Eddie might be part of the problem Arak had warned of. But the man had become much more sociable and even listened when Amos sprinkled in comments about finding true life through Christ.

He had long ago learned not to apply the bludgeon of spirituality that had been popular with some of the church goers he grew up with. It often served to alienate people and could also lead to "casting pearls before swine". Sadly, as Scripture declared, some members of the race called human were indeed *fit only for destruction.*

It was something he'd wrestled with for a long time. Only years of evangelistic forays and observation had finally convinced him that not everyone would listen to the Truth even if you could just calmly lay it out for them. Only the Holy Spirit could discern when such a situation had altered and he seemed interested in Eddie these days. He'd certainly taken an interest in Matt. So be it; Amos would strive to do his part whenever and wherever he was led. For now, more earthly matters needed attention. It was time to alert the crew regarding preparations for the upcoming pump tests. He was preparing to do just that, using the PL phone, when "Mac" walked back into his office.

"Hey Amos, how'd it go?"

Amos hung the phone back up, "Well Mac, the jump went fine but there's still a lot of scrap lying around on top of the sheet."

"Not good. I wonder how much of that stuff got through the system to the turbines."

"I'd say some of it had to. There's a lot of bells missing sections or completely gone."

"Damn," that was pretty strong language for Mac, "have you looked in on the Deck crew to see if they're finding anything?"

"No, but I do know it's still pretty 'crapped up' in there. Fitz wants a 'suit' to go in and look things over soonest, but the sheet and drives are keeping the HP guy's pretty busy. I guess I could talk to RB about maybe rigging for one tomorrow."

"Can't be tomorrow. If you're going to let Dormer make a jump, I want you as close as possible during the whole op."

"OK by me. Anybody decide whether it's going to be the sheet or a Drive yet?"

"Nope...You know the drill. Third shift is not going to be making any for while after that Spent Fuel snafu. We'll have to see what the guys on first do before we'll know."

Amos sighed, "Sounds like hurry up and wait again. You know Mac, we could get in another jump per shift if they'd let me train some of our guys with the tooling. It's not really rocket science."

"I know; bounced that off Roger again last night. Answer's still the same. No more guys go ANM till the new budget figures come out."

"I guess Eddie lucked out getting in under the wire, huh."

Mac's face took on a serious demeanor, "Amos, keep a close watch on him. I've never had much faith in leopards that change spots."

Amos paused, "I know…I can totally relate. But I've seen people straighten up and fly right before. I think he appreciates the chance you're giving him."

"Hah, let's see how appreciative he is after he's been in one of those suits for a couple of hours."

Amos laughed, "Yeah there is that. Hope he hasn't got any claustrophobia. Mac, can we get these guys in fifteen minutes early tonight and set up the details on maintenance before those pump tests?"

"Yeah, thanks for reminding me. Can you handle the announcement and track down the ones in the O-zones?"

A "zero-zone" was an already noisy area where you wore ear protection and heard absolutely nothing that went out over the plant-lines.

"No problem, consider it done."

And with that they went back to the task of rebuilding and maintaining one of man's more serious, and dangerous, technological marvels. An even more dangerous "marvel" had now introduced itself into the equation. One which might impact not only lives, but devastate the entire geographical area.

The powers of the dimensional realms watched all this unfold well aware that another crossroads in Earth's spiritual history was racing right alongside these events. As the old saying went, you could cut the tension with a knife; or in this case…a sword.

CHAPTER 19

NEXT MORNING, Jenny again found Amos out back on his small dock. The boat was in the water, the gear loaded and ready to go. He immediately engaged her on the idea of going with him, but she was hesitant.

"So how about it....You ever do any diving?"

"Well, yeah, I've snorkeled some with my dad. The Keys once, some of the springs, but Amos...spear fishing?"

"Why not, I'll be doing the shooting...you can watch for sharks."

"Very funny."

"You think I'm kidding...I just need a couple, so I'm going to try and take both from one of my bigger holes. Once I start shooting, you can get in the boat with Bubba and holler if any show up. You'll spot em a lot sooner than I will. Jerry does it sometimes when he's home. Saved me from a 'close encounter' once or twice."

"Oh yeah, what does Bubba normally do? Bark when he sees one?"

"Nah, haven't been able to teach him that one yet...Are you saying you'd bark?"

Jenny snatched off a flip-flop and whapped Amos soundly on the shoulder.

"Ow,...OK...You win...Just holler."

Jenny was still eyeing him with mock ferocity, "Let me ask you something Mikals, you any good at that nuclear stuff you do?"

He looked blank for a moment, "Uh...yeah, I guess so."

"Good, 'cause you ain't never gonna make it in comedy boy."

Amos burst into laughter ruining Jenny's attempt to keep a straight face, "Are they all as feisty as you in Jacksonville?"

She continued in her best southern drawl, "Son, in Jacksonville, folks got better sense than to mess with an Alexander...you hear me?"

He was still grinning from ear to ear, "Are they all as pretty as you?"

Although Jenny started to blush beet red, she again kept the straightest face possible and glared at him, "Don't go tryin' to get out of it with flattery big boy."

Amos dropped all pretense at levity, "I wasn't; I thought the same thing the other day when you were caught in the bush."

Well, that just about "de-winded" her sails. They were both quiet for several long moments.

"That's a nice thing to say Mr. Mikals; thank you."

"You're welcome Miss Alexander...still like to hear you bark though."

Something between a squeal and a growl erupted from Jenny and the flip flop returned to battle stations. Amos was off like a shot. What could pass for a small Indian princess was on the war path right behind him. After several seconds puzzlement, Bubba let out a low "groof" and bounded off in pursuit. It would take some time before the more serious matter of supplying the day's fish fry could again be addressed.

Eventually, however, Jenny found herself on the bow seat of Amos' little v-hull, zipping west down Fish Creek. The natural beauty had lost nothing from her first look and, if anything, she had an even deeper sense of appreciation for the peace and wonderment of this massive estuary system.

They passed some islands substantial enough to have full size pines and palms towering over the brushy under-growth. Other places were the domain of the Mangrove tree. They created islands of their own as they crowded against each other with "banks" made of tubular roots dipping claw-like into the shallows. Some shorelines were composed of small, eroded lime rock ridges that tumbled down to mud flats or sandy, light grey beaches. Many of these beaches were thronged with bird life ranging from pelicans and gulls, to Great Blue herons. Smaller avian cousins could be seen swooping gracefully over the assembled throngs, while others darted along the waters edge stopping repeatedly to peck at potential snacks.

But, along many stretches, the water simply merged into huge, Everglades looking, needle grass plains. Plains that wandered far out onto the horizon, particularly to the south. Amidst all this variety, scattered tributaries and smaller creeks wandered intermittently off into the distance on either side. As they were approaching one of these intersections, Jenny watched an Osprey cease its restless circling, fold its wings and streak down into a watery collision causing spray to explode in every direction. It instantly re-emerged and continued in low level flight as it manfully struggled to gain altitude grasping what appeared to be a foot long mullet. She glanced back at Amos who smiled and nodded. The high pitched whine of the little outboard made conversation difficult. Then they cleared a large bend and were suddenly face to face with the vast expanse of the Gulf of Mexico.

As they zoomed past the boundary, where the irregular needle grass and mangrove line gave way to the open sea, she saw the water color change and they shot out over the large, deep "hole" where Amos said their first breakfast had originated. It appeared to be about ten or twelve feet deep with sheer, cliff like sides all around. Even at this speed she glimpsed movement and saw several large shadows streak away towards the rocky cover of the far wall. Then they were out on the perimeter of the huge, endless grass flats streaking over the crystal shallows where it appeared the water was barely deep enough for their little craft.

Amos called the wide, flat blades Turtle Grass. It stretched away in every direction like a green carpet captured under a glassy, clear surface. Here and there were bald patches which, she'd seen previously, were rock and sand areas. In these areas the depth would be somewhat deeper and the fringes were composed of the root structure of the surrounding grass clinging tenaciously to the white sand bottom.

What she'd learned on their first outing was that some of these same areas housed ledges and caves. Here, close to shore, the grass was growing in two to four feet of water and the rocky areas were not much deeper. As you progressed seaward, the depth gradually increased. On their previous trip, Amos had stopped over a series of three good sized holes, grouped together in five or six feet of water, that he had called singularly "Appointment Hole". When asked about the curious name, he'd only smiled mysteriously and said, "ask me later." She now realized she'd forgotten to do that.

A shout broke her reverie and she looked back to find him pointing southwest. Out a couple of hundred feet in that direction, the glassy, calm surface was alive with boils and froth. As she watched, a dolphin broke the surface briefly and was gone; then another and another. Her eyes widened. There were perhaps six or seven of these gorgeous marine mammals, traveling fast in close formation and coming in their direction like a well aimed torpedo. What on Earth. First, she was shocked to see such large creatures in such shallow water. Secondly, why were they heading in their direction in such an apparent frenzy?

Another shout from Amos, "Hang on." And he put the extended tiller handle hard over and hammered the throttle wide open shooting away from the approaching horde. Now she was really mystified...and a little concerned. Did these normally harmless creatures represent some danger he was aware of? Bubba had bounced up from his place on the floorboard, or deck, and positioned himself in a wide stance with both front paws on the boats gunnel. His jaws were open with his tongue lolling out in an expression of pure pleasure. Then, the dog that never barked, let out a couple of happy yips that sounded like canine merriment. What the heck was going on?

She looked back to where the dolphin pod should be, only to see they had turned parallel with Amos course and were pacing them a mere fifty or so feet away. They were leaving huge oversized "vees" on the waters surface similar to bass in a pond. Only these vees were punctuated with large frothy swirls at regular intervals from the powerful up and down motion of their tails. This action was mixed with high speed lunges to the surface where they were apparently taking big, deep "dolphin breaths". She could hear some of the explosive exhalations even over the singing of the little Suzuki. Then, as she watched, one vee separated itself and angled in their direction. Two seconds later she was looking right into the smiling, intelligent face of an eight foot Bottlenose.

He swooped gracefully alongside the speeding little boat as if trying to communicate. Bubba was letting out more of those happy barks and leaning over as far as he could towards the sleek, gray torpedo form. Then with an effortless burst the creature shot ahead of them and criss-crossed several times in front of their bow. At this performance Amos again veered to a new heading.

Jenny looked back and watched the surface track of the dolphin also swerve, but back in the direction of the pod. Then the whole group seemed to explode into a more rapid pace, change course and again start to close on them. This was crazy. Then suddenly, in an instant, she was surrounded by dolphins.

They were on every side streaking along in perfect formation with the boat. A small, involuntary yelp escaped her as a full grown adult suddenly leaped clear of the water close enough to touch. For a long second their eyes met, then he was back under the surface. Another smaller one repeated the performance on the opposite side.

Time had once more ceased for Jennifer Alexander. She was no longer aware of any other thing in "life". The incredible, and unexplained, spectacle, which danced and gyrated all around her, became all she knew. She felt the whipping breeze from the boat's travel and the cool jets of spray blowing in from the mammalian acrobats, but her mind had gone into auto-pilot as her eyes darted first this way, then that, recording and glorying in the experience. The biggest grin from her childhood would not have eclipsed the one she was now wearing.

Then, as if on some silent command, they were gone. Her head swiveled the horizon seeking for them and found the tell-tale surface print of their travels off to the left moving out to sea as rapidly as they'd come. Amos began to throttle back and Bubba once again relaxed into silence and reseated himself. Jenny turned to face Amos, not realizing her mouth was hanging open while the grin was still trying to be in place. Amos laughed out loud and brought the throttle to idle. As soon as the RPM's settled he pulled the outboard out of gear and shut it down. The sudden silence had that intense, ear ringing quality to it. Their momentum caused them to coast silently, suspended over the slowly undulating green bottom like some magic carpet ride.

"Pretty cool, huh."

Jenny blinked a couple of times and tried to regain her senses, "Amos...what was that?"

"Racing."

"Racing?"

"Yeah; we do it all the time."

"We?"

"Me...and them."

"The dolphins?"

"Yes."

"I have never even heard...," she trailed off.

"Yeah, it's a little weird. They won't do it like that with any other boat I know of. Some of the guys have tried. See, not that many years ago, the fishermen around here would shoot at them."

"Shoot at them?!"

"Yeah, they were considered competition for the mullet."

"That's terrible...isn't it also against the law or something?"

Amos smile had a sad quality to it, "You're not in Kansas any more Toto. If everything that's been done around here illegally was common knowledge, we'd have considerably fewer neighbors."

"Like what?"

"You mean besides shooting at protected marine mammals...Let's see. Well, even I don't want to know how much drug trafficking has gone on over the years. I've heard some stories and you only have to look around to imagine how easy it would be. You see all those canals and creeks going off into the marshes, I've been so lost in there it took me half a day to find my way out...in the daylight. Once, while I was lost, I stopped on one of the bigger islands just to get in the shade. Guess what was on the island with me."

"I have no idea."

"A still."

"A still...you mean like, moonshine still?"

"Yep, I've seen them in pictures and this was definitely the real deal. Course' it looked like it hadn't been used in years."

"Holy cow...its Ten Thousand Islands, only farther north."

"Yeah, and in the good old days, a lot more convenient."

"So it's not like that around here anymore?"

"Who knows…I'm sure things still go on. Wanna hear something funny. I've been told that some of the individuals who were into that sort of thing are now afraid because of the UFO's."

Jenny rolled her eyes, "That's the first thing Clarice accused me of. Being a reporter chasing a UFO story."

She stopped and thought a moment, "Are there UFO's around here?"

Amos thoughtfully gazed around them at the currently placid waters. The boat had settled into a slow tide-borne glide over that glassy surface. Still, there were disturbances all around if you looked. Some large, some small, but it was obviously a busy place down below. Many of these he'd learned to recognize even at a distance. The tracks left by his racing buddies or the tell-tale double swirl of a ray's wingtips vortexing the surface. Even the big cluster of super-vees the schools of Tarpon left when they passed through each year. And you would always do well to notice some really big vee traveling all by itself, usually evidence of a top predator's presence. On a choppy day you'd never notice, but days like this transformed the whole place into a gigantic aquarium complete with "signatures" on its surface.

He turned back to Jenny, "Someone's out there. I've seen stuff flying way up high, traveling really fast, suddenly stop and change direction like nothing we've got. I've seen three of them shoot together and stop like they're having a conference, then explode off in different directions at warp speed."

They stared at each other for a few moments. Then Jenny said, "Amos, after what I saw in Rome, I don't doubt much anymore. Who could they be?"

Another thoughtful pause on Amos' part, "Well see, that's the thing, they have to be under the same jurisdiction we are."

"What?"

"Jen, they must belong to God just like we do. Whatever or whoever they are. That's his playground out there...all the toys are His."

Jenny thought a moment, "I guess I never thought about it quite like that."

"Makes sense though, doesn't it?"

Now Jenny looked thoughtful, "Deran."

"What?"

"Deran...he says he's originally from some place called Deran."

"Oh, yeah...well in a way, there's your proof. Remember the verse where Jesus talks about other 'sheep pens'?"

"Uh-huh...John 10, I think."

"That day, I asked him about these things we see...he said I was right about that verse."

"You know", said Jenny, "in Rome he talked about a Deran conversion...said it was different."

"We have just enough clues to go crazy wondering."

"Well, it'd sure sound crazy to most anyone else."

Amos made another scan of the area, "We may never know for sure till we get there, but one thing's for sure today."

"What."

"We'll go hungry if we don't get busy. It's still a little bit of a run out to the deep water and Eagle Ray."

"Eagle Ray?"

"Yeah...one of the 'outer' holes; eight or ten feet of water with big ledges and big fish...sometimes big sharks. First glance I ever got, there was a four foot, spotted Eagle ray swimming right through the middle; named it after him."

He turned and, with a grunt, pull started the Suzuki, and then pointed the bow out towards the limitless, blue-green horizon. As the hull surged up onto a plane and began picking up speed, Jenny watched the ever changing sub-sea panorama flash past while her thoughts strayed again to Rome. Then to the other beautiful sea she'd recently spent some time with...the dream world.

PYTOR SQUINTED to re-focus gritty eyes and continued to stare at the grey ribbon of Interstate 10 which seemed to reach out forever. On either side were pine woods and more pine woods. This monotonous landscape was combined with intermittent, lonely exits containing a solitary, or at most, a scraggly pair of competing service stations. The lack of scenery, and an endless array of AM and FM frequencies, containing mostly static, had reduced his razor sharp senses to a certain level of numbness. Considering his cargo, this was risky indeed...but necessary. His non-descript vehicle would not attract attention, his accent might. So it was stay on the road and speak little when fuel stops were required. This despite the fact he knew he was heading for one of the vacation Mecca's of the world where even some of his old countrymen sometimes found themselves with a few blessed weeks of warmth and entertainment. That is, if they were placed highly enough. In the old days he would never have been one of those chosen few.

This was a tough, nerve wracking way to see Florida. However, Samir's information had been deemed adequate for a green light to be given to operation "Peregrine". Now he was traveling across the highways of the so called "Greatest Nation" intent on doing his part to wreck some of that greatness. No nuclear device had ever been detonated by unfriendly forces on American soil. The dubious honor of being its caretaker was not lost on him...neither were the risks.

The Americans loudly proclaimed the integrity of their court system and sense of justice. But Pytor knew, from the experience of a few hapless comrades, how quickly a man and his existence could disappear into those hallowed halls. If he was caught in possession of this weapon, there was a good chance few would ever hear of it. And a pretty good chance he would never be heard from himself. That thought brought him to his senses and he shook his head to clear the cobwebs of fatigue.

In the trunk was the innocuous looking case that housed the long ago stolen SADM. It was uncertain whether this discrepancy had ever surfaced in the whirlwind world of nuclear testing in the fifties and sixties. If so, no official record was available...it had been checked and rechecked. Likewise, no effort had been made to further camouflage the device since it looked like nothing more than an army-surplus footlocker. Even the cylindrical weapon itself would be hard to decipher to an untrained eye. It could be passed off as most anything your imagination could come up with; sealed munitions storage, an antiquated guidance unit, whatever. Unless you were in range of a Geiger counter, all would be well. There were plenty of those residing at the intended destination but, once in range of the facility, the local radiation signature would mask the diminutive weapon with ease.

Samir had assured their superiors of his ability to make the insertion into the reactor building...but Pytor was unconvinced. It sounded as if too much hinged on the cooperation of an, as-yet, un-verified civilian. He would never have moved the weapon without more confirmation. He was also sure that fathead, who called himself Kabir (Great One), was getting carried away with the thought of such glory at the expense of both security and perhaps the lives of those in the field.

OK, admittedly, it was a stroke of diabolical genius to place such a device internally inside an American nuclear facility. If successful, it would ascend to center stage of the terrorist world as the greatest feat ever accomplished by any organization. Such a detonation would devastate the immediate area and spread high level contamination for untold miles. How far and where would depend largely on the prevailing winds. The instructions were specific to set the internal timer for a 3–11:00 p.m. window local time; something to do with a secondary target. As fortune would have it, the prevailing sea breeze off the adjacent Gulf waters should be in full swing at that hour blowing onshore with gusto. If all went well, the body count would be impressive now and for years to come.

Not only that, much of the local area would assume some of the same characteristics as many of the test islands and sites used so abusively by the Americans to create these nightmare weapons. A useless pit of contamination surrounded by many square miles which would not be habitable for generations to come. It was quite probable enough of the core would survive so that, with the cooling disrupted, the reaction would go supercritical causing massive secondary damage. This should result in a chain reaction of explosions that would further the carnage, and increase the radiation plume.

In the end, it would mean not only the loss and damage caused to the reactor facility, but the loss of use and untold casualties from the employees of the adjoining fossil fuel plants as well. It would surely result in contamination of hundreds of square miles of Gulf waters and even the potential ruination of the subterranean aquifer system. Yes, it was a pretty grandiose scheme, and success would render much of Florida's west coast a no man's land.

Regardless of how it might play out, there was no doubt about one thing...you didn't want to be anywhere in the vicinity when the SADM did its job.

CHAPTER 20

MIDNIGHT-THIRTY FOUND EDDIE once more occupying his favorite stool at the Inn's worn and battle-scarred bar. He was in a bit of a daze after a long, ground breaking shift at the plant. He'd done it; he was officially an ANM crew member. It had been more intense than he expected. The suits were a challenge to work in and the over the shoulder scrutiny by the technical supervisory crew made you feel as if you were performing on stage. But he'd pulled it off. Mikals had even complimented him on doing a nice job. He had to admit it; he owed the guy for taking a chance on him...and convincing McMillan.

It was sort of comical. Under other circumstances no one would pay you this kind of money for that kind of work. All he'd done was use a fancy looking vacuum apparatus and some tools to remove metal shavings and debris off a small area of the damaged tube sheet surface. The only tricky part was using oversize dental-pic type tools to dislodge the pieces jammed in the cracks while wearing the bulky "space suit" gloves. There were a lot of them too. It was going take a bunch of trips to clean that sucker out. All the better for me, he thought. He hadn't even picked up much exposure on his dosimeters. His thoughts were interrupted by the arrival of Sammy on the stool next to him.

"What is up, Edward?"

"Hey dude, just decompressing...long night in the suit."

"Ah, you have been playing 'Reactor Ranger' again," Sammy grinned.

"Yeah, that's us...the Few, the Proud, the Contaminated."

Sammy just shook his head, "Better you than me my friend."

"Hard to turn down the pay buddy." He looked around at the mostly deserted bar room, "Speaking of, you talk to 'Smith and Jones'?"

About that time, the bartender arrived to take Sammy's order. When he'd deposited his drink and left, Sammy leaned in slightly towards Eddie,

"Ah...yes, I did in fact speak to one of them. He gave me this." He reached into his pocket and pulled out a small wad of bills. Eddies eyes widened as he saw they were hundreds.

"Holy crap dude," then he caught himself, "put it away," he whispered.

"You do it," said Sammy quietly and handed the bills to him.

Eddie looked around with a slightly panicked expression then shoved the cash in his pocket.

"Look Sammy, I didn't agree to take their money. I didn't agree to anything."

Sammy held a finger to his lips, "Relax Edward, he said this was earnest money...to show their sincerity. He emphasized there were no strings attached and no hard feelings if we do not want the job."

"How much is there?"

"Five hundred dollars."

"Damn."

Eddies weary mind tried to surge into a higher gear; he hadn't seen this one coming. What he was also unaware of, was the absolute laser focus of temptation being directed at him by unseen forces...and he was wavering.

"Are you OK Edward? We should perhaps just walk away from this. I am maybe sorry I ever laid eyes on them."

"No...it's alright...I, uh, just gotta think a minute. They say anything else?"

Sammy looked at the floor a moment, "This will seem crazy."

"Yeah, well too late...this whole thing is crazy; what?"

"Out of curiosity, I ask him what they thought we could do...or rather you could do, inside the plant to cause such delay. He said the easiest way is to fool the computers. They claim to have some technical device that will trigger the computers in the uh, operations room...is that right?"

"Yeah, operations; it's where the main computer stuff is."

"Yes, uh, operations...a device that will show problems where none really exist."

Eddie looked confused, "I don't get it."

"Well, apparently, if the computer thinks there is a problem, it will not start the reactor till the problem is fixed."

"Oh, yeah, that's old news...especially if it's in the cooling system."

"He mentioned that too. At any rate, it is supposed to be able to keep them busy chasing their tails for a good, long time."

Eddie was again in thought, "I don't know Sammy…who would have access to that kind of technology?"

"I would say people with connections and lots of money. I also believe they are involved with some competitor in the power industry."

"Hmmm, could be…might be FPL. They're already selling power out on the grid that we usually supply. This is starting to make more sense."

Samir was exulting inwardly, "He also pointed out that every glitch would require investigation and testing by the mechanics…is that not you?"

It was Eddie's turn to think exulting thoughts, "Yeah, it would be. How's this thing supposed to get all that done?"

"That is the part where we, er, you fit in. It must be placed close to the reactor so that the signals appear to originate from the, how do you say, sensors?"

"Yeah, it's covered up in em…So the deal is we have to get this thing in and hide it close to the vessel," said Eddie thoughtfully.

"Uh, vessel?" feigned Sammy.

"Containment…Containment vessel."

Eddie's mind was working now…Fifty grand…He was thinking of the D-ring bust. It had made the dungeon area around the reactor the "kiss of death". As far as he knew no one ventured down there anymore for fear of reprisal. Then the light went on; the dump run.

"Any idea what this contraption looks like or how big it is?"

"Uh, he said it would fit in a large suitcase."

"I need to know for sure…I got an idea."

"He mentioned something else…it's pretty heavy."

"Why, electronic stuff ain't that heavy."

Samir thought himself pretty clever but kept the demure expression, "It seems that the transmitter part must be protected from the radiation to work reliably. It is encased in lead sheeting."

A small flag of suspicion flashed through Eddies mind and was squashed almost as fast. It was a logical jump to the protection theory and greed was in the driver's seat now. But if the thing was too heavy, the D-ring was out.

"How heavy we talking?"

"About a hundred and fifty pounds."

Eddie's jaw dropped, "Dude, that's crazy. They think I can waltz in there with a hundred and fifty pound package like I'm carrying lunch. Forget it."

Now Samir launched into reverse psychology mode; he sighed, "I think you are right Edward. If they wish to do something so crazy, they should hire experts. We should walk away and let someone else do it."

"Someone else…who they gonna get if we turn em down?"

"I do not know, but they seem very intent on going through with it."

Eddie was silent, thinking, "Crap…I guess for that kind of money you could get ex-military guys if you wanted."

The dump run light flickered back on, "You know, this still might be doable."

"What?"

"Listen Sammy, you're in this up to your gills; you're gonna have to get in deeper. And we might need someone else."

"Why?"

"Cause dude, if this thing weighs that much you can't really move it too far by yourself...no offense."

"Ah no, not offended, but where would I be moving it to?"

"The dump."

"The plant's dump?"

"Yeah, if it was done during third shift, there's virtually no one watching that area."

Samir contained his glee, "But Edward, even if I could do that, how would you get it inside...especially by yourself?"

Eddie smiled with a sly expression, "I know something that just might work."

WELL, that hadn't gone as bad as it might have. It was one thing to read a Scripture about Almighty God saying *"Come let us reason together"*; it was another thing entirely to do so face to face. And yet, that's where Arak had just come from. His mind felt as it always did after one of these sessions with Father. It was as if things had to spool down mentally and return to a sense of reality.

Even with the affection that was evident, creations just didn't stand face to face with their Creator and feel like it was some little conversation between family members. Anyone who let that thought surf through their thinking had never tried it. This was particularly so if you were advocating something you knew was against Father's usual "code of conduct". But this time it had been encouraging.

271

He was keeping abreast of a plot to utterly devastate things on Amos little part of planet Earth. Nothing was truly hidden from the "eyes" of God. But whether that devastation would be allowed to come to fruition was still apparently in question. Arak was well aware that Father had been forced to witness greater tragedies than this simply because he was God and his words were inviolate. He had granted these creatures a will like His own and would not often interfere in matters they were intent on orchestrating; good or bad. However, Lucifer's game of bending the rule book was paying dividends.

He had suspected as much upon hearing of the intervention on Jenny's behalf. That had been a marked departure from protocol. The common denominator was the individual degrees of faith of those involved. He had to smile. If any two beings on Earth had reason to feel their faith lifted above the norm, Jenny and Amos were probably it. And he was a player in that scenario. There was no use denying it, he was both proud and gratified at Father's trust.

Not a destructive pride, rather one that tuned outward and glorified the source of these decisions and actions. That was a pretty accurate description, he thought. No being could work in harmony with the Great I Am without some of that glory being shared with them. It was the same "sharing" Jesus had spoken of in the Earth Scriptures. However, those words, sacred as they were, didn't do the actual experience justice. So many things here fit that comparison.

And so, Father was intently watching the situation. The First Ranks involved were reporting directly on any open discrepancies; a list that was growing longer by the Earth day. And now Arak had a green light for maybe a little bending of his own. It would depend on how things transpired from this point...but he was hopeful.

ANGELS AND DEMONS, poisonous snakes, nuclear reactors in peril...You would think there was no way anyone involved in such insanity would be able to relax and let their guard down. You would have failed to reckon with the power of the Holy Spirit.

Arak had surmised correctly; one end result, of all this apparent chaos, was that the members in the drama were operating on a plane of faith never before experienced. When dealing with a mind that has already begun to see Earthly life as a temporary passing through, while heading for a destination of indescribable joy, your average everyday threat of death and destruction loses a little of its steam anyway. Such was the case for Amos and Jenny prior to beginning this "adventure". Now it had been intensified to a finely honed edge.

The unflappable Jim fit with them like a peg in its matching hole. And Bubba; well what can we say about Bubba. The world could use a few more canines who take the title Man's Best Friend as solidly to heart as that furry bundle of muscle.

That is not to say their awareness level dipped below safe parameters. Still, the day after Jenny's introduction to marine motorsports with the dolphins, the four of them were once more gathered in Amos' "two dollar" kitchen with its million dollar view. The subject of discussion had nothing to do with the more epic experiences of late; dinner was again the topic at hand. The usual fish fry had given way to plans for ribs on his small grill.

Amos had secured another day's leave from the plant and, earlier, had raced out to Appointment Hole with Jim. The two of them had snorkeled for a couple of hours while intermittently recounting dive stories and getting better acquainted. Jim had pronounced these "holes" as one of the more stunning underwater experiences he'd had in years.

He found the size of the fish inhabiting such shallow water incredible. The passage of a ten foot hammerhead through their area did nothing to detract from that mind set. However they weren't shooting and offered nothing of serious interest to the apex predator. They had simply gotten in the boat and watched him gracefully circle a few times before losing interest and moving on.

Now Jenny was busy peeling potatoes as Amos kept bumping elbows with her while preparing ingredients to bake what he termed his "Famous Tug Boat Biscuits". Jim had appointed himself grill-master and was wandering in and out eyeing the condition of the charcoal mound as it slowly combusted its way to a satisfactory glow. Bubba was happily dividing his time between the kitchen preparations and keeping Jim company, secure in the knowledge Amos would never let him miss out on barbeque.

Despite this idyllic setting, the conversation did finally wind its way around to the more serious matters at hand and possible defensive maneuvers.

"You're not worried?"

Amos looked at her quizzically, "About?"

"Not being at the plant."

"Oh, OK; there's so much I could legitimately 'worry' about, you lost me. You mean if something was to happen."

"Yeah."

"The way I see it, I've been forced to be some kind of common denominator. If the Devil really wants me silenced, and that's where he plans to do it, then he'll wait till I'm there. And if he can't wait and wants to come here, then the nuclear part should be out of the equation; kind of a win-win."

He looked at the expression on Jenny's face for two seconds and then they simultaneously started laughing.

"Amos, that has got to be the worst win-win of all time."

He looked sheepish, "Yeah, maybe I should phrase that differently."

"Oh no, I understand exactly what you mean. I just don't think many people would think of it in a win context."

"Win what?" asked Jim coming through the door.

"Oh nothing, Amos was just hoping Lucifer and his buddies would show up here for dinner."

"That's not exactly what I meant."

Jim stared questioningly at the two of them, then looked down at Bubba, "Oh to be young again...or not. Well, I'm putting these ribs on...if you're expecting guests, tell me now. Come on boy."

With that Jim and Bubba marched sedately out the door and headed for the grill. Amos and Jenny looked at each other a little open mouthed and again started laughing.

"Not much rattles him does it?"

"You have no idea. When he was a teenager the bets ranged from President to the electric chair. People still have a hard time believing he's a church guy."

Amos gazed out the kitchen window and eyed the pair of characters tending his grill. They were back-dropped by that sweeping panorama he'd come to love.

"When I was a kid I thought the 'Jesus Freaks' sometimes used religion to hide from the world. I thought of them as weak...and I guess some were. I got in a couple of scraps defending a few in high school."

"You sound like dad...always sticking up for the under dog."

"Maybe; I wouldn't mind that...your dad is one of the neatest guys I ever met."

"Don't you mean cool?" grinned Jenny.

"That too...but there's something else."

Jenny waited silently.

"Whatever is going on these days, it seems to be attracting quite a variety of folks to the Cross. And one variety I've noticed, are the warriors."

"Oh...another common chord for you guys. Dad has a whole little study on that. He'll take you on a Bible tour of all the warriors God has used throughout history. Know who his favorite is...David."

"Oh yeah, a man after God's own heart. Know who mine is...Peter."

Jenny's mouth fell open. "Peter...your favorite is Peter...mine too."

"Really, why...I mean after all he denied Jesus, right?"

"Yeah, cause nobody else had the guts to be in the courtyard with him."

"He's the only guy that knows what walking on water feels like too...no one else got out of the boat."

Jenny looked serious, "I haven't met many other people who stopped to consider that, it's always the three denials thing."

"I know."

Now she was quiet for several more long moments, "Amos...if we're not out of the boat yet...I have the feeling we're about to be."

He gave a small sigh, "Jen...I can feel the water lapping at my heels...And I don't want to let Him down."

"You won't," said Jenny quietly, then reached out and took his hand.

CHAPTER 21

WHILE THESE ACTIVITIES were underway at Amos' place, Matt Robbins was flying the "Bird" north along the Gulf shoreline for yet another visit to CR3. To his east, and a thousand feet below, the islands of Ozello lay scattered across the estuarial plain like some nomadic fishing village from another era. He now knew approximately where Amos lived by keying in on the much more "modern", if dilapidated, appearing marina. It had a double wide boat ramp and one big metal building with racks for storing boats. There was a weathered looking asphalt parking area, perforated with weeds, and a small concrete block office building. He'd never seen much activity around it. Southwest lay the undulating row of scattered dwellings on the bank of Fish Creek which included his friends place. Maybe the one of the best friends he'd ever have.

After all these years his mother's prayers had finally been answered; he "got it". Now, looking back across that same divide, he wondered why he'd never been able to grasp it before. Must be like Amos had stated; man says prove it and I'll believe it...God says believe it and I'll prove it. Amos...the man was an epic part of his life now. He'd certainly never heard God's purposes explained the way he did it. You could look in his eyes and see the absolute conviction he had. And Matt was starting to understand why.

Every morning found him with his face in the Bible. And like as not, he'd be reading it at bedtime too. He was hungry to know what instructions, history lessons and warnings Almighty God had chosen to give man. He'd had several chances to talk with Amos about passages he was studying; both in person and over the phone. He was always impressed by the knowledge the young man had accumulated. He was confident that if you could start a Scripture, most times Amos could finish it. But lots of church people could quote Scripture. Amos also brought a clarity and understanding to it that made the whole stage of Creation come to life like some hit Broadway play.

God had designs and purposes for everything and every part of His "Great Plan". Man was a small, but important, component of it. And that was now both exhilarating and sad for him to think about. Most people would never bother to explore the possibility. They would look around themselves and search the Earth, even the heavens, to know and understand the created things; without ever getting to know the Creator. Now...Matt knew Him. Under a starry sky the night before he had tried to open his heart to God and apologize for his old life. It wouldn't come out. Instead a small flame seemed to kindle in his heart and as he looked up at the night sky it felt almost like he was looking at that mighty face. In an indescribable burst of joy he whispered to that starry countenance, "I know who you are". It was humbling to think that God was just as delighted with the exchange as he was.

The Scriptures were so right...all things were being made new. He acknowledged he was a work in progress, but that was as it should be. He was beginning to understand the geography of "time" as God had laid it out here on Earth. There were peaks and valleys in all of history and in every life. There were some appointments and destinations that would not change or be denied. But interspersed, and instrumental to the placement of these, were the myriad wanderings of beings with the right to choose their own path. Admittedly, in this life, some had more freedom to do so than others.

He lived in a free nation and in relative luxury compared with much of the world. He'd never appreciated that fact more than now. It shamed him to think how callously for-granted he had taken such things in the past. The lives of those called to the fields of less fortunate nations as missionaries, suddenly made more sense as well. They battled to bring some quality of life to the poor and struggling trapped in such circumstances, while lacing it with a dose of ultimate Truth. The confidence that there was a destination that overrode and over shadowed this "life, no matter what cards you were dealt here.

Truth; now there was a subject he once thought he was a student of. What a sad joke. There wasn't enough "absolute truth" floating around anymore to support a row boat. Everyone lied...mostly for some sort of gain. From the Whitehouse down to the local authorities and all through the "citizenry", lying was so accepted, people no longer gave it a second thought. Yet God had said "*Thou shalt not lie*" and then went on to promise liars a one way trip to the

Lake of Fire...the second death. So what was the biggest lie? That there was no God? That there was no Hell? That there was no "destination"? How had a nation, which had once adopted "In God We Trust" as a motto, ever gotten so far off track? Now he knew the answer; Sin.

Amos had talked about what he termed "Sin Number One". The first step towards Hell in a person's life; failure to acknowledge God's sovereignty. Yeah...that made sense. The first step towards a life of self worship would be to remove the chief obstacle. The one you were intended to worship by design. It also removed the "light" of truth, which illuminated those sins, so you could continue to do them in the darkness with a clear conscience. He'd certainly made a science of that one.

So why did it all seem so obvious now. It was a little weird that someone like him could have their mental state reprogrammed this far, this fast. There was only one explanation, the Gift. He understood from reading and talking to Amos how powerful the presence of the Holy Spirit was. The Bible specifically called him the Holy Spirit of Truth. Now Matt understood that was what had transpired the other afternoon.

Amos had brought some sudden truth to his table because of his own obedience to God. Then the Holy Spirit had taken time to body slam the point home with conviction. Could he have resisted and walked away? Ordinarily he would have said yes; but that strange dream with his mom and the taxi's? Reading about the seeds and the different ground? It all seemed to have been set in motion for some purpose. He thought...I feel...I feel as if I'm beginning the greatest adventure of my life. No, that wasn't quite right. Something had happened that now made life an adventure in itself...maybe it was purpose. What God thought his purpose should be still seemed a little mysterious. But, from now on, he would find Matt an obedient co-conspirator.

A voice had been in his head-set for several seconds now, "Matt...hey Matt...we going to Cedar Key?"

"What...Oh, holy smokes...Sorry Charlie."

Crystal River 3 was fast disappearing to their starboard quarter. Matt had flown right by it.

"Hang on Charlie", he said and put the Bird into a swooping, military grade dive. The plant reappeared on the windscreen and zoomed into focus at warp speed.

"Wheeooo!" bellowed Charlie over the headphones. Matt just smiled.

He reversed the turn and lined up his usual landing zone with barely a reduction in the rate of descent. At the last second he threw the chopper into a powerful flare and bled off the airspeed. They seemed to barely slide over the restricted area fencing, then transition into a perfect skids down landing. He left the power spooled up for a few seconds and looked over at Charlie.

"Holy Hell...what has gotten into you?" but he was grinning from ear to ear.

Matt throttled down and cut the fuel flow. After their mock bomb run it seemed suddenly peaceful in the cockpit. Only the whine of the turbine spooling down penetrated the Dave Clark head sets.

Charlie was still looking at him with a question in his eyes, "I mean it...you've been different now for days...what's up?"

Matt was treated to that light mental "tap" on the shoulder he would come to know so well. He smiled back at Charlie, "You know what...If you're really interested, I'd like to tell you about it."

Matt Robbins, evangelist, had just stepped up...to center stage. And in Heaven...the Angels sang.

NOT LONG AFTER MATT AND CHARLIE LANDED, a nondescript sedan pulled in and parked near the same spot where Jenny and her dad had been sitting the day before. Pytor's nerves were on full alert and he felt uncomfortably exposed this close to their intended target. His orders, however, were clear. Contact Samir, and make use of the facility's background radiation to mask the SADM against any mischance detection. He sat quietly and eyed the activity surrounding the nuclear structure. Slowly he relaxed to a small degree. The huge area involved, along with the number of civilians racing about, actually made pretty good cover.

He knew the Gulf of Mexico lay just beyond the vast complex; he could smell the salt marshes on the breeze. According to the Intel, there was a debris area on the far side where workers removed non-radiant materials for disposal or incineration. Samir had hinted that this was an avenue past security but no details were forthcoming. Pytor was surely not going anywhere near the restricted zones in broad daylight. Nightfall would be a different story.

Over the years he and his teams had infiltrated far more deadly arenas of interest. Still, only now did he begin to have some faith in the info obtained thus far. The stream of traffic in and out of the massive complex made any attempt at safeguarding it an operations nightmare. The fact that he was sitting at this range, eyeing a US nuclear facility, while in the company of a tactical grade weapon, was heady stuff. A small smile moved the corners of his mouth.

While he was in the act of picturing a huge mushroom cloud over a burned out and shattered version of the scene before him, a lift bed truck, bearing the livery and logo of the power firm, entered his view. It materialized from where he surmised the "dump" area to be located. This could be the very disposal assignment Samir had spoken of. A golden opportunity to observe the security check on re-entry, but his eye level view was partially blocked by the adjacent vehicles. His thoughts raced around a moment, then he reached into the back seat and snatched up a black ball cap bearing the famous Caterpillar equipment logo. Placing it on his head, he got out of the vehicle and leaned against it while lighting a cigarette. He was already clad in work type clothing and boots and could easily be mistaken for just another worker taking a break. A big muscle-bound one.

He looked as relaxed as possible while eyeing the activity going on some three hundred feet away. The truck carried a driver and two men standing in the bed itself. Those two were in animated conversation and appeared oblivious to all else. Another small smile; blue collar workers did not vary much the world over. He could easily imagine the mundane topics of wine, women and song that were dancing through their dialogue. Looking at his watch he thought it unfortunate for them that they were on this particular shift. Today was perhaps one of the last they would get to experience.

The mechanical gate began to retract on its large rubber wheels and a chunky, uniformed security guard waddled out carrying some long handled device. He engaged briefly in conversation with the man driving the vehicle. After a moment, he passed the drivers window and thrust the device under the truck. Pytor saw the afternoon sun glint momentarily off a polished surface. Of course; a mirror. Perhaps they were more alert than it first seemed. That notion was squashed by the haphazard and half-hearted look the guard gave the under carriage. He glanced briefly into the bed, said a few words to the men standing there and then returned to the driver's window. After some more inane appearing chatter, he waved the vehicle through.

That was it? This was security at an American nuclear facility? Pytor slid back into his driver's seat and slumped there in mild disbelief. Then the smile once again creased his rugged features.

AT LAST; it was going to happen. Father was going to send him back in to intervene on behalf of Amos' little group. It appeared the diabolical operation Lucifer had concocted involving the Eastern Fanatics, was not to be. Instead, Arak would be permitted to elaborate, to a degree, on the identities and plans that were swirling around this obscure little backwater like some forming tornado.

Armed with such information, he was sure Amos could employ his own talents, and the Spirit's guidance, to formulate some counter action against the increasingly grim plot. One which Father had now deemed too far "out of bounds". The sense of relief that coursed through the mighty angel's own mind was shared by his fellows; including his long time mentor, the esteemed Raphael.

"Arak, my son, timing will be paramount on this one."

"More so than usual I gather, sir?"

Raphael nodded, "You cannot go in early nor can you be late. I am familiar with your trademark tactic of misdirection as far as entry points. If you plan to employ this once again, you must allow for both the secondary transfer and any obstruction Lucifer may manage to place in your path. He too is aware that ploy exists. Should he delay you as he did last time, things may alter to the point we cannot legitimately prevent a bad conclusion."

It seemed Arak had felt the burden and pressure of war-time tactics and decisions all his life. And that included both Deran and the Kingdom. But this time the weight of responsibility seemed to rest on his massive shoulders like the globe he'd seen on the mythical Atlas statues of Earth. Probably more accurate this time, he thought uncomfortably.

Father had shown him that these actions, which centered on Amos, had ramifications and repercussions that swept out across the Earth, and its "time", like tentacles. Tentacles that could be either positive or negative based on the variety of outcomes possible. This was one of the mysteries of the Great Plan.

Every created being of "free will", had an existence which was laid out like a massive roadway map. One that showed every major highway, minor state road, two lane by-way or little dirt trail. The intersections were the decisions, great and small, that entity made along the journey termed "life". Each one had results, good, bad or sometimes indifferent. New avenues and directions were constantly presenting themselves based on the choices made. And these "life trails" crossed and re-crossed one another creating a truly limitless number of scenarios involving many other lives. Often at the most unexpected or unforeseen of moments. It was a maze no other mind in the Cosmos would be able to follow or keep track of.

Only Almighty God knew the direction and possibilities of each and every single or series of choices. He also knew the array of possible outcomes that flexed and changed in a fluid manner based on these decisions. Even the series that would eventually culminate in that one appointment no Earther got to miss...Death. Along the way, the options were entirely at the whim and discretion of the particular individual.

So while a human could never actually fool God about their direction in life, you could sure disappoint Him or surprise Him with the ones you decided to take. Sometimes you could even warm that mighty heart. It was one main reason why He had created man; fellowship. And because of the plan for the Earth, involving the momentous sacrifice made by the Christ, He was more than willing to let His own Spirit act as navigator along the way...Not many took Him up on the offer these days.

So now, despite the indifference and disloyalty, which had descended like some spiritual plague to infect the majority of the little planet's current occupants, Father would once again act in the manner befitting that title...He would try to protect His children...even from themselves.

CHAPTER 22

THE RIB DINNER had come and gone in pleasant, satisfactory style. Now, once again, the little group was seated at Amos' picnic table eyeing the approaching sunset. The weathered table had assumed a status of its own during the events and drama of late. Not only had it been involved in several memorable moments, it was also strategically placed on a small projection of land which was part of the shoreline comprising Amos' southerly property line. When seated here, one could catch the breezes, view the surrounding marshes, and enjoy a stellar view of each glorious sunset. All in all, it made a pretty nice "conference room".

Jim was listening to the two younger members spar over who had KP duty. He was not surprised at the apparent affection which seemed to be blossoming between them. He doubted any two humans had ever met under stranger circumstances; or had a more dynamic spiritual bond thrust into their lives. As a father, he had no doubt he could count on Jenny to keep things in line on that front. And he harbored no doubts about Amos' intentions either. The fact was they made an almost perfect pair. If it were to progress to a totally serious level, he'd gladly welcome Amos into their little family.

He brought himself up mentally with a start. One, here he was supposedly older and wiser and he was getting the cart before the horse like a teenager. Two, they would all have to survive whatever was coming at them to return to such mundane concerns.

"OK; you made a bigger mess with your biscuits than I did with the vegetables," said Jenny.

"Did you eat any of them?"

"Of course...so what?"

"Did you enjoy it?"

"Oh, so now you're fishing for more compliments. We already admitted to the royalty of your biscuits oh master tugboat chef."

Jim broke in, "Tugboat chef?"

Jenny looked at her dad, "That's right, you missed that part. He doesn't just call them tugboat biscuits, that's where he learned to make them; in Jacksonville of all places."

Jim looked at Amos quizzically.

"When I was in my late teens, I got a job on some river tugs that pushed oil barges on the St. Johns. It was just dumb luck. They needed someone to dive under the boats once in a while and I showed up wearing a dive t-shirt looking for work. That was about ten in the morning on a Thursday. The guy picked my brain for a while then told me to be back at the dock at four. Till then I had hardly ever been away from home. It would be forty two days before I saw it again."

"Wow," said Jim, "that's almost a military crash course."

"It felt like the military. Anyway, the two jobs for deckhands were loading the petroleum products, for which we had to take the Coast Guard test and get a license, and cooking. I didn't much mind loading the barges but after a while it was boring. Cooking was less time consuming, or boring, and those guys love to eat. When they gave me a shot at it, I scrounged up an old Betty Crocker cookbook of my mom's and happened to find that biscuit recipe."

Here he smiled, "Then I sort of customized it."

"Which he will not tell you about," interjected Jenny. "I should have paid more attention a while ago."

"Well," said her father, "no denying they're tasty, what happened?"

"I guess you could say the crew became biscuit addicts. I made them every morning for breakfast and again for dinner."

"What...twice a day...did any of the crew wind up as round as the biscuits?" exclaimed Jenny.

"Not really, it's pretty physical out there. Even for the wheelhouse guys. I don't remember any of them ever being really overweight."

Jim had a sly smile, "Not like the church people you wrote about, huh?"

Amos paused, surprised, "You saw that?"

"Duh," stated Jenny, "how'd you think we knew where to find you? Dad's been reading your stuff for a while."

"You know, in all the excitement, I never thought to ask. Guess I figured God just set it up somehow."

"Yeah," said Jim, "technically that's probably true. You've been obeying him by writing stuff no one really wants to hear; we're just some readers that happened to come along."

It was Amos turn to grin, "Yeah, just came along. I imagine we'll have to wait to find out everything that's really gone on behind the scenes during all this."

Jenny's face took on a more pensive look, "Don't count on it. I saw what's going on in Rome, remember."

At that moment Bubba sat up from where he'd been tracking the conversation and gave his low "groof".

The other three stopped and listened intently. Jenny felt prickles run up her spine. Any time Bubba went on alert, she now expected something serious to follow. Amos pointed back to the northeast.

"One of the mullet guys is coming."

Sure enough the whine of an outboard motor was growing steadily closer. Bubba had sprung to his feet and now he raced off down the easterly bank. He'd no sooner reached the point made by the intersection of the distant canal when a reddish brown boat shot out into the bay. It looked like it had been built backwards. The outboard was housed in a square box just behind the bow and the driver was straddling the bow with one leg on each side. A pole of some sort protruded from the motor to his right hand.

The craft executed a sweeping, high speed turn and headed in their direction. As it straightened out they heard the motor RPM start to wind up. The next second Bubba streaked past and then the boat screamed by trying to catch him. The driver was a burly, redheaded man with a full, Viking looking beard and as he shot past he raised his right arm and waved energetically.

"Yo, Preacher!"

Amos waved just as enthusiastically, "Yo Barney, go get him."

In a few moments the boat was gone around the far bend and they could see Bubba hitting the brakes where the next canal fed in. It wasn't possible to pick the winner from where they sat.

As the wash from the little display lapped at the rocky seawall, Jenny eyed Amos, "Let me guess, more racing."

"Uh, yeah...don't know who likes it more, Bubba or the guys."

"What kind of boat is that?" asked Jim.

"A 'well' boat. Notice how high it was in the bow? The prop is just under the boat itself. Gives them more clearance running around these shallow waters. That rig will run forty miles an hour across eighteen inches of water. Jerry let's me use his a lot. I've been running along in water so shallow you don't dare stop; you just stay on a plane and keep hoping."

"Yow, that would be a little scary."

Jenny looked thoughtful as Bubba arrived panting happily, "I thought they didn't go out at nights any more."

"Most don't...Barney couldn't care less...I think he is one of the aliens."

"Speaking of," said Jim "I saw some lights and activity last night that fits your description."

Both youngsters looked at him, "Pretty high up, with what appears to be normal color lights for aircraft...red, green, clear; but move in that fast, stop, start motion you talked about."

"That would be them...as far as I know. Guys like Barney claim to have seen them closer up. One thing they all agree on is they're wedge shaped. Sort of like a flying wing."

Jenny plopped her head on her arms, "Please, please...don't add aliens to our list of things to worry about."

"Sorry, I think they were already here," said Amos.

Jim laughed, "Check it out...three Bible thumping church goers talking about UFO's."

"Other sheep pens," chuckled Amos.

"Oh, sweet Lord above, you win...I'll do the dishes," said Jenny and stood up.

Amos grinned up at her, "Take Bubba, I think he's too tough even for the aliens. I'll be in to help in a second."

Jenny glared at him with her trademark mock ferocity, "You'd best be, Mr. Mikals."

Amos raised both arms in supplication, "Yes bwana missy, I be there."

Jim laughed, Jenny spun to hide her smile and Bubba fell into step. The two men sat a while in contemplative silence soaking up the scenery around them. Then Amos spoke,

"Jim, what happened to her mom?"

"Cancer...seven years ago."

"Very sorry to hear that." He thought to himself...that's the second mom gone seven years I've heard about lately.

Jim looked out over the marshes, "Not to worry Amos, she was a true believer if ever there was one. I swear sometimes I can feel her watching us."

Amos was silent a moment, "Yeah, like my granny, Etta."

"Etta...I like that...Jenny's mom was Christine."

"Granny, put me on the path early...after my parents broke up. I was eight years old. I can't know for sure, but I think she stepped in and saved my soul."

"Hmm...not sure I'd have done so well without Jenny's mom either. She definitely helped finish getting the rough edges off; knew her since we were kids. Fact is, in high school, her parents didn't even want her speaking to me."

Amos chuckled, "Why is it I find that so easy to believe."

Jim grinned back, "And I suppose you were always a choir boy?"

"Nope, I'm afraid what we have here is a table of miscreants somehow redeemed for the Lord's purposes."

Jim was again thoughtful, "Amos, this thing goes wrong, watch over my daughter."

He also paused, "Jim, I would be honored to accept that responsibility, but I'm afraid if this one goes wrong, we won't have to worry about it...Still, if anything leads to that, you can count on me. Speaking of, I better go keep my promise before Pocahontas comes back and scalps me."

Jim smiled and nodded as Amos departed. Then he looked back out at the vast, marshy prairie to the south. He could hear her voice in his mind repeating those familiar words, "James Alexander, you be careful."

He looked up at the crystal blue sky which was backlit by the orange and gold colors of sunset, "I'll try my best honey...Maybe put in a good word for us with The Boss."

At that moment a towering thunderhead, perched on the southwest horizon like some giant, translucent anvil, let go with one of those faint rumbles that seems to echo on forever. Jim just smiled and bowed his head.

BLONDE CREW CUT, square jaw, piercing ice blue eyes and a Marine Corp. physique...Eddie's first glimpse of

Sammy's third party was a little disconcerting. It got worse when he spoke. All this guy needed was a glass of vodka and the Kremlin for a back drop.

"I am pleased to meet you."

Eddie almost filled in the unspoken "Comrade", "Uh, same here...How was the drive from Miami?"

"You know, same old scenery...boring."

Eddie did know, he'd made the trip often enough, but some little warning bell prevented his asking more specifics, "Yeah, that run down the Trail can be a hassle...So you guy's used to work together?"

Sammy jumped in, "Not exactly; when I ran the grocery for my father, Peter used to drive for one of the companies which delivered to us."

Eddie just nodded. It was another late weeknight at the Orange Blossom and there were only a few diehards in attendance. Most of them pretty well sloshed.

Sammy seemed to pick up on his discomfort and launched into a conversation with Peter. From this, he deduced that the man and his family were, in fact, Ukrainian and had settled in a small Florida town called North Port. There was apparently a good sized enclave of these foreigners at that location. This skillful, and mostly false, dialogue succeeded in allaying some of Eddie's misgivings.

They had set up camp in one of the booths along the wall and now Sammy leaned in conspiratorially, "I have explained our situation to Peter. We have known each other for many years. He will help with whatever is needed. Additionally he does not feel his involvement requires a full share, I will pay him a suitable sum from my own takings."

Eddie knew it was too late to get out of this. His instincts told him he had not dug deep enough into the whole matter, and now it looked like he was "in for a penny, in for a pound". He sighed mentally, so be it...the money would ease the pain. For the time being he had better stay sharp and get the thing done without any screw-ups. Sammy had been a decent enough guy all along; he'd have to trust this Peter too.

"Fair enough dude." Eddie didn't care what Sammy made...as long as the fifty G's came his way. And where he had previously thought of insisting on a meeting with "Smith and Jones", he now couldn't care less. The fewer people who saw his face, the better. And the sooner this thing was done, the happier he'd be.

"OK, here's what we need to do." Eddie outlined the first stage of his master plan, which really wasn't all that bad. He had purloined lots of items during his years at the plant. Among them was a good supply of the Radiation Hazard tape and the extra large, opaque yellow bags used for on-site collection from the hot zones. All such waste was clearly marked with the Milli-Rem reading and stored for relocation to one of the waste sites around the country. In the case of CR3 that meant Barnwell, South Carolina.

Eddie's plan was for Sammy and Peter to sneak the device into the dump area after placing it in one of the yellow bags and taping it securely with the hazard tape. He instructed them on how to label the MR reading sufficiently high so that anyone accidentally stumbling across it would give it a wide berth. An unfortunate event like that might result in the alarm being raised. Then again, maybe not.

There had already been one incident where some contaminated lumber accidentally made it to the dump site. Only to be discovered by one of the guys who initially thought he could use it on his living room remodel. He had carted it home without opening the outer covering only to discover the inner warning layers in the presence of his wife and daughter. When the dust settled, and the facts were laid out, it became clear no one in management wanted the story to go any further. The event had already become a plant "urban legend" with said worker supposedly receiving some "remodeling" money to keep quiet. Eddie didn't know about that but he had seen the wood. That part was true and nobody was broadcasting it. His little endeavor might get the same treatment if things went awry.

Once they were successful in reaching the relatively unguarded dump area, they could place it in one of the empty fifty-five gallon drums which were always in attendance. They would need to mark the drum so Eddie could pick it out on the nightly run. He would take it from there.

"So dude," he said to Sammy, "Will this thing fit in a drum? That's twenty four inches at the opening and about thirty five high. And where is it now?"

"I do not know for sure about the sizing. I am supposed to pick the unit up tomorrow. We will not know actual measurements until then."

"Well, that's the best I got. If it doesn't work out, I'm not sure we can pull it off."

The taciturn Peter had not offered any comment during Eddie's recital of his plan, but those chilling eyes seemed to be measuring and taking in everything, including their surroundings. Now he spoke,

"It will probably work. I suggest we get some rest. By lunch tomorrow we should have the details, yes?" He said this while eyeing Sammy.

"That is most likely; I will make contact as early as possible."

"Fine by me dude; I'm ready for some rack. You got my number, I need to know ASAP."

And with that, they said their goodbyes and parted company. This resulted in somewhat of an additional scramble as several of the assigned "watchers" and First Ranks made their own dimensional departures to report to their commanders. Those left behind continued the vigil aware that every move these humans were making seemed to turn the screw a little tighter on an already tense situation. It looked like serious trouble loomed on the horizon...no matter which way this thing went.

"DO YOU NOT NOTE THE PATTERN?" inquired Lucifer.

"Ah, Sire, I fear I do not."

Buferan was standing before his diabolical leader staring at some strange figure which seemed to be made of fiery, glittering lines. They hovered on the tips of the most awful "fingers" the Earth would ever know. It was like a mobile or mosaic that pulsed with some inner power. These lines crossed and re-crossed over darker ones that seemed to repeat at regular intervals. The result was a three dimensional, cylindrical figure with tapering ends. Often, where the lines intersected, bright pinpoints of color were present. Some were ruby red, others an emerald green.

Buferan's confusion was not surprising. Lucifer himself had performed the "study" that resulted in this display and no other creature had knowledge of it. He had even shielded it as best possible from the One himself. He was unsure what measure of interest this attempt might have aroused but he was hopeful that the multiple avenues and feints had muddied the water sufficiently to avoid attracting that massive, troublesome intellect...at least for a short time. The fact was such a hologram had appeared only once before in all of Earth's history. And this one would soon be nothing but a memory.

"You have often wondered about the actual details of the capture of Kurtanus, have you not?"

"Yes Majesty."

"You see before you the answer."

The bewildered countenance of the massive under lord continued for several moments. Then there was a mental start that widened the giant, serpent-like eyes.

"That is Earth and those are the entry points of the Deranian."

"Bravo," said Lucifer, "they are indeed; but for two Deranians. Look closely."

He scrutinized the figure intently then sighed, "Sire, I must confess I do not understand."

The evil smile, of that most damnable of creatures, crept across the fearsome visage, "It is of little consequence, but I will enlighten you. You are aware of His love for the mechanics underlying the act of creation."

It was a statement and Buferan only nodded.

"You are also aware these humans share that affinity," another nod.

"Well, although I have yet to visit Deran, I am convinced the natives there also mimic that trait. These patterns fit a well known Earth concept; something they call the 'the golden ratio'. However, our little Deranians have each thrown in a twist of their own. While every entry point is essentially a mathematical extension or retraction of the one used before, it is always uncertain whether the progression will be to the east or to the west. In addition the subsequent secondary transfer, for which they are so renowned, employs another rational shift based on an obscure formula. One, which I admit, took some little while to unravel...especially for Arak...behold."

The cylinder seemed to rotate briefly and a new point of fire burst into existence amidst the other lines and points. Then the continents of Earth appeared as well, laid out in glistening, inky black lines. A grunt issued from Buferan.

"Yes, you are no doubt familiar with that particular locale, are you not?"

A matching evil grin exposed the hideous maw of his subordinate, "It is where we captured Kurtanus."

"Yes, and you wondered how I knew where to send you. The answer is before you."

Buferan's eyes widened yet again, "I see it...We almost always knew, or suspected, the destinations but that would always prove too late to attempt an action. The most vulnerable moment was upon entry. You used this to reverse his course from the suspect destination?"

"Again, bravo, that is exactly what happened."

Buferan's eyes glittered with pent up malice "Sire, are you telling me you can apply this to the other Deranian as well?"

"Yes, watch." The cylinder again rotated and the peninsula of Florida appeared with a bright emerald point ablaze over the tiny village of Ozello. The great, satanic leader snapped his huge fingers over that point. A new pair of lines appeared originating at the emerald juncture and then went racing away in opposite directions. Buferan watched spellbound. The cylinder seemed to quiver and the lines became wavy and indistinct.

"This is where their clever little formula is applied. I believe the whole matter has something to do with back tracking or locating one another."

Suddenly the figure stabilized and resumed its original state. Buferan recognized the continent of Europe and the point of his latest confrontation with that most troublesome Third Rank.

"This was how you directed us to his location last time?"

"I was able to get you close enough to lay the deception."

"Which very nearly succeeded."

"Yes...in the case of Kurtanus, he blundered in much closer and we were fortunate to choose the correct of the two possibilities. Since that time I have unraveled their little feint to a higher degree; again, observe."

The lines and points resumed their wavering, fluid look. Then the cylinder rotated once more before again resuming its stable form. A new series of lines emanated from the Ozello point. Once again the globe began its rotation, this time westerly, and came to rest at the junction point of the first pair of lines. It lay in the vast expanse of the Pacific Ocean far away from any land mass.

Buferan eyed it skeptically, "That, Sire, is a possible point of entry?"

"It is...it fits their little spiral system exactly."

"I have never known the Deranian, or his counter part, to use the waters before."

"Nor do I believe he will do so now. To miscalculate that possibility, however, would be unfortunate. As you well know, our best chance to assemble the necessary strength, and make the capture, is immediately upon entry...at the moment of highest vulnerability."

"Yes Highness, I understand. It would be a great misfortune to choose the wrong point. Where does the other point lie?"

The gigantic, evil smile wreathed its way across Lucifer's face once again. The cylindrical model of man's little world began another slow rotation in the opposite direction. Then, with the slightest of tremors, it stopped. The face of evil glowed with a terrible pleasure. Buferan's malignant countenance worked its way through a surprised moment, and then the same unearthly enjoyment transfixed his features as well.

Highlighted by the pulsing alternate colors, in the precise congruence of two of the fiery lines, lay his enemy's suspected point of re-entry. Possibly the exact location where the damnable Arak would make his next foray into the Earthly dimensions. And into the realm of the potentially lethal influence of this ungodly duo. It was almost poetic. There, at the intersection, sat the most influential and famous location in Biblical history...Jerusalem.

CHAPTER 23

F OUR IN THE MORNING. Although the air was still warm and sultry, the heat and humidity were nearing the daily low point for early summer in Florida. Rows of mercury vapor lights burned uniformly across much of the eastern CR3 parking lot. In the glow of these lighted areas, insect life teemed and swarmed, flashing endlessly through the hypnotic radiance. Occasionally the swoop of a bat would appear and some moth, or other insect, was subtracted from the roster of those in desynchronized orbit around these tiny artificial suns. Still, several deep pockets of shadow remained. Some of the darkest zones were near the front rows where a line of mature scrub oaks cast shadowy, distorted caricatures along many of the concrete medians.

A respectable number of vehicles thronged the area attesting to the 'round the clock' effort involved in refurbishing the atomic generating apparatus. The giant complex, elevated well above its surroundings, resided atop its perch like some medieval fortress of old. That complex had none of the shadowy pockets and dark zones found in the parking area. It sat brightly lit like a military operation preparing for combat. The air around it rang and thrummed with the roars and growls of support devices and machinery engaged in this most intricate and dangerous of ballets. A formidable dance floor where science combined with commerce to feed man's insatiable appetite for power.

None the less, you could sense the human side of the equation was not as indefatigable as their mechanical counter parts. There was not a soul to be seen. A sense of false quiet seemed to co-exist within the mechanical cacophony. These were clearly the slowly pulsing hours of the "dead of night".

From one of the darkened areas came movement. The shadowy figures of Samir and Pytor materialized next to the auto that had delivered the former Russian commando and his plutonium based nightmare. As planned, the vehicle had remained parked with its terrible secret residing nonchalantly in the trunk like a forgotten suitcase. With all the vehicles swarming in and out on every shift, no one paid the slightest attention to another middle aged sedan resting amongst the others...hide in plain sight.

Pytor unlocked the driver's door and got in. No light shown. Even a kindergarten terrorist would never leave the interior light functioning. This terrorist had his master's degree. He unlocked the passenger door and Samir joined him holding a canvas gym bag.

"Will it fit in the drum?" asked Samir.

"Only if we remove the device from the case."

"What of the timer?"

"It is inside the outer covering of the unit. There is an access panel."

Samir pointed to a large area of darkness beyond the CR3 entrance, "The dump is in that open section west of the main gate. It is mostly unlit, although there are sometimes fires smoldering from the days refuse."

"Security?"

"None; at this hour there are not even workers present. This shift rarely makes an appearance outside the perimeter."

"Shall we open the case here or look for another location?

Samir eyed the surroundings swiveling slowly left to right. "We do it here. If anyone approaches I will engage them in conversation. If possible we are just new workers waiting to clock in. If there is a problem you will have to decide whether termination is necessary. But remember, any scrutiny or disturbance at this point will likely result in 'Bird Cage' becoming our only option."

Bird Cage was a last ditch, worst case scenario. It consisted of arming a pre-set timing device on the weapon, leaving it in the trunk and ramming the main entry gates. With approximately ninety seconds of existence left, the duo of terrorist would engage any and all resistance with the cry of Allah on their lips. Well, only one would be screaming about Allah, but the other would probably inflict more damage without saying a word.

Not that it would matter. Anything within a half mile radius would not exist in its original form after the first second elapsed. Any living entity, within three miles, which looked directly into the artificial star that was briefly spawned, would never see again. In between those two zones, would be varying degrees of destruction and contamination. Given that ground zero would be adjacent to the actual containment facility, it was quite possible the radiation and fallout would get some kind of assist from the devastation of that structure. As glorious as that mental picture could be made to look, neither man really wanted to test the theory.

A grunt issued from Pytor, "Let us then be careful."

"Agreed, shall we prepare the device?"

Both men exited the sedan and Pytor quietly opened the trunk. Unexpectedly, they were seized with a moment's hesitation as they gazed in the dim light at the plain, olive green housing. After a few seconds Pytor swung into action, turned the lock-hasp catches and raised the upper half of the shell. They again paused in silent awe. To the untrained eye, the simple, canvas covered cylindrical housing would evoke no special response. To the two man audience that beheld it, it was a regular terrorist Mona Lisa.

Samir broke the spell, "How do you set the timer?"

Pytor eyed him a moment, "That is best left to me."

"Agreed, but what if something should happen to you? I would not even be able to complete the necessary final act."

The Russian thought for a moment then aimed a small penlight at the SADM. He reached under a flap on the camouflaged fabric liner and tugged back a large brass zipper exposing the silvery metal of the weapon itself. In the center of the opening was an obvious access hatch. There were two butterfly shaped, folding thumb screws at one end. Pytor flipped these upright, then twisted them in opposite directions. They popped up about an inch as if spring loaded. Then he pulled firmly up and a hinged panel about four by six inches popped open. There was a rubber gasket around the recessed lip and a series of switches along with two dial type gauges on the underlying panel.

"Old American technology," said Pytor, "in truth, some of the toughest ever produced. And what they term, user friendly."

He walked Samir through the steps necessary to set the delay or time of day then showed him the secondary arming switches.

"What of the master circuit? Must you open this to arm the weapon?"

"Once you have completed the timing, secure the hatch if possible. It is not necessary but it will delay anyone who might tamper with it. The emergency switch has now become the arming switch for the timer.

He reached a little further under the fabric exposing a recessed area where another metal cover had obviously been removed. There were scars where the hinged plate had once been. Below, in the well beneath, was an aircraft style switch with a flip up safety cover. Pytor did just that exposing a simple red toggle.

"A little custom addition is involved here. Once a timing sequence is chosen and this switch is thrown, simply reversing it will not disable the weapon. The circuit is locked from that point until detonation. Any changes in the timer will no longer be honored by the firing circuit."

Samir scanned the deserted parking area, "The last variable is whether to arm it ourselves or have the American do it."

"Why would that be necessary?"

"What if he is delayed in retrieving it? There is no guarantee as far as delivery into the facility."

Pytor was thoughtful for several moments, "Then, if it is armed, we risk detonation outside the reactor."

"Precisely."

"It would still be a great feat."

"But not nearly so great as planned," said Samir.

"So what shall we set it for?"

"One hour."

"And we rely on this man to activate it."

"Yes."

"What of Kabir's detonation 'window'?"

Samir shrugged...it was of little consequence to him when the explosion occurred, but it must be inside the reactor, "There is no help for it. We cannot now control the delivery schedule."

They were interrupted by the sound of the distant gate machinery grinding and rattling into action. Without a seconds hesitation Pytor quietly lowered the trunk lid and both men slid into the shadows on their respective sides. A dark colored sedan pulled up to the security shack and was still for a moment. Then it continued out the entrance and headed east on the main access road. Both men eyed it as it passed. Pytor's hand had unconsciously rested on the butt of a Czech CZ-52 automatic pistol where it nestled under the back of his shirt. The car passed without incident but the terrorist's already taut nerves were ratcheted up another notch.

"It is time we made the placement," said Samir.

Wordlessly they returned to the trunk. Pytor manipulated the switches and one dial gauge then turned to his partner, "It is done."

Then he looked thoughtful for a long moment, turned and appeared to recheck or redo his handiwork.

"Yes, it is as it should be."

Samir stared for a long moment at the open hatch, "Very well; close it."

Pytor did as bid, locking and folding the butterfly screws, then zipping the outer cover closed. Samir retrieved the gym bag and produced a yellow plastic rectangle. With as much stealth as possible he slowly unfolded and opened a large, standard issue containment bag. Certainly when Eddie had purloined it, he never imagined where it would wind up. He folded the upper area back and squashed it on the pavement into a rough bowl shape. Pytor leaned over the SADM, rested his legs against the car's bumper and, with a low grunt, lifted the nuclear weapon into his arms.

Using his knees he began lowering it towards the yellow plastic where Samir met his efforts. Together they positioned it upright and gently nestled the weapon inside the "rad-bag". After folding the excess portion over, Samir produced a roll of yellow tape clearly marked with the repeating words "High Radiation". He started to peel the tape and it made a typical tearing sound. It seemed unnaturally loud in the quiet of the night and both men glanced nervously about. He continued and proceeded to securely seal the neck with the tape.

"That should do," whispered Samir.

He placed the tape back in the bag and brought forth a large permanent marker. On a number of places he wrote in large letters 720 MR. Seven hundred and twenty millirems; that would earn the respect of any would be investigator who stumbled upon it. He briefly wondered what the actual exposure rate was but shrugged it off. Risk was part of the calling.

Samir aimed his own pen light at the SADM, "Position the access area towards me."

Pytor rotated the package so the over-flap of the zipper portion was visible through the translucent plastic. Samir placed a large black asterisk on the cover area and then wrote in large letters on the near end, UP.

"Alright, it is done. Make sure that end is facing up in the drum."

With only a nod, Pytor bent his iron physique to the task once more and set the cocooned weapon back in the trunk. They quietly re-entered the auto. Samir reached into the gym bag, removed a small spray can of modeling paint and then slung the bag into the back floor board.

"We must exit easterly first and return I think."

Pytor looked over towards the main gate, "Yes, let us go out and then back up for a distance."

Without a word Samir started the engine and prepared to back out of the parking space. He bumped the shift selector to reverse for only a moment before continuing to neutral. The car crept backwards and he bumped reverse once more. The backup lights barely had time to blink. It was enough; the momentum carried them clear. When the motion was almost at a stand still he engaged drive and they began to idle quietly towards the far exit hugging the shadowy darkness provided by the oaks.

As they approached the entry both men craned to see if there were any visible headlights on the long roadway leading back to US 41. Nothing; their luck was holding. They were already past the point where they were visible to the guard shack. None the less, Samir pulled around with the front of the car facing west, stopped and then began slowly backing away from the plant entrance. For a long minute they crept along in this fashion while he used the edge of the asphalt and centerline stripes to navigate in the gloom.

Finally he stopped, "Far enough?" he breathed to Pytor.

"I think yes, let us proceed."

First the fog lamps then the headlights appeared; Samir dropped the selector again to drive and accelerated to a modest speed. The CR3 entrance was soon upon them. They drove sedately past without a glance, just two workers on their way to one of the coal fired plants in the distance. In a few more seconds the dump perimeter appeared ahead on their left and Samir let off the accelerator. Pytor noted it was much as Samir had diagrammed it the night before. There was a six foot chain link fence topped with barbed wire, but at about the halfway point he could see the double swinging entry gates standing ajar; amazing.

There was one large pile of debris that still smoldered to the left of the entry and along the fencing he could see numerous fifty-five gallon drums which stood like rotund, irregularly spaced sentinels. This was the tricky part. They had been steadily losing speed, now Samir downshifted through the gears as their momentum continued to bleed off. At the last second he tapped the brakes while simultaneously switching off the lights and swinging in through the open gate. The sandy soil helped drag them to a stop and Samir killed the engine. It was nicely done.

They sat silently in the trampled entry area and scanned for evidence of human activity or notice of their little maneuver. They were some distance now from the lighted areas and all appeared quiet. Pytor looked about at the drums, some of which appeared lidded, others not. Several had the lids leaning against them or lying nearby. His eye quickly chose a convenient example less than twenty feet away.

"That one," he whispered and pointed to it.

"This close to the front gate?"

"Why not; they are everywhere and all appear similar."

Samir shrugged. It probably made as much sense as any and they had perhaps used up their portion of luck in this matter. Both men got out, repeated the action of removing the SADM and rested it on the ground. Pytor strode over to the chosen drum, lifted the lid and looked in with his pen light. There were several pieces of cardboard and some fairly large chunks of Styrofoam. He paused in thought a moment, then removed these placing them nearby before quietly laying the drum on its side.

He returned to where Samir waited nervously by the weapon, his head constantly swiveling toward the lighted areas. He nodded at the package,

"Let us do this."

With both men the burden was quite manageable. They crab-stepped over to the drum, then placed it on the ground length wise, lined up with the open cavity.

"You have the up mark, yes?"

Samir flicked his pen light at the end, "Yes."

Pytor straddled the weapon, and clasp it with both hands. He lifted the end nearest the drum and Samir quickly slid the throat under that portion.

"Again," he hissed.

Pytor slid to the far end and lifted while Samir pushed. The device was well over half way in.

"Stand it up."

Pytor did so effortlessly. There was a slight metallic thump as the SADM settled onto the drum base, but the fit was excellent. Samir reached for the lid, "Wait."

Pytor collected the packing scraps and shone his light into the opening. He quickly reinserted the pieces then gave a satisfied grunt. Samir looked into the drum. Not bad, it looked almost as if someone had measured and fit the apparatus for shipping. The "up" and two of the 720 MR's were still clearly visible...perfect.

At that moment headlights appeared on the entry road to the east. They were some distance out but the duo quickly realized the closure rate was fast. The car was obviously taking advantage of the absence of traffic to fly down the two lane byway. A guttural curse, in foreign dialect, issued from Pytor. Samir hurried to place the lid over their handiwork and quickly forced a couple of the bendable tabs back down. Then they both raced for the car.

The headlights were rocketing towards them. They were caught in a dilemma. If they were spotted sitting in this area, there might be questions raised. Now the expletive issued from Samir...in English. The paint!

He had left it on the seat. Pytor was advocating they get in motion. Samir knew that, minus the paint, it would be difficult for Eddie to cull out the correct drum without attracting undue notice. Things were unraveling fast. Then, without any warning, the approaching automobile suddenly decelerated and slewed into the brightly lit main entry of the nuke facility. It was the same dark sedan, identifiable even at this distance. The gate began its slow traverse once more as both terrorist breathed sighs of relief.

"Probably a food run," said Pytor remembering the chubby guards he had observed.

Samir just shook his head and wiped at the bullets of sweat. He exited the car and ran to the drum. At the base, facing the center of the refuse area, he sprayed a small two inch dot of runny white paint then returned swiftly to the vehicle. They backed out, mimicking the strategy used in the parking lot, and accelerated down the access road headed east to US 41.

In the dump area, the little blob of paint slowly began to dry. A terrorist attack, of nuclear proportions, had just been ear marked with a small can of "Testors Primer White" spray paint. Something more appropriately found on a twelve year old modeling table...Nothing human was aware of the irony.

CHAPTER 24

EDDIE'S NERVES were fraying fast. The dump run would take place shortly, but he was scheduled for his first "Drive" jump in two hours. Given that situation, there was not much way to explain any interest in getting involved with the trash truck detail. It would be so far out of character, someone would notice.

Their little escapade had also introduced a new tension into his lunch meeting with Sammy. It had been pretty apparent in the man's eyes and manner. He had repeated the information concerning the drum, and the actuating of the "jammer", a number of times.

"I got it dude, I got it...that part doesn't worry me. It's getting the thing through the gate."

Sammy seemed to fidget all over, "Edward, that is your part of the bargain; you must somehow deliver."

"Let me tell you something Sammy, my biggest interest right now is staying out of prison. If things look too dicey, I'm not touching it."

That seemed to strike some chord inside the "man from Miami". "You are right," he sighed "do not do anything to get caught. In fact, if it looks as if there is no way to make it happen, just try to activate the device where it is. Perhaps it will do some good, even at such a distance...and we can get at least partial payment."

Samir had begun to think any version of disaster at the facility was better than nothing at all. Even a detonation where the SADM was sitting would pretty much shut down this part of the world for the foreseeable future.

"Dude, that thing would have so much concrete and lead between it and Operations, there ain't no way it'd reach them."

Actually, Eddie thought he could pull off the insertion in such a fashion as to be totally non-culpable...even if the alarm was raised. He had rehearsed each expression and nuance for every scenario he could imagine and most left him the hero for having spotted the thing. Chances were, even if his plan for the guard shack went south, he would still be in the clear. He would also know where the device was taken for storage and might be able to trip the switch at a later date. It would depend on the level of interest, and how high up the ladder that interest went. At the maintenance level it was just some junk that accidentally got out like the lumber had. As he sat there, he realized it was probably time to play hard ball with "Smith and Jones" too.

"Look Sammy, the thing's pretty much in place. Even if it's discovered, they'll take it inside because of the MR reading before they ever find out it's not radioactive. I'm pretty sure I know where they'd park it and I guarantee I'd be able to turn it on at some point. It might have enough reach from safe-storage."

This was a new twist. Samir and company had always assumed that if the weapon was discovered it would be the end of operation Peregrine.

"Uh, what is safe-storage?"

"The holding area next to the tool hatch where the 'rad' stuff is stockpiled for the trip to Barnwell."

"Tool hatch?"

"The main access for big stuff in and out of the R/B. Because of all the work, there's loads of 'hot' stuff drummed up and waiting."

"Inside the Reactor Building?"

"Only place they got dude, there's no room in 'Aux' for the kind of crap we're piling up. Once or twice a week the heavy equipment swings the hatch open and we lift the old stuff out and bring in whatever new gear is waiting. Most of the hardware being replaced inside wouldn't fit through the pressurization hatch anyway. It all comes in, or goes out, through there."

Samir was trying to remember his briefings on these structures; his own interest was piqued. "How big is this hatch?"

"Gotta be twelve or fifteen feet at least. I watched the sunset from it one evening. Bet the public would freak over that. Here's some guy standing in a nuclear R/B with the reactor at his back, wearing his little 'mop-up' suit and staring out through an opening the size of one of those pools you buy for your kids."

"Edward, you are kidding me; how is that possible. What about contamination?"

"Listen man, they got fans with twelve foot blades in there. We always trick the newbie's into walking across the catwalk in front of em'. They'll suck you right up against the screens like a bug. Those babies only job is to pull fresh air in through one-way stacks and exhaust it through the biggest bank of charcoal filters you ever saw. Trust me; I've worked the filter crew a couple of times changing em'. Point is, the R/B's always at negative pressure. When I was standing at the hatch that night, it felt like a spring breeze sucking in the whole time."

Samir's mind was racing again, wondering if there was some way to take advantage of this new info.

"Does the dump vehicle pick up from this area as well?"

"Once in a while. Most of the stuff we 'can up' is headed for South Carolina."

Sammy sighed, "I guess we are stuck with the original plan...Just do your best Edward."

"Yeah, well, here's the deal; once that thing's inside you can collect from Smith and Jones and then I'll throw their little switch."

"What?!...Edward that was not part of the deal."

"I wasn't in much on making that deal, but my butt is the one on the line here now."

Samir examined Eddie's face. There was a determined glint to his eyes and he surmised any resistance might arouse suspicion. He decided to play along.

"You are right Edward. There should be some compensation for us as well. But here is the thing; once it is in place and active they have every incentive to keep us happy, especially you. Think about it. You turned it on; you can turn it off. You will be in control. You could probably increase your fee if you cared to. I gather money is very cheap to these people."

Ah...the demon of greed. On the "other side" a wicked smile appeared on Buferan's unholy excuse for a face; for he was attending personally and closely to this little intrigue. Sometimes it was too easy. Take your average human, throw in a little hatred or fanaticism; stir in some money and voila'. Violence, destruction and best of all...souls harvested by the grimmest of reapers.

Samir watched as Eddie's mind ran the calculations. The bulb came on and he suddenly grinned back at the terrorist...teased, hooked, played...dead.

So tonight Eddie was stewing in a state of mental sweat. Finally, though, he gave a shrug of resignation. There was no way he could attempt his little subterfuge this shift. It was going to have to wait.

THERE WAS A BLINDING FLASH followed by something Arak had not experienced in centuries...pain. His sight was instantly gone, yet he knew this was the work of Lucifer. He tried with all his considerable might to stem the waves of agony rolling through his being...to no avail.

There was a roaring in his ears that had the same hurtful effect on his audio senses. His "physical" self was completely immobilized; the only sensory input present was the pain. It felt as if he'd been dipped in molten lava and left to harden inside a shell made of flesh eating fire. He did not understand exactly how this was made possible, but at the core of his mind, he knew he had somehow been shackled by the demons. Trapped... as Kurtanus had been.

He tried to cry out to Father and to the Spirit. It was as if his thoughts were caged inside this living hell with him. He knew no one heard and that redoubled the hopelessness already being slammed forcefully against his mind. It tore an agonizing roar from him which was also heard by no one. No one, that is, except his captors.

If a demon of Hell can said to be "happy", Buferan and company were in that state. But their glee was of a fiendish nature. The same they harbored watching hapless humans destroy their souls with sin. A delight that could only be experienced by causing the misery and destruction of another. Twisted pleasure, of a sadistic nature, refined to the highest degree in the known universe; pure evil.

The original team from the Basilica encounter had been positioned using Lucifer's damning counter intelligence and success was now theirs. The hapless Arak had materialized in the very jaws of their trap. He was now destined to spend the rest of Earth's current age in the company of those most horrid of Arch-Demons and one brother Deranian... neither of whom would be aware of the other. This totally encompassing prison of hopelessness and pain was a like precursor to Hell itself. There are not adequate words to portray the first condition...much less the second.

AND ON THE EARTH, in the "dimension" of man, a new phenomenon is observed.

Amos is in the R/B making preparations for the night's work which will include Eddie's Drive jump. These are inherently the most menacing of the required procedures and they are treated like Extra Vehicular Activities in space; no room for error. By the large wall clock, it is exactly 5:29 p.m. when Amos suddenly clutches his head and drops to one knee. Ron Bennett, the Aussie, is nearby and is the only one to observe the apparent seizure. He races to kneel by his friend's side.

"Amos, Amos what is it. Look at me mate."

He lift's Amos' chin and looks into his eyes. There is a vacant stare that scares the HP Tech. As he watches though, the eyes begin to focus and Amos appears to recognize him.

"Ron...what...where..." Amos is looking around the area as if searching for something.

"Easy mate... let me see those eyes again."

As he's trying to look, Amos stands up and shakes his head. Ron steps in front of him, produces a pocket light and checks the man's pupils. They appear normal. He grabs his wrist but, although accelerated, the pulse is steady and strong.

"Amos, what just happened?"

He refocuses on Ron, "I...don't know. There was a pain... Something's wrong..." he falters to a stop.

Jenny, he thinks...No...Something else. The tell tale impulse of the Spirit does a reverse race down his spine.

"Amos, look at me. You need to get to the infirmary. Something serious is going on."

He looks Ron in the eyes even as clarity begins to reassert itself, "Yeah...Yeah, Ron you're right; but it's got nothing to do with my health."

"Whaa-tt...Amos, I just saw you knocked pretty well to the floor."

"Listen, you're going to have to trust me on this one. No report. No infirmary."

Ron eyes him for a long moment. There's no one in this facility he would trust any more than this man. His track record, his whole demeanor exudes a confidence and stability that are rare these days. Nevertheless, this is a nuclear reactor we're talking about.

"Are you on a jump tonight?"

"No, I'll be assisting on Eddies 'Drive' at seven thirty."

Another long pause as he scrutinizes Amos for any signs of distress. He has to admit, he looks totally normal now. He glances around the area. The whole thing appears to have gone unnoticed. "Amos...anybody but you, it's no show..."

"Ron, I know it looks bad, but please, trust me...just this once."

"Ok, mate...just this once. Anything else happens we go downstairs; agreed?"

"Agreed. Now...I gotta go make a call. Get Dormer prepped if I don't get back in time, OK?"

Ron watches Amos leave hurriedly for the hatch. In fact he follows him down one passage and is in position to see him form up with the small group waiting out the current cycle. He isn't talking or looking around, just standing there seemingly lost in thought. The cycle concludes, the huge steel hatch opens and the crew members inside enter the reactor area. Amos' bunch takes their place in the chamber and the performance is reversed. Ron walks back towards the Drive staging area mentally scratching his head...and totally determined to watch Mikals like the proverbial hawk.

THAT SAME 5:29 P.M., Jenny is standing looking out Amos' southerly living room window. She has just concluded some light cleaning, giving the little domicile an abbreviated version of a woman's touch. Jim is on the small dock with Bubba, idly casting a lure out to the center of the bay and playing it back. The same "over surge" strikes her.

She clutches her head as her mind screams out in terror. But it's not her voice. She stumbles forward then does a small pirouette and collapses on a comfy old couch that backs up to the large window.

As quickly as it arrived, the shot of agony passes. She's left dazed, slumped back and staring through the large sliding screen doors which face the front yard.

"Dad"…her voice is weakened; she tries again, "Dad!"

An answering shout reaches her and seconds later Jim and Bubba race through the lanai and into the living room.

"What…What's wrong?" the distress in his daughter's voice is evident.

"I…I don't know…"

Jenny attempts to describe the event, unknowingly, in much the same terms Amos will use. As she is searching for more words, the house telephone rings. Jim picks up the mobile handset lying on an end table.

"Mikals residence….Oh, hey Amos…aren't you at the plant?"

"What!?…" Jim listens intently for at least a minute, then,

"Yeah, well you're not gonna believe this."

The two men compare notes for another minute or two. Jenny listens wide eyed as the dual strike is revealed, then Jim hands her the phone.

"Hey…No, I have no idea."

"Yes…I guess it was right around 5:30."

"No, no I'm fine now. What about you?"

"No, don't come home, you've missed enough work lately because of us…

"I know, I know."

"Just hang in there...what...Alright I'll ask dad about it...Yeah, I know where the stuff is, I was doing a little sorting and cleaning while he was fishing..."

"You're welcome..."

"I guess you'll know if the SX is in the drive, right...OK...Bye."

Jenny clicks the handset off and looks at Jim, "What do you think about staying here tonight?"

He looks at the hallway leading back to the bedroom area, "Well, they're small but he's got the room. You sure you want to sleep in the same house with that snake?"

"You've seen that cage of his. You want to try breaking out of that thing?"

"Point taken...how do you feel now?"

Jenny looks down for a long moment, "Like there's something I should know...but I don't."

"Can you elaborate?"

More moments pass as she canvasses the experience mentally.

"It feels like I heard a cry for help, but it was cut off."

"What...well it wasn't Amos, thank God."

"No, but he got hit the same time...what's up with that?"

It's Jim's turn to rub his chin and sit in contemplation. Jenny recognizes the familiar pattern and waits patiently. Suddenly her dad cocks his head toward the ceiling, then turns and stares out at the marshes.

"Oh no..."

Jenny pales slightly, "What...what's, oh no?"

"Alright, bear with me. What's the single biggest denominator between you and Amos?"

With no hesitation, "Arak."

"And when you first encountered him, what was going on?"

"Those demons, that Buferan, had him trapped in the..." she falters to a stop...Then,

"Oh no."

CHAPTER 25

A MOS RETURNED to the R/B shortly before Eddie's scheduled jump. He was still mentally poring over his earlier, unnerving, experience. However, this mental sleuthing had been distracted by run-of-the-mill obligations concerning maintenance work details and the underlying knowledge of a newbie getting ready to make a Drive jump. He caught Ron staring at him several times and smiled inwardly. The man was a credit to his ranks and Amos didn't blame him for being concerned.

He listened as Ron gave Eddie the standard drill regarding safety and emergency procedures. This was not the same animal as a Sheet jump. Eddie was about to go toe to toe with apparatus that had been in close contact with the fuel cells. The danger and exposure rates were maxxed out during these operations. Almost all support personnel would be in respirators, even though they would not be entering the "tent"; the nickname the crews had given the large polyethylene structure that comprised the actual work space.

When Ron concluded, Amos began helping Eddie don the one piece space suit required for serious hot work. He could see the man was a little tense but that too was normal; who wouldn't be? He had no way of knowing Eddie's "other" problem which continued to worry at his mind.

"OK, Ed, this isn't really a big deal procedure wise. You've seen me do the gasket job twice now, right."

"Yeah."

"Just be sure that surface is spot free. If they find a speck of old material, we'll have to set up another complete jump and Fitz will have our heads. It's better to take a few more MR's, and get it right, than take a whole 'nuther bunch going back in on the same drive."

Eddie's normally snide demeanor was nowhere to be found tonight, "Amos, how hot are these things. I mean no one's said anything about Rem numbers yet."

Amos looked him in the eye, "Eddie, when that tip is coming down, it's pretty intense. No way to change that. The trick is to get it straight into the bore and then pile those pouches around it fast and deep."

Eddie just nodded, his eyes still widened to a degree.

"Hey...It's not that bad. You can do this. Just stay calm and focus on it."

Ron was listening and watching. Amos knew that if the "space cadet", another crew nick name, looked too shook or nervous, the HP technician would call the jump off. That would also be the last time they were offered the opportunity. He held up a palm towards Ron, then shuffled the suited Eddie a few steps away.

"Hey, I don't blame you if you're concerned, but don't let that rattle you. The actual work is easier than splitting cases on a Honda. For you it should be a snap."

At that, Eddie seemed to relax a little, "Yeah...yeah, I know you're right Amos. Just got a lot on my mind these days."

Naturally, Amos figured this was the rent, girlfriend matter. Still, a little burst of caution blossomed in his mind. However, considering the night he'd had so far, he chalked it up to his own nerves being a little keyed up.

"Well buddy, this is one of those times when we all have to leave personal matters outside or on the shelf; you gotta stay sharp."

"Gentlemen," intoned Ron from the sideline; "time to start your engines."

Amos grinned at Eddie, "C'mon dude, let's do it."

Eddie managed a grin back and then looked at Ron, "Yeah, no worries mate."

That seemed to break the tension. Ron laughed and quipped, "That's the spirit, old chap."

They walked over as a group to the base of the stairway that lead up to the work deck inside the tent. Here Ron helped pull the helmet portion of Eddie's suit over his head and then zipped the wetsuit style zipper up the back to the helmet base. Eddie was now ensconced in the exposure rig and receiving air through the open ventilation tube that hung down from the back side of the helmet. The brass fitting at the end of that tube was where the life sustaining air would be piped in from a nearby purification station. Until that air was applied, the heat build-up in the suit would get worse by the minute.

Ron carefully used duct tape to place a secondary seal over the zipper flap. Then he used the same to wrap Eddie's wrist and pants cuffs to keep them streamlined and out of the way. Lastly he taped the airline securely to the suit itself so it wouldn't flop around. The inlet fitting wound up about waist high. He reached over to a rack that looked as if it contained hose-lines similar to those found in a garage or shop. Each ended in a coupler designed to mate with the suit's inlet. These were housed under rubber safety plugs, color coded blue and white, and clearly marked Breathing Air.

Ron selected the nearest line and, after removing the end cap, snapped it onto Eddie's suit. Immediately, cool, purified air washed down through the helmet's foam padded crown bathing him with welcome relief. The suit assumed its slightly inflated shape and the wearer was now under positive pressure. Hopefully this insured any punctures or cuts would bleed fresh air out, rather than let deadly, isotope laden air in. Ron went carefully over the seams and joints, at one point spraying the outer surface with a pump bottle of soapy water to make any leakage visible. Lastly, he cupped his hand over the exhaust fitting while eyeing the air flow pressure gauge. He gave a satisfied grunt and turned to Amos, "Our turn."

At that moment the tall, lanky form of Fitzgerald materialized in front of Eddie, "OK in there son?" he shouted.

Eddie nodded and gave him the thumbs up.

He turned to Ron and Amos, "You guy's have the platform on this one. I got a valve build going at number seven."

"Fitz" tried to observe every Drive jump that went down while wearing a respirator and stationed on the platform outside the large slit that acted as an entry door. Said slit had seen its share of activity and both edges had been repeatedly duct taped leaving little doubt as to its location or purpose. He gave a slow, rotating look at the surround-ing area and his eye lit on something.

"Amos, some numb-nuts left a screwdriver on the roll out mat."

Amos stopped adjusting his respirator straps and looked over at the mat. Sure enough, off in one corner lay a small Phillips head screwdriver. Probably left over after adjusting some piece of equipment.

The "Roll Out" mat represented the last line of defense for the mechanic inside the tent. If something went terribly wrong, like a major tear in the suit, all personnel were trained to virtually dive off the work platform and onto the extra thick mat below. A second HP tech, also in full respirator, waited there for the duration of each jump with a short bladed case cutter and a pressurized respirator nose piece close at hand. The drill was to cut the victim free of the suit helmet and place the fresh air mask of the respira-tor over their mouth and nose.

Any damage to one's suit which interrupted the flow of air, or exceeded the capability of the breathing system to force air out, would leave the technician inside vulnerable to a lung full of radioactive isotope with the next breath. Some of these had half-lives of more than a thousand years. Your chances of survival in such a case were not good, to say the least. To date, nothing untoward had required this rescue operation be put to the test, but no one wanted to make a jump like this without the option available.

Amos waved at the other tech, Scott Billings, who was busy fiddling with the air lines going to his station. Even at this short distance the background noise of the gigantic fans, and other full time machinery, made conversation difficult. When he had Scott's attention he pointed to the screwdriver. The man's eyes took in the mat and then the tool came into focus. He strode over and picked it up, then turned and gave Amos an eye roll and a thank you motion.

Fitz gave the whole area another once over then, "OK, looks like you guys got it from here." He placed himself in front of Eddie once again, "Work as fast as you can, but don't rush it and get sloppy...be careful."

Another nod from the space suited Eddie.

Amos and Ron finished cinching on their respirators and Amos signaled Eddie to proceed up the short flight of wooden stairs to the work deck. He and Ron followed in tandem safeguarding against a trip or fall while keeping the feed line to the suit clear of any obstruction as it snaked along behind. Once all three were poised in front of the entry, Amos looked up at a third story catwalk and exchanged signals with the Polar Crane operator who was waiting patiently on station.

The Control Rod Drive units had been previously removed from the reactor head and were stored in a giant lead lined rack off to one side of the containment vessel. It resembled a military missile system with the stainless outer tubes projecting out of the rack in evenly spaced rows. Each wore a large colored tag indicating its rebuild status. A temporary catwalk had been positioned along the upper level of the vessel next to the rack. Another worker stood there ready to make the mechanical connection to the selected assembly.

On Amos' signal the operator picked up a plant line and his voice boomed and echoed through the area. The announcement of a Drive "move" was quickly responded to by the few remaining workers on other tasks and they vacated the area. Most had been through the drill before and were already gathered at the hatch laughing and talking. This had become the norm since any incident during such a move would result in their immediate departure.

With the excess personnel clear, the giant crane rumbled to life and began a slight rotation on its tracks. The operator was fine tuning its relationship to one of the units carrying a red tag. The green tagged ones had already been through the process. Once satisfied with the alignment, the huge ball and hook, which dangled beneath a giant pulley and cable arrangement, began a slow descent towards the selected assembly. The waiting tech on the catwalk also wore a respirator in addition to the basic cotton outer jump suit, head covering, gloves and plastic boots that were donned by any and all employees prior to entry into the hatch.

As the hook neared the selected unit, the speed decreased even further and the catwalk attendant began giving signals to the operator. Finally he raised a balled fist and all motion ceased. He reached down and produced a heavy, triple hook safety chain with a large eye on the upper end. With some effort, the eye was hoisted onto the large utility hook, leaving three smaller hooks looped up and attached to the main body. Upon signal, the operator bumped the apparatus lowering it one increment at a time.

Another balled fist and the appendage was at the correct level. The tech retrieved each hook, fed it into a designated slot on the large stainless housing, and then signaled for a slow upward motion. The chains tightened and the movement again stopped. The catwalk attendee gave each one a visual exam, and a hearty tug, then gave the operator the up signal. The giant crane motor once more added its growl to the roar of background noise and the Drive assembly started to rise. The technician beat a hasty retreat to the edge of the catwalk and stooped to retrieve a long aluminum pole with a padded S-hook on one end.

The assembly continued its slow rise. As the narrow "lead screw" end appeared, the tech reached out with the pole and, using the hook, snared it. The business end of the Drive looked somewhat like a jousters lance and ended in the corkscrew tip that actually engaged the fuel cell. The pole device was simply to dampen any movement as it cleared the rack. It also kept the tech somewhat away from the immediate area of intense radiation. As soon as it cleared, he removed the tool and beat another hasty retreat down the stairway. His moment of increased risk was past for the moment. With any luck the procedure in the tent would take long enough that his counter part on the morning shift would have to do the reverse dance to return it to the rack.

The Drive was now at the correct level and the crane operator began a swivel procedure to bring it in line with the tent. Eddie watched the large, missile-looking apparatus dangle in space with widened eyes. *They were in the valley now and had the dragon by the tail.*

Once aligned, the rotation ceased and was followed by a linear motion down the giant dual tracks which brought it bearing down on the tent location. As soon as it appeared to hover over the upper opening, Amos signaled Eddie to enter the enclosure. Girding his mental loins, he clumsily stepped through the slit while Ron fed the airline in. His first job was to relay signals to Amos, who passed them on to the operator. It was imperative to precisely center the tip over the tubular, twelve inch opening that went down through the stack of leaded-concrete barrels. Although no one wanted one of these screamingly "hot" units hanging in exposed surroundings any longer than necessary, it could not be rushed.

Eddie watched as the Drive tip entered the sister slit in the "roof" of the tent. He was momentarily spell bound. Like a bird captivated by the serpent's eyes, he couldn't look away. He shook himself and quickly looked down at the receiving point, gauging the alignment with the approach of what, in his mind, had taken on the proportions of a demon's spear. There was no way to physically feel or assess the intensity of the radiation fast approaching his face plate, but mentally it felt as if electricity were being fed into his mind and body. His thoughts recoiled at the sensation, sending imaginary spikes up and down his spine. He was using every ounce of self control to stay focused as he watched this "messenger of death" prepare to pass eighteen inches from his face.

It was at that very moment, the unthinkable occurred.

There was a loud pop and a continuing hiss filled the tent. The air coupler had separated from the inlet fitting on the suit. Amos and Ron saw the line drop to the deck at Eddie's feet and there was a split second of shocked disbelief on both men's faces. Eddie was only aware that the cooling breeze, that had been saturating the suit, had suddenly ceased. His keyed up mind worked against him as tried to analyze the malfunction while fighting to maintain concentration on the slowly traversing Drive tip. Problem was, in the next few breaths, the highly contaminated, frighteningly radioactive air, lurking around that tip, would be pulled up the small inlet line and into the helmet. Eddie was two or three breaths from certain death.

As the split second of surprise elapsed, Ron and Amos exploded into action. Amos leaned through the slit, caught the surprised Eddie by one arm and dragged him towards the entry. As Eddie clumsily cleared the threshold Amos used his free hand to grasp the suit inlet line. He snatched it loose from the duct tape, then bent the tubing double in attempt to kink it shut. Eddie had no idea what was going on but stood pliant while this was happening.

The next thing he knew he had been bodily propelled on stumbling legs as Amos drove them both off the platform and onto the roll out mat. It wasn't a clean landing. They impacted in a tangle of arms and legs with Amos holding onto the kinked air line with both hands like he was swinging from it. Scott had seen Amos burst into the work area and was waiting. As soon as they landed he pounced atop the hapless Eddie who, by now, was in a shocked state unsure of what was happening.

Straddling the man's chest to immobilize him, Scott brought his face plate together with Eddie's and screamed, "Hold still; hold your breath." When he'd seen that the man understood, he drew the case cutter along the chin area of the plasticized material and flipped the face plate as far back as possible. He cast the cutter aside, grabbed the nosepiece and placed it firmly over the hapless ANM's face. Amos released his death grip on the inlet line and stood up.

He quickly surveyed the work area. The operator had observed the pandemonium in the tent and frozen the action of the crane. Problem was, this left the Drive tip suspended and bathing the area with hi-intensity rays and particles. Ron had descended and was hovering over the feed line apparatus while monitoring Scott and Eddie. Amos made a snap decision.

He placed his faceplate close to Billing's, "Scott, keep him there, OK."

The man nodded. Eddie realized something had gone seriously wrong and was lying quietly while his eyes darted from man to man. There was no way Billings was letting him up till he could fasten the straps around his head, but the remains of the helmet made that impossible at the moment.

Amos turned to Ron, "RB, let's go."

With that he charged up the stairs to the tent entry. After a surprised moment, Ron followed him. When they were at the entrance Amos placed his faceplate on Ron's and simply said, "Relay for me."

With that he burst into the tent wearing only the cotton contamination gear and his respirator.

Ron's "Wait, Amos, don't." died on his lips. It was too late.

Amos was signaling "down" repeatedly and after a moment Ron relayed it to the operator. The fearsome tip finally resumed its vertical descent. As it neared the throat of the secondary containment, Amos made one slight horizontal request on the alignment. A few seconds later, the tip slid cleanly into the opening. In a few more, he signaled for the stop. He commenced piling the heavy lead pellet pouches around the shaft protruding out the opening until they were three deep. There were a lot of dangers still lurking in this bad scenario, but the dragon had been momentarily caged.

Ron was motioning to him and Amos put his respirator plate out the slit.

"Amos, you need to get out of there."

"Put down the paper first."

He nodded in understanding and started down the stairway. At the base was a rack of what looked like over-size rolls of brown packaging paper. Ron brought one up to the platform and rolled out a good sized portion, then using his own cutter, sliced the section cleanly off. Amos stepped through the slit onto the paper. As soon as he cleared the tent Ron was on him checking the tension of his respirator straps.

"That was crazy, mate."

Amos just nodded. Then he began stripping off his cotton outer wear. He looked down to where Scott had managed to get the rest of the helmet off Eddie and fasten the respirator straps around his head.

"We need to find out," he stated to Ron.

Ron leaned in toward Amos faceplate. "On both of you."

"I'm probably good, check Eddie."

Ron nodded and started down the stairs. Scott had Eddie on his feet and was helping him shed the "suit" while standing on a similar section of brown paper. He looked at Ron, then down at the brown paper "floor.

"Probably a waste of time; whole area's gotta be crapped up."

The Aussie gave a shrug, "Do it anyway, mate; can't hurt."

The paper floor was there to attempt to corral as much contaminated material as possible. Even dust particles, that made contact with a source, came away dangerous. It was sort of a radiated version of germ warfare. In fact, if you pretended the stuff could spread like some deadly bacteria or virus, you'd not be far off on the mechanics involved.

Amos had shed his white contamination suit and rolled it up in the paper. He was now wearing his lightweight blue FPC jumpsuit and a pair of the generic brown cotton gloves which were available all over the plant site. He placed the wadded suit and paper in a drum at the stair base marked "Radioactive Waste" then joined the techs at Eddie's side. A small crowd had materialized at the far end of the hallway leading to the hatch. Amos waved them back, signaling the possibility of airborne contamination. Ron had started to sweep the area around Eddie's face with a small Geiger counter. It was a short range model designed for just such purposes and immune to the larger sources around it. Nothing registered; a good sign. He swept Amos upper shoulder and head area and got the reverse. His little foray into the tent had left its mark.

He turned to Scott, "Better roll the hallway and get everyone out. Wait, let me check you. Billing's came up positive all over from contact with Eddie's suit. This was getting more difficult. He swept his own person and came up pretty clean.

"Alright then, I'll do the hallway, you guy's are obviously getting the shower."

The emergency wash station next to the hatch had multiple shower heads and special ventilation and debris removal areas. Ron motioned the others into a huddle.

"Here's the deal; I'll clear everyone out and roll the hall. Then when I signal, I want you to come down one at a time starting with you."

He pointed at Eddie, who nodded, then continued, "The fans have probably gotten any airborne stuff by now, but hold your breath if you can." Indicating they should strip off the emergency breathing apparatus and have Eddie make haste to the shower area.

Amos was on pins and needles to check him for internal contamination but recognized the wisdom of following Ron's expertise. All three nodded in turn. Bennett grabbed a four foot roll of the brown paper from the nearby rack and proceeded to unroll it down the hallway, pushing it open with his feet. He bent it around the corner and was out of view for a long minute as the remaining trio waited silently. Amos knew he was shooing the remaining crew out the hatch before going on with the mini-rescue operation. He reappeared shortly, minus his respirator, and gave them the signal to proceed.

Scott looked at Eddie, "Ready?" Eddie had realized the nature of the mishap by now and was resigned to following the lead of the others. But, he too knew his moment of truth had not yet arrived.

He nodded and took a deep breath. Scott released him from the face piece and hose assembly and he took off down the hall. Ron was waiting at the shower room, the water running amidst wisp of steam. De-con water needed to be on the warm side. He ushered Eddie under the stream and then directed him to strip while the water poured over him. He didn't even hesitate. He'd been here long enough to even see male and female co-workers sharing these showers as they scrubbed to remove unexpected contaminants from some incident. Getting "crapped up" wasn't all that rare. Breathing it inadvertently was. And that was on the minds of all those involved.

The word had gotten out and a team of three maintenance guys, along with McMillan himself, stepped out of the hatch while Eddie was showering.

"What happened," asked Mac.

Ron filled him in on the details.

"You 'breathe' him yet?"

"No...getting ready to right now. Let me get Amos first."

Ron reappeared at the end of the hallway and motioned to Amos. He repeated the trip that Eddie had taken, but retained his respirator. Once it was flushed thoroughly he'd remove it while under the shower. He rounded the corner to find Mac and his team gathered around the de-con entry. Eddie was toweling off near the front of the tiled area while one of the men from Mac's bunch stood by with a clean jump suit and some plastic boots.

Without hesitation Amos plunged under the shower stream looking up and washing the boundary where the face mask met his skin. Then he removed it, did the same full strip and began a thorough scrub down. He could see Ron was having Eddie blow into the counter, but couldn't hear the conversation. Finally he turned to Amos and gave him the OK signal. A huge weight lifted for Amos; Eddie hadn't inhaled any of the contaminants inside the tent. His turn would be next. Although they all had faith in the military grade respirators, no one had ever worn one into the enclosed work area with a live Drive unit before.

As soon as Amos was towel clad, RB held the little counter up to his mouth and nostrils, "Blow through; nose first."

Amos complied and the needle stayed put.

"Blow through the mouth...hard."

Another negative reaction. There were cheers all round and a couple of high fives and shoulder slaps. The "Reactor Ranger" community shared some of the intensity of a real Ranger platoon. Only here, you would never see the enemy that killed you. None the less, death was a constant background companion on drills like the one that had just gone bad.

Mac spoke up, "Alright, lets have a look at the suit. Ops will want it sent back for testing."

Mac's crew and the trio of Amos, Ron and Eddie all donned paper mask from the rack outside the shower area and walked the hallway edge back to where Billings was still waiting. They took care not to touch or disturb the brown paper. The crew stopped well short of the immediate area. Decontamination here was most likely going require suiting a couple of more guys up. Ron edged up to the paper floor where Scott had waited patiently knowing exactly what was going on around the bend. He pointed at Eddie and Amos and gave a questioning motion.

"No worries mate," shouted RB and gave him the high sign. The man mimicked wiping sweat from his brow.

"Scott," shouted Amos, "check the inlet line."

Scott leaned over and retrieved the helmet portion. He stretched the air feed away from the contaminated suit. They all watched as he began a slow track with the counter moving from the brass entry fitting towards the remains of the helmet. As soon as it neared the fitting, the alarm sounded and the needle went wild. Scott continued the sweep and about six inches from the helmet, the device quieted down. He repeated the procedure and then turned a solemn face towards the waiting crew members. They were stone silent now. Eddie's last inhalation had nearly dragged death into the helmet with him.

RB placed a hand on his shoulder, "Well mate, it managed to get six inches from your face." He turned and pointed at Amos, "That bloke just saved your life."

CHAPTER 26

A S AMOS HEADED SOUTH on US 41, the highway was over-lit by a brilliant full moon. Ordinarily one of his favorite astronomic sights, he was not paying much attention to it tonight. The events of the evening were still swirling and tumbling through his mind. Not only that; his spiritual "antennae" were on full alert as well. He'd had far too much going on to think about the "attack" earlier, but now it was nagging at him. It hit Jenny simultaneously; that was a telling point. In his heart he already knew it must somehow concern Arak.

When he got to his place, he found the others gathered in the kitchen looking glum. Even Bubba appeared solemn as he strode over for his welcome home petting.

"It's that bad isn't it," stated Amos.

Jenny nodded, "Pretty sure it is."

She proceeded to once more go over the info concerning the possibility of capture and imprisonment Arak had described. As the enormity, and apparent finality, of the scenario sank in, a real sense of gloom settled on their spirits. Then, after a period of silence, Amos seemed to shake himself awake as if from some bad dream.

He looked at the other two, "I refuse to accept this as final."

They just stared.

He stood up and continued, "Look, I can believe that we're right about what happened; I feel it too. But I don't accept it as the end of him...or us."

Questioning looks.

"I feel like I'm preaching to the choir here, but bear with me. I'd bet you can both name other times, or situations, where God came through for you in a miraculous way."

Nods from both.

"Well, if he'll do that for us, why not for Arak?"

Jim spoke up, "Amos, I see your point. I believe your point. But we're in a strange place here where Scripture doesn't have much to say."

"Agreed," stated Amos, "but the Holy Spirit has plenty I'll bet."

The first flicker embraced the room.

Amos continued, "The mechanics of faith do not change, as best I can tell. Right now it's as if a good friend is sick...real sick...what do you do?"

"Pray," said Jenny, "believe."

"Yes, exactly, we do what Scripture has taught since the beginning and we do it with all the faith we possess."

Jenny sighed, "I'm afraid mine's a little wobbly right now. I mean, why go to all this trouble to involve us in this...this situation, stuff no one I know has ever seen, and let him end up like that?"

"That's the part I don't accept. This isn't the end. There's still some kind of war raging. It involves danger, not just to us, but also to a bunch of clueless civilians. Think about this. Arak knew all about this possibility, told you about it first thing, do you think that would have stopped him from trying?"

The inner glow intensified.

"Wouldn't even cross his mind," said Jenny and her dad nodded.

"Then let's do it. Let's do what we have always believed in."

Amos sat back down, they joined hands and he began,

"Almighty, Father God, we gather here as instructed by your Son's words, knowing that where two or more gather in his name we are one in spirit with you both. But we acknowledge that, humanly, we don't always know what to pray for...or how. Let the Spirit of Truth pray with us and for us. Let Jesus, at your mighty right hand, intercede on our behalf.

"We would bring before you the situation with our brother Arak. Your own Holy messenger. How marvelous you made him. And how he loves to do your will. Even here on the Earth, which we know is not a world he has ever called home. Yet he fought for you, and for us, against the evil cast here amongst us so long ago. Evil that must someday itself be used to achieve your purposes...which are sometimes a mystery to us. So be it Father; your will is often fraught with danger. It was so even with your own son when he was here. How can we expect any different if we are standing for you and trying to walk like him.

"Father, I also do not have adequate words of thanks. You were gracious to send your warning...and to send new and dear friends to help carry the burden of it. And now the burden grows heavy because of what we fear for our fellow servant. Mighty though he is, it seems he has met with an awful fate. I will not mince words with you, oh God, we desire your personal attention, blessing and intervention in this instance. And we come directly before your throne with boldness because of what your own mighty Christ accomplished on our behalf. Together, we implore you to order action against those who hold him captive. To make war in that world against all that is going on here on the Earth, or in any other realm we are unaware of, regarding this matter. And to give us the strength to tighten up our own spiritual armor, gird our faith and carry the fight to these unholy adversaries, both in the spirit and in the flesh.

"In this Father, you will find our hearts unified as commanded. Even as our spirits are unified in You our Creator. Please accept both our petition which, we place before you under Jesus own name, and our thanks and praise for your attention to this request...Amen."

His amen was echoed by the other two and then Jim spoke up, "Thanks for the reminder Amos."

"No thanks necessary. But I do have another request. I almost lost a guy tonight..."

He was interrupted by Jenny's gasp, "You mean killed?" "Yes."

He went on to tell them of Eddie's narrow escape and add some insights into the infrequent, but real, dangers of the nuclear world. Ones which didn't often get much public airing. After the details were examined and the questions answered, he suggested they offer a prayer for the man. He sensed that any such encounter might make an individual re-examine whatever faith they possessed or claimed internally.

So once again they united in prayer. This time for a fellow human being's deliverance from judgment, and the wrath to come. Then Jim announced his intention to hit the sack and Amos, Jenny and Bubba wandered out to the dock under the bright moonlit sky. Jenny sat beside him and their feet dangled just above the water. That silvery surface shimmered and danced with the ripples and splashes of numerous species feeding in the customary shine of the lunar cycle. The reflected image of the moon flickered in time with the ripples.

Jenny once again reached over and clasped Amos' hand. It gave his heart a warm feeling he'd never experienced before. They sat quietly, speaking only occasionally, and let the peace and beauty of the night, and the warmth of each other's touch, act as a balm for their weary souls.

It was under that sky, with the calls and cries of the night time marsh denizens, mixed with the splashes and gurgles of the marine ones, that they would share their first kiss. A chaste little goodnight kiss, but none the less, a landmark in time that would stay with each of them for the rest of their lives...However long that might last.

THERE WAS LITTLE DOUBT Father knew he was here. It would be beyond foolish to think that even the current tumultuous state of affairs on the Earth would distract that limitless intellect long enough to miss the absence of an Arch rank angel. Of course he had all the authority needed to make such a visit but, under other circumstances, he would have certainly discussed the matter beforehand. Come to think of it, God himself seemed to be going along with, if not actually approving, some of the rather unusual activities being spawned by the misadventure and "rule twisting" in this particular saga. One which had now taken a sad turn.

Raphael stood on a high mountain overlooking one of the sparkling seas of Deran. None of the inhabitants knew he was here. He had desired to once more see Arak's home world and prepare himself for the task of telling his family of his fate. And to be truthful, mourn a little. No one knew the length of the current Earth age. Nor did anyone know how long a Third Rank could resist the tortures that such a confinement implied. Father had always seemed to adjust the "age" matter according to how his will was being acted upon and whatever timeline suited him for concluding it. Raphael's job was to support and enforce the array of dictates for any particular world or matter; not suggest or decide those policies.

Oh, he wore no false humility. He was quite aware of the standing the Cosmos accorded him at Father's pleasure. He was a contemporary of Michael and Gabriel and answered to none but the Great I Am. Any thoughts of grandeur because of this must have been burnt out through those same ages. For an indescribably long time, he had only felt humbled by the concerns and responsibilities that went with such power. The mantle of that power rested heavily on him today.

He let his eyes soak in the eloquent version of Creation these particular beings called home. This "perfected" world was another testimony to the absolute flawlessness with which Father completed his own very long range plans. Raphael had visited here a few times during the centuries of unrest incited by the Ag's. It had borne some of the same conflicting patterns one could observe on the Earth of today.

Always a stunningly visual planet, with vistas also somewhat similar to the Earth, it had been tainted by the presence of evil among its inhabitants. Perhaps a slightly different category than the one encountered now in the den of Lucifer himself, but still, a spiritual atmosphere that left a stain on everything around it. That said, those misguided zealots had never come close to consuming their entire world in a maelstrom of lawlessness and sin, such as the Earth was currently succumbing to. And now another of those, who had been a champion against some of that evil, had fallen. And he, Raphael, would be the messenger of that fall to those who loved him best.

He could "see" where Lonius was at the moment. In fact, he was somewhat familiar with the stone compound Arak's family called home. It was a large, functional estate situated on the shoreline of this great sea. The living quarters were three stories tall and had a glorious view of both the waters before and the snow capped peaks on the horizon behind.

Arak's father was not currently in those living areas. He was in a massive side building tinkering with one of his mechanical devices. It was a pastime which many of the male inhabitants, and a few of the females, seemed to share here. They were infatuated with many forms of locomotion ranging from sailing vessels to things quite a bit more powerful. One never knew what form their freedom of expression might take next but, with their enhanced abilities to manipulate matter, it was safe to say it would probably be fast. Ah well, it was time to pay the visit. There would be no need to send ahead or announce his presence.

Lonius was indeed occupied inside the huge structure. The cavernous opening, which acted as the main entry, faced the sea and there were other smaller ones scattered about so that a pleasant breeze was nearly always present. The walls were lined with various sized benches, obviously hewn from the local timber, and finished with an artisan's pride. On many of these were objects and contraptions that would have required an inside knowledge to even guess at their purposes. All this was clearly visible throughout the giant structure because the "stones" that made up the overhead centerline, shone with a natural luminosity of more than sufficient wattage.

Near the center of this oversize workshop, Lonius' tall, sinewy form was crouched wrestling with a strangely glowing, metallic coil which protruded from an opening on the lower side of his current project. It was his largest, most ambitious ever and took up much of the useable area. He held an oddly shaped tool with which he appeared to be trying to coerce one end of the coil to mate with a similar shaped piece above it. At length a grunt, followed by an exclamation of success, announced the connection had been made.

Several openings on the curved side of the massive device erupted into a similar turquoise glow, as did two of the large apparatus lying on nearby benches. This was co-joined with a large audible hum that seemed to pulse with some form of latent energy. He gave a loud exclamation of victory with both hands raised like a fan at an athletic event. Then a grin of satisfaction settled on the handsome features, only to be instantly transformed into a look of surprise.

For at that same moment, a furious high energy sizzling erupted from the open space in front of his workshop followed by a veritable thunderclap of displaced atoms. Before his shocked eyes, Raphael, the ancient Arch who had been his son's longtime mentor, flashed into physical presence in all his glory. And that glory was substantial.

To behold an Arch in the fleshly dimension was to see all the great sunsets and works of art combined and then embodied with a detectable sense of almost limitless power. Only the appearance of Father himself could have shocked Lonius more. But the next second, he knew.

Neither spoke as he walked out into the bright daylight and stood before the towering Raphael.

"It is my son?"

Raphael nodded.

"Is it as Kurtanus?"

"Yes."

His mind fell in upon itself. Images of his son cascaded there, but the central focus that screamed out in his head was...Loss...More loss.

"Father may 'summon' you. I did not officially alert him to my coming. You do not need me to tell you of his fury and pain."

"Why is this creature allowed to continue?"

"You are perhaps the only one on this world who can now answer that."

"This Hell? This contest in which he engages this demon?"

Another nod.

"Elder, I have not the understanding as to why Father allows such evil to continue. Or the explanation of its spread. He is God, I am not; but I will not abide the loss of my son quietly."

Raphael eyed Arak's father with understanding. He felt that way sometimes too, but one did not defy Father,

"There is little we can do at present."

"You say we, have you some thought on the matter?"

"The same thoughts I had with Kurtanus. The desire to wage an attack and right great wrongs."

Lonius shouldn't have been surprised. He knew the brotherhood that existed amongst all Father's creations once they moved past their "testing" stages. They shared almost a single mind when it came to loving and protecting one another. It was one of the most wonderful pieces in the nearly incomprehensible puzzle known as The Great Plan.

"Will Father act this time?"

A silence ensued during which Raphael turned and looked out over the sea. Then,

"I have not the authority to say...but I do not see Him altering his intentions regarding the Earth over this matter."

Lonius looked down a moment, "And will you act this time?"

"You forget yourself Lonius; I am an Arch...Sad to say, I have seen much greater tragedies than this. Besides, it is possible that both Kurtanus and Arak will be restored to us at the end of days there."

"And it is also possible they will not successfully endure this 'captivity' for that period."

"Many things are possible," agreed Raphael.

"I was taught that with God, all things are possible."

"You may appeal to Father yourself. Again, He may summon you."

"You are his spokesman."

"I do not speak for God in this instance. As I said, I left with no audience beforehand."

"Do you doubt He knows you are here? Or may even be aware of these details as we discuss them?"

"Lonius, neither of us is foolish enough to doubt his power."

"Yet you are here; uninterrupted and unchallenged."

A sad smile graced the wondrous features of the giant Arch angel, "It is not hard to see where your son gets his spirit."

A similar one rested now on his father's face, "Yes, he was born to push the boundaries it seems. The price he now pays is a hard one...for us as well."

Raphael seemed suddenly lost in thought. He spoke almost musingly, "He has always been impulsive, yet some of Father's best works have benefited from that streak in his nature."

"He told me this Lucifer is defying some of Father's dictates on that world."

"Indeed," said the great elder thoughtfully, "he has been testing those waters."

"And without reprisal?"

"Yes"

"Why would that be?"

Raphael seemed to snap back to the present, "I have a number of theories, none of which have I the utmost confidence in."

"But something is different...or amiss?"

"Possibly...You and I are here trying to second guess the Ancient of Days. Another circumstance and it might be amusing...even to Him."

"Elder...Raphael...I know something of your fondness for Arak. However, that will not trump my love as his father. I vow to you that I will either rescue or avenge my son...even should it cause the end of my existence."

"It will not comfort your heart if I tell you I do know how you feel. Or that I also share your desire for a reckoning with this creature. More so than you are aware. But there is little you are able to do. You are far removed from the Earth and, short of a 'summons', you are not a transitional being." Here he stopped and eyed the large "project" that currently occupied Lonius work space. "Even were that not so, you underestimate the power of the one you would face should you enter the air of Earth and his influence."

Lonius gazed up into the angels face and their eyes locked, "Never the less, my vow stands."

Some long moments passed while the giant elder once more turned and gazed out at the crystalline sea. Lonius glanced around as well marveling at the incandescent hue which the presence of one of Creation's original members cast over the entire scene. Suddenly, Raphael shook his massive head and grunted as if coming to some realization or conclusion. Then he turned back to Lonius,

"I am going to ask you to do something for me. I wish to leave something in your care."

With that he reached down to an oversize, chain-mail looking belt studded with gems which sparkled around the huge waist. With obvious reverence, he slowly removed one of his most cherished possessions. As he did so, Lonius' eyes widened and his mouth actually fell open as a shocked expression enveloped his countenance. Raphael held it out to him, but he could not move to take it.

"Elder, no other may carry such things."

"What you say is true...until this moment. Maybe I have been too long in the company of your son. Father may deal with me harshly, but perhaps he will acknowledge my right to this; take it."

Lonius reached out and his hands trembled, "I...I do not have sufficient words...You honor me beyond my understanding."

"Yes...and let honor and truth dictate your every move...or it will certainly destroy you."

Lonius bowed to the angel, "Yes Elder, it shall be as you say."

Raphael retuned a slight bow, "Now...I must return to my duties and to Him." He paused once more. "Lonius...I am sorry about your son."

"I...we...appreciate your feelings...Raphael."

The angel nodded, "Until we meet again...Father of Arak."

With that the crackling, electrical sound returned at a near deafening level and the air shimmered around them with what seemed to be the entire spectrum of color. Raphael was suddenly encased in this aura of flashing power like some huge rainbow had been fed into an equally large, swirling, tornado-like vortex. The next second, Lonius was literally blown backwards a step by the explosive displacement of the giant Arch's departure.

A few moments later, it might have been a dream. Except for the heavy, pulsing object he held in his hands. It was both incredibly beautiful and awesomely frightful. For at that moment, a moment which none had so far equaled, a being of the flesh held more power in his hands than any other in the entire known Cosmos...before or since.

CHAPTER 27

NEXT DAY, Eddie knew he should probably take this one off. Even Mac would understand. "Dead" his mind would whisper every so often, "You'd be as good as dead"...and he would be. But for the intervention of Amos, today would be the first in a short countdown to something he now understood he was completely unprepared for; the end. The end of this life, the end of hopes and dreams, the end of thinking, "Someday, I'll get it right."...Someday would never come.

His mind raced around looking for answers to the quandary involving the "jammer". OK, he had to be straight with himself. He had a whole new way of looking at his co-workers now. The obvious concern they had felt for his plight, the selflessness of what Mikals had done; it was all now part of his...new reality. But did that have any impact on his plan with Sammy? Should it have? He had intentionally avoided meeting them at the Inn before work to keep any pressure from him, or his un-nerving friend, out of the equation. But should yesterday really change anything about the original plan? No, he decided, it shouldn't.

Any delay in getting the plant back on line did most of the guys a favor. The ANM work would continue and the pay with it. That made sense, right? He was actually even doing Amos a favor. In fact, he'd do him another one. When he collected from these mystery guys, he'd find a way to slip some of it to Amos. Yeah, that was a good plan. He'd work out the details later. His job now, was to somehow get the contraption in the door. To do that, he'd best show up as usual and see where thing's went.

When he did check in, Eddie found himself something of a celebrity. Word of any such incident didn't take long to get around amongst the tight knit fraternity of nuclear workers. A seemingly endless stream of well wishers, from both the outgoing and incoming shifts, accosted him as made his way through security and began the uphill walk. Any other time he would have found a way to bask in the attention. Today he needed to focus. Getting on the trash run would be easy enough, the rest he was going to have to play by ear.

He carefully stayed on the Aux side and helped with the routine chores, while still having to field comments and questions about yesterday's mishap. Gradually though, things resumed something of their normal tempo. As the sundown hour approached, and the refuse had been collected and categorized, he sought out Amos and apprised him of his intent to go outside. He managed to subtly insinuate that he wasn't quite ready for the R/B yet and, as expected, got no resistance.

The non-radiated stuff was still accumulating at a fast pace. Everything from boxes and packing to the lumber that was used as scaffolding and temporary support for re-welds and inspections. This, in addition to the everyday detritus from so many people engaged in such a wide variety of task, often added up to a pretty full truck.

Eddie watched the guardhouse staff do their exit inspection on the truck and crew. He noted, with some relief, they were back to their old haphazard tactics. The "hot" lumber thing had gotten them on their toes for a while, but seemed to have faded from memory pretty quick. So much the better.

As they entered the dump site, he casually glanced in the direction Sammy had indicated. To him, the painted drum stuck out like a beacon. Damn, he was going to have to try this. His nerves jumped and tingled as he fought down the rush of adrenaline. They were backing in now to one of the smoldering piles and Eddie jumped down and pretended to survey the site. The others began off loading a number of large cardboard cartons and tossing them onto the smoking ashes. It didn't take long for the cardboard to flare up. Eddie wandered over to Jeff Hutchins and, with a mental gulp, engaged the first gear of his plan.

"Yo, Jeff, wanna grab some barrels for the hatch; they were looking low the other day."

Hutchins looked at him and then eyed the barrels ringing the perimeter, "You sure Ed, Amos didn't say nothing about that."

Eddie shrugged, "With all the excitement yesterday, I doubt anyone thought of it. I just noticed they were running low. You know, he's always telling us to look ahead and think about what's needed and all that."

Hutchins gave an answering shrug, "Yeah, I guess so. It'll give us a chance to hang out at the hatch for a while anyway."

"Yeah", agreed Eddie, "best view in the house."

It was true. That portion of the raised escarpment provided a pretty scenic look at the point where Crystal River entered the Gulf. And while the crew had mended its ways in many respects, outside details still carried an implicit license to relax a little. A quick break from the chaotic and noisy environment inside.

Next second Jeff played right into his hands, "Let's grab that batch by the gate. Hey Phil, help Eddie load some of those drums, will ya." He looked at Dormer, "What say...a half dozen?"

"Should do", stated Eddie as he walked toward the row housing the SADM.

Here though, he rearranged his original intent. He rolled out a drum three down from the marked one, grabbed it by the rims and began hauling it towards the vehicle. Phil arrived and grabbed the next in line. They parked them both in the truck bed and headed back across the sandy entry area for more. Eddie repeated his performance and Phil reached out to do the same.

"Oof...what the crap?" the barrel hadn't budged at his tug. He repeated the effort with another experimental yank and then just stood back.

Eddie covertly watched this as he headed for the truck. Phil mentally scratched his head and then shifted to the next drum in line which immediately responded to his efforts in a normal fashion.

Eddie met him on the return and pointed at the marked drum now standing alone from its brothers, "What's wrong with that one?"

"Don't know...feels like it's full of something."

"Not supposed to be, you check it?"

"No."

"Better take a look."

Eddie stalled a few moments pretending to re-lace his boot. Phil came striding back over and Eddie fell in step as they approached the drum. He noted that one of the co-conspirators had half heartedly bent a couple of the tabs over on the lid. Phil grabbed a hold and gave it a strong yank. It barely responded.

"Whatever they got in there it's pretty heavy."

"Yeah? Lets take a look," said Eddie.

Phil used his gloved hands to pry back the tabs and then forced the lid off.

"Uh-oh."

"What?"

Phil looked at him. "Dude, it's a containment bag." He looked back in the drum with narrowed eyes. "Oh *&#...Look."

Eddie played his part perfectly, "Holy crap...720...Put the lid back on Phil."

The man complied and then started backing away from the container, "What the $#@* is that doing out here?"

Eddie was ready, "Another screw up...just like the lumber."

Phil looked at him blankly then turned to Jeff Hutchins, "Hutch, you better look at this."

Hutchins walked over, "What?"

Eddie took over, "We got another Barnwell load that's slipped out here man."

"Oh crap, are you sure?"

Phil spoke up, "Just take his word man, its marked 720 mr."

"Whoa, that's pretty hot...What the heck...Who are we supposed to tell about this?"

Eddie pretended to be in thought, "Well...if we raise the alarm, Hector, Bill or somebody is history."

Hutchins looked at him, "Whatdya mean?"

"I was in on that last fiasco with the wood. If this gets out they're gonna clean house on the gate crew."

The guards were on a first name basis with nearly everyone. They were well liked and hardly a soul in the plant harbored any ill feeling toward them. Almost to a man, they were just older retirees trying to supplement their small pension checks.

"Judas priest," said Hutchins in disgust.

It was time, "Alright, here's what I think. One, I don't care what kind of crap they got in that drum, it's too hot to leave outside."

Phil broke in, "Yeah, no kidding, 720mr...I don't even want to stand here with it."

Eddie continued, "He's right and that'll make it way worse if it hits the fan again. The lumber wasn't nearly that high"

"So what are our options?" asked Hutchins.

Eddie didn't realize it, but his ANM status, and yesterday's high profile escape, had left him with a perceived air of authority within the maintenance crews.

"Let's just take it to the hatch with the others and put it back inside."

The other two looked at him quizzically for a moment.

"Can we do that?" asked Phil.

Hutchins was deep in thought for a moment, "Yeah...I guess that's better than getting the whole place in another uproar...or getting Hector canned."

Eddie pretended to be in thought as well, "When they gonna open it again."

Phil spoke up, "I heard Mac talking about some new valves coming in tomorrow. They gotta open it then, even though the drummed stuff isn't supposed to leave till next week."

Hutchins was still thinking too, "720's too hot to just leave lying around; we may have to turn it in."

Eddie's heart rate sped back up but he played it cool, "Yeah, you're right; much as I hate to do that to Hector...or any of em'."

This little parlay was starting to get sideways. Eddie was scratching hard mentally but he wasn't coming up with anything. Then he had a flash, "Jeff, let's just take it to the hatch and put it with the others, then pretend we found it there."

"What...Why?"

Eddie thought he had hit on it, "Then it'll just be a piece from the Barnwell run that got missed. No one'll know who to blame, Hector's clear and we look good for finding it."

Hutchins chewed mentally again, "Might work."

Phil was all the way on board, "Oh yeah, that would save Hector's %# and get this sucker back inside."

Eddie pushed his advantage, "Alright, let's get it done and over with. I don't wanna hang around it any more than we have to."

The others voiced their assent and the deal was done. Jeff backed the truck up to the line of drums and they threw a few other empties on board. Then the three of them tag teamed the SADM's drum into the bed. Eddie edge-rolled it in amongst the cluster of empties and they set out for the entrance. It went off without a hitch. The guards had seen so many empty drums collected from the dump area that Hector, who actually was on duty, didn't give them a second glance. The remote probe assembly he had available to check outgoing loads for radiation stayed securely in its rack; another chance missed.

The truck crew continued up the hill and around to the far side of the Reactor Building. To Eddie's relief, he saw there were still only three other empty drums residing outside the huge maintenance entry. They would even look good for having followed Amos' directive to show a little initiative.

The drill was repeated in reverse and the cluster of empty drums was soon staged neatly outside the hatch. The drum with the SADM was still in the truck bed.

"What now," asked Phil.

Eddie and Hutchins exchanged glances, and then Eddie spoke, "I might have a better idea. What if we just bring it back in through the south side roll-up and wheel it back to the R/B like it's more junk from Aux?"

Hutchins looked concerned, "Should we tell Amos what really happened?"

Eddie wasn't too sure about this himself, "I suppose we could. Wait a minute; if we do that we can't be sure how far up the ladder it might get kicked. Maybe we should just try doing it like nothing's special and see how far we get. If Amos shows up we can always use the hatch story."

Hutchins hesitated and then shrugged his shoulders. With that they retraced part of their route and detoured to the southerly truck entrance on the far end of the Auxiliary Building. At this point the whole thing took on an appearance of normality and they off loaded the drum and parked the vehicle with hardly a glance from anyone.

They returned to the inner workings of the Auxiliary complex and quickly made their way to the receiving area serviced by the big roll-up door. Hutchins silenced the alarm, they opened the entry and rolled the drum inside. After re-securing the area, it was decided that Hutch and Eddie would do the deed. They corralled one of the industrial grade drum dollies, retrieved the SADM's drum and set out for the air lock.

Parking their load outside the suit-up area, they donned the cotton overalls, booties, gloves and hood that comprised the basic R/B entry gear. As luck would have it one of Eddie's pals had the "duty".

"Yo, Steve, what's new?"

"Boredom," replied his friend.

It was true; no one particularly enjoyed air-lock duty after the first few times. It consisted of continually operating the valves and locks to allow traffic in and out of the R/B. Being the "nuclear gate keeper" had a certain panache' when you first got the assignment, but it soon became tedium.

"Yeah I know what you mean. You seen Amos?"

"I imagine he's suiting up as we speak. They're gonna try and finish stage one on the sheet tonight."

Eddie was careful not to show his relief, "OK, no matter. We just gotta park this with the Barnwell run and get back to Aux anyway."

"Whatever dude; going to the Inn after work?"

"Could be," said Eddie, and it dawned on him he and Sammy might have something to celebrate tonight.

With that they entered the lock, along with their clandestine cargo, and waited through the cycle. When the opposite hatch opened, Ron Bennet was waiting there with a couple of others.

"Hey, Eddie, how you doing old man?"

Eddie was thinking fast but the HP guys didn't involve themselves much with maintenance, "Right as rain thanks to you and Amos."

"No thanks required mate, Amos is the one took all the risk."

"I know you did your part R. B., I'm grateful."

He was not too surprised to find he was being sincere. It was part of that new reality. Now if he could just get this damn "jammer" off his hands, he could start trying to assess where this new outlook was leading to.

"Nothing to it Ed, just hope to never go down that track again."

"Makes two of us I'm sure," grinned Eddie.

Ron gave a chuckle and slapped him lightly on the shoulder, "Come by later and watch Amos pry chips out of the sheet."

"See ya' Ron."

Ron headed into the lock as Hutch and Eddie took off down a back corridor headed for the far side of the R/B. This was where the drums of tainted material were collected for transfer. There was no traffic on their round about pathway and shortly the innocuous looking drum, with its cargo of instant destruction, was once again hiding in plain sight.

As he and Hutch headed back the way they had come Eddie breathed his first real sigh of relief. It was done. Fifty thousand bucks was his. Now the question was whether to sneak back in and look for the "on" switch or let it wait till he collected his cash. Sammy was right; he was in the driver's seat now. He wondered why he didn't feel better about it.

On the "other side" Buferan was again gleeful. First the take down of his old enemy, now the destruction of Mikals and thousands of his fellow humans. It didn't get much better than this.

"WE HAVE NO WAY of knowing when the device may be activated."

"It does not matter. We are well away from the immediate effects and we dare not leave the actions of the American to chance."

It was a little before midnight and Pytor and Samir were in the parking lot of the "Inn" discussing their next step. It was largely out of their hands now and Pytor was for leaving the vicinity immediately. In his mind their job was done and his additional pay was due; whether Samir's side of the bargain came to fruition or not. His counterpart, on the other hand, wanted nothing left to chance regarding Eddie's involvement.

Samir glanced at his watch, "It is almost time for him to leave the facility. Obviously nothing has occurred thus far. Let us wait and be certain the device is in place."

"Why...If he fails to keep his end are we to attempt its retrieval?"

Samir looked at him thoughtfully, "I had not considered that. It is clearly too valuable to abandon."

The steely eyed Slav stared back at him, "Understand this...I have fulfilled my obligation on this matter. If such a task is put forward, I reserve the right to turn it down...or receive additional compensation."

Samir looked away to hide his distaste. With these people it always revolved back to the money. He too appreciated the finery one could purchase with the American dollars, but that was not the driving force of a true Jihadist. Still, he knew he would never cross this man unless it was over the barrel of a weapon.

"I do not think Kabir would disagree with that."

With a grunt Pytor lapsed back into his customary silence.

A short while later, Eddie's old, four wheel drive Ford pickup entered the lime rock parking area. As he exited, Samir gave a low whistle. After a moment Eddie's eyes adjusted and he saw him motioning. He walked over and joined the strange duo, taking a seat in the back.

"Well, my friend?" said Samir as calmly as possible.

"It's in," replied Eddie.

Samir's heart leapt, "And is it activated?"

"Nah, no chance to do it tonight. Had a thought about that again anyway. We should get paid first."

The terrorist too had canvassed that possibility after their last discussion and he'd come up with a counter plan of sorts.

"Ah, I had the opportunity to suggest that to one of the proprietors. He was not very receptive to the idea. Apparently they have some sort of tracking device that allows them to drive by and tell the approximate location and whether the unit is operating by checking its frequency. I should have thought of that before. At this level of technology that does make sense."

Eddie wasn't sure what made sense anymore, but he was getting real tired of taking such risk and being forced to keep company with a man like Peter...who looked like he'd kill you over a sandwich.

"You know what dude; I don't care what they say. If I get caught messing with that thing, my cover story is blown. I got half a mind to just let it take the trip to Barnwell and no one's the wiser."

At that, the thick shoulders of Peter began to rotate in Eddie's direction. He draped one big arm over the seat and Eddie could almost feel the twin lasers of those strange blue eyes staring into his soul.

"Edward...we agreed to do a job...I agreed to do a job. That job is not finished until the activation is verified. In my upbringing, such failure becomes a matter of honor. Would you truly expect me to have my honor besmirched because you are reluctant to turn on a switch; or have become the victim of greed?"

Eddie's heart began to race. The implicit threat was clear as crystal. He cringed inwardly. He knew he had gotten in over his head when he met this guy. He was no "friend" from Sammy's neighborhood in Miami. Or maybe he was. Miami was a place where hired muscle could easily be found. Whatever the case, his future was now in this guy's hands; but only to a point. He'd just faced death in an environment more frightening than anything these two had to offer. He'd keep the bargain and then they could go hang. And if he didn't see the cash tomorrow night, he'd personally put the damn drum on the front row of the South Carolina run.

He stared back at the darkened countenance, "I tell you guy's what. I will make every effort to turn the thing on by 5:00 tomorrow. You have your boys do their drive by sometime between then and quitting time. Have them repeat it if there's no signal in case I'm held up. Then tomorrow night we get paid. After that I'm done. I'll put it somewhere it won't get taken out on the next load and leave it running, but that's it. Do not expect me to change the batteries or anything else that comes up after that...got it? And the dough better be here tomorrow night or off it goes."

Pytor gave a wicked smile, which Eddie could just make out in the dim lighting, then extended a big paw in his direction, "Edward, your terms are completely acceptable."

Eddie couldn't see it, but a similar smirk was on Samir's face as well.

WELL, apparently that was that. Father had been less than pleased with his visit to Deran, but stopped short of demanding he recover the "keepsake" left with Lonius. Looking back he knew...no, he'd already known, that its mere presence would introduce some temptation into the Deranian's mind. But, despite that, it would also be something that might keep him occupied while the loss of his son was so fresh. He knew there was no way Lonius could act on his wish to avenge that loss...unless Father intervened or assisted. And now that was not going to happen. Ah well, there had been no real indication that it would.

What he hadn't expected, was for things to be suddenly suspended just as they were. He had felt sure there would be a scramble to send in a replacement or maybe a small squad of "Second's" to deliver Arak's original info. But it now appeared that Amos and company were on their own. The most recent reports offered a few surprising turns but did not indicate the trio at the heart of the matter had deduced the true severity or nature of the threat.

Raphael sighed deeply; it seemed he would once again be forced to watch the forces of evil shortchange human lives. He had seen many tragedies and horrors inflicted on these helpless, and sometimes innocent, members of Earth. Yet his soul still recoiled as it had the first time. Truly, when Judgment arrived, this world would pay a high price for the blood soaked path Lucifer had led them down. This matter of free will might produce the next "generation" of rulers and potentates, but it had certainly spawned its share of devils as well. Someday there would be Hell to pay...literally.

Right now though, it looked as if the repercussions were going to land hard on Amos, his friends and untold others on his little piece of that globe. In many ways it made no sense, even to his ancient and experienced mind, but he had pushed the boundaries as far as he dared on the matter.

Scripture taught the fact that God could sympathize and feel the pain of His creation's suffering. Raphael understood that perfectly; the ache in his own heart was now constant as well.

CHAPTER 28

A S AMOS CLEARED SECURITY the next day, and began the familiar uphill walk, he had the pleasure of watching Matt Robbins bring the Bird in for another "Charlie" visit. He liked the man and knew that he and Fitz went way back in the nuclear world; both military and industrial. None the less, Fitz never failed to give his old friend an earful about how his "inspections" were slowing progress. Charlie, for his part, was like the proverbial duck; Fitzgerald just rolled off like water.

Amos could hear the turbine spooling down on the far side of the R/B and made a note to try and see Matt before they departed. These afternoon visits were usually over well before dark as the duo had to fly back to temporary headquarters on the outskirts of Miami. There were no NRC offices in Florida. All official activity was spawned in Atlanta in the Region II office. The mash-up at CR3, and some planned activity at one of the Turkey Point reactors, had resulted in the stationing of a temp-team in South Florida.

His thoughts also kept returning to the situation with Arak. He had to battle that hopeless feeling that fought to attach itself to his thinking. Oh, he had faith that God heard their plea, but even so, His will was often out of sync with that of man. Amos sometimes felt life seemed far longer during certain periods than others. Older mentors had schooled him on how time seemed to have flown by as you approached the twilight years. But right now, time felt like it was creeping by and every tick held a shadow of menace. Thankfully, he wasn't doing any hot work tonight. A break from that intensity was welcome under the circumstances. And then, there was Jenny.

It was becoming obvious they had touched each others hearts. What a crazy way to finally meet the "right" girl. And another worry he had to harbor in the back of his mind. She was in this thing as deep as he was. Happenstance or direct will of God, it didn't matter They were fellow warriors now, engaged in what was apparently becoming an epic battle. Had he heard such an outlandish tale from anyone else, he had to admit, he'd have wondered about their mental state. The sheer "insanity" of all that had transpired exceeded some of the big screen's own efforts. But, unlike some movie or newscast, chances were, most of the facts on this one would remain a closed file.

As he prepared to officially enter the complex, his thoughts and those of the Holy Spirit seemed to mesh with that accustomed suddenness. He felt the reaction up and down his spine that often announced when such a moment had arrived.

"Uh-oh, what now?"

He stopped in his tracks and slowly scanned the area. Nothing seemed unusual, but he now knew not to place too much weight on that fact. The next moment Eddie cleared Security and stepped out into the afternoon sun. Was there something going on here that involved Eddie? That question kept coming up. Or maybe tonight was the night he would get a chance to really lay the Gospel out for him? He would like to put it down to nerves but, again, he had weathered too much lately to drop his guard. He gave a wave to the man, who was still far down the hill, and turned to once more enter the "Valley of the Shadow"...unaware how accurate that moniker was steadily becoming.

AS FOR EDDIE, when he slipped back to "safe storage" that afternoon, first shift had already shuffled and added to the drum count. It took him a few anxious minutes to locate the little paint dot. During the early shift movements no one would have noticed the weight; there were probably several in the accumulation that out-weighed the "jammer". Problem was, he needed to park his somewhere it wouldn't attract attention and would be exempt from the next Barnwell load-up. He decided to make a short patrol through the hallways serving the area and see if some place caught his eye. He was preparing to head back down one passageway when the thought struck him. "Smith and Jones" might already be cruising by checking for a signal.

He strode back over to the SADM's resting place and stood staring at the innocent looking drum. There was not much chance of being disturbed in this area, particularly at this time of the shift. But before he messed with it, he should probably position it at the back of the pack so it would be convenient when he was ready for the move. He used the tilt and roll technique on several of the others to clear a path and then strenuously did the same with the device's drum positioning it on the row nearest the hallway. The thought occurred that he should perhaps complete the surveillance of his surroundings before going any further but curiosity finally set in.

He'd risked much to get this thing in-house and had never even laid eyes on it. According to Sammy, he would have no trouble locating the switch under the plastic bag because of the asterisk. Should he go ahead and turn it on? He pondered a few seconds while multiple unseen entities figuratively held their breath...for opposite reasons.

Nah, better get it moved first. What if it immediately sent some whacked out message to Ops and someone came prowling to check it out. He'd better make the relocation before he risked opening the thing. He continued his original plan to recon the area.

As he proceeded down the hall, he noticed a mainte-nance cart with a couple of nearly full Rem bags on board. He snagged it and began pushing it through the circular outer hallway as if looking for more debris. He hadn't gotten far when one of the dog-leg openings to a machinery room caught his eye. Almost all equipment areas were entered through these ninety degree bend type entries which acted as blockades to damp the radiation from sources inside. This one had a High Radiation sign strung on a chain across the opening. A sure bet you didn't want to mess around inside without first using a probe to check the exposure rate. There was a "personnel" Geiger counter on a small rack to one side of the doorway and some shelving stocked with supplies on the other.

Eddie had no idea what type equipment resided within, but it was obviously pretty "hot". The short hallway would make an ideal spot to camouflage the drum. He plundered around on the shelves and found a roll of Radioactive Waste tape. The bright yellow tape, with its magenta colored lettering, would announce to one and all that a container was actively being used to collect material from a hot work zone. If he labeled his drum with the tape, and parked it here behind the chain, it might be a long time before anyone received an assignment to go past that point; or bother taking notice of its presence. It would look like a dozen others in the area waiting to reach the full mark and be shuffled out to storage.

He abandoned the cart in its original location and went in search of a drum dolly. It didn't take long to come up with one. They, like much of the other maintenance hard-ware, led an unsettled life here in the heart of the chaos. Although procedure had "a place for every thing and every thing in its place" rule during actual operation, that dictate had become somewhat flexible as the rebuild dragged on. He returned to the storage zone and loaded up his quarry grunting as he threw his weight back to elevate it. As he passed the maintenance cart another thought struck him.

He could probably plunder around inside the drum right here and pretend he was loading stuff for transport. He did a quick scan and the decided it was time to commit. He rested it nearly against the cart and looked at the lid. Phil's half-hearted bends on a few of the tabs were still all that held it in place. He undid them with his gloved hands and pried the lid free. The 720mr markings were clearly visible but he realized the switch portion must be hidden under the Styrofoam packing and cardboard. Crap, he was going to have to unpack some of it. He carefully began removing pieces and placing them onboard the cart with the already full bags. The asterisk quickly came into view.

Eddie had broken out in a light sweat now and his heartbeat was accelerating. This was the very pit of danger as far as getting caught. The vinyl bag was slippery under his cotton gloves so he pulled them off. He tried to rip the place where the asterisk was to no avail. These were not your everyday lawn and leaf bags. He remembered a case cutter on the supply shelf at his planned destination and strode hurriedly away to retrieve it. His luck held and he returned and quickly made a slit through the asterisk.

There was the flap in the fabric covering. So far so good. Wait a minute; this thing was wearing some kind of camouflage. Was the device military? That made sense; where would those corporate jokers get the kind of technology we were talking about here. What if it was stolen? Nah, everything in this country was for sale these days. With the money they apparently had, it probably wouldn't be hard to find a military guy or manufacturer to buy it from. Still might be stolen though.

Eddie cared not at all for that scenario; it only made his involvement that much more criminal. Rats...there was that new feeling again. His conscience had never been much of a problem before this. Now he felt like some kind of traitor to the other guys...and to Amos. Amos would have never gone for a deal like this. Was it too late to get out of this thing? Probably...unless he wanted to be looking over his shoulder for Peter every night. With a large mental sigh he reached in and pulled back on the zipper.

There was the other opening Sammy had spoken of. It had some kind of door with fancy screws holding it shut. The one he wanted was higher up. It didn't take long to find it. He looked at the hi-tech switch-cover for a moment and then flipped it up exposing a bright red, flat sided toggle switch. There was no on/off nomenclature or any labeling, but there was a small indicator light adjacent to it. That must be all the info you needed to be sure it was transmitting. Eddie reached for the switch...something stopped him. This was getting ridiculous. His mind was playing tricks on him. One side argued he forget the whole thing and the other was playing out the scene of getting his money and finally being done with this. He had truly never experienced such a mental tug of war. The money won out.

You would think that such an inter-dimensional, climactic moment would have something special to set it apart. Instead, all you would have been able to observe was Eddie's activation of the switch followed by several whirs and one loud click from within the device. That along with the illumination of the small red indicator light...Nevertheless, D-day had arrived. But in this case, it was only one hour long.

A sixty minute countdown to a thermonuclear blast inside an active reactor facility has begun. There is an exposed, freshly fueled core and a full set of spent fuel rods in the nearby storage pool. As anticipated, the afternoon sea breeze is in full swing blowing onshore with gusto. Ultimately, the exposure-based death toll will be astronomic. Humans, pets, wildlife; nothing will be spared. Contamination of both the Gulf, and the underground aquifer system, is also pretty much a foregone conclusion. Water supplies, dairy and farming, the fishing industry... gone in the blink of an atomic eye.

The immediate local destruction will be something like a squadron size B-52 carpet bombing. CR3, and its adjacent sister plants, will largely cease to exist. With the containment and cooling systems destroyed, the newly replenished core will quickly go supercritical. The ensuing secondary explosions will spew untold amounts of radioactive contamination and multiply the disaster factor exponentially. The aftermath and contamination will shut down the West Central coast of Florida for a thousand years. Tampa, Orlando, Disney World...these will become ghost towns. The backlash of such an occurrence takes on the proportion of a scaled down Armageddon...And no one has a clue.

CHAPTER 29

WHILE EDDIE was inadvertently placing the entire geographic area in peril, Amos was pursuing one of his favorite idle moment activities. Picking Fitzgerald's brain about the mechanics of "Fission for Power" and listening to some of the less than public nuclear history lessons he'd gleaned over the years. Fitz would shortly be joining his old pal Charlie for the scheduled Auxside inspections but, for now, Amos had him to himself. They were in the main reactor area solemnly discussing the trauma dealt to the Three Mile Island facility. Something which stilled weighed quite heavily on the collective consciousness of the industry.

Fitz had personally managed the team that sought to assess the internal damage caused by the accident which had resulted in a core melt down on reactor number two. The timing of the accident with the release of a Hollywood movie, "The China Syndrome", about a troubled nuclear plant, was eerie.

The movie put forth the possibility of a runaway core burning or melting its way through its vessel and into the Earth's crust "to China". Now Amos was listening attentively while Fitz described the utter destruction, of nearly indestructible materials, inside the involved containment building. Evidence of the incredible heat that had bloomed from the stricken reactor. He concluded his tale with a sobering look on his face,

"Amos, ever since that movie and all the hoopla over the accident, everyone keeps yakking about one of these things going out of control and burning through the Earth. The fact is, if that one didn't...I'm not sure they will. And we have no idea why not."

Both men were silent now as they stared up at the massive reactor head which towered on its equally huge rebuild stand beside them. Sometimes man got involved, or chose to play on a playground, where he was not always in charge and didn't get to make all the rules. These beasts certainly fit in that category.

EDDIE REPLACED THE PACKING, put the lid back on the drum and re-bent several of the tabs to insure anyone wishing to look inside would at least have to make an effort. He would wait till he got to the entry way to add the Rad-Waste tape. He resumed ferrying his cargo towards that point and was relieved to again not run into anyone. He wheeled it right up next to the chain and set it down with a thump. Then something strange happened. The little Geiger counter outside the entry way gave a couple of chirps.

He looked at it in surprise. What's that about? Must be really hot in there for it to do that. He was tempted to take a quick glance into the actual cubicle but common sense dictated otherwise. Oh well, he'd park this thing behind the chain and beat feet out of here; for good. He was reaching for the yellow warning tape when the counter repeated its performance, only with more chirps than before. Now, that was weird. Those little ones were calibrated for close range. The only thing getting close to it was him. Ah nuts, he must've gotten crapped up messing with those other drums.

He took the unit from the shelf and it did the same thing in his hands. But not like it was reacting to him. The signal wandered and fluctuated as he moved it around. He stepped back into the center of the hall and used the small probe with its coiled wire lead to give himself a quick sweep; nothing. OK, the batteries must be failing; he'd seen them get erratic when that was the case. He flipped it over and looked at the status needle next to the power compartment. It was in the green. Curiouser and curiouser.

He shrugged and turned to replace the unit and as he did so, it let out a determined series of warbles. He'd walked right by the drum on his way to the shelf. Eddie froze for a moment and just listened to the counter. Man, it was really excited about something. This wasn't one of those temporary reactions to all the background stuff. He waved it around experimentally and as it passed over the drum it emitted a high pitched squeal and pegged the needle.

Confusion...There were a few moments of total disorientation as his brain tried to connect the dots. Then a wave of uneasiness washed through his soul. No, wait a minute; they must have crapped up his drum while they were shuffling things around this morning. The best thing to do was get the thing parked and get out of here. Some voice in his head would not agree. He had to be sure. He walked the probe right up against the drum's surface...and it pegged again. But there was no evidence of contamination or smears on the surface. Now a sick feeling surged into the pit of his stomach. It just wasn't possible. Was the jammer radioactive?

His gloved fingers tore at the tabs and he snatched the lid back off. He moved the now steadily singing probe towards the top of the yellow plastic. It didn't even get close before it again loudly exceeded its limits. Whatever was inside this thing was off the scale. Suddenly a horrible series of lights started switching on in Eddie's head. Sammy...the accent, and then Peter...another foreigner. The military look to the "jammer"...and it was apparently super hot...Oh no...Oh no...Oh no.

Panic...Panic was trying to overtake his mind...was it possible...Oh God, Oh God. It was almost a plea for divine intervention. He spun and looked both ways subconsciously wishing for help of some kind. Then he froze. Wait...Wait...Wait...He could just turn it off. He ripped off his gloves and snatched at the packing slinging it out on the floor. He found the switch, jerked the safety cover up and thumbed it to the off position...the light stayed on. His eyes began to bulge and his mind started to succumb to an overload of panic stricken melt down.

He caught himself and gulped some deep breaths. It was just not possible. There had to be another explanation. "Alright stop," his conscious mind shouted at him, "think." He had set whatever this was in motion by throwing that switch. Maybe the other door had the actual power circuit that controlled it. He snatched the case cutter up and swept a long incision down the Rem bag. It didn't take long to figure out the flip up wing screws and then he was looking at the apparatus inside. Some smaller switches and a couple of clock looking dials; what the heck, timers?

His blood went suddenly cold and the original fear leapt back to clutch at his heart and mind. The left hand clock was clicking off seconds...in reverse. It was backing down! And the margin showing was fifty three minutes. He started to reach for the other switches then snatched his hand back. He was afraid now to touch any of the "controls". Sheer terror was again starting to engulf his thinking.

Now his very being did do just that; cry out in total sincerity to God for help. And suddenly, at that point, all the residual, spiritual selfishness evaporated from Eddie's inner being. The Holy Spirit had been advancing towards this moment even before the disastrous Drive jump. Operating in that anonymous and secret parallel with the very "Mind of the Cosmos", his influence had, at this most terrifying of moments, shone the divine light of true reality into the heart, mind and soul of one Edward Allen Dormer.

In a micro-instant, as time ceased to be a factor, Eddie made his peace with every failed moment of a life lived outside the dictates of the massive will and power of the Creator who had made him. All the information he had ever been exposed to, in churches, at funerals, street preachers...even more recently with Amos, rushed at him like a reverse kaleidoscope of realization. And in that instant he surrendered his heart back to God and accepted what the Firstborn over all Creation had come to Earth to do on his behalf. It was accomplished before the timer had managed to deduct another second.

In an already crazy sounding story, yet another milestone was breached. A "loser" in the greatest game life has to offer, became a winner for all eternity...And knew exactly what he had to do.

Eddie raced back down the hallway and took the first opening that led back to the central reactor area. He burst onto the busy floor, almost at the base of the giant stand that held the reactor head. And there, like a godsend, standing in conversation, were Amos and Fitz.

Eddie was still wide eyed, "Amos, I need your help." He looked at the other man, "You too Fitz."

Amos glanced at Fitzgerald and then back at Eddie, "Sure Ed, what for?"

He actually hung his head for a second, then, "I've been tricked into something; something real bad I think. We gotta go...now!"

With that, he raced back the way he had come. The other two looked at each other for a one count and then took off after him. There was no mistaking the urgency in Eddie's eyes. They caught up with him when he paused at the hallway juncture, but he immediately bolted off down the oversize, curved version that paralleled the outer containment wall. When they again caught up, he was standing amidst some packing scraps next to a debris drum that was parked in front of the entry to a restricted equipment room.

"This...this is supposed to be a piece of computer equipment," said Eddie breathlessly pointing inside the drum.

Both men eyed the exposed section of the yellow bag housing the "jammer" without really seeing it.

Fitz spoke first, "Uh, OK, what about it."

"It's hot...real hot."

Fitz looked non-plussed, "Then why isn't it in storage? It must be junk if they canned it up."

Once more Eddie cast his eyes down, "We didn't can it...it's from an outside source."

During all this Amos recognized the intense hammering the Spirit was once again imparting to his mentality. He looked at Eddie and again at the piece inside the drum,

"From where Ed, how would it get in here?"

Oh God, it hurt to say this, "I brought it in. I know I'm in trouble; but I didn't know what it was. I still don't, but its really hot...look."

With that he grabbed the counter and stuck it on the device. Both men now realized the little unit had been quietly chirping intermittently on its stand, but they sometimes did that. Hey, it was a nuclear plant. Now it sang its off key warble that signaled the end of its capability and clearly announced a warning to anyone within range. Both men's eyes widened and Fitz bent over fearlessly to look inside. Eddie placed the unit back on its shelf while Amos stood watching Fitzgerald.

Suddenly Fitz's whole body seemed to convulse and his eyes took on Eddie's same bulge. He grabbed both sides of the slit in the Rem bag and forcefully snatched it open.

"Oh my God," he nearly shouted. Then he did a similar sweep in both directions as if seeking some answer or guidance.

"What...what is it?" asked Amos as calmly as he could. Fitz was one cool customer and his reaction had already "spooked" his own nerve endings.

Fitz stopped suddenly and seemed to be catching his breath. Then he peered again into the drum. He pushed the distorted Rem bag around and seemed to be inspecting the contraption inside. Then his eyes went even wider and another "Oh my God," quietly escaped his lips. "It's armed and counting."

"I didn't know, I didn't know," Eddie was repeating.

Amos training took over, "Know what Eddie...tell me, NOW!"

Fitz interrupted the exchange, "He didn't know it's a US Government 'suitcase' nuke."

Like some cue from a more lighthearted skit, both Eddie and Amos echoed at the same time, "A WHAT?"

Fitz's own military background, which included quite a bit of knowledge about these particular weapons, now re-engaged as well. He eyed Eddie as he began a hurried explanation,

"This is a 1960's military weapon called a SADM...Special Atomic Demolition Munition...This one's obviously stolen and...and...Just how the hell did it get in here Dormer? Never mind...Amos, the timer on it has been modified...I don't dare touch it. There were several that had an immediate detonation safety lock if you tampered with them. No way to know which this is."

He leaned again to look inside the drum and pulled the yellow plastic aside, "There's forty eight minutes showing on the clock. That's not enough time to get a bomb crew or figure out how to disarm it. But it's time enough to get it out of the facility. The question is...to where?"

Amos had managed to calmly process the info Fitzgerald was pumping out. The past days all seemed to have been meant to prepare him for whatever was in the works. And now, the great secret was out...and it was a doozy. An icy clarity settled on his mind and soul,

"There's absolutely no way to defuse it or disarm it?"

"Probably is...but not in...,"Fitz glanced down, "forty seven minutes."

That inner voice had already helped crystallize some of Amos' thinking,

"There's a way..."

Both the others stared expectantly at him.

"Have Matt put it in the Bird, drop it in the Gulf."

Several seconds passed in silence as they both processed the idea Then Fitz spoke,

"That's not a good thing, but it might be the only way to get out of this without a really major disaster. I'll go with him and watch it on the way out."

"No; I'll go" said Amos. The finality in the statement and the look in his eyes almost sealed the deal without another word.

"Why you," said Fitz, "I know more about them...and I'm older," he added solemnly.

"When I get back, I might explain it to you...both of you...but this thing was always about getting me."

In a world that had strayed so far from God, men didn't often get the chance to feel the true power of His Spirit. That power and authority now rested tangibly on this young man and his words. Eddie had suddenly come to understand something about that. Fitz was an old dog without much in the way of new tricks; but it hit him just the same. Calm settled on their nerves and both remained silent.

"OK here's the deal; right now only we know about this. Don't cause a panic. Don't tell a soul. We'll have to fill Matt in but everyone else is out. OK?"

They both nodded.

"Fitz, go out to Matt; you know he won't be far from the chopper. Explain it to him. Eddie, let's get this thing out to Aux and take it to the back side roll up...quietly."

They both hesitated for a second and looked at Amos. He said softly, "Guy's this is the real deal, we have to try our best to stop it. Peoples lives are in our hands...just do it."

Fitz had been under the spell of that strange calmness surrounding Amos. He wasn't quite sure what to make of it. The whole thing felt almost dream-like; or rather like some nightmare. But he just placed his hand on Amos' shoulder and said, "Good luck, Amos," and hurried back down the hallway en-route to give Robbins the shock of his life.

Eddie was still eyeing him, "Amos...I never meant for anything like this to happen...And now I understand...About you and Him," he pointed up.

"Tell me about it on the way," said Amos as he grabbed the dolly and began to reposition it under the drum.

With that, they beat a retreat to the air-lock where they were briefly reunited with Fitz while waiting out the current cycle. All three eyed each other, but not a word was spoken. They had not bothered to replace the lid and Amos fought a desire to look inside at the timer. He was sure the other two shared that concern.

CHAPTER 30

FINALLY, they were through. As they wheeled the lidless drum through the access passageway, one of the attendant Geiger counters gave a loud warble and began chirping constantly. The attendant, Eddie's pal again, gave him a raised eyebrow look.

"You takin' hot stuff out?"

Fitz stepped in, "Yeah, Ops has gotta have a look at it."

No one argued with Fitz. Steve just shrugged and they proceeded to quickly de-suit from the R/B outer wear. Then, with another clandestine glance, Fitzgerald hurried away and Amos and Eddie resumed their trek to the backside of the Auxiliary complex. When they arrived, Amos silenced the security alarm and proceeded to activate the giant steel door. The cold mechanical atmosphere, under the industrial fluorescents, began to recede as the bright sunlit afternoon came into view.

There had been little conversation as they made their way through the maze of the auxiliary building. Too many stray ears were all around the hectic platforms and work sites in some places; in others, the machinery was just too loud. They rolled the dolly out into the surreal silence and peaceful backdrop that only this part of the perimeter had to offer. The hatch area, including the zone where Matt landed the Bell helicopter, were just around the corner out of view. Eddie tried to resume the same conversation he'd attempted during the frantic trip from the R/B.

"Look...Amos...I had no idea and I can explain what I thought it was...."

"Ed, there's no time. I believe you weren't aware it was...a bomb. But the rest will have to wait...OK?"

He sighed, "Yeah man, but I need you to believe me."

"I do... Now get it around to the chopper; I gotta make a call."

"Amos...now...to who? Oh, yeah, I guess the cops right."

"No, not the cops. You guy's just get it loaded."

The "new" Eddie stared a moment at him, "Ok, you got it...I'm sorry."

"I know...now go...go."

With that they parted company and Amos raced back towards the only "real" telephone available in this section of the building. They called it the booth; a raised office area which was soundproofed against the tremendous noise levels present when everything was engaged and producing power. Amos used his master key to enter and sat down in a well worn office chair parked in front of an equally 'broke in' desk. He rang the switchboard, got an outside line and dialed his home number. The machine picked up; he'd expected that.

Before he departed, he had helped Jim and Jenny get his boat in the water and configured for a run out into the Gulf. They planned to snorkel Appointment hole and watch the sunset from one of the best spots on the planet...this part anyway. Even with the horrific intensity of what was happening, the image of the two of them made a wistful smile fleet across his face. He hoped, no, he prayed, he'd see them again. However, the substance of that prayer needed little vocalization at the moment. A kindergarten believer could have felt the hum of energy linking his own small spirit with that of the One who is guardian of all that exist. The oneness spoken of by Jesus in John's gospel.

Now he proceeded to leave a terse message quickly detailing the situation. As he ended the most terrible sit-rep their little team would ever have to hear, he added quietly...Jen...Just in case...I love you. Their faces, smiles and voices continued to flicker through his mind as he raced for the roll-up door. As he got nearer he could hear the turbine on the Bird spooling up. A mental hurrah flashed into his thoughts. Matt wasn't asking questions he was going with the same impulse that was driving Amos. The nano-seconds were clicking by in slow motion and his mind was now keeping pace.

Was all this somehow prearranged by God? Matt's conversion. The chopper being here in the "hour of need". Would they make it? Time was definitely ticking but they should have at least a half hour left. The Bird was capable of well over 150 mph; theoretically they should have room to spare. He'd have to ask Fitz to be sure. A suitcase nuke? It was like something out of the movies. It wasn't physically very big. How large was the explosion from such a weapon?

He rounded the corner of the Aux building and immediately felt the air currents coming off the chopper's big four bladed rotor. The drum was lying on its side against the R/B wall where the prop-wash had evidently blown it after the device was removed. Eddie was inside the passenger section taking directions from Fitz. They seemed to be trying to lash it to the steel legs beneath the rear seats. Amos ducked in under the spinning blades and watched as Ed finished cinching the camouflaged unit to the supports. The outer fabric covering actually had webbing and buckles that appeared to have been designed for just such operations. He motioned to Fitz with a wristwatch motion asking about time.

Fitz grasped his shoulder and leaned him in to where the original zipper clad flap was open. He pulled it back so Amos could see the dial; thirty one minutes. Amos sidestepped down the fuselage to where he could look over at Matt who was already strapped into the right hand seat. He was wearing his headset and obviously going through pre-flight checks. He caught his friend's attention and signaled an OK query with his hand. Matt stared a moment and Amos imagined he could see him rolling his eyes behind the dark Ray Ban Aviator glasses. Then he nodded and motioned for Amos to get on board.

Amos gathered Fitz and Eddie and hustled them away from the shrieking, windy tempest. When he could make himself heard he shouted,

"If you can wait here till we get back, do it; but don't give out any info you don't have to."

"Amos, people are going to notice starting as soon as Charlie realizes that chopper's gone," shouted Fitz.

"Fitz, it's in your hands, but we need to sort some of this out before the chaos begins."

They both looked at Eddie and Fitz said loudly, "The sorting starts now...right Dormer?"

Eddie just looked down and then nodded.

"Fair enough...you guy's...pray."

They nodded in unison and Amos sprinted for the open door of the Bird. He clambered in and they watched it slam shut.

Squeezing into the cockpit, he settled into the left hand seat and began fastening the lap and shoulder belts. As soon as they clicked into place he felt as if he'd just gotten on a ride at the fair. The chopper fairly leaped off the ground and they were away and over the perimeter fence before he even had time to glance back at Eddie and Fitz. Matt looked over at him and pointed to a light green headset and another set of Ray Bans resting on his console. Amos placed the headset over his ears and immediately heard Matt's voice.

"Mikals...it would be too much to hope this is another of your practical jokes, right?"

"Fraid not Matt...It's a long story I'm sure, but I only know this last little part right now."

"And that thing is really a nuke."

"Seems so."

An exasperated sigh came to Amos through the pilot's mike, "So, after all this time avoiding the reactors and what-not, I'm strapped in here with a miniaturized A-bomb anyway. How much time we got?"

"About a half hour...Which brings me to a favor I need to ask."

"Yeah?"

"Can you take us down and stop by one of my holes?"

Matt turned to him, "One of your grouper holes...what the devil for?"

Amos was quiet for a second, "When we get back, I'm going to tell you the weirdest story you're ever likely to hear."

Matt interrupted him, "Uh, you want to take a look in back and rephrase that?"

Amos did glance back at the bomb, "Actually, this is only one chapter...and I'm pretty sure it's not over yet."

"Yeah, roger that, so why the hole?"

"The future Mrs. Mikals is there, and just in case...I want to say goodbye."

Matt turned again and stared at him, "That girl you...Jenny...Well I'll be...Which way?"

CHAPTER 31

I N Amos' little aluminum V-hull, perched on the crystal clear water over Appointment Hole, Jim and Jenny were sipping cokes and munching Doritos. As they snacked, they watched the wide variety of large and small denizens swarm in and out of the cracks and crevasses below. Occasionally one would stop and hover, staring warily back up at them through the "looking glass" surface.

"This is so cool. It's like a saltwater aquarium... only better."

"I see cool has made it into your vocabulary."

"Very funny pops...Whatdya think would happen hanging around you two all the time?"

"Some of the things that are happening come as a total surprise."

Jenny blushed a little. She knew her dad was referring to the blossoming affection between her and Amos.

"Well, it comes as a little bit of a shock to me too."

"Hey, you know what, it does my heart..."

Jim stopped in mid sentence. A high pitched whine had been registering in his mind for several seconds but it was now increasing to a familiar whup-whup accented roar. He scanned to the north and his eye detected a bright red chopper about a half mile out, on the deck and racing right at them.

"Uh, Jen...stand by to abandon ship if need be."

Jenny had followed his gaze and was also eyeing the approaching "Bird" with some concern. In mere seconds the chopper was upon them. It suddenly flared upward, threw on the brakes and came to rest hovering a hundred feet from their position. Then it gently settled till its skids were only a few feet off the water and crept towards them nose first. The rotor turbulence had turned the clear surface into a choppy froth and blown them south, hard up against the anchor line. It stopped its progress while still far enough out to keep them clear of the direct down-wash off the blade tips.

Jim had picked up Amos' spear gun and placed it across his lap. He doubted it would be much use against an adversary equipped with a fancy-looking new chopper. They probably had some fancy, new guns too. But training and habits die hard and no one was endangering his daughter without taking the best shot he had available. As he was considering pulling the bands to armed position, the figure in the pilot's compartment to their right came into focus waving both arms. Then that same side cockpit door was forced open against the down force and the chopper rotated to place them face to face with the occupant. NRC was in bold black letters on the fuselage. The waving figure pulled off his headset and glasses and both Alexander's mouth's dropped at the same time.

"Dad...it's Amos," shouted Jenny; stating the obvious.

He was motioning to them pantomiming using a phone. Then he pointed back inshore towards home. Now he was holding his hand over his heart and then he threw Jenny a kiss. The door closed as suddenly as it had opened and they had one last glimpse of Amos waving at them. Then the thing spiraled around to face west, jerked its tail rotor skyward and accelerated out to sea at warp speed.

The surface was still unsettled as rings of ripples vibrated away from their position in every direction. After the horrendous thunder of the blades and turbine, the afternoon quiet had that ear ringing intensity. Only the ripples and the distant, fading roar were left to prove it had ever really been there.

"Dad..."

"Yeah, I know...something has obviously happened...You get the phone thing?"

"I think so...I'm guessing he called the house...Probably left a message," said Jenny.

"The rest was pretty clear too." She blushed again but her dad continued, "So; do we head in or wait around here. Chopper like that doesn't have fuel to wander around the Gulf forever. They gotta be back here sometime fairly soon. Where would he be going straight out like that?"

"Maybe to a ship or something?"

Jim's mind was racing and he was listening hard for some kind of impulse or guidance. He figured his daughter was too. Yet they hadn't come up with much of anything so far. Given the last few days, that in itself was odd...even a little scary.

"OK Jen...lets hang out here a while, see if they come back. If it gets to be too long, we'll go check the house."

"Yeah...OK...Dad...I got a bad feeling about this."

Jim didn't reply...He was starting to feel it too.

MEANWHILE, Amos and Matt raced westward with their unwelcome passenger. Matt had brought them up to a much higher altitude, intending to have their "package" well below and behind them when it contacted the salt water; just in case. Amos had left the cockpit and was seated over the SADM where he could see the timer. Problem was, no one had been paying any attention to the secondary dial face; another custom modification courtesy of Kabir's people.

It was sitting silently, its indicator lined up unmoving with the number fifteen. Pytor had set it on his second trip into the compartment that night to help stymie anyone savvy enough to know the original timing system. The fifteen represented an operator induced error which could affect the timing positively or negatively. Making the actual detonation sequence occur late or early. In this case fifteen minutes late...or early. Pytor had keyed it for the negative value.

Where Amos looked and saw twenty two minutes left on the clock...there were only seven.

CHAPTER 32

S O THAT WAS IT. The steady stream of First Rank
reports were clearly painting a picture of victory for
Lucifer. Yet, Father still seemed immoveable. The
palpable, breathless hush, which had become a trademark
of this little adventure, had descended into a crushed
silence. Even members who had not been close to the action
were gathering now to hear whatever news came in. None
of it was good.

In the early stages, Raphael had been hopeful that this
drama would induce Father to lift the curtain dimensionally so that some of the Kingdom family could watch the
events unfold on Earth in "real time". This was something
he'd been witness to on a number of occasions during the
planet's tumultuous history. Some of the humans involved
in such events were now here on the other side of that
experience looking back. Any Earth believer, studying the
scriptures deeply enough, could find reference to this sort of
possibility. Unfortunately, that number was not a large
one.

Now he was glad they would not have to see the fiery,
mortal end of this little champion who had resisted so

heartily the wiles the devil hurled at his earthly existence. Not that this regrettable finale would reduce the standing that resistance had garnered him. The real tragedy was that many, who might possibly have joined in that acclaim, would probably be eternally absent.

Their complex road map of life would see many undulating avenues and trails, involving the possible influence of one Amos Mikals, snuffed out. Just the recent activity in and around that influence had produced some deep changes in several others. The one called Eddie was indeed something of a surprise. It was this latent power in the message that drove the Gospel forward on their tattered little world.

Conversely, the design and wickedness of Lucifer was such that, by attacking those who sought to impart Truth, he often weakened and distorted that message. The "Cheap Grace" syndrome, which had been spreading slowly amongst the very establishments claiming to represent Truth, was one direct and damning result of these attacks. In this case however, it seemed both the messenger and, to a great extent, the message, would come to an abrupt finish.

First Arak...and now the man he had been sent to warn of this very possibility. He figured the demons must be dancing with delight. Ah well...the Earth would rotate on at Fathers behest until His will was satisfied; so be it. But it was with a heavy heart that Raphael waited for the final page to turn on Amos' once promising life there.

THE DEMONS, and their King, weren't exactly dancing, but there was definitely a smirking, celebratory mood. As the watchers raced effortlessly along the dimension wall, with the Bird in plain sight, one would occasionally peel off and zip the latest status back to some unholy superior. They knew the other side was doing almost exactly the same thing. It was even possible that the One was monitoring much of this himself. It wouldn't matter. So sure were they now of the outcome, that Buferan simply waited with his boss in the "throne room" leaving his lieutenants to gather the reports and apprise him periodically.

"Pleasant is it not?"

"Greatly so, My Lord. Only the original intent would have been more satisfying."

Lucifer waved one mighty appendage, "It is of little consequence, most of the ones in range are ours already."

A hateful grin danced beneath the glowing eyes, and then the Ruler of Evil continued, "I believe we can leave the principality in Manoc's hands after this...I see no interference of significance arising from these ashes."

"What of the girl and the others who fell under Mikals' spell?"

"Retain the watchers, but bide your time before making any move to finish the job. He will not be pleased by all this and, though our strength now grows, it would be foolish to engage the Arch's unnecessarily before we complete the final phase."

"Your wish... as always, Sire."

IT HAD BEEN CALM BEFORE, but now the afternoon had arrived at a state of complete breathlessness. The waters surface was completely mirror-like with only the swirls and disturbances created by a frolicking, or sometimes fleeing, fin indicating the busy life cycles beneath. At one point, a large Loggerhead materialized just off their bow, contemplated them with that ageless look of turtle wisdom, then sank down and swam gracefully under the boat. After some moments spent nosing around the coral encrusted rock formations, he swooped off like some big, pendant shaped submarine. All these glories were scarcely noticed by Jim and Jenny.

That same breathlessness gripped their hearts. They sat torn between this silent offshore vigil and a burning curiosity as to the phone business. For Jenny, it was an equation based on proximity. Amos was out there somewhere on the horizon. To return, he must backtrack this way; she should be waiting for him. Her dad had easily deciphered the lettering on the helicopter; Nuclear Regulatory Commission. So whatever this was about involved the plant in some pretty dramatic fashion.

Government aircraft did not take unauthorized passengers on joyrides. Something very serious was afoot; and it almost had to be the "something" they had all feared. The very warning that lay at the center of this entire fracas. An insane sounding drama which stretched from Heaven itself, to one of the most famous religious landmarks on Earth, and then on to a tiny fishing village lying nearly on the other side of that world. How it could possibly involve a mad dash in a helicopter, out into the "no man's land" of the Gulf of Mexico, was a total mystery.

And, for now, they were essentially neutralized. Forced to sit in agonized apprehension while Amos and someone else, who obviously had to be Matt Robbins, dealt with whatever terrible plan Satan had conjured up. It seemed it had already cost them any chance at future help, or fellowship, with one of the most magnificent beings she had ever imagined. And now her soul and spirit virtually trembled with the certainty that some sinister, untold danger was in play here; danger to the man she had come to love. As it turned out, the wait was not a long one.

At 5:13 p.m. Eastern Standard Time, multiple equipment ranging from seismographic oil exploration rigs to DSP spy satellites far above the Earth, recorded an explosion or disturbance at 28 49 30 N; 83 25 15 W in the Gulf of Mexico. Subsequent examination and verification pointed to an aerial nuclear detonation of one to two kilotons. While not considered large by modern weapons standards, it none the less caused major behind the scenes alarm bells and quietly raised reaction levels across the entire Eastern Seaboard. A mad inter-agency and military scramble to pin down the source, or lay the blame, revealed little to nothing at first. When a few facts did finally surface, the circle of "need to know" entities first narrowed, and then closed. Information to the public would be typically sketchy and skewed. The two closest observers would never be interviewed.

From the vantage point of Appointment Hole, both Alexander's had been steadily gazing westward lost in their concerns for Amos and company. Suddenly a point on the distant horizon seemed to erupt in an intense rainbow colored aura or haze. It was followed by a bright flash that over-rode the suns own brilliance for several long seconds. After another set of seconds, there was a faint rumble like far off thunder. They sat staring in silence...then,

"Dad...what was that?" There was a tremor in the question.

"I have no idea sweetheart...One thing though...it wasn't the chopper."

"Oh God", she whispered, "are you sure."

"Pretty sure...that was big. Bigger than any aircraft could make...unless it was carrying ordinance."

"But that's exactly the direction they went."

Jim was silently processing his own statement. Ordinance; he'd seen plenty of that dropped in his day. Napalm, HE...but that flash looked ominously like something he'd only seen in films. And that was just not possible. Or rather he didn't want it to be possible. The last two weeks had rearranged most definitions of "possible" he'd originally clung to.

"Jen...sweetheart, we'll wait about ten more minutes and then we better go check that phone...OK?"

"Dad...do you think something happened to them?"

He looked into his daughter's frightened eyes, "Honestly...I don't know. They may come tearing back by here any time now."

But they did not; even though the duo overstayed the ten minute deadline. It was with a steadily increasing feeling of dread that they finally pulled the anchor and headed in.

CHAPTER 33

WHEN MATT AND AMOS lifted off from the plant escarpment, Fitz immediately began grilling Eddie for more details. He listened for several minutes as he came clean about the details of getting the "jammer" into the plant. Eddie now painfully realized the extent of greed and gullibility it had required for the two terrorist to play him into this game. And Fitz, who could be as hard nosed as they came, recognized true remorse when he saw it. In this case, repentance had played a large part in that as well.

After he extracted the info, he left Eddie to await the choppers return and headed in to catch up with Charlie. Due to the physically insular nature of the huge facility, and the absolute pandemonium which was currently reigning within, only the two remaining participants knew anything untoward had occurred. Charlie didn't even yet know his pilot and ride were absent. If at all possible, Fitz intended to keep his word to Amos until they could compare notes, but he was chomping at the bit to get someone in position to way lay the two terrorist Eddie called Sammy and Peter.

In the meantime, he engaged Charlie and pretended to be paying attention to welding inspections that were currently in progress on several of the main cooling lines. All the while on 'pins and needles' to see, or hear from, Amos or Dormer. He also had to wonder how long he could harbor info on a crime of this magnitude before being culpable himself. As the minutes dragged by, his attention strayed so often he caught Charlie giving him several questioning glances. Looking at his watch, he knew the time limit had expired; still no report from Dormer. Finally he could stand it no longer.

"Look Charlie, I got a couple of things I need to check on."

Charlie gave him a sardonic look, "You're telling me. You act like you're waiting to go on patrol in Cambodia."

Damn, the guy knew him too well, "Yeah, well close, but no cigar. Let me run check with one of my people and I'll tell you all about it."

"Fitzgerald, you're gonna do whatever you're gonna do. Go get whatever has your skirt bunched up taken care of and then come on back. We should be on eight by then."

All he got was a "Be right back," and a backside view of his old friend hurrying away. A little inkling of concern rippled through his mind, but he just shrugged and tried to get his thoughts back in sync with the X-ray technician.

Fitz went out the personnel door on the west end of the Aux building and half trotted around the corner to where he'd left Dormer. He found him parked in the southwest corner of the perimeter fencing staring out to sea.

"No sign of them?"

Eddie looked haggard, "No, but I think the thing went off."

"What? Are you sure?"

"Saw a major flash about fifteen minutes after you left." It was true; the raised facility embankment had given Eddie an even better view of the distant flash than that of the Alexander's.

Fitz did the calculations in his mind, "That doesn't jive up with the timer."

Eddie let out a huge sigh, "I know...and they're not back."

The sinking feeling again struck Fitzgerald's stomach as his mind wrestled with the available facts. He had dealt with these weapons in the late 60's at the Nevada Test Site center. There had been so many permutations of the timers involved it was anybody's guess which version was in play here. Could they have messed with it and caused a safety-lock detonation? Probably not, Amos was smarter than that. The horror of possible loss of life was now joined by the realization that it might also involve the megabuck chopper. And he had, so far, not alerted even his friend; much less the authorities. It appeared time had run out on that option.

"OK Eddie, we'll wait a few minutes and if there's no sign we're going to sound the alarm...starting with Charlie Barnes."

Eddie just nodded.

BUBBA WAS WAITING patiently for them on the dock. He wasn't dancing around and didn't react to their arrival except to peer over the dock's edge into the boat. Then he settled back and watched as they tied up and off-loaded the

gear. Now that they had returned, there was some sublimi-
nal hesitation to charge in and be confronted by whatever
might lay in wait on the message machine. Once the
equipment and gear were up on the dock though, the time
had come. They waited through the short announcement
cycle and suddenly Amos voice filled the small living room.
Bubba's ears shot up and Jenny had the momentary
realization that he had probably never heard Amos voice on
an incoming message.

"Hey you guys, listen up. It would seem whoever is
backing this thing actually managed to sneak a bomb into
the R/B. Our head guy recognized it...calls it a 'suitcase'
nuke. Yeah, you heard right...nuke. It was set for a one
hour delay and we have about forty five minutes left on the
timer. Matt and I are taking it straight offshore to deep
water and dropping it. I gotta go, but I had to let you
know...Oh...You probably wouldn't, but don't say anything
till we get back and figure out just what happened
here...OK...More on that later..."

There was a short pause, then, "And uh...Just in
case...Jen...I love you." Click; and he was gone.

It was suddenly all too clear. Jenny sank into Amos' favorite old chair which faced a small wood burning stove.
Her eyes filled and tears began sliding silently down her
cheeks. No hysteria...No sobs...Just two trickles of tears
and a forlorn expression of shocked pain on her young face.
Jim's own face mirrored that shock. He walked over, sat on
the arm of the chair and placed an arm around her shoulders. She looked up and his heart fractured a bit more at
the hurt in her eyes.

"Dad...Why?"

"Don't know honey...Only He knows."

"But Arak warned us...We were supposed to stop it."

Another long pause, then Jim whispered in a husky voice trying to control his own pain for her sake,

"He did stop it...Our Hero was a hero all over again."

At that, Jenny did break into sobs. And all her dad could do, was hold her while she cried.

CHAPTER 34

ANOTHER TIME LIMIT came and went. True to his word, Fitz began with Charlie, who took several repetitions to be convinced it was not a prank. When he was finally standing where he and Matt had landed just hours before, the absence of the million dollar chopper spoke volumes to the credibility of the tale. He immediately contacted the Region II office in Atlanta, who in turn contacted the Jacksonville FBI field office. Another helicopter, carrying a squad of agents, was airborne from Craig Field within the hour enroute for the same landing zone Matt had used.

After conferring with Atlanta, Charlie led the trio to the Operations building where, at his request, the Site Shift Manager contacted William Franklin, the Operations Manager. He was in his office in less than half an hour and was brought up to speed on what details they had. Now a quandary of sorts faced the small group. Eddie had the most vital knowledge of what had happened, but protocol demanded he be incarcerated immediately. Fitz dissented with that plan claiming that, once local law enforcement entered the picture, any security regarding the facts was history.

"Do that and the Tribune will be at the front gate in twenty minutes," was how he put it. This was something management definitely wished to avoid.

So Eddie was remanded to Fitzgerald's care and responsibility. His mind was in a terrible state. He realized that he was now a murderer, as well as a terrorist. His recent acceptance of the "true reality" was a grand thing and he knew in his heart it had been real, but he also knew he was in deep trouble. The pain in his heart over Amos was perhaps worse than his fear of the punishment due him. The man had done nothing but try to help and advance Eddie's life, not to mention saving it. He had also been instrumental in waking him up to that final reality. And in return, it had cost Amos his. He figured he must be the most miserable creature on the planet...Florida for sure.

DESPITE THE VARIOUS REPORTS from monitoring agencies, distant sightings by the public, and a couple of commercial aircraft "call ins", the powers that be initially insisted it had been an errant flare fired from a passing vessel. In many minds, the facts would not support this claim but no further information was being offered. Later someone would put forth the theory of a secret missile test by a US submarine. For now, other than a brief sound bite on local channels, there was little mention of the mystery light seen over the Gulf. Given the persistent UFO sightings associated with this particular locale, many resident conspiracy buffs labeled the extra-terrestrials somehow responsible.

Clandestinely, the government sent aerial equipment to detect and monitor any fallout from the detonation. They found the levels low, dispersing quickly and located well offshore. No one considered it necessary to try and locate the aircraft; you couldn't find something that had been vaporized.

A couple of ambitious news teams applied pressure on the local authorities for a better explanation, with no success. They didn't know anything either; the fix was definitely in. So, despite the chilling reality of the plutonium bullet that had barely been dodged, the over-all flap would be short lived.

Even in the plant, things were so mysterious and tight lipped, the crews weren't sure what had gone down. Some of the rumors contained small segments of accuracy, but word was to leave it be for now. Only at the upper levels were the facts explored and examined in hushed tones. Those at the very top of that cadre were beginning to speak Amos and Matt's names in reverent tones. As they reconstructed the timeline and overall blueprint, the immensity of how close the call had actually been, had a sobering effect. Many of them would now be scattered atoms and most of the others in grave, if not fatal, peril. Along with families, friends and virtually all those in the area which they held dear.

But, in the end, it would get almost completely hushed up. Leave it to agencies like the NSA and other so called protective entities to dissemble and obscure the facts. One must wonder when the last time the governing body, elected under the guise of serving and being responsible to

the people, was actually transparent about much of anything. It certainly wasn't going to start here.

Perhaps the only satisfying part of the finale involved
Pytor and Samir. The FBI field team took stock of Eddie's
information, loaded him into a borrowed FPC sedan and
headed for the Orange Blossom Inn with zero hesitation.
They found the two terrorist occupying the same booth
where they had parlayed with Mr. Dormer. Having eyed the
little blip on the evening newscast, they were arguing
quietly about whether the SADM had somehow been
involved. Samir's insistence to remain in the area until they
heard from Eddie, or had some confirmation of a detonation, sealed their fate.

For his part, Eddie found this the only brief satisfaction
he was going to get for the duping that had been worked so
craftily upon him. He walked casually up to the duo,
flanked by two huge agents who looked like refugees from
some NFL dinner party, and calmly announced,

"Peter, Sammy...I'd like you to meet Mr. Smith and Mr.
Jones."

Pytor's reflexes had his hand behind him and the butt
of his CZ 52 in his palm before the intro was finished; only
to find a copy of the ubiquitous, all American Colt .45 six
inches from his nose. The jig, as they say, was up. However,
the two terrorist posed a similar problem to Eddie...they
knew too much. Since the sedan's capacity was already
strained with a total of four agents and Mr. Dormer, the
two hapless Jihadists found themselves cuffed individually,
then together and placed unceremoniously in the vehicle's
trunk.

As luck would have it, a Citrus County Deputy eyeing the parking lot from across US 41 caught the action and converged on the scene, weapon drawn, demanding that they "Show him their hands." In the end, they showed him their credentials, had him cancel his call for back up and assured him that one word of inquiry would prove fatal to his career. They left the hapless officer muttering less than complimentary epitaphs regarding, the "Feds".

That would be the last time Eddie ever saw or heard of his former compatriots. He felt lucky not to have wound up in the trunk with them. He was actually sent home with Fitzgerald after it became conclusively apparent that he was in deepest regret, denied not a thing about the incident and seemed to presently be his own worst enemy, judge and jury. Unknown to any, there were also powerful forces working behind the scenes on his behalf. So an already unorthodox saga added yet another oddity to its list.

LATE THAT NIGHT, Jenny and Jim saw the minor bit of information being given out by the local news; it barely registered. They had officially checked out of their room on the Homosassa River and relocated to Amos' place. They both felt the emotional need to remain close to his home front as the shock and pain wore on. They also needed to be there for Bubba whose instincts told him there was trouble.

He interspersed vigils on the front steps with ones spent at dockside and would spend lengthy periods lying next to one of them with his chin on his paws; not at all his normally enthusiastic self. When one or the other got up or walked outside, he went along like a shadow, silently keeping watch. When the one a.m. hour came and still no Amos, he just settled down on his personal throw rug by the little wood stove and watched them with mournful eyes.

"He knows," stated Jenny.

"Animal that smart must have senses we don't even understand," replied Jim.

"Dad, what are we gonna do?"

He was silent for several long moments, "I'm not real sure. Do you feel any kind of input...anything."

"Just that I need to stay here for now...be close."

"OK, so it's not just me."

"But what about tomorrow? What about all we know?"

Jim smiled a sad smile, "Hon...how much of what we know do you want to try on the Federal authorities?"

Jenny looked about the comfortable little living room and a single tear slid down one cheek, "I guess...I just wish people could know what he...what they did for them."

"Jen, you heard that nonsense about a flare. They aren't going to let this cat out of the bag would be my guess."

"How is that possible?"

"Listen, I saw it lots of times in the military. If the public knew half of what goes on behind the scenes sometimes..."

She sighed again, "Yeah, I know that too...I'm just feeling so...so lost."

"You pray about it?"

"Only a little...I feel...I feel like He knows how I'm hurting, but my heart and mind are in some kind of limbo...or something. I can't focus the thoughts."

"Yeah...I think I'd describe mine as 'Spiritual Shock'. Let's face it; we've been here before."

"Mom."

"Yes...Not the same scenario, but the same kind of loss. And just like your mother, we have no fears about their futures."

"But that won't diminish the pain," she finished for him.

Jim sighed, "Unfortunately not."

"Dad, there are going to be a lot of loose ends here."

He looked at her questioningly.

"The only family Amos ever mentioned is his brother. Aren't we responsible for finding him and maybe explaining what happened? Should we try to bring his truck home or what? And there's got to be people at that plant who know something."

Jim looked thoughtful, "Yeah, they're missing a really expensive chopper and two employees. And Amos said their head guy recognized the weapon. I think he's the one we'll need to get hold of...you know who he might be?"

"Just about has to be that Three Mile Island guy...Fitz?"

"That's right...Fitzgerald. OK...tomorrow we'll see about contacting this 'Fitz' person. Tonight, let's try to grab some sleep so we'll be halfway clear to handle whatever comes."

Jenny agreed, they shared a long, tearful hug and said goodnight. Jim retired to the small bedroom at the end of the hall. Jenny turned out the lights, sat on the couch with Bubba's head in her lap and stared vacantly at the reflection of the moonlit marshes in the double glass doors. The silent tears returned for a while. Then, at some point, she slumped over and ended up curled in a ball with the dog's muscular shoulder under her head. After a while, Bubba's big golden cat eyes slowly began to droop too. Daybreak would find them pretty much in the same position.

CHAPTER 35

EDDIE AND FITZ were back in Operations before 9:00 the next morning. During the night, the first team of agents had quietly departed with their detainees. A second FBI team had materialized in a trade mark black sedan followed by a new, but non-descript, panel truck of the same color. As unobtrusively as possible, this team ran test and collected prints and evidence from the areas known to have played parts in yesterday's mysterious "attack". Normally, given the same scenario, the first culprit to look for would be trace radiation. Faced with the scene they had to work with, that became something of a quiet joke.

In fact, if truth were told, most of the involved personnel were less than happy to be clambering around inside an active nuclear facility. Much less one with parts scattered all over the place and a live core glimmering up at them from its deep, stainless steel "pool" of borated water. To add to that discomfort, they were being escorted by two carefully selected senior members of the crew who could not resist playing a little to their fears. The end result was that they collected what they could in the swiftest possible fashion and vacated the area vowing not to return unless ordered to do so.

What was collected shed not much light at all on the bizarre story. An empty drum and a partially shredded Rem bag. Additional clandestine testimonies from Jeff and Phil as to how the drum in question was brought inside. And a hodgepodge of prints and forensic matter that would reveal nothing new at all. Crew members involved were told a skewed version of what had happened. None were brought into the covey of individuals aware that a tactical nuclear weapon had made a visit to their own atomic workplace.

It was amidst this activity, which was blended with the usual daily chaos, that Fitzgerald was apprised, over one of the plant lines, that he had a personal call on line four. Making his way to the same phone inside the "booth" Amos had used, he picked up the receiver and was then connected to that outside line. A male voice with a faint but decided southern drawl met his ear.

"Mr. Fitzgerald?"

"Yes...who is this?"

"Sir, you don't know me, but I'm a friend of Amos Mikals."

Fitz's heartbeat skipped and then accelerated, "Uh, OK...Do you know where he is right now?"

"Sadly, I'm afraid I probably do."

Fitz mind was racing. He needed to confirm what this guy knew.

"Uh-huh...Can you tell me about it?"

"Mr. Fitzgerald, you had a most unfortunate incident at your plant yesterday. I believe it cost you Amos, a pilot named Matt and a very expensive helicopter."

An involuntary exhalation escaped Fitz and he remembered Eddie saying that Amos had called someone during the pandemonium of getting rid of the bomb.

"OK...Mr uh..."

"No need to know that just yet."

"OK...fine...You definitely have my attention...Can you tell me anything new we don't know about all this?"

Something that sounded like a sad chuckle came over the line, "I could...you probably won't accept it."

"Would you tell it to the authorities too?"

"Probably not...Tell you what...I'll agree to tell you about it and then you can make the call regarding the authorities."

To Fitz that sounded strange or ominous...maybe both, "Uh...OK, that will work...Go ahead and tell me what you know."

"Not on the phone...You know where Smokey's Place is?"

"The barbeque joint?"

"Yes."

"Yeah, I know it."

"Let's meet there at 11:30."

His mind was still trying to catch up, "I, um...I don't know if I can do that...I mean get away with all that's going on right now."

"Well sir...this is the only chance you're gonna get...I'd suggest you take it...Alone."

"Alone," Fitz echoed, "Well alright...I think I can work it out. Wait a minute...There's another guy here who knows more than I do. You know who I'm talking about?"

"No...who?"

"Guy named Ed Dormer."

It was Jim's turn to think fast. This might be the other piece of the puzzle. Hadn't Amos mentioned some guy named Eddie a couple of times? Of course, he was the one that nearly got killed working on the Drive rebuild that night.

"OK...Bring him with you."

"I don't know about that either. They're watching him pretty close right now. He's lucky they haven't locked him up."

"Work it out if you can Mr. Fitzgerald, but I'll be watching to see who shows up at the restaurant. If you really want to get some facts, respect my privacy. I can assure you I'm nothing to do with what happened at your plant...More a bystander who was drawn in on Amos' behalf. Sit on the south bench out front."

Click; he was gone. Fitz stared at the receiver a moment, slowly placed in its cradle, then looked at his watch. This was unexpected. Did he dare break the rules again? He thought back to his last minutes with Amos. There had been that "feeling" when he took charge. And last night Eddie had tried to tell him some strange story of how he had this miraculous change in the middle of all that was going on. Sort of an "Old Time Religion" thing. The odd part was...he did seem different now. Even with the trouble he was in, he had some of that same calmness about him. Ah, hell...he knew he was going to do it...why fight it. He headed out to Ops planning to somehow corral Eddie. With the Feds off on other business, he'd only have to deal with Franklin. As he went, he rehearsed the story he'd give the man; he was getting a little too good at this.

In what passed for downtown Crystal River, Jim hung up the pay phone in front of the Seven-Eleven and got back in the SX. He thought a moment then got back out and called Jenny.

"Hey...OK, it's on for 11:30...No, I'm not coming to get you...Let me check things out and if it's kosher we'll go from there. If it's not, they'll only have me....Yeah, I'm sure...Just pray at 11:30 alright...Bye.

JIM WATCHED as a tan Ford Crown Victoria entered Smokey's parking area; it fit the situation. It was now 11:25, there were two men inside and they were really giving the place the "once-over". They parked, got out and were looking all around as they headed for the prescribed bench. One reminded Jim of an older version of himself; he was well over six foot and lanky in form. The other was much younger, and shorter, with a stocky build and jet black hair. They sat down on the bench and carried on a quiet conversation while both heads swiveled periodically.

He let them sit for about five more minutes. Lunch was picking up and a number of patrons were in the process of parking and entering. Finally he fired the SX up and exited the little strip mall across from the barbecue house. He went south to a turn lane in the median, made the u-turn, then pulled into a feed and tack operation that was the restaurant's southerly neighbor. He got out and ambled around the corner coming face to face with the pair on the bench. As soon as their eyes met, they knew.

"Mr. Fitzgerald...and Eddie, I presume?"

Fitz looked back at him with a pair of intense blue eyes that also reminded Jim of his own, "You seem to know us...but we don't know you."

"Call me Jim."

"Alright…Thank-you, Jim…What's this all about? Other than the obvious?"

"Let's wait a minute and see if any of your boys show up."

"Boys…you mean cops or something," stated Fitz.

Jim said nothing.

"Jim, you can put that out of your mind. One, I went to some lengths to explain our absence. Two, I keep my word. And three; I don't believe even 'they' are sure they want to hear any more about this."

"Meaning they aim to hush up what really happened…what a shock."

Fitz had already begun to notice some common ground with this guy…beyond the strange physical similarity, "Yeah, imagine that…a Government cover up…what's the world coming to?"

There were several more moments of silence. Then Fitz said, "You seem to know parts we don't know and vice-versa."

"Oh, I'm pretty sure I know most of it."

"Well I sure didn't see you around when the thing was going down."

"Wasn't…but Amos left me a situation report and even dropped by in that shiny red helicopter."

"You saw them?"

"Yes…When they were on their way out to get rid of the thing."

A long silence; then Fitz said, "OK…guess you do know most of it. What can you add to what we know?"

"The beginning; but not here."

They all glanced around at the parking and entry areas which were getting busier by the minute. Jim was praying fervently inside that he was about to do the right thing. It felt right, but it would mean involving his daughter with these two. So far the younger one had not said a word. He seemed distracted or depressed.

"Where then?" asked Fitz.

"Get your car; pull up near the entrance. When you see a blue and white Nissan pull out next door, follow it."

Fitzgerald looked at Eddie who just shrugged, "Ok...Jim...In for a penny, I guess."

Jim nodded and left the way he'd come.

CHAPTER 36

THE TRIP OUT to Amos' place took a good twenty minutes. Along the way Jim repeated the prayer that he not endanger Jenny in any way. When they finally pulled into the lime rock driveway, he pretty much felt peace about it. Jenny materialized on the front steps followed by Bubba. Jim stopped so the dog could get a fix on the company at his own pace. The other two just froze in place as the big, scarred bulldog did his jungle-cat amble towards them.

"Amos' dog," said Jim.

For the first time Eddie spoke, "That's a good looking pit." He knelt in place and stretched his hand out towards Bubba. Bubba could scent the familiar smells unique to the "plant" environment on these two. An unmistakable blend of industrial solvents, fuels and a burnt taste left by the treated air. He accepted Eddie's intro pats and looked calmly up at Fitzgerald.

"Not one I'd like to pick a fight with," remarked Fitz.

Now Jenny spoke, "You have no idea."

They all turned to her, "This is my daughter, Jenny."

Both men muttered greetings.

Jim continued, "You want to know the beginning, it starts with her...and Rome."

Jenny eyed her dad but remained silent.

"Rome?"

"Well, yeah...that and the Black Mamba."

"Black Mamba? OK, wait...I'm sorry, I don't mean to be your echo, but what in God's name are you talking about," asked Fitz.

Jim smiled, "Funny you should put it that way." He turned to Jenny, "Well kiddo, you up for it?"

She looked down for a moment, then sighed, "He'd do it for me...Guess I'll do it for him."

"Gentlemen," said Jim, "best come inside...and sit down."

As the afternoon marched past, the improbable little group reconstructed the entire tale to the best of their ability. As could be expected, Fitz was suspicious of the idea of angels and demons, but kept his council. The fact was, there had been a terrible attempt made on numerous lives in a most incredulous fashion. And there was indeed a huge, bad tempered Black Mamba housed on the premises.

Eddie was a different story. He accepted what was said without question and filled in the details of the foreign terrorist and their cleverness against him. He did not try to downplay his guilt and when he got to the instant of his conversion in the midst of the most terrifying moment of his life, both Alexander's just nodded. He could sense the attachment; he was now among his own kind.

Fitzgerald had broken off long enough to phone CR 3 and give a plausible explanation as to their continued absence. He confided to the Shift Operations Manager that they were in pursuit of some additional info and left it at that. Even under the strange circumstances, no one argued much with Fitz. Fitz, on the other hand, was in great conflict within. All these years he'd styled himself as an agnostic when it came to religion. But if he were to accept the crazy sounding story these two were giving...he'd been wrong; about a great many things.

The heat of the day was fading and they decided to retire to the distinguished picnic table for sandwiches and iced tea. No one had stopped to eat and the meal was just what the doctor ordered. The conversation had garnered a more natural feel now and, despite the bizarre aspects of the subject matter, they had become fairly relaxed with each other. Fitz had just started asking Jenny some detail about the snake event when he suddenly froze in place. Not stopped...froze. Mouth open, hand raised...his eyes didn't even blink. The others were staring at him in shock when Jenny noticed,

"Dad...where's the breeze?"

Eddie was pointing at the bay while trying to swallow a bite of sandwich, "Look afth thuh waater," he said with his mouth full. They turned to find the little riplets that had been dancing eastward, borne on the now absent sea breeze, in the same condition as Fitzgerald. Suspended in time and space.

"Oh," gasped Jenny pointing up, "look."

There above their heads, maybe thirty feet up, a loose formation of three gulls hung motionless like some stuffed attraction in a museum. Their eyes were still focused on the sandwiches.

Jenny spun at the waist to check on Bubba. He looked back at her with a canine look of surprise in those eyes, but he was fine.

"Dad, everything's stopped except us."

It was true. The only possible description was that time seemed to have just taken a time out. Other than the three of them and their dog, not a molecule was stirring. There was also an absolute ringing silence. It was decidedly more eerie than anything even Hollywood could portray. Then the silent unmoving sky above them began to change color.

There is blue, there is sky blue, but the "Royal" blue that began to shade the air above them had not been seen in the Earth's skies since time immemorial. It was as if some giant painter had begun directly over their heads and was using a spray gun to slowly mist the air a new color from some other-worldly palette.

They sat in stunned silence as the atmosphere surrounding them was casually turned into a gigantic inverted bowl of translucent, supernatural blue. Just the scale of it was unimaginable. Then Eddie, who was facing west, and had managed to subconsciously finish his bite of sandwich, pointed in that direction. "Uh...Look." When they turned there was a distinct anomaly at that point on the huge "bowl".

At first it looked like a giant kernel of fire. Then the flame gyrated and flexed as if it was trying to assume some kind of shape. They were staring uncertainly at this distant spectacle when suddenly, without warning, it burst, as if from within, scattering huge firework-like arms of color in every direction. More hues and brighter colors than any they'd ever witnessed. It was a magnificent display that dwarfed any Fourth of July finale man had ever conceived of. But the biggest surprise was yet to come. The gigantic "arms" of dazzling color suddenly reversed course and started to collect or reassemble. They began pulling inward towards the epicenter and, with a flash brighter than anything preceding it, a huge figure literally exploded into existence.

Only Eddie could find his voice and all he could manage was a muted, "Oh wow."

They did not know it yet, but they were looking at the massive, winged back of one of God's own Arch Angels. It would have been hard to decide whether the colorful "flames" surrounding him were incendiary or electrical. They danced and changed shape and color in an endless wave of patterns like wind rippling across a field of grain. It was apparent the giant arms were crossed in front and on the left, from their view point, a long projection, which appeared to be the business end of an equally gigantic sword, extended diagonally upward. It too glittered with colors that pulsed in time with those of its owner. Given the distance, they could only guess at the tremendous size he must be up close.

Jim cleared his throat. The sound seemed ultra loud and strident in the vacuum like stillness.

"It looks like...he's standing guard...or something."

"Look," said Jenny, suddenly pointing due South.

As they watched, the performance was repeated and another gigantic warrior took up a post that loomed out over the marshes in that direction. Then the spectacle was repeated twice more to the other points on the compass. The little trio now found themselves perched inside a giant inverted coliseum with an Arch Angel poised at the four geographic corners.

To put it mildly, it had been an historical period for Jim and Jenny. Eddie too, had been subjected to more life changing events in a shorter period than he would have dreamed possible. But folks, even so, what they were now experiencing was on a scale guaranteed to buy you a rubber room in the state hospital of your choice. The three of them were also feeling somewhat suspended; and nearly in shock. They now waited with a shallow breathlessness on whatever could possibly come next.

Sixty seconds went buy...They remained silent...Two minutes...Nothing changed. The air felt charged by the unheard of coloring, but nothing stirred. The huge sentinels themselves made not a single movement except for the pulse of the "flames".

"Dad...?"

Jim looked at both youngsters, "Guy's...you tell me...I have no idea." He paused then looked up into the gorgeous blue canopy overhead,

"Father God," he began and the other two automatically bowed their heads, "We see what you are doing here...But we have no idea what it is you want from us...if anything. But hear our confession Father, when we say that we are yours. We have fought this fight with your will foremost in our hearts. We have lost our friend and your own warrior sent to warn him. But whatever further you require Lord, you need only ask...We your servants are waiting...and listening."

After a second Jenny and Eddie intoned together, "Amen." The next second there was an ear splitting clap of thunder that rattled everything and totally destroyed the silence. All three momentarily cleared their seats by a respectable margin and Bubba sprang to his feet with them. This "blast" was instantly followed by a shrill whistling sound mixed with an unearthly low pitched hum; like the two frequencies were competing with each other for the attention of all available ears.

At the same instant, a shadow appeared and blotted out the luminescent blue light from above. Their eyes jerked skyward and all three mouths fell open in unison. Jim's mind was racing faster than his heart as he now realized the "thunderclap" might have been a sonic boom. There was a craft of immense proportions settling through the atmosphere of the blue "bowl" and descending straight for them. As it descended, the sound continued to grow in volume.

It was shaped like a giant, lengthy triangular wedge with no sharp edges or surfaces. What appeared to be the front, or nose, was an ovoid shape like the business end of a Manta Ray. The after portion thickened noticeably, swelling into what looked like twin tail fins of a vertical, rapier-like configuration. It had a coloration much like the huge guardians on the perimeter and the different hues undulated across the underside in those same breezy patterns. But this surface had a molten metallic look. Like it had been cast from some giant reservoir of painted mercury. There were four large downward facing "vents", two forward and two aft, that showed a vaporous exhalation of sorts and seemed to be the source of the ear splitting noise. No sooner had he noticed these than the sound was cut off like a giant switch had been thrown.

The ship, if that's what it was, continued its slow descent amidst the renewed hush that again asserted itself over the scene. It seemed to be gently lowering, as if it were lighter than the air around it. Even as he sat in rapt wonder, Jim thought that it must be somehow magnetically based to do that. There was no sound, but there were a series of locations around the hull that were alternately glowing and flashing with a liquid looking turquoise color. As it towered above them, he judged it must be as long as a football field. It was positioned in an alignment that poised the forward port side over the bay closest to them with the rest extending diagonally southwest out into the marshes.

This semi-molten looking behemoth settled to within ten feet of the bay's paralyzed waters with the outer surface of the forward section no more than forty feet from where they sat transfixed. They could make out a low hum emanating from it that seemed omni-directional and surrounded the area. It was not unpleasant but gave the impression of some immense power source straining at the leash. There was no "hover" in the sense of the word. It just stopped; frozen in place as much as everything else. The smooth rounded sides swept upward and towered over them by several stories. The port side, of what would be the fuselage section, angled away and swept gracefully back towards the tail; the thing was huge. It just hung there humming that throaty tone.

Jim had noted the apparent absence of any visible hatches or openings, but suddenly an outline appeared in the forward section aligned directly with their location. It formed a large, squashed oval with a flat portion at the base and was probably twenty feet high at its apex. The next second, the molten, colored surface inside the outline began to systematically and uniformly recede. It started at the center and moved outward, as if blending back into the surrounding hull. The process was completed in less than half a minute. The maw that was exposed showed nothing; just inky darkness. For several long moments, there was no further movement. Then, what appeared to be some sort of catwalk, or gangplank, began to seemingly "grow" out of the flat portion of the opening. It was more solid in appearance than the outer surface but had those same turquoise lights flashing down the sides. It was easily large enough to drive a tank across.

The little bunch at the table was sitting in an utterly stunned silence with their nerves ramped up to maximum pitch. It seemed highly probable they were about to get a visitor of some sort. Jenny's mind was playing back all the data she'd been getting since this began about UFO's and aliens. She'd been in Rome. She'd seen an angelic being and three demonic ones. Those giant "guardians" in the distance looked like some of Arak's really big brothers. But this thing looked more like...like a spaceship. As she watched the "catwalk" slowly completing its trajectory in their direction, she recalled Amos' comment about such matters. He'd said whoever was out there must belong to God too since, "it was His playground and all the toys are His". She breathed a silent prayer this was so.

CHAPTER 37

THE OVERSIZE RAMP had reached the shoreline. It hung just inches from the surface, suspended as if the very molecules of air were supporting it. The turquoise impulses flashing along the side rails were now the only observable activity. The dark of the opening remained impenetrable. Bubba, who had again been sitting silently taking in the whole spectacle, suddenly got to his feet once more and paced cautiously over to the foot of the giant gang way. He glanced back once at the others, then turned and seemed to scrutinize the distant entry point.

Eddie found his voice, "Uh...do you think maybe we're supposed to go out there...in there?"

They all looked at each other with widened eyes. Eddie was the first to stand. Jim and Jenny followed, still glancing uncertainly at each other. They walked over, joining the dog at the ramp's base, and stood staring at the pitch black, cavernous opening looming before them.

Suddenly, without warning, a giant figure, that well fit the scale of the entryway, materialized from out of the darkness. All their eyes bulged and Jim felt the hair on his neck stand straight up. But Jenny's wide eyed stare swiftly narrowed to a purposeful focus. Then she swayed a little on her feet and subconsciously placed a hand on her dad's arm.

"Arak," she whispered.

And indeed it was. But not as Jenny had seen him in Rome. This was the fleshly, armor clad, gladiator appearance some on Deran were more familiar with. Their eyes met; then their hearts and souls engaged. Jenny was off like the proverbial shot. She raced across the oversize gangplank and hurtled herself into the waiting arms of the giant, winged warrior who caught her like a little china doll. After a few seconds of further, silent eye contact, he held her gently to the huge chest plate and they could hear her sobbing quietly. A sound that seemed to be mixed with both joy and sorrow. Jim and Eddie were once more frozen in shock, transfixed by the sight. Bubba waited quietly by their side.

Jenny lifted her head and looked up at her giant friend. Then she noticed his wrists. There were scars that looked like burns on both. He followed her eyes and all were treated to the sound of that deep, penetrating bass voice,

"The shackles...I will bear them from now on...in this form...Much as our Savior does his."

Jenny sniffed, "As long as you're back."

Arak shifted Jenny so that she was perched against one huge forearm and strode across to where the others were still waiting with widened eyes. He placed her gently on her feet and straightened to his full height.

"James...Edward, greetings from both the Father and the Son." He glanced down at the bulldog, nodded and rumbled, "Bubba."

Jim found his voice and looked up at the giant, "Sir...Arak..." he stopped and exhaled a large sigh. "It's an honor to meet you...and a joy to see you safe."

"Trust you, that I am equally honored. Your attention to a father's duty has helped bring us this determined little warrior." As he spoke, he glanced at Jenny and inclined his head towards Jim.

"Thank you," Jim replied. Then he pointed at the massive, quietly humming ship, "That...I could not have predicted."

Arak turned and eyed it as well, "Truthfully, nor could I. It is a 'hobby' of my father's; but I suspect he may have recently received input from someone very high up. It transcends both the size and expectations of his original design...by some considerable degree."

"Your father?"

"It is a long story."

"Arak...what is all this," asked Jenny solemnly.

The mighty warrior also slowly surveyed the scene. When he spoke, his voice was soft...reverential,

"Among other things, it is Spiritual History rewritten. Never has such a stronghold graced the Earth of man. Nor indeed is it foretold. The shield you see above is of the Spirit himself. The sentinels at the four 'corners' are all senior Archs."

"Archs," interrupted Jim slowly, "as in Arch Angels...Woow."

"Indeed," replied Arak. "Such power could easily unhinge a galaxy...yet here it is...in plain view of mortals. I myself am deeply honored. You, frankly, cannot fathom it yet."

Another soft sob broke the stillness. They all turned to Jenny. "I...if only I...we...hadn't lost Amos."

A strong, clear voice issued from the darkness of the ship's portal, "Yeah...that would be a shame...I thought we were just getting started."

Jenny side-stepped around Arak and stared at the entry in wide eyed, speechless shock. A much smaller, sandy haired figure appeared in the giant hatchway. He was clad in a dark blue FPC jump suit and work boots as if ready to resume his duties in the CR3 reactor building.

His name exploded in a shriek of unalloyed love and joy that seemed to push even the blue in the surrounding skies to a further level of luminosity, "AAAMMMOOSSSS..."

For the second time, Jenny literally flew across the big, flashing walkway. She catapulted herself into Amos' arms, who also managed to catch her, albeit without the casual power of their big friend. Only this time she bestowed several kisses that had been reserved for no one else in all of Creation. While they were locked in this embrace, Bubba slammed into Amos legs and joined the celebration. A moment later a taller, dark haired figure, still wearing those "Aviator" glasses, emerged into the light.

"Man...nice to be missed, huh."

Amos left one arm around Jenny's waist and half turned with her to face the stranger, "Jen...Matt; Matt...Jenny."

Matt held out his hand, "I believe we met briefly at, uh... Appointment Hole." He eyed Amos... "Right?"

Jenny unclasped Amos and reached up to hug the pilot, "Oh, Matt...welcome home."

"And this is my dog Bub...er, our dog, Bubba," he smiled at Jenny.

Then all three faced the group ashore and after a pause started their way with the dog in tow.

Eddie had excitedly followed Jenny part way up the ramp, but then stopped uncertainly. Now the three of them met him, all four, along with Bubba, standing on the walkway of some other-worldly piece of technology. There were tear tracks on Eddie's face.

He looked first at Amos, and then at Matt, "I thought I'd killed you."

Amos reached out, took his hand then grabbed him in a brief bear hug, "Nah man; greatest adventure of my life."

Matt drawled from beside him, "Doesn't necessarily mean we need to try it again."

"Amos, how is all this possible?"

He let his eyes rove the scene a moment, "Jen, all I can say is what Scripture teaches...With God, all things are possible."

She also looked about and then returned her gaze to him, "Son...these are some serious things."

Matt spoke up, "Amen to that...and you should see where we've been."

Amos was looking around and his gaze came to rest on the picnic table, "Fitz is here?"

Jenny followed his eyes, "Well, yes...and no...I think."

Amos smiled, "This might be the first time anyone has gotten the last word with him."

They joined Arak and Jim who had been quietly watching the joyous reunion. Jim reached out his hand and Amos used it to pull him into another hug. Both men's eyes looked a little liquid.

"You made it," said Jim in a husky voice.

"Yeah...well this one was definitely by the Grace of God. I still can't quite get my head around some of it." He looked at Matt, "Not sure we're supposed to, huh."

At that moment a tall, as in seven foot plus, figure repeated the performance of materializing in the large opening. He was clad in a faintly military looking uniform with a belt load of strange equipment strapped around his waist. He wore high top boots that shimmered with some similarity to the large craft he was standing on. His face had the sort of chiseled features seen on the American Indians in photographs and paintings. It was crowned with a mane of longish, dark hair accented with grey. It seemed probable that he was the ships "commander". What appeared to be an oversize, medieval looking sword of some kind was strapped to his back. It protruded up over his left shoulder and had a sparkling rainbow luminescence similar to those of the giant Arch's on the perimeter. He slowly took in the scene around him with the penetrating gaze of a bird of prey.

Arak said simply, "My father, Lonius of Deran."

Lonius strode down the gangway and stood next to his son. He placed his fist over his heart and said, "Greetings to each of you," then slowly rotated his head once more looking studiously at his surroundings. "So...This is Earth...'Firma-Cognito'...Very beautiful...I had never thought to see it."

Jim spoke up, "Lonius...correct?"

"Yes"

"Thank you sir, for what you have evidently done for us."

"Rather thank Father, for what he has done for us all," stated Lonius.

Jim emulated the salutation with his fist over his heart and smiled, "Agreed."

Jenny looked at Amos. "Where were you two when that thing went off...we saw it."

"Yeah...how long ago was it?"

She looked surprised, "You don't know?"

"Uh, no, not really," he glanced at Matt, "time's...kinda funny when you're not, uh...here."

"Well, for me, you've been dead for over a day."

"Really...only one day...who else knows?"

Jenny turned back towards the immobilized Fitzgerald, "Him...and a few others for sure. You didn't answer my question."

Amos looked up at Lonius, "It was somewhat as you see it here," said the elder Deranian.

She looked thoughtful, "So there was...a blink in time; like this?"

"An appropriate analogy."

Jim looked at Matt, "I guess it's too bad about the chopper. They're gonna have a hard time hiding that one."

Matt looked mystified, "Hiding?"

"Yeah...despite what you guys did for them, appears they're trying to sweep the whole thing under the rug."

Matt looked a little concerned, "Oh man, which means Charlie thinks I'm dead and the Bird's history."

Lonius broke in, "It is this 'Bird' I wanted to ask you of; may we off load it in that open area?"

He was pointing at the vacant lot to the east of Amos' place.

Jim shared an incredulous glance with the others, "You have the helicopter?"

Lonius just nodded.

Matt was eyeing the open lot and the various structures, utilities and foliage near it, "Yes sir; that will do just
fine."

"Then I shall attend to it. May Father continue to watch
over you all...Frankly, I do not envy you this...'war', but I
hope to see you again at some future point when it is
concluded."

Jenny gave him a smile, "I very much hope to see Deran."

Lonius smiled a small, knowing smile in return, "And so
you shall my dear, so you shall."

Jenny glanced at Amos who just shrugged. Then Lonius
turned to Arak,

"My son, Father has instructed me to have you return
this to Raphael. I think He hopes it will also assist you
against any further 'interference' while you are here or
during your transfer home. Considering what it did to
Lucifer's 'unbreakable' shackles, I doubt he would care to
face it in your hands."

With that, Lonius reached over his head and began to
withdraw the giant, glittering sword. A stunned hush
enveloped the little group. As it cleared, a sense of awe
seemed to descend upon the very air around them.

"Is that..." began Jim then trailed off.

Lonius held it out in front of himself with the tip towards Heaven. It pulsed with the incalculable power stored
within. He said solemnly, "It is the 'Sword of Raphael'; a
chief amongst the Archs." He glanced at Arak, "And a true
fellow and brother if ever there was. He risked much on
your behalf when Father's will was not yet clear," and here
he surveyed the scene around him once more, "on this most
astonishing of developments."

They were silent a moment while they considered this statement, and all that was before and around them. Then Jenny broke the silence as she looked over at the suspended Fitz,

"I take it he is not one of...us?"

Arak rumbled an answer, "Not at this time...and his is running out."

"Well, forgive me if this is foolish, but what if he could see all this?" She waved an arm across the scene, "How long could he remain in disbelief?"

Her dad replied, "Sweetheart, you already know that answer."

She sighed and Amos tightened his arm around her shoulders, "I know...faith has to come first."

Arak rejoined, "Truly...else it is no faith at all. Little sister; we met in the Basilica strictly because you already had the 'Spirit of Truth' inside you. The fact is, none of you," and he looked at them all, "has experienced anything that your heart had not already acknowledged was possible, because of His presence."

They were silent, again thoughtful; then Amos spoke, "Possibilities...He's often spoken to me about that." Here he too took in the surroundings with another long glance, "Will we be allowed to share any of this?"

"That, I think, is between you...and Him," stated Arak.

"Not like anyone would buy it anyway," shrugged Jim.

"If only people took more time to consider the 'possibilities'," Amos mused aloud.

Arak reached out and placed a giant hand on his shoulder, "Amos Mikals...It has been your obedient effort to convey such a message, that has resulted in... this," and he waved the other massive arm around them.

Lonius stepped over to face his son who still towered over him in his "fleshly" form. He was holding the sword, parallel with the ground now, in both hands similar to an ancient Samurai ceremonial pose.

"Arak, my son, I well know you are a fitting and worthy conveyor of this. When you do return it to Raphael, please present to him, and to Father, my most heartfelt love, respect and thanks. In His mercy he has restored you to us, and these to each other."

Arak took the sword and it instantly shifted its coloration to a new pattern mixed with more emerald green. He held it raised point up, as his father had, and slowly turned it from side to side.

"Father...It shall be so."

"Now," said Lonius, "I must return Matt's earthly mechanical marvel to him." He rotated his head making eye contact with each of the others, "Until we meet again."

With that he repeated the fist gesture while the others chorused their goodbyes and then strode back into the ship. They waited expectantly and it wasn't long before sounds could be heard emanating from somewhere on the upper portion of the vessel. It might be a "celestial" craft, but apparently heavy equipment shares some universal grunts and groans. In seconds the folded joint of a giant appendage appeared. Somewhat like an enlarged version of the Space Shuttle cargo arm.

As they continued to watch, the Bell helicopter emerged over the periphery of the upper deck. It was seemingly unscathed and suspended in some fashion at the business end of the apparatus. It might as well have been made of Styrofoam. The cargo "crane" effortlessly cleared the ship's hull and swung slowly around to face the empty lot. When the motion ceased, the upper section began to lengthen itself until the Bird was poised above an open space. Then the chopper seemed to detach itself and ride slowly downward, suspended by an improbably slender, metallic looking rod or cable. In no time, the NRC's pride and joy had returned to Earth, none the worse for wear. The little group stood in silent admiration and Jim just shook his head in utter amazement.

He gave a chuckle, "I'm not sure how much more my mind can take today."

The giant Third Rank cleared his throat behind him, "I fear the 'day' may not be over yet."

Jenny looked up a little warily, "What do you mean by that?"

The others brought their attention back to him as well.

"The efforts of my father to locate me, supplemented by the Lord himself, as you see, revealed the methodology by which I was targeted for capture. Unless strictly forbidden, I intend to use that information...and this," he raised the Sword, "to attempt the release of a brother Third Rank. I am sure he has been relocated, but I believe I can now predict the coordinates of his imprisonment."

"But you are just now out of that trap yourself...won't you be back in the same danger?" asked Jenny querulously.

"Yes."

They fell silent. The ships arm had fully retracted now and she sat unmoving. All that could be heard was the hum of that bridled power in some apparent state of intense idle.

Amos pointed at the ship, "Will you receive any help?"

"It will be minimal at best."

Matt spoke up, "Does it mean going back to..." he shrugged, "you know?"

"Briefly."

Amos gave a sigh, "How long?"

"By your sun, less than what was required here...probably."

Jenny had experienced a mixed rush of emotions at this news. She had just gotten Amos back. And for that matter, Arak too. Now the original messenger, who had triggered perhaps the most amazing story ever destined to be hidden in the annals of Earth, intended to boldly attack the very forces she'd seen evidenced in Rome.

She looked up at this giant "brother" whom she loved with all her heart, "I'm in."

There was total silence as that portent sank in.

Then Jim said, "I'd guess we're all in."

Arak put his fist to his chest, then extended it in front of himself. The others formed a semi-circle around his massive form and one after the other touched theirs to it.

After a moment, he turned to the catwalk and held his arm out in a welcoming gesture, "Shall we?"

Eddie's heart was racing unlike anything his life experience had to offer. He knew he wanted to be a part of all this. Here, there, it didn't matter. He could feel the eternity in his soul that was part and parcel of the bargain.

He looked up at Arak, "Where are we going?"

"We shall begin at my original destination...Jerusalem."

EPILOGUE

I F THERE HAD BEEN some way to capture the last act of our unparalleled little drama, it would have played out like this.

The "ship" retracted its support gear, the hatchway returned to its matching fluid state and there were several motionless minutes, broken only by the sound of the powerful hum. Then, without warning, it reversed trajectory and began to rise silently towards the brilliant, blue "ceiling" above. As it neared that membranous boundary, the unearthly hum-whistle reappeared with a vengeance. The acceleration through this translucent "shield" was heralded with the same mind rattling boom as before. Then the Archs at the four corners vacated their post like a simultaneous explosion of multi-colored, miniature Super Novas. And lastly, the ultra-blue of the vast protective covering also reversed itself...and was gone.

As the lens continues to pull back, we see the afternoon resume its cheerful, breezy action. The little dwelling is shrinking rapidly as the geographic view of the local water ways and islands, slides from a tight focus to a larger "big picture" view. One that continues and soon reveals the Gulf and its adjoining shorelines. We are on our way to a satellite panorama of one of God's favorite masterpieces.

In His presence there is cheering and celebration. For you see, the curtain had indeed been drawn. A great crowd of witnesses has watched from the grandstands as these nerve wracking proceedings unfurled their finale upon the Earth. They are a glad hearted, joyous gathering, even though they have been forced to watch as those newly delivered from Lucifer's snares, have turned and willingly gone now on the offensive.

All are aware of the danger these will face. None are in ignorance of the "black" power that still overshadows the little planet's existence. But they are also aware that none of this can ultimately change the eternal destination and glory that awaits these warriors of Jehovah. All will conclude as it has been written...in His good time.

Oh...two more things.

Let us zoom, for a moment, back in to our distinguished picnic table. Here we find Fitz, who has also "returned" to action. He is shaken and somewhat mystified for, from his viewpoint, the others magically vanished whilst he was in mid sentence...Wait till he turns around and sees the helicopter.

In the massive, but dark and oppressive, hallway, which leads to the "throne room" of the other guy, Buferan has finished collecting final reports from those watchers assigned to the Mikals case. He must now make his report to the Dark Lord. His thoughts are in chaos as the magnitude of the "interference", which their own insolence has brought down upon them, begins to sink in. He feels like screaming in rage, or maybe roaring in pain, but he leaves us with only two words from the giant, fanged maw...

"Ahh...crap."

Dear Reader,

If you enjoyed this book (Arak-An Angel's Story) please do two things:

1.) Use your Amazon account to locate the book's page in their store and leave a favorable review. Reviews drive the placement of any book in Amazon's promotional hierarchy.

2.) Stay tuned for book two of "The Warrior Angel Chronicles": Arak-Soul Collector